D0291844

WHAT THE HEART WANTS

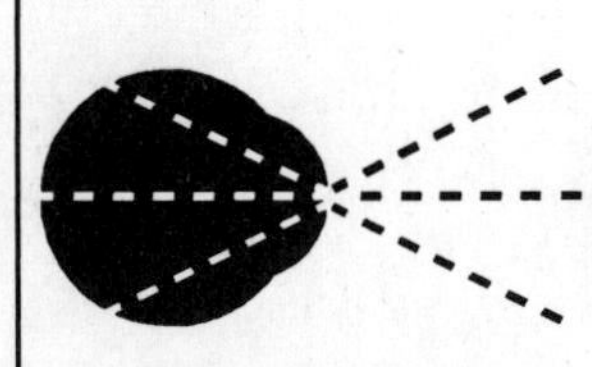

AN ANGEL RIDGE NOVEL

WHAT THE HEART WANTS

DEBORAH GRACE STALEY

THORNDIKE PRESS
A part of Gale, Cengage Learning

GALE
CENGAGE Learning™

Detroit • New York • San Francisco • New Haven, Conn • Waterville, Maine • London

Thorndike Press® Large Print Clean Reads.
The text of this Large Print edition is unabridged.
Other aspects of the book may vary from the original edition.
Set in 16 pt. Plantin.

LIBRARY OF CONGRESS CATALOGING-IN-PUBLICATION DATA

Staley, Deborah Grace.
What the heart wants / by Deborah Grace Staley. — Large print ed.
p. cm. — (An Angel Ridge novel ; 3) (Thorndike Press large print clean reads)
Originally published: Memphis, TN : Bell Bridge Books, 2010.
ISBN-13: 978-1-4104-3477-7
ISBN-10: 1-4104-3477-X
1. Man-woman relationships—Fiction. 2. Tennessee—Fiction. 3. Large type books. I. Title.
PS3619.T348W43 2011
813'.6—dc22 2010052371

Published in 2011 by arrangement with BelleBooks, Inc.

Printed in the United States of America
1 2 3 4 5 6 7 15 14 13 12 11

For Kim Faucett, Wendy Pitts Reeves, Susan Maxwell, and Janene Satterfield for bringing me back to my first love, writing, and for believing that I could when I wasn't so sure.

ACKNOWLEDGEMENTS

The author would like to acknowledge the invaluable guidance of her Goddard College faculty advisor, Victoria Nelson, whose input on this novel made it rich and helped raise this book to the next level. This book would not have been possible without the support and encouragement of Regina Tingle, Katy Zirbel and the rest of the Goddard-Port Townsend MFA community. And last, but never least, for the Debs and Bell Bridge Books, Deborah Smith and Debra Dixon, for this amazing opportunity and for believing in the Angel Ridge series.

WELCOME

Hi, y'all. Welcome to Angel Ridge and Happy Fall. Dixie Ferguson's the name, and I run Ferguson's, the town diner. You won't find better food or service in any restaurant you'd care to compare us with. Oh sure, there's a deli down the road inside the Angel Ridge Corner Market that's started doin' steak night on Fridays, but Ferguson's hasn't suffered a bit from the competition. There's room enough for two eating establishments in this town. I always say, you gotta make room for newcomers or you'll stagnate. Variety is the spice of life, after all.

Speaking of newcomers, we got us a new shop owner in town. Name's Candi Heart. I know, it's a little different, but ain't nothin' wrong with that. Look at me? Candi means to do something with Madge's old beauty shop. You know, the pink storefront kitty-corner across Main from the diner?

But before we get to that, let me take a

second to tell you a bit about the place I've called home for most of my life — Angel Ridge. Population three hundred forty.

It's a picturesque town in the valley of the Little Tennessee River, established in 1785. In the early days, its first families — the McKays, the Wallaces, the Houstons, the Jonses, and the Craigs — staked their claims on hundreds of acres of the richest bottomland anyone had ever seen. They built big ol' homes near the meandering river and operated prosperous plantations. Well, all except for the Craigs. They were traders and craftsmen. Men of commerce, as it were. Meanwhile, the town developed above the river on a high ridge.

In the early 1970s, the Flood Control Board came in and bought up most of the property along the flood prone river, and those stately homes that some called relics of a bygone era, were inundated in the name of progress. But those who built more modest Victorians near town up on the ridge? Well, their homes are still standin'. Of course, the families who lost theirs to the newly formed Tellassee Lake moved up to the ridge as well and built elaborate Victorian mansions such as this quaint little town had never seen.

Most of the families I mentioned earlier

are still around. These are hardy folks. Why, in all the time they've lived here, they've endured Indian attacks, floods, divided loyalties in the Civil War, and yes, even feuds. The older folks are still marked by the hardships of the past, but the young people of the town hope to move beyond old hurts to create a new generation made strong because of their roots, yet free of the past.

You've picked an interesting time to visit our little town. It's a restless time between summer and fall, when the days get shorter, the glorious colors of the trees have faded to gray, and people aren't quite ready to settle in for the winter. In short, it's the time of year that gives a body the heebie-jeebies, if you don't mind me sayin'. You know, like when something that can't be explained happens, and somebody says, 'Could have been a ghost,' and the most logical of minds sit back and say, 'Can't rule it out.'

And that brings me back to the town's newest resident, Candi Heart. She arrived unnoticed by most, a woman of the mountains who will never draw much attention, except that strange things started happenin' right away. Crime became the rule, rather than the exception, which was bad for the town, but good for our sheriff, Grady Wallace.

A Wallace has held the office of sheriff in Angel Ridge since the town was chartered. This Sheriff Wallace, however, isn't cut from quite the same cloth. You see, Grady's a man of action who craves excitement and needs plenty of activity, and he's seen precious little of either in the ten or so years he's been our sheriff. Well, let's just say that since Candi Heart came to town, he's had plenty to keep him busy, what with the stream of crimes that follows her around. And then there's the mystery surrounding the woman herself. Suffice to say, Candi's not quite what she appears and leave it at that.

If you've traveled this way before, it's likely you met Candi and Grady, but their story was so fascinatin', I think you'll find it's worth goin' back in time a bit to hear it. In fact, hearin' it might give some of you hope that you can walk in your own skin and start over in a place where you'll not only be accepted for who you are, but welcomed and loved.

So have yourself a cup of cider, sit back, and enjoy your time in Angel Ridge.

Dixie

PRELUDE

At the intersection of longing and love is
deceit and truth

Longing set this one on a path to find
home and vocation
But a web of secrets formed around her,
entangling her in their intricate web
The kind of complex web that can only
form
from long-held secrets.
The more she tried to free herself, her
longing,
her past, her future
The more tangled in its silken weave she
became.

People came, friend and foe alike
One by one, they cut the web
Some with hate-laced knives slashed
Caring hands cut through the weave just as
effectively,

Not knowing the end result would be the same.

The town stood witness to her fall
As she crashed to the earth
Exposed and utterly vulnerable
Her secret lives, lies and truths
Stained her skin and lay in mounds at her feet
Her foes sat in judgment as a jury,

But love came . . . with gentle hands
Love dried her tears
Love covered her shame
Love sheltered her with compassion
Love accepted her anyway
Love embraced her
Love welcomed her home.

Prologue

The misty morning fog hugged her body like a lover's embrace. As it swirled about her, she tipped her head back, long dark hair a shadow shifting down her back as she rotated her neck from side to side, a worshipful expression transforming her face.

She extended her arms with palms up to the sky as she communed one-on-one with the Creator. A thin, white linen gown, made nearly translucent by the cool mountain mist, clung to her body. The music of the hills sang through the tall pines the cry of the hawk soaring majestically overhead, the sound of the gentle deer and her fawn making their way to the creek, squirrels scurrying to put up their nuts for winter, and rabbits stilled and watched, not wanting to intrude on her sacred meditations. The pungent scent of the earth rose to mingle and blend with her own.

She was one with these mountains that

had sheltered and nurtured generations of the women who were her ancestors — her heritage. But even as she communed completely and easily on Laurel Mountain with the Creator and His wondrous nature, something troubled and intruded on her meditations. A curiosity . . . no, a need for a different kind of communion. One with people not of the mountain, but rather the outsiders of the Ridge.

She couldn't explain the call of Angel Ridge. Women before her, like her mother, had experienced the same longing, had tried to assimilate with the people below the mountain and had been cruelly rejected, returning to the mountain to live a singular existence.

The prospects of such a life quickly brought hot, soul-wrenching tears to the surface. She stilled as they fell from her eyes, scalding her face, fracturing her peace. She lowered her hands and focused on the town on the other side of the river — Angel Ridge. She was all alone now. The time had come to make the town on the far ridge her home. Surely her peace must be there, somewhere in this strange longing she had inside, because the mountain of her ancestors had held no contentment for her since her grandmother's death.

The spirit of the mountain and her grandmother would go with her, guiding her steps. She'd only need to close her eyes and look to the mountain to hear their voices. They would comfort her if times became hard. On her deathbed, Aunt Ruby had told her hearts on the Ridge had been prepared to accept her, but that there would also be those who would not welcome her. She'd have to use her gift of discernment to recognize those she should trust from the others.

She'd seek shelter in new friendships even though she'd never known a friend or had anyone her own age to talk to. How she craved for this new kind of communion. She prayed there would be those in the town who would welcome her as the mountain always had, but perhaps these bonds would take time to form. Patience and caution should be her first friends.

She would go now and find her place there. She must, or she sensed she would never again know peace.

"Lark! You there, girl?"

"I'm here, Uncle Billy!" She scrambled down the slope to the back door of the cabin. Stripping off her nightgown, she stepped into the dark cotton skirt she'd laid out the night before and hurriedly buttoned her shirt. "Coming!"

She jammed her arms into her sweater and lifted the old, hard suitcase, weathered brown with age, that she'd filled with her things. It had been her mother's — the one she'd packed all her things into the day she'd left Laurel Mountain to settle in Angel Ridge. Shivering as she gripped the handle, she looked around the cabin one last time. The uneasiness was still there. Why wouldn't it leave her be?

She closed the cabin door and rushed down the well-worn path to the river bank. Uncle Billy sat in his fishing boat. The deep lines of his face told his age to be only a few less than his sister, her precious grandmother. She smiled and handed him her suitcase.

Instead of taking it, he said, "You sure about this, girl?"

"Yes, sir." She said the words, but the uneasiness settled in her core like a dark warning she ought to heed.

The old man took her suitcase and stowed it under a seat. "You've got the look of your mama, exceptin' for your Aunt Ruby's eyes."

"She always said it was so I could see the world right and true, because my mama never did." That was about all Aunt Ruby had ever told her about her mama.

"I reckon she was right." He jammed his hat down on his head, then without looking at her, said, "You know, you don't have to live in Angel Ridge. You can live in Maryville just as well."

"I thought of that, but if I'm in Angel Ridge, at least I'll know three people — you, Aunt Verdi and Miss Estelee. I know y'all will be there for me if I need you."

He nodded, but his mouth was set. He turned and pulled the line to start the motor. The gas smell hung in the moist heavy morning mist, settling in her throat. She coughed as they slowly pulled away from the riverbank. She looked up at the mountain trying to get one last look at the cabin she'd called home most of her life, but the mountain mist clung to the trees and bushes, obscuring its rough lines.

She closed her eyes, the memory of it etched on her mind. She'd make a good life for herself in Angel Ridge. She had to. There was nothing for her on the mountain. Everyone had left years ago. But Aunt Ruby had refused to leave, so Lark had stayed on until her passing.

It had been her elders' time, just as now it was her time — time to follow her heart and her dreams to see what would come of them.

The crossing was slow because the lake that separated the mountain from the other side was wide. After a time, Uncle Billy pulled the boat alongside the little dock he'd built at the edge of his property. Standing, he tied it up just as the sun rose over the backside of the mountain. He lifted her suitcase onto the dock, hopped up alongside it, then offered her a hand.

She stepped out of the boat, smoothing her skirt and looking around. Not much had changed. His meager house sat on a little rise with a view of the river and the mountain.

"I'll give you a ride into town, then. My truck's just up there."

"Thank you."

"Where will you stay?"

"I'm not sure. Maybe Miss Estelee's. She's the only person in town I really know. And, Uncle Billy, I'll be callin' myself Candi now, so please don't call me Lark in front of anyone."

"Candi?"

"It reminds me of Aunt Ruby. It was her nickname for me. She always said I was sweet as candy." She got in the truck and after her uncle had settled behind the wheel, said, "Uncle Billy, you think it'd be best if folks didn't know Aunt Ruby was my grandmamma?"

He raked a hand down his weathered face, considering. In the end, he nodded his agreement and started the truck. "Not everybody understands mountain ways."

"Was that why my mama had trouble when she moved to Angel Ridge? Folks knew she was Aunt Ruby's daughter?"

"Your mama went about tryin' to belong here all wrong."

"It must be hard trying to figure out how to get on in a world that's different from anythin' you ever knew."

"Some people up there don't have no happiness in 'em, and they got a lot of say. So, don't be surprised if makin' a place for yourself in that town takes some doin'."

"Do you think anyone will remember my mama?"

Uncle Billy looked at her long and hard. "It's been a lot of years . . . for your sake, I hope not."

As they started on the road to her new life, the uneasiness in her middle twisted painfully, and she wrapped her thin sweater closer around her.

"Drop me at the end of Main Street, Uncle Billy."

He didn't speak, but his silence did. Maybe he was remembering what happened to her mother. She might have asked him to tell her the story Aunt Ruby had not, but Candi kept silent as well. Whatever had happened to her mother in Angel Ridge all those years ago needed to stay locked in the past. Aunt Ruby always said that diggin' up bones just made holes to fall into. Best to let 'em lie.

Uncle Billy pulled over, and the old truck rattled to a stop. Rusty hinges spoke their protest as Candi opened the door and stepped out into the chill, gray morning.

Mist hovered on the lake below and obscured the mountain she'd called home her entire life. Fitting, that. She should look at what was in front of her and not what was behind. She closed the door and lifted her suitcase out of the truck bed. Uncle Billy drove away, leaving her alone on the brick sidewalks of Angel Ridge.

Candi closed her eyes, drew in a long, cleansing breath and then put one foot in front of the other. Signs in shop windows read, "Closed," but some lights were on behind the wide windows of the storefronts. One man swept the sidewalk outside Wallace's Grocery. He looked up as if to call out a greeting as she came near, but words died half spoken on his lips. He gripped his broom, rubbed his eyes, blinked, and then looked at her again. As if not liking what he saw, he hurried into his shop and locked the door.

She stopped, puzzled by his strange reaction, but then kept moving. She felt the man's eyes on her as he watched her from his store's windows. Uneasiness crept up the back of her neck, but she kept moving.

Shops lined both sides of the street that U-ed at the end to come around to the other side. Fading grass took up the middle holding park benches, a large gazebo, and a great bronze angel perched atop a brick pedestal. Fitting for a town that legend told was named for an angel that saved its earliest settlers from an Indian attack.

Candi walked down the street passing the drug store and soda fountain, McKay's Bank & Trust, around the horseshoe where the library stood, the courthouse, the Baptist Church and the Presbyterian. On the other side of the street, there was a lawyer's office, an empty storefront, another building with offices, the post office, and a hardware store which stood separate from the line of storefronts. Each one was a different color: black, brown, blue, yellow, and the vacant one, which drew her attention, was pink.

She'd planned and dreamed of having a

shop most of her life, one filled with all the color and activity that had been lacking in her life on the mountain. She'd even come off the mountain for a time to study at vocational school so she'd be ready when the time came. She had a storage shed full of promise, waiting for the dream to become reality.

A "For Rent" sign with a telephone number on it stood in the corner of a wide bay window. Candi pressed her face to the glass trying to make out what might be inside. The front room was empty, and it looked like the space was narrow and deep. She backed up a pace to look up. Windows above promised that maybe a living space could be arranged upstairs.

Well, pink certainly would be the right color for someone named 'Candi.' The thought brought a smile to her face.

Candi turned to look around the early morning town devoid of activity. Diagonally across the street was a restaurant with a rustic sign that read, "Ferguson's Diner." A red, flashing neon sign that declared it "Open" invited people to come inside. Maybe she could ask someone there about the pink building.

As she approached the red brick building with cheery yellow and white striped awnings, she could see through the long row of large windows that the diner was crowded. Candi hesitated. Not being used to them, crowds made her uncomfortable. She took a deep breath to shore up her courage and opened the door. A bell clanged alerting that a new customer had arrived. It seemed that all eyes focused on her, curious about the stranger who had just walked in.

"Good mornin'," a woman bustling behind the counter said. "Come in and take a seat. I'll be with you in a second."

People focused back on their meals and conversations. Candi sat at the bar and removed her knit cap. She smoothed a hand over her hair.

The tall, smartly dressed red-haired woman soon returned and placed a thick white cup in front of her. She poured coffee and said, "What can I get you, hon?" She took a pencil and an order pad from her apron pocket. Candi frowned. That pocket was big red lips. Interesting.

"*Um* . . . Nothing, thank you. I was wondering if you could tell me who's renting the pink building in town."

"The beauty shop?"

"Is that what it is?"

"Yeah. The lady who ran it moved about a year ago. You thinkin' to rent it?"

"I'm not sure."

"Well, Bud DeFoe owns that and most of the other buildings on that side of Main. He runs the hardware store just across the street." She put her pad and pencil away and added, "He's usually here this time of day, but he had to see to a truck unloadin' a shipment of lumber this morning."

"Thank you."

The woman leaned against the counter and said, "You're new in town."

It wasn't a question. "Yes."

"I'm Dixie Ferguson."

Dixie Ferguson . . . she must own the diner. She had a warm smile that reached her eyes and seemed like a nice person, but Candi couldn't be sure on such short acquaintance. Better to keep her guard up until she knew her better.

"My name is Candi. I'm pleased to meet you."

"Likewise." Dixie grabbed a cloth and swiped at the counter. "What brings you to Angel Ridge?"

"I'm looking to settle here. Thought maybe I'd open a business."

"You're a hair dresser then?"

"No. I just liked the building. It . . . stands out."

Dixie smiled. "It does that. I'm partial to

pink myself, as you can see."

Now that she mentioned it, Candi noticed that Dixie was dressed in a pink turtleneck sweater with a fuchsia floral scarf that matched the lips on her pink apron.

"So, what kind of shop you thinkin' about opening?"

Candi shrugged. "I was thinking of opening a sundries shop."

"Sundries?"

"This and that."

Dixie frowned, but nodded and said, "I see. Well, if you need any advice on getting business licenses and navigating town ordinances, let me know. It'll be nice to have another woman running a business in town."

"That's very kind. Thank you, ma'am."

"Please, call me Dixie. 'Ma'am' makes me sound like somebody's mother, and I'm not about to be a mother anytime soon."

Candi smiled. "Dixie, then."

"Order up!" someone called from the back.

"Duty calls. You sure I can't get you anything to eat? Never let it be said that someone left Ferguson's Diner hungry."

"I should be gettin' on." She had a lot to do before the sun set, the most important of which was finding somewhere to stay until she found a place of her own. "I'll try to come by for supper."

"You do that. Fried chicken's the special tonight." Dixie turned and impressively took up four plates of steaming food. "Welcome to Angel Ridge," she said, and headed to a booth in the back to drop off the food to waiting customers.

Candi left a dollar on the counter for the coffee, then stood, picked up her suitcase, and headed for the door. A beauty shop . . . that might make people happy, especially since there didn't seem to be another one in town. But becoming a beautician would require going to school, and she needed income now. She had some money that her Aunt Ruby had left for her, but she wasn't sure how long it would last.

She had to be practical. Aunt Ruby had taught her to have good common sense if nothing else. Rely on what you know and what seems practical, that's what she'd say to her if she was standing next to her right now. She'd had a plan when she come off the mountain. No need to be changin' things now. Just because the building had once been a beauty shop didn't oblige her to keep it a beauty shop. She needed money now, and that meant sticking to what she knew. She was passable good at arranging flowers, and she would sell the salves and tonics that Aunt Ruby had taught her to make. Everyone liked flowers and they would also like the natural remedies. And then there were the clothes and such she'd been collecting since school to sell. That was it. Stick to the plan. It was a good plan.

She stepped back out on the sidewalk, the bright sunshine and a sense of rightness lightening the uneasy feeling in her stomach a bit. She took a breath and crossed the street to the hardware store. Might as well talk to this Mr. DeFoe. If the money in Aunt Ruby's strong box wasn't enough to rent out a shop, better to know now so she could make other plans.

CHAPTER 1

An hour later, Candi was unlocking the front door to the pink building that might become her shop. The rent sounded reasonable. In fact, she had more than enough money to get by for a few months. But, what did she really know about what reasonable rent was? Mr. DeFoe had said he was gonna be tied up with that lumber shipment a little bit longer, so he'd sent her ahead with the key and a promise of meeting her in half an hour to see if she was still interested.

Dixie had mentioned helping her with getting business licenses and something about town ordinances. And then there was the matter of her lying about her name. Could she sign a lease and get licenses all under a false name? What if they checked her out and figured out she was a fraud? What then?

Candi stepped inside the cool interior of the building and smoothed a hand over her hair after removing her knit cap. Clearly there was more to think through than just finding a place to have a business. She wished she had someone to talk to. Someone she was certain she could trust. Maybe she'd plain old put the cart before the horse. No matter. She was here. Might as well have a look around.

Mr. DeFoe had told her the shop included a room upstairs. At first she'd thought that if she decided to rent the place, maybe she could live there, but she'd been disappointed to learn that it would take a day or so to get the utilities turned on. He'd also said something about a town ordinance prohibiting residential spaces on Main Street.

Candi sighed. Oh, well. She wasn't really all that keen on living in town anyway. She was used to living off the land. A small house with room for a garden where she could raise the herbs and flowers she'd need for her natural remedies would be more the thing. She'd ask around about rentals, but first, she'd have to find a place to stay tonight.

One thing at a time. First, she would explore the shop. The front room was wide, with dark wood floors. A bay window next to the front door allowed plenty of light and would be good for a display. She'd have to see about getting a sign, but she'd need to decide on a name first. *Candi's Sundry Shop?* No, too long.

Candi followed a long hallway towards the back of the building. Part way back, she found a door to the right with another directly across from it. Large matching rooms opened up beyond the doorways. This was more space than she'd imagined when she'd thought of having her own shop. There was plenty of room for displaying different kinds of merchandise. She loved the high ceilings with decorative punched tin and antique ceiling fans hanging down. Those would be nice in the summer.

Still, what would she do with all this space? The front room would work for candies and flowers. The two rooms off the long hallway leading to the back were much larger than the front of the shop. She hadn't considered having to spread things out, but she could have two boutiques to sell different kinds of clothing. She could divide up the skincare and perfumes between them, too. She could call it *Candi's Boutique.* She liked the sound of it, but wondered if it made it sound like clothes were all she was selling.

She returned to the hallway and continued to the back of the shop. This is where the previous owner had operated her beauty shop. Here there were sinks and cabinets against the walls with mirrors and chairs with hair dryers attached to them. There were even raised chairs with tubs at their base. She wondered what those were for. They looked like foot baths. Very strange.

Whatever would she do with all this equipment? The practical thing to do would be to advertise for a hair dresser, but she wasn't sure she wanted to share the space with a stranger. Still, she'd give it some thought.

This was a huge room. It was near as big as the dining room at Ferguson's. A room opened off the far side of it that had shelving and a worktable in the middle. This would be a good space to store her herbs, dried flowers, oils, and other ingredients she would use to make her remedies. The heavy door would help keep the inside nice, dry and cool. She'd stored a good many dried herbs, flowers, and some jars of creams and essential oils in the spring house in anticipation of setting up her shop. After she let the shop, she'd have Uncle Billy take her back to the mountain so she could get them.

"Hello?" A deep, masculine voice called from the front.

The voice did not belong to Mr. DeFoe.

Candi backed out of the storeroom, and cautiously replied, "Who's there?"

A tall man with wide shoulders wearing a uniform appeared in the back room almost as soon as Candi got the words out.

"I think that's my line."

A frown creased the man's wide brow, and a badge on his jacket declared him a lawman. His hand rested on his gun as he eyed her suspiciously. That made him the second person in town today who'd looked at her that way. Aunt Ruby said to never trust a lawman because they were all crooked, always looking for something to harass you about. She felt her hackles rising.

"I'm perusing the shop, sir. Mr. DeFoe gave me the key." She held it up for him to see. "I might be interested in renting it."

He took off his dark brown cowboy-style hat and raked a hand through reddish-brown hair cut short, but not short enough to conceal its tendency to wave. A ruddy complexion and freckles that went along with his hair color sprinkled across his nose and cheeks making him look younger than the creases on his forehead indicated. A jagged scar on his chin marred what might have otherwise been wholesome features.

"My apologies, ma'am." He approached and held out a hand, "I'm Sheriff Grady

Wallace."

Candi reluctantly gave him her hand, but retrieved it after only a brief shake.

"When I was making my rounds this morning, I noticed the front door standing open and came in to check it out. This building's been empty for nearly a year now, so naturally, seeing that door open led me to believe that someone had broken in."

"Naturally?"

"Well, sure. Someone might have been looking for shelter for the night, or teenagers could have been up to some mischief."

"Well, I'm not a teenager, and I didn't spend the night here, nor would I," she said.

"Oh, I wasn't implying that you would."

"What were you implying, then?"

"I'm sorry. I didn't get your name."

"I didn't give it."

He took a breath, twirled his hat on his hand, and smiled. "How about if we start over."

She stared at him blankly. She had no idea what he meant.

"I'm Sheriff Grady Wallace," he said and extended his hand again.

She looked at it, frowning. "We already shook."

He smiled again, like he wanted to put her at ease, and twirled his hat again. "I apologize for bustin' in on you. I imagine I must have given you a fright."

"You did that."

"You have me at a disadvantage. You know my name, but I don't know yours."

Great. She'd have to give him her name. He'd asked her point blank. She sighed and said, "Candi."

"Just Candi?"

"Heart."

"Excuse me?"

"My name is Candi Heart, sir." Candi Heart? Saying it out loud to a stranger, it sounded stupid and unnatural. What was wrong with her? She should have decided on Jones or Smith or Collins or anything, but Heart? At first, she'd thought it was catchy and memorable, but now she just thought it sounded like some kind of fancy lady. She was *not* that kind of lady.

He chuckled and rubbed his fingertips across the scar on his chin. "Your name is Candi Heart?"

"Yes, sir. I reckon you could say my mama had a sense of humor." She waited and watched, hoping the explanation made the lie go down easier.

"Please, call me Grady."

"Oh, I couldn't."

"Why's that?"

"Because you're the law, and a body ought to show the proper respect."

"Well, Ms. Heart, we don't much stand on ceremony around here. If you're plannin' to live in Angel Ridge, you'll find that out soon enough."

Candi didn't know what to say to that, so she didn't say anything at all. He was quite a bit taller than her, and the fact that he was the sheriff, and that he still had a hand on his gun, made her uncomfortable. She remembered again Aunt Ruby's warning about lawmen. Best to not say too much.

"So, you're a hair dresser?"

He sure was nosey, askin' all his questions. "No, sir."

"I'm sorry. I just assumed that you might be since you're thinking to rent Madge's old shop."

Candi continued to watch the man carefully. He seemed completely at ease. Confident and in control. Wonder how he did that when she felt like she might bust right out of her skin? She wished he'd get on his way.

"Mr. DeFoe will be coming by soon, and I'd like to look around a bit more before he comes, if that's all right with you . . . sir," she added.

"Of course. I'm sorry to hold you up." He put his hat back on, and smiled widely this time. "I'll just be on my way. But first, I need you to do something for me."

Candi frowned. What could she possibly do for him? Still, she'd be crazy to get crosswise of the law her first day in town. "I'll do my best, sir."

"Call me Grady."

"I couldn't —"

He held up a hand, halting her words. "Now, I insist. You callin' me 'sir' makes me feel old before my time."

Dixie Ferguson had said near the same thing earlier, but that was different. She could call Dixie by her first name because she ran a diner where interacting with people on a personal level was appropriate. This, however, was the sheriff. She couldn't imagine ever calling him by his given name.

"I'm just bein' respectful, sir. It's nothin' to do with your age. It's to do with who you are — the sheriff."

"I appreciate that, but if it's just the same to you, I'd like you or anyone else in town to call me Grady. I've lived here my whole life, and as I said, we don't stand on ceremony in Angel Ridge." He looped a thumb in his gun belt and rocked back on his heels. "Would you be willing to give it a try?"

She took a breath and tried to at least act like she had relaxed into his easy manner, but found it terribly difficult. She chewed her lower lip, considering, and then said, "I'd be willin' to try, say in a week or so, but certainly not with my just havin' met you. I'm sorry, sir."

Her words made a frown crease his brow again. "You mind me asking you where you're from?"

She'd had about enough of his questions. "Yes, sir. I do."

"Why's that?"

"Meanin' no disrespect, but unless I've done something wrong and there's some official-like reason that you'd be askin', I don't see as it's any of your business."

"I see." He pulled the brim of his hat down lower on his forehead. "My apologies. I don't mean to offend. Most folks around here would call asking a newcomer in town where they're from just makin' conversation."

"Is that why you asked? Because you were just 'makin' conversation?' " She looked deep into his hazel-colored eyes to discern the truth of his words. He looked right back.

"I was just curious. Your accent isn't like what you hear in our foothills. It has the sound of the mountains in it."

So, he was an observer of people and their ways. Candi supposed he'd need to be in his line of work. She'd have to work on being more neighborly. If she was going to run a shop, folks would expect her to be friendly, but she didn't see how that meant she had to tell everybody her business. Still, she'd do well to hold to Aunt Ruby's old sayin', *You catch more flies with honey than vinegar.*

"You're right, Sheriff. I am from the mountains." She'd let him take that as he would. She wasn't about to tell him she was from Laurel Mountain.

"Hello!"

"Back here, Bud."

The sheriff called out to Mr. DeFoe, but didn't break eye contact with her. *Let him look as long as he wants,* Candi thought. *He's not gonna see anything but a stranger who's just arrived in Angel Ridge.*

"What are you doin' here, Grady?"

At last he looked away to speak to Mr. DeFoe. Finally able to breathe again, Candi took a long, deep breath of the cool musty air filling the back room.

"Like I was tellin' Ms. Heart here, I was doin' my morning rounds and saw the front door to the building standin' wide open. Since the place has been vacant for so long, I figured I ought to check it out."

Mr. DeFoe slapped the sheriff on the shoulder and offered him his hand. "Well,

I'm much obliged, Grady. Appreciate you keepin' an eye on things around town."

The sheriff took Mr. DeFoe's hand. "That's what you pay me for, Bud."

"That it is."

"I'll leave you to your business, then." The sheriff swung his gaze back to Candi and touched the brim of his hat. "A pleasure meetin' you, Ms. Heart."

Candi nodded, but didn't say anything. Words sometimes were unnecessary.

"Bud," he nodded to Mr. DeFoe and left them alone.

"Well, what do you think about the place, little lady?"

Candi's gaze remained focused on the doorway that the sheriff had disappeared through.

"Ms. Heart? Candi?"

Candi blinked and looked back at Mr. DeFoe. "I beg your pardon, sir. You were sayin'?"

"The shop. What do you think?"

"It might do. It's more space than I need. I haven't looked upstairs yet, but I'm not sure that matters much since the downstairs is the retail space. I guess it'd do for storage." She moved around, looking. "Needs cleanin' and the walls could do with a fresh coat of paint."

"Oh sure, sure. We'll take care of all that if you decide you want the place."

She thought he was eyein' her funny, and she didn't like it none too much. The look in his eye put her in a mind of that man across the street she'd seen first thing this morning.

"As you can see, it's been empty for some time. The McKay woman that owns the bank across the way has been after me night and day to get some businesses operatin' in some of these vacant buildings on this side of the street. Says so many empty storefronts and offices makes the town look rundown." He took off his cap and rubbed his shiny head. "I guess when you're rich as Midas, recessions and bad economies don't bother you none too much."

Candi folded her arms and tried to get a read on Mr. DeFoe. "I suppose not."

"Tell you what. I'll make you a deal. You sign a twelve months' lease on the place by the end of this week, and I'll give you the first two months rent free and waive the security deposit. After all, the place ain't doin' nobody any good standin' empty."

"That's a generous offer." But still, Candi had to settle some things in her mind. Her instincts told her to rent it, but she didn't want to make any rash decisions. Better that she at least sleep on it. "I'll be in touch by the end of the week, then."

Candi held out the key, and Mr. DeFoe reluctantly took it.

"All right then. You stay as long as you want and look around. I'll come back by later to lock the place up."

"Thank you." He was still giving her that peculiar look. So she said, "You're looking at me in a familiar manner, sir. I don't mind sayin', it makes me a mite uneasy."

Mr. DeFoe blinked and leaned back on his heels. He wadded his cap in his hand. The older man looked to be somewhere in his sixties, bald on top with neatly trimmed gray hair on the sides. He was average height with a bit of a paunch. His clear blue eyes held a sadness that had Candi looking away.

"Forgive me. I don't mean no disrespect. It's just that you remind me of somebody I knew a long time ago."

Candi nodded, but still didn't look in his eyes. She didn't want to know about the hurt and secrets that lived there. She had enough trouble of her own. Then, all of a sudden, it hit her. Oh Lord, what if he'd known her mother? That was trouble she didn't need just now.

"I'll just be going then," he said.

She nodded and kept her back to him as he left, holding her breath. When she heard the front door open and close, she let it out long and slow. With everyone gone now, Candi shook off that unsettled feeling Mr. DeFoe had left her with and looked around the shop, imagining the possibilities. Possibilities she hadn't considered when she'd been dreamin' of this day back on the mountain. She felt elated at the prospect of running her own business, overwhelmed at the responsibility, but mostly, she experienced a feeling that had been her constant, cold companion these many years.

Alone.

CHAPTER 2

Grady took off his hat and set it on the lunch counter of Ferguson's Diner. He clasped his hands and puzzled over the strange encounter he'd just had with Candi Heart, if that was really her name. There was something about her. Something he couldn't quite put his finger on.

"Hey, Grady."

"Dixie."

She set a mug in front of him and poured coffee.

He drank and thought. It's what he did. He observed people. He understood them. He trusted his gut, but this woman, he couldn't get a good read on her. The signals she put out were all mixed up. She didn't seem the type to make trouble, but she'd been awfully guarded with him. Mountain people could be that way, though. His father had found that out the hard way. Best to just leave 'em be.

Dixie swiped at the counter and leaned towards him. "What's got you all introspective this morning?"

Grady shrugged. "A newcomer."

"So, you met her, too?"

"Yeah. Down at Madge's old beauty parlor."

"Interesting lady."

Grady set his mug down. He had to agree. "Yeah. Interesting name, too."

"What, Candi?"

"Candi Heart."

"Her name is Candi *Heart?*"

"That's what she said."

"Who would name their child Candi Heart? That's just cruel. I bet she got teased somethin' awful in school; but now that she's grown, it puts you in mind of a stripper, doesn't it?" Dixie chuckled as she poured herself a cup of coffee and took a sip. "Well, I'm glad she didn't tell me her last name when I met her because, you know me, I would have been tempted to make a smart remark, as I'm like to do, and that would have been a bad idea with her seemin' so skittish and all."

"Yeah. Skittish. I thought so, too." A stripper. Leave it to Dixie. He supposed she was pretty enough in a natural sort of way, but he couldn't imagine her as something so exotic.

Dixie straightened away from the counter. "What did you do, Grady Wallace?"

"Nothin'."

"*Uh-uh.* Spill it."

"I was doin' my morning rounds and noticed the front door of Madge's shop standing open. So, I went in to check it out."

Dixie rolled her eyes. "Please tell me you didn't bust in on her guns blazin' and scare the living daylights out of her."

"Well, I probably had my hand on my gun when I came up on her in the back of the shop. I didn't know who or what might be back there, after all."

"Oh, Lord. Welcome to Angel Ridge."

"She said she's not a beautician, so what do you think she's plannin' on doing with the shop?

"I don't know. She said something about sellin' sundries."

"That's an odd choice of words. Is that what she said?"

"Yeah, she said 'sundries.' I thought it was odd, too, but to each her own. Nothing wrong with bein' different. Look at me."

That many shades of pink on anyone else would make them look like a carnival act. "You make it work, Dix."

"Thank you."

"I asked her where she was from because she doesn't have our accent. She said she was from the mountains."

"I can see that."

"Yeah, but it was a non-specific answer, and it just makes you wonder." He took another sip of his coffee.

"Not especially."

"Huh?"

"What's to wonder? There's a new woman in town, and she's interested in opening a shop. She doesn't have to tell us where she's from or anything else for that matter." She slapped a towel down behind the counter and said, "I need to get the prep started for lunch. You need anything else?"

"Just a doughnut to go."

"Typical." Dixie lifted the dome on the cake plate and put a doughnut in a bag. She poured coffee into a cup and put a lid on it. "You comin' back by later?"

"I'm not sure."

"Well, I'll see you when I see you then, and in case you're interested, the town's newest resident said she'd be by for supper."

With that, Dixie turned and walked into the back. Duly noted. He ought to just let the mysteries of Candi Heart be, but he couldn't. It wasn't in his nature. Oh well, he tried not to miss Dixie's fried chicken anyway.

Grady picked up the bag and coffee, then walked out into the less humid air that heralded coming fall. He squinted up into the sunshine. Another beautiful day stretched out in front of him with nothing to look forward to but long hours of sitting in his office or walking around town. He'd love to get in his Jeep, drive up into the mountains, and spend a few days hiking.

He juggled the coffee and bag to retrieve his sunglasses from a pocket in his jacket. He was restless. Nothing new there. He'd been restless for as long as he could remember, and that wasn't likely to change anytime soon. His father had been sheriff in Angel Ridge, his grandfather had been sheriff, and his father before him, and his before him. Tradition ran deep in this town, and he was tangled up good in it.

Growing up, he'd known early on he didn't want to follow in the family tradition, so he'd done everything he could to rebel against it. He got in more trouble than any other kid in town. He still held the record for most suspensions from Angel Ridge High School. Add to that shoplifting from Wallace's Grocery and DeFoe's Hardware, vandalism, defacing public property. It had taken him the better part of two weeks to clean that black spray paint off the angel monument after a Halloween prank, but the best part had been the whole town knowing he'd done it. These people would never expect someone like him to be their sheriff.

But then his dad had gotten himself shot in the line of duty. Things hadn't been the same after that. His dad hadn't been the same. When he died a few years later, everyone in town had expected Grady to take his dad's place. His mother had needed him close by since he was her only child. How he wished he wanted to be sheriff; it would make life a whole lot easier. Truth was he was flat out bored. The last major crime that had been committed in Angel Ridge had been when his father was shot by Tom Hensley from Laurel Mountain. Years of bad blood between the moonshiner and the lawman came to a head when Hensley's daughter turned up dead in town. Accidental drowning had been the official cause of death, but there must have been more to it than that for Hensley to come to town and call Grady's daddy out.

Word was that Hensley's daughter had come to town one summer, a beautiful stranger who'd gotten the local men all stirred up — the single and married alike. Once, he'd asked Miss Estelee about it. The town's oldest resident who'd always had her finger on the pulse of the town was likely to have answers. She'd said that was a dark chapter in the town's history, better left closed.

Too many unanswered questions. The only thing Grady hated more than being bored were unsolved mysteries and people with secrets. He'd never been able to let well enough alone.

As he walked down Main, he glanced across town square toward the pink building that stood out like a sore thumb. Candi came outside and stood there, looking up at the building. The front door of the bank opened and closed behind Mrs. McKay. She focused on the stranger across the street like a missile honing in on its target and headed towards her. Grady sighed. He'd best run interference. Harriet McKay would chew someone like Candi up and spit her out. He quickened his pace and caught up with the ladies just as Mrs. McKay was introducing herself.

Grady nodded at Candi, who gave him a frown that clearly showed she was annoyed with him for turning up again. Ignoring that, he said, "Morning, Mrs. McKay."

The thin older lady with shoulder length artificially dark hair turned and looked down her long pointed nose at him. "Sheriff Wallace."

"Fine morning."

"Indeed. Don't let us keep you. I am sure you must have important business to attend to."

Grady was trying to come up with a semi-polite conversational maneuver to ignore the woman's pointed dismissal, when Miss Estelee appeared out of nowhere and saved him from it.

"Howdy-do all! Fine mornin' to be alive and livin' on the Ridge, ain't it."

"Miss Estelee!" Candi exclaimed, a transforming smile lit every inch of her plain face. Pleasantly so, he had to admit . . .

"As I live and breathe. I woke up this mornin' and knew it was going to be a good day, and here you are to make it so. Come here and greet me proper."

Candi fairly launched herself into Miss Estelee's arms, hugging her like she'd never let go. So, the town's newest resident knew the town's oldest resident. Interesting.

"Oh, I'm happy to see you. I've got your room all ready."

Candi stood back and looked at Miss Estelee. Was that surprise on her face?

"You do?"

"Of course. I knew you were coming. We best be getting on. The day's a wastin', and we got catchin' up to do. Grady, Harriet."

Candi picked up her suitcase and linking her arm with Miss Estelee's, the pair made off down the sidewalk at a brisk pace.

"Well, I say, I wanted to ask that young lady a few questions." She turned and looked at the pink shop and then back at Grady. "Did you see her coming out of this building?"

Ignoring that, Grady said, "I'm sorry, Mrs. McKay, I just remembered I have an appointment at," he looked at his watch, "oh, sorry. I'd best be going, or I'm gonna be late."

He moved out toward the courthouse in the opposite direction Miss Estelee and Candi had taken, leaving Mrs. McKay standing alone on the sidewalk in front of the garish pink building she'd made no secret of disliking. He thought he heard her say, "*Tsk, tsk, tsk.* Young people these days!" but he just smiled, and kept walking. The morning's diversion had broken the monotony of another day as sheriff of Angel Ridge.

He turned back toward the courthouse,

thinking he might add running a preliminary background check on one Candi Heart to his growing list of things to do.

Candi followed Miss Estelee up the old brick sidewalk that led to the unusual shaped front porch of her house. It looked to be older and a different style from the other Victorians lining the street that ran along the ridge. Two matching wings capped by large bay windows stood on either side of the porch making a V-shaped front and a trapezoid porch. The gingerbread in the high eaves of the house and on either side of the porch posts had angel's wings.

As Miss Estelee opened the front door, Candi turned and looked out at the breathtaking view above the lake with Laurel Mountain rising up on the other side. The bright sunshine had cleared the morning mist. Miss Estelee was right. It was a beautiful day on the Ridge. She'd dreamed of this day so long, she could hardly believe she was finally here in Angel Ridge . . . for good.

"Don't leave the door standin' open. You'll let flies in."

"Yes, ma'am."

Candi came inside, pulling the door closed. She set her suitcase down and looked around the comfortable front room to the left of the foyer. Miss Estelee was removing her coat and hat and hanging them on an old wooden coat tree.

"Mercy! Where's your coat? Come warm yourself by the stove."

She opened the door to a square, black stove that stood at the side of the room, and then sat in a comfortable-looking rocking chair. Candi unbuttoned her sweater and shivered as she hung it on a vacant hook on the coat tree.

"Look at you. That's no kind of outfit to be wearin' in this cool weather."

Candi looked down at her drab, well-worn short-sleeved blouse and long cotton skirt. They were old and ill-fitting, but clean and the best she had left. "I suppose I need to go shopping." She smoothed her hand over her skirt and sat in a chair opposite Miss Estelee. "Should I ask how you knew I was coming?"

"Come to me in a dream last night. Woke me up from a dead sleep, so I got up and started getting the rooms upstairs ready for you. I ain't used them in years, and they were a mite dusty."

"I didn't know where I was going to stay tonight. I had thought to come by to ask you if you knew of a place that would take me."

"Nonsense. You'll stay here for now. Oh, I'm sure you'll want a place of your own, but it'll do me and you both some good to have you here, safe and sound. Ruby would have wanted me to see to getting you settled on your first days with us."

She picked up her knitting from a basket beside her chair and the needles started clicking out a pleasant rhythm that reminded her of her Aunt Ruby.

"I don't like to put you out, ma'am."

"It's you that'll be put out, mark my words." Miss Estelee cackled and slapped her knee. "I've lived alone for so long, I'm like to forget you're on the place. I'll prob'ly worry the life out of you, gettin' up at all hours and comin' and goin' as I'm wont to do."

"I'm happy to see you, ma'am."

"It's good that you're here, honey. I reckon you'll shake things up in this old town, Lark Hensley." She cackled again and shook her head as she started a new row on her knitting.

She smoothed her hair back toward her braid. "About that, I'm callin' myself Candi Heart now."

Her mouth flattened and her eyebrows went up into a straight line over her round glasses. "Call yourself what you will. It won't change who you are."

"Well, I don't want to go dredging up my family's past. I mean, there's no point in folks around here knowing that I'm a Hensley. They'll just make assumptions they shouldn't."

Miss Estelee put her knitting aside and gave her a direct look. "Like you got Ruby's gift?"

Candi shook her head. "No, ma'am. She taught me to have common sense and about her mountain ways of usin' what the land gives us for food and healing, but I don't know things the way she did . . . the way you do."

"Ruby told me different."

Shaking her head, Candi looked away and said, "She wanted me to, since I'm the last of her line."

Miss Estelee tapped her foot on the polished hardwoods as she rocked a steady beat, back and forth. "She also told me you was denyin' the truth of it. That'll lead to nothin' but heartache." She stopped rocking and leaned forward as she said, "Your mama would testify to that if she was still with us, God rest her soul."

Candi had heard of her mother's failed attempt at leaving the mountain to live in Angel Ridge her whole life. It was used as a deterrent to having a dream of something more, less solitary and isolated. "I'm not my mother, ma'am. I didn't even know her. And besides, you're forgettin' about me leavin' the mountain to go to school."

"Ruby didn't like it none neither."

"I know. She worried herself sick. At least I finished before she needed me to come back and care for her."

"Ruby's leaving has been a sad time for me. I'm the last of our, *um,* generation now."

Candi reached out and took Miss Estelee's wrinkled hand in hers. "I miss her, too, but having you here is a comfort. It's like still having a bit of Aunt Ruby with me."

Miss Estelee patted her hand in much the same way as Aunt Ruby had. It was warm and familiar and very comforting. Right.

"I tried to ease her mind about me comin' here; about my dreams of havin' a shop in town," Candi said quietly. "She still worried."

"She knew you'd come here when she was gone. That you'd have to. You're a woman now; you've been a woman for some years. It was good of you to stay on the mountain to care for Ruby in her last days, but a woman can't spend her days alone and isolated in a mountain cabin. That's not how God meant us to live. Even Eve had

Adam. People shouldn't live that way. It's not natural." She shook her head. "You should have gone to school with other children."

"Aunt Verdi was a school teacher, you know. She taught me well enough to pass all the same achievement tests as the kids in school. I took the college entrance tests, too, then got into vocational school."

Miss Estelee just shook her head as if she hadn't heard her. "You're gonna need lookin' after, and I'm here to see to that. I promised Ruby I'd do my best."

Candi clasped her hands in her lap. "I'm too old to be looked after, and I'll only trouble you for a place to stay until I can get something of my own."

"You might be old in years, but you've lived alone most of your life on that mountain with just an old mountain woman for company. There's a sight of life you don't know nothin' about."

"I'll get on just fine," she said.

"As I said, I'm here to see to that, because I'm afraid the road won't be easy for you, Little Lark."

"Candi," she reminded.

"Call yourself what you want. It won't change who you are."

"I'm not plannin' to change who I am,

Miss Estelee." She felt frustration rise and took a deep breath to settle it. "It's for the best." She stood and walked over to a cabinet to look at the collection of porcelain angels inside. Interesting . . . they were all male warrior angels with swords and horns.

"I see you've got your mind set."

"Yes, ma'am."

"All right. I'll abide by your wishes."

"Thank you."

"I'm guessing you plan to use what you learned at that vocational school now."

"Yes, ma'am. I studied retail merchandising and want to open a shop in town."

"You'll need to rent something, then."

Candi nodded. "I had just finished looking at the old beauty shop when I ran into you this morning. I like it, but I'm not sure about signing a lease right now. I just got into town, after all, and there's so much to consider."

"I reckon so."

"What do you know about Bud DeFoe?"

Miss Estelee hesitated. "He means well."

Candi frowned. "He owns the shop in town I'm interested in renting."

Miss Estelee rocked a steady rhythm. A clock ticked loudly in the silence, but she didn't elaborate on her statement.

"Is he a bad person?" Candi asked.

"Not bad, but he could mean trouble for you."

She'd gotten the same feeling about him. "He said I reminded him of someone he knew a long time ago. Did he know my mama?"

"There's a number of folks here in town that knew your mama, and your granddaddy, too, for that matter, but that was a long time ago. Time makes memories fade, but," her eyes narrowed on Candi, "we might need to help that along. If you don't want these folks connectin' you to the Hensleys, you'll be needing to make some changes."

"What kind of changes?" Candi said cautiously.

Miss Estelee nodded as if she had set her mind to something. She stood slowly, got her feet under her, and made her way over to an old telephone on a side table. She picked it up and dialed a number. After a moment, she said loudly, "Hello? Dixie? This here's Miss Estelee . . . Fair to good today. Fair to good . . . *Uh-huh.* Listen, I know how busy you are, but I need a favor, and I'll be beholdin' to you if you can help me out . . . Can you take off from the diner after you get lunch a goin'? . . . I know . . . Yeah, yeah. It's real important. I got my grandniece here, and she's a needin' someone to take her into town, and you're the person to help her do what she'll be needin' to get done."

Grandniece? Candi wondered what Miss Estelee was up to.

"About two? *Uh-huh,* two hours'll do just fine. We'll meet you at the diner. Thank you, darlin'. Bye now." Miss Estelee hung the phone up.

"Grandniece?"

"Well, since you're creatin' a new identity, no harm in you makin' me your great aunt. It's a harmless fib that'll serve us well."

"And what do we need Dixie to help us with?"

"So, you've met her?"

Candi nodded.

"You'll see. Now, get on upstairs and settle in."

With that, Miss Estelee disappeared into the back of the house. Candi retrieved her suitcase and walked up the stairs wondering just what the afternoon had in store for her. If she were honest, she'd admit that she was excited and felt more alive than she ever had. Today was the beginning of a whole new life for her, and she couldn't wait to begin it.

Chapter 3

That afternoon, Candi went with Dixie "to town," as Miss Estelee called it. Town was Maryville, a small city just outside Knoxville that wasn't far from Angel Ridge. Dixie said it boasted that it was "twenty minutes from anywhere."

The first stop was a beauty shop. As she sat in the beautician's chair, Miss Estelee's words rang in her ears. *If you're gonna live in town and run a shop, you'll need to look like town folk. If you don't want folks knowin' you just came down from the mountain, then don't look like you did. Get your hair styled and some new clothes.*

The beautician handed Candi a book filled with different hairstyles while she undid the long braid hanging down her back. She'd never had a "hairstyle," and, she had to admit, as she thumbed through the book, she wondered if one of these haircuts and some make-up would make her pretty.

But which to choose . . .

Thank heavens for Dixie. She took charge of the situation, and Candi was happy to let her. She talked to the woman about keeping the style long, but easy to care for. She also mentioned something about a glosser and some red highlights to brighten it up. Candi smiled. Red highlights. That might be fun.

Even with keeping her hair long, the beautician still cut off more than twelve inches and promised to donate it to an organization that made wigs for women with cancer. The end result had her shiny black hair softly framing her face. She looked like a different person, and she loved the highlights.

Dixie dug in her bright pink leather purse and handed her a tube of lipstick. "This'll have to do until we get you to a make-up counter." She had to admit, red shiny lips and the hair put more confidence in her step. Several more whirlwind stops included a large store in a shopping mall for make-up, shoes, a purse, panties and a bra that made her look curvy! Blue jeans, slacks, a skirt, two sweaters, two t-shirts, and then one more stop at a discount store for a hair dryer, styling brush like the woman at the beauty shop had used, and other essentials. They got her a cell phone, too. She'd so wanted one when she'd been in school, but there was no use for one on the mountain where there were no cell towers.

She didn't want to think about how much money she'd spent. Miss Estelee had given Dixie cash for the purchases, but she'd refused. She'd pay her own way. It was bad enough she had to trouble the dear lady for shelter. She had the money in Aunt Ruby's strong box and more in their secret hiding place if she needed it.

As she stood just inside the door of Ferguson's, she looked around and, at last, felt like she fit in.

"Here you are! Come and let us have a look at you."

Miss Estelee waved from a booth in the middle of the diner. A handsome older gentleman with a snowy beard and rosy cheeks sat with her.

When Candi stood next to Miss Estelee's booth, she smiled and said, "Evenin', Miss Estelee. Sir."

"Well, ain't you a sight. Pretty as a picture, ain't she Charles?"

"She certainly is."

The older gentleman stood, took her hand and kissed it. Candi blushed.

"This here's Doc Prescott. Doc, this is Miss Candi Heart. She's my grandniece."

"I'm pleased to meet you, sir," Candi said. The man had kind eyes. She disliked lying to him, or anyone else for that matter, but it couldn't be helped.

"The pleasure's mine. Indeed, I'm the luckiest man in Angel Ridge this evening to be having dinner with two such lovely ladies."

"You old charmer, you," Miss Estelee said. "Sit, sit. You're both puttin' a crick in my neck."

As Candi slid into the booth next to Miss Estelee, she noticed that the older lady's cheeks were glowing. "Are you well, ma'am?"

"Right as rain. Look at you! I can't get over it. Your hair is just beautiful, and those colors you're wearin' are real becomin'."

Dixie joined them and handed Miss Estelee the untouched roll of cash she'd been entrusted with.

"How'd we do Miss Estelee?" Dixie asked.

"Right fine. Thank you for seeing to Candi, darlin'. You're an angel, but what's this?" she asked, indicating the money.

Dixie jerked a thumb in Candi's direction. "She insisted on payin' for everything herself. She was set on it, too, and I'm not about to get in the middle of that battle. Have y'all ordered?"

"No. We were waiting for you ladies to arrive," Doc Prescott said.

"Specials all around?" Dixie asked.

They all nodded. Candi was starved. Now that she thought about it, she hadn't eaten since breakfast.

"Three specials!" Dixie called out.

"We'll need four, Dixie. I hope you don't mind," the Doc said to Candi and Miss Estelee. "I asked Grady Wallace to join us."

"Make that four specials!" Dixie said and went to wait on other customers in the crowded diner buzzing with customers.

Candi could have groaned at the doctor's revelation. The sheriff would be joining them? The last person she'd expected to see again today was the town's inquisitive sheriff.

"I reckon you two spent the afternoon fishing," Miss Estelee said, nodding at his fishing vest complete with flies attached to it.

Doc Prescott's smile was wide and unrepentant. "It was a slow day. Grady just ran up to the courthouse to check in with Woody. Oh, here he is now."

Doc waved at someone behind her. Candi braced herself and tried to paste a pleasant expression on her face. *Flies and honey. Flies and honey.*

Grady approached the table and offered Doc Prescott his hand. He felt like a new man after their afternoon of trout fishing. There was nothing like standing knee deep in a creek in the woods on a clear autumn day to change your perspective.

"Evenin' Doc, Miss Estelee, ma'am —" The word died half spoken on his lips.

"Sheriff," Candi said.

"Miss Heart. I hardly recognized you."

That was true enough. The woman seated across from him hardly resembled the girl he'd met this morning. A cloud of styled, shiny black hair framed her face and fell down her back nearly to her waist. She wore a dark red sweater, belted at the waist, and she had on something shiny, black, lacy, and low cut underneath the sweater.

He dragged his eyes back to her face. Big mistake. Red lipstick emphasized full lips he'd totally missed before, and long thick black lashes framed pale green eyes. Wow . . . what a change.

"Sheriff, this is my grandniece, Candi Heart, but I suppose the two of you have already met."

Miss Estelee was looking from him to her niece with interest. The woman missed nothing, but he had nothing to hide. Nothing wrong with enjoying the company of an attractive woman. He wouldn't call her beautiful, but there was definitely something intriguing about her. The way she looked at him just drew him in.

"We met earlier," Candi supplied.

"That's right. Grady was standin' there when I came up on you this mornin'."

"That's right," Candi confirmed.

Grady watched as she fidgeted with the napkin in her lap and avoided looking at him. What was it with her? She clearly disliked him, and he couldn't for the life of him figure what he'd done to merit such a reaction from her. It was almost as if she'd decided to dislike him on sight, and maybe that was a good instinct on her part. He'd come up empty on the preliminary background check he'd run on her this morning. Candi Heart, if that was her name, was a mystery. He loved a good mystery, and this one was begging him to solve it.

He'd have to take a different tack. Win her over. He rubbed the old scar on his chin. Well, never let it be said that Grady Wallace couldn't charm a lady. Even a reluctant one. He smiled, easing back against his seat, and said, "How was your first day in Angel Ridge, Candi?"

Miss Estelee saved her from replying. "She hardly spent half of it here. Candi and Dixie went to Maryville to do a little shopping. Don't she look right smart?"

"She does indeed," he said slowly, letting his gaze travel from her face down, and then back up again. A blush colored her cheeks more becomingly than any store bought make-up could.

"Hey, Dixie! Are we gonna get to eat somctime tonight? We been waitin' for —"

"Keep your shirt on Vernon! I'm working as fast as I can," Dixie called from behind the lunch counter.

Candi frowned, distracted by the loud conversation around them. She was still avoiding looking at him.

"So, you'll be stayin' with Miss Estelee for now?"

"Yes —"

"Yeah, Dixie. The service around here keeps gettin' slower and slower," someone else said.

Dixie came from around the counter balancing an impressive number of dishes. She plunked one down in front of the customers at the table next to theirs, then turned and said, "Look here, Gil Henderson, if you've got a complaint about the service, file it with the complaint department."

"You oughta hire some help."

"Well, that's a brilliant idea, Gil." She clapped her hands and said, "And if I need any more business advice, you'll be the first person I ask. In the meantime, stick a sock in it. I'll get to you as quick as these two legs can carry me, and, I might add, standin' here chattin' about the state of the service in this fine establishment has delayed your meal another five minutes."

"Dixie?" Candi said in a soft, husky way that Grady had to admit got under his skin a little.

That halted Dixie's progress back to the kitchen, but typically Dixie, she didn't seem at all annoyed. She just said what was on her mind, and then got on with it. Grady had always liked that about her.

"Yes, darlin'? You need more tea?"

"No, thank you. I was just thinkin', I'd be more than happy to help you out this evenin'. After all you did for me today, it's the least I can do."

"Nonsense. You've not had supper yourself."

"I'm not really all that hungry."

Candi chanced a brief glance at him, then grabbed her purse and said to Miss Estelee,

"You don't mind do you, ma'am?"

"Course not. You go on and do whatever you want. I'll be home waitin' to let you in whenever you're ready."

Grady was about to volunteer to walk her home when Dixie said, "That's real nice of you, Candi. I'll give you a ride when we finish up. Miss Estelee's right on my way home anyway."

"Sounds like it's all settled then," Doc Prescott said cheerfully.

Grady frowned. This wasn't working out at all like he would have preferred. Candi stood, and he did as well. She gave him that look he was getting too used to from her — like she was oddly annoyed with him and curious at the same time. He didn't know what to say, so he just smiled and said, "Good to see you again."

Her frown deepened. Without replying, she turned and followed Dixie to the kitchen.

Doc Prescott chuckled. "I don't think she likes you much, son."

He crushed his napkin and set it on the table beside his iced tea. "What was your first clue?"

"She don't mean nothin' by it, Grady," Miss Estelee said. "She's not much used to men."

Interesting. "No brothers?"

"No daddy or mama either. Her grandparents took her to raise when her mama died, but her granddaddy died when she was just little. So, it was only her and her grandmamma."

"I'm sure she had to deal with boys in school," Doc said.

"I could say more, but I'd be talkin' out of turn. I got no place tellin' you her private business. If she wants y'all or anyone else to know, she should tell you herself."

He'd like nothing better than to find out more of her "private business." Candi emerged from the back in one of Dixie's crazy aprons carrying plates of food. At least the red bird on the bright yellow apron matched her sweater. Those high-heeled boots were gonna get uncomfortable, but she sure looked good in 'em.

She deposited the food at Gil Henderson's table. "Can I get you anything else?" she said in soft husky tones that made a man want to lean in closer to her.

"No. Just a little more tea when you get a second."

"Oh! I see how it is," Dixie said as she dropped off the food for Grady, Doc, and Miss Estelee. "You beller at me that you can't get anything quick enough, and it's 'when you get a second' with anyone else. Don't worry, hon," she said to Candi, "he'll be yellin' at you, too, after he gets used to you."

Candi smiled, falling in with Dixie's good-natured banter. "I guess I'll have to learn to yell back, then."

Dixie chuckled. "Candi, I think we're gonna get along just fine!"

Grady fiddled with his food for a good fifteen minutes while he watched Candi move efficiently around the diner, charming everyone she came in contact with, more than a little envious that she hadn't seen the need to charm him. That was it. Her elusive quality was charisma. People were drawn to her, and he was no exception.

Doc cleared his throat. "Grady, you plannin' on eatin' that or torturing it?"

He threw his napkin beside his plate and rose. "Excuse me."

"You feelin' all right, son?" Doc asked.

He turned back toward the booth. "Yeah. I'm just not hungry. I've never seen so many people in here. I think I'll make myself useful and help out in the back."

As he approached the kitchen area, Candi had just turned toward the kitchen as well, with two empty plates in her hands. Grady followed a few steps behind as they walked through the silver swinging doors.

She set the plates near the cluttered rinsing station and then turned right into him. She braced her hands against his chest while he steadied her with hands at her waist.

"Grady! What are you doing back here?"

So, she *could* use his name. He had to admit, it sounded good in her husky alto. He also noted she hadn't moved away. He flexed his fingers, enjoying the feel of her a little more than he should.

"I thought I'd lend a hand." He nodded at the mound of dirty dishes beside them. "Won't be the first time I've washed dishes here."

"Order up!"

Bill Ferguson set two specials in the window, his words jolting Candi into action. She took a step back, breaking contact with him.

"Thanks, Bill," she said, grabbing the steaming plates and then hustling out into the diner like she was escaping a fire. Grady smiled. For half an unguarded second, the wariness had left her eyes and she'd looked at him — really looked at him. She'd nibbled her full lower lip and curled her fingers against his chest. When his grip had tightened, she hadn't pulled away, even when a spark zinged between them. Grady rubbed his chin. Maybe she wasn't as immune to him as she'd like him to believe.

"You gonna just stand there grinning like an idiot or are you gonna get started on those dishes?"

Bill was the oldest of the Ferguson clan. Blake, a local contractor, came next, then there was Cory, an attorney in Knoxville. Dixie was the baby.

"I'm on it." He grabbed an apron, looped it over his head and tied it around his waist as he pulled the rinse wand down.

"Uh-huh . . ."

"What?"

"I know that look, Grady."

"I don't know what you're talking about, Bill." He rinsed dishes and stacked them in crates to push through the washer.

Dixie breezed through the door with more dirty dishes to drop off. "What's he doin' in here?" she said to her brother.

"What's it look like?" Grady said, an edge to his voice.

"He's trying to get the inside track on that little lady you got waitin' tables."

"And you're surprised?" Dixie asked.

Bill chuckled.

"Three more specials," Candi said as she came through the swinging door with more dirty plates.

Grady noticed when she looked at him that the wariness had shuttered her eyes once more.

"Thank you, Candi. You've been a big help tonight."

"You're welcome," she said softly, careful to avoid looking at him again.

"Don't let these two harass you. If they try anything, be sure to let me know."

"Dixie, darlin'," Bill said, "you're gonna give this little lady here the wrong idea about us." He slung an arm around Grady's shoulders. "Why, you couldn't find two finer, upstanding gentlemen than me and Grady here."

"Please." Dixie rolled her eyes. "Pay them no mind, honey."

Doing just that, Candi asked, "What should I do with the tips, Dixie?"

"There's a jar behind the counter out front. Drop the money in there, and we'll deal with it later." Dixie handed her a drink pitcher. "You refill glasses, and I'll make more tea."

Candi smiled and nodded, then went back out into the diner. Even though it hadn't been directed toward him, he enjoyed seeing her smile so much more easily tonight. Maybe she was finally letting her guard down. People shared information when they let their guard down.

Dixie walked over and poked him in the chest. “Look here, Grady Wallace, don’t think I don’t know what you’re up to.”

“Who, me?” He put his hand over his heart to lend sincerity to his words, but his grin must have killed the effect.

“Yeah, you. Charm’s your favorite weapon with women who don’t know any better, and with Candi being new in town, you’re thinking to use it to learn all her secrets.”

He kept rinsing and stacking as he spoke. “It’s my job to check out newcomers.”

“Especially the pretty ones,” Bill added.

Dixie shot him a look, then swung her gaze back to Grady. “She’s Miss Estelee’s kin. That’s good enough for me.”

“Or so she says.”

“Right. Let me get Miss Estelee in here so you can accuse her of lying.”

“Who’s lying?” A surprised looking Miss Estelee came through the door as if she’d been eavesdropping.

“No one, ma’am,” Grady said quickly before Dixie could say anything.

“I’m glad to hear it. There’s nothing worse than one who bears false witness.” Her astute gaze moved around the room, stopping briefly at each set of eyes. “Dixie, I wanted to let you know that I’m headin’ home. Thank you again for takin' Candi into town today."

"It was my pleasure, Miss Estelee. Now don't you worry, I'll see Candi gets home safe."

"Oh, I'm not worried. Between you and the sheriff, she couldn't be in better hands."

She turned to Grady then. That was odd. Had she just winked at him?

"Evenin'."

"Evenin', Miss Estelee," Dixie said. She frowned and then added, "That's strange."

"What?" Grady asked as he put another crate of dishes in the washer.

"Why'd she bring you into the conversation when we were talking about *me* bringing Candi home?"

Grady shrugged. "You ought to know better than to puzzle over something Miss Estelee says. She doesn't make sense half the time."

Dixie's frown deepened. *"Hmm . . ."*

Grady smiled. They were all playing right into his hands.

CHAPTER 4

At seven, Dixie turned the lighted "Open" sign off and set the lock. "Whew! Is it me, or did we serve fried chicken to everyone in Angel Ridge tonight?"

Candi sat at the lunch counter sipping a glass of sweet iced tea. She hadn't been on her feet this long since the day after Thanksgiving, that semester she'd done a merchandising internship at Belk. She still loved it. Helping the customers here tonight had been energizing.

"How about some blueberry pie and ice cream?"

Candi's mouth watered. "Sounds good."

Dixie dished up the dessert and set it on the counter. Grady came out from the back, pushing a mop and bucket on wheels.

"You don't have to do that, Grady," Dixie said. "Bill usually mops. Can't anyone do it to suit him."

"I sent him home. He was dead on his

feet. The twins kept him up most of the night last night."

"Look at you, bein' all thoughtful."

"Don't let it get around," he said chuckling.

The sound of his low laugh skittered all the way down Candi's spine. The smell of bleach filled the air, burning her nose, and thankfully killing the effect. It smelled clean and fresh, making Candi want to get started cleaning up her own shop.

She popped a bite of pie into her mouth. "*Mmm* . . . the pie is delicious, Dixie."

"Glad you like it, hon."

She pulled the tip jar out from behind the counter and upended it. Bills of various denominations and coins bounced across the lunch counter. Candi watched as Dixie silently counted the money while she ate, and Grady mopped ever closer to where she sat.

Candi wondered why anything he did should be of any concern to her, but she hadn't been able to put him out of her mind since she'd run into him, literally, earlier. Something about him unsettled her.

"Boy! You racked up."

"Pardon?" Candi said, pulling her attention back to Dixie.

Dixie pushed the stack of money towards

her. "Here you go. That's quite a haul on tips. All well-deserved."

"Oh no, Dixie. You keep that."

"*Uh-uh.* You earned it. I insist."

"But I didn't do this for money. I did it because I wanted to help. I so appreciated what you did for me this afternoon."

"No thanks required. Now, take the tips. They belong to you." She grinned. "Go rent a building or something."

She looked at the stack of money in front of her. It was more than enough to cover their afternoon shopping excursion, or to put away for rent on the shop. Candi looked up at Dixie. Given the determined set of her jaw, she guessed arguing further would be useless. So, she took the money and put it in an envelope in her purse. "Thank you. Again."

"I'm the one to be thanking you. Feel free to work the lunch or dinner rush anytime."

Candi smiled. "If you need me, all you have to do is call."

"Deal." She gave Candi's hand a warm, friendly pat. "Hey, Grady. Did Bill put the pies in the ovens before he left?"

"I'm not sure."

She looked back at Candi and said, "Let me check, and if he didn't, I'll take you home."

"Dixie, you don't need to drive me home. I'd enjoy the walk on such a nice night."

Dixie held up a hand. "Oh, no. I promised Miss Estelee I'd see you get home safe."

"I could walk with her," Grady offered.

Candi laughed nervously. "I don't need looking after."

He had mopped his way to stand beside her. A fact that had not escaped Candi's notice.

"My mama raised me to be a gentleman. There's no way I could stand here and watch a lady leave to walk home alone after dark."

"Which is why I'll be driving her home," Dixie said.

"Maybe we should flip a coin."

Candi wasn't about to sit by while these two argued about something so silly. She lifted her purse strap to her shoulder and headed for the door. "I'll be fine. Goodnight."

Candi unlocked the door and turned to wave, only to find them staring at her with slack jaws. She smiled as she moved slowly down the sidewalk towards Miss Estelee's. She heard the door to the diner open and close. She didn't have to guess who was hurrying to catch up with her, which didn't take long with his long strides.

"Sheriff," she acknowledged without looking at him.

"You don't seem surprised."

"I'm not." She turned to him then. "This truly is unnecessary."

He shoved his hands into the pockets of his jeans and shrugged. "Humor me, then."

"You say that like I have a choice."

He surprised her by saying, "You always have a choice." He paused, then continued, "I'd feel better if you'd allow me to accompany you. I'm sure Miss Estelee would as well."

She sighed. "That's not playin' fair."

He matched his steps to hers. "Why does it offend you that we want to see you home safely?"

"I'm not offended. Just uncomfortable. After all," she chanced another glance at him, "I hardly know you."

"You're among friends here in Angel Ridge. You're safe."

She smiled. "And yet I need to be 'seen home safely' as you put it?"

"Now, you're twisting my words. I meant you're safe with me."

Candi wished she could believe that, but felt sure she wasn't safe with any lawman. And even if Grady weren't a lawman, she still wouldn't be safe with him for entirely different reasons. All her senses heightened when he came around. She didn't need that. Not now.

"You don't believe me."

He was very perceptive. She pondered her response, remembering it wouldn't be wise to offend the town's sheriff.

"I suppose . . . it's too soon to tell."

He chuckled. "Very diplomatic response."

They turned onto Ridge Road. Just like the day, it was a perfect night. No clouds, plentiful stars dotting the night sky. A big, orange harvest moon took center stage brightly lighting their way. Soft lights twinkled behind lace curtains of homes more than a century old that lined one side of the street. The heels of her new boots tapping against the brick sidewalk were the only sound besides the flowing river below the ridge.

They continued in silence, which suited her since they couldn't seem to manage a civil conversation. Their encounter in the kitchen flared unbidden in her mind's eye. He'd felt warm and solid under her hands. In that unguarded moment, she'd looked in his eyes and glimpsed someone she'd like to believe she could trust. Someone who, maybe, she might even like to get to know, but a person should never proceed recklessly based on something as unreliable as impressions, supposed or imagined, in unguarded moments.

Not paying attention to her footing on the uneven bricks of the sidewalk, she caught her toe and pitched forward. Grady gently clasped her arm and saved her from falling face first.

"Careful. These old sidewalks can be hazardous." They continued on their way, but he didn't take his hand from her arm. "It's too dark down this stretch of the road. Town council should —"

Screeching tires and bright headlights cut his words off. A truck was weaving and barreling towards them, the muffler unnaturally loud in the quiet night.

"What the —"

Candi didn't take time to think. She let instinct take over. Lowering her shoulder, she tackled Grady, knocking him sideways over a row of prickly boxwoods. She heard a grunt, fabric ripping, felt the bush's leaves scrape her face and hands all in one instant as the truck careened onto the sidewalk where she and Grady had been standing only a second ago.

Grady rolled as they hit the ground, taking the impact of their landing with her on top of him. The truck sped away, heading towards town.

"Are you all right?" Candi asked.

Grady felt a rush of heat cover his face and throat. He was used to being the rescuer, not the one being rescued. He wasn't sure he liked that feeling, but he wouldn't complain about the feeling of Candi pressed to his body from knee to shoulder. "I think that should be my line."

"I'm fine." She didn't seem to have any interest in moving.

Damn it. He'd like to savor the feel of her on top of him a while longer, but he needed an ID on that vehicle. They could have been killed. Someone might be injured yet if that driver wasn't stopped.

He eased Candi to his side and stood. The truck disappeared into the night, its lights now off, the only sound its loud muffler as it moved further away from them.

"Great." He knelt next to Candi. "Are you sure you're all right?"

She got her elbows under her, but didn't move further. He steadied her with a hand at her shoulder as she squeezed her eyes closed.

"Dizzy?"

Candi nodded.

He grabbed his cell phone and called his deputy. Woody answered on the first ring.

"Yeah, Boss?"

"I got a truck headed towards town traveling erratically at a high rate of speed. Can you pursue? I'm away from my unit."

"I'm on it. Description?"

"Negative."

"Older black Ford truck, two door, with a dent in the hood."

Grady pulled the cell phone away from his ear and looked at Candi incredulously. How had she known what Woody had asked? She must have heard. It was pretty quiet around here most evenings.

"Got it," Woody said. "I'll call when I pull 'em over."

As he disconnected the call, Grady could already hear the siren going as Woody pulled out from the courthouse in town. He returned the phone to his pocket and just stared at the woman next to him. Her hair was mussed with boxwood leaves sticking out of it, her skirt was torn, and a bloody scratch marred her cheek. She was completely disheveled and, at the same time, completely appealing. He had so many questions, he didn't know where to begin.

"I'm sorry if I hurt you," she was saying.

"I think you got the worst of it." He took off his jacket and draped it over her shoulders, then rubbed his hands up and down her arms to help warm her and get the blood flowing normally again. "How did you see that truck com—"

"I dropped my purse. I probably have stuff scattered all over these people's yard."

It was then that he noticed Dan and Mardi Harris peering out their living room window. He waved to let them know everything was all right. Dan moved away from the window. He'd probably be out in a minute.

Candi was crawling around on her hands and knees trying to gather her things. Grady pulled a flashlight out of his pocket, clicked it on, and helped.

"I'm sorry," she said again, her voice a little more shaky now that the adrenaline was wearing off.

Grady brushed her hair back over her shoulder so he could see her face. "Stop apologizing. You've got a cut on your face."

She shied away from his touch, his nearness. "I'm fine."

She grabbed an envelope with money spilling out of it, shoved it into her purse and stood. Now where had that come from? That was more than the night's tips.

"Grady? What's going on out here?"

Dan Harris was coming down the sidewalk towards them.

"Evenin', Dan." He chanced one more look at Candi before responding further. She was sitting still now, looking at the ground, the backs of her fingers against her injured cheek. He handed her his handkerchief. She took it and pressed it against the scratch.

"Sorry to trouble you folks," Grady stood and shook Dan's hand.

"What's the trouble?"

"I was walking Miss Estelee's niece, Candi here, home, and a truck came out of nowhere and ran us off the sidewalk. We had to dive into your boxwoods, but I don't think there's any damage other than a few bruises and scratches on us." He chuckled, and looked at Candi again. She still looked rattled.

"If you don't mind, Dan, I'm gonna see to Candi, and then I'll head into town to try and track that driver down."

"Now, don't you worry none about them bushes, Sheriff. They been standin' more than a hundred years. You couldn't hurt 'em if you tried. You go on and do what you need to." He leaned toward Candi and said, "Where's my manners? I'm Dan Harris, ma'am. I've known Miss Estelee my whole life. I'm pleased to meet you."

Candi looked up then and made an attempt at a weak smile. She nodded, but didn't speak.

Grady grasped Candi's arm and said, "Can you stand?"

"Of course," she insisted, but allowed him to help her get to her feet. He let her stand there a second till she got her legs under her.

"Y'all be careful, now," Dan said with a wave.

Grady steered Candi back to the sidewalk, keeping a hand at her elbow and a close eye on her. Miss Estelee's was only a couple of houses away, but when Grady looked up, he found her heading towards them with Doc Prescott close behind.

"Lawsy day! I heard tires screeching and by the time I got out onto my porch, I saw y'all flying over the Harris' boxwoods. What in the world?" She took Candi into her arms and hugged her tightly. "Darlin'? Are you all right."

"I'm fine, ma'am."

Doc Prescott caught up to them then. "She has some scratches," Grady said. "You should have a look at her, Doc."

"Of course. Here now, Estelee. Let me get to her."

"I'm fine," Candi insisted.

Miss Estelee swept her with an all-encompassing look. "Oh, your sweet face is scratched and your new skirt is torn." She clicked her tongue, and then turned on Grady. "Young man, I told y'all to see my grandniece home safe, and just look at her!"

She was right. He should have been paying closer attention, and he should have been walking street side. What was wrong with him? "I'm sorry, ma'am."

"It's not Grady's fault."

"Well, of course it is!"

"We can stand here arguing about fault, or we can get this poor girl off the street and into a comfortable house where I can have a look at her," Doc Prescott interjected.

He was right. What was wrong with them all? Without giving it a second thought, he swept Candi up into his arms and moved quickly towards Miss Estelee's house. She could have a concussion, something could be broken, or worse.

"Grady!" Candi exclaimed, "Please . . . put me down."

He set his jaw and tightened his grip, expecting her to struggle. "I will, as soon as I get you inside."

She sighed and held onto his shoulders as he moved as quickly as safety permitted.

CHAPTER 5

"Now Grady, you don't need to stand around here. We'll see to Candi. You get out there and find this maniac that tried to run you and my grandniece over."

"Yes, ma'am. I'll check back later to see how she is."

Candi hated all the fuss they were making. Doc Prescott was presently checking her for broken bones while she lay on the sofa in the parlor. "I'm fine," she repeated for what felt like hundredth time.

"You can call later, after you put that person in jail, and not before," Miss Estelee said as she pushed Grady out the door. As soon as he was gone, she hurried back into the parlor. "Is she all right, Charles?"

"Looks like a few scratches, some bruising, and a tear in her skirt are the worst of it." To Miss Estelee he said, "Could you get me a basin of water and a washcloth? I want to clean the dirt out of these cuts, and then get some ointment and bandages on them." To Candi, he said, "Then I want you to take some ibuprofen and get to bed, young lady. You've had a full day."

Candi tried to sit up, but a wave of dizziness overtook her, and she eased back into the cushions of the couch.

"Dizzy?" Doc Prescott asked.

Candi squeezed her eyes shut and nodded.

"Oh, Lordy," Miss Estelee said.

"I checked her head. There are no knots, but that doesn't necessarily mean she didn't hit it. Maybe we should take her to the ER for a CAT scan to check for concussion."

"No, please. I just tried to sit up too quickly."

He checked her head again anyway. "Did you lose consciousness?"

"No."

"Any tenderness?"

"No, none."

He rubbed his snowy beard, frowning. "Well, it's likely just the trauma making her lightheaded. Nothing a good night's sleep won't cure."

"Couldn't I just soak in the tub to clean the scrapes?" Candi suggested. "That will help with any soreness I might have tomorrow. I can put the ointment on myself before

I get into bed." She really needed some time alone to regroup. All these people hovering were smothering her. She tried to breathe deeply, but couldn't quite get a whole breath in.

Miss Estelee seemed to understand. "I think that'll be fine, Charles. I'll keep an eye on her. If anything changes, I'll call you."

He offered her his hand and helped her into a sitting position. He checked her eyes with a penlight, then had her follow his finger . . . up, right, left, down.

He turned the light off and stared at her for a long moment.

"All right, but I insist on helping her upstairs, and I'll stay until she's in bed. I want to check her again before she goes to sleep."

Miss Estelee looked at Candi and waited.

She nodded her agreement. "All right." Anything to have a few minutes alone.

Less than an hour later, she was lying in the softest bed she'd ever slept in under a mound of quilts. The hot bath had helped calm her spirits. The vision of the man in the truck racing towards her and Grady hovered at the edge of her consciousness, but the pain pills and the bath combined to keep it there as she drifted off to sleep.

■ ■ ■ ■

A young woman with sleekly-styled blonde hair steps off Uncle Billy's fishing boat, hugging her sweater close and trying not to choke on the nausea from the outboard motor's fumes.

She stands on the riverbank looking lost as the boat disappears from view. The lake parts and separates a little, then smoothes back over as if the boat had never been there.

She hefts a suitcase and walks a well-worn path to a cabin. She stares at the ground, not missing a step, like she's walked it many times before. Sadness pulls at her pretty features.

My dreams, all my dreams . . . she moans, *oh why did I have to wake when all I want to do is sleep for the rest o' my days . . .*

An old woman stands on the porch wearing a faded cotton dress and stained apron, both drab from many washings. Her black and steel hair hangs in a long, thick braid down her back.

I been expectin' you, missy . . .

The younger woman hesitates, almost like she knows that when she sets foot on that porch and enters that cabin, it will be an end to all of her sweet dreams.

She steps up onto the porch and sets her suitcase down on the rough-hewn planks. She slides her hand around to the base of her back, rubbing it.

The old woman comes and puts a gnarled, age-bent hand on the girl's belly. Neither speak, but both close their eyes and breathe in slow and deep.

A calm stillness marks the woman's time-weathered face. *The circle of life continues. Another generation to carry on our ways after we're gone.*

The young woman nods, a tear trickles down her cheek. Regret for wrong choices ages her features as she looks into the dark cabin, but a deep acceptance soon replaces it.

She picks up the suitcase and walks inside. The old woman follows and shuts the door.

Weeping . . . the weeping of a soul mourning, the sound so sad it hurts to hear it.

Pacing . . . Trees and water . . .

A woman moving among the shadows.

Pacing . . .

Crying . . .

Waiting . . .

Water lapping against the shore, the trees so near.

Too near . . .

Too far . . .
Pacing . . .
Crying . . .
Waiting . . .
My heart . . . oh, my heart . . .

The water rises up to the trees now. The woman moves like a ghost among their shadows.

Crying . . .
Waiting . . .
Stillness . . .

She steps onto a small dock, but looks over her shoulder to the trees as if she's not comfortable outside their shelter. Mist rises from the murky water that's almost even with the wood planks she stands on.

Her eyes change. She looks straight ahead.

Hope.

A smile breaks on her beautiful face.

Love.

She holds out her hand and takes a step forward.

My heart, oh my heart . . .

She takes another step forward. The ancient, narrow dock sways and creaks, but she takes another step, the transformative smile still defining her face.

My heart . . . oh, my heart. Come to me!

Another step. A horrible crack. She slips into the water in one fluid motion, the smile still on her face, love shining in her lovely eyes.

Ripples circle out around the spot where she sinks.

Ripples . . .

Quiet . . .

Stillness . . .

"Hough . . ." Candi sucked in a breath as she sat up in bed. She looked around, disoriented. Where was she? She pushed the hair out of her eyes. Light streamed in around the white shade pulled down behind lace curtains. What time was it?

A bedside clock declared it was just past dawn. As she moved from the dream to wakefulness, she remembered. She'd left the mountain yesterday. She was in Angel Ridge, sleeping in Miss Estelee's upstairs bedroom. She was sore. She held up her hands and looked at the bandages over bruising scratches. There'd nearly been an accident. She'd had to jump out of the path of an oncoming truck. She'd fallen. Grady.

A dream. She'd been dreaming about a woman coming home to Laurel Mountain and Aunt Ruby. A woman so sad, looking for a lost love? And then, she'd drowned.

Candi stood and walked to the dresser sitting against the wall. She leaned in to examine the scratch on her cheek and looked into the face of the woman in her dream.

Chapter 6

Grady strolled into the office early the next morning, surprised to find everyone already there and working. He looked at his watch. He was in an hour before he usually was.

"You guys usually come in this early?"

"Woody and I come in at seven most days, Grady. Here are your messages." Clara, his administrative assistant and dispatcher, handed him several slips of paper, then turned back to her computer and resumed typing at a furious speed.

"Here's the report on the reckless driving incident last night," Woody said.

Grady took that as well and scanned it. "My office."

Woody followed him and sat in the chair across from his desk. Grady removed his coat and shoulder harness, then hung both on the coat tree standing in the corner. He needed coffee. He hadn't taken the time to stop by Ferguson's to pick up any. He'd swung by Miss Estelee's to check on Candi, but no one had answered when he knocked on the front door.

"Here you go, Grady," Clara set a steaming cup of strong black coffee in front of him. "Remind me to recommend a raise for you at the next town council meeting, Clara."

"Will do."

As she spoke, she was already shutting the door and returning to her desk. He had a top rate staff. Why hadn't he noticed that before?

"Tell me again what happened last night, Woody," he said, taking a long sip of coffee as he read the report in front of him. They'd gone over all this last night, but maybe he'd missed something.

"Sure thing. As soon as I finished talking to you, I saw the truck come into town. It took the turn from Ridge Road to Main pretty much on two wheels." Woody shifted in his seat before continuing. "I pursued. He headed straight for the Tall Pines-Lower River Road fork just north of town.

"By the time I reached the fork, there was no sign of the vehicle. I took the left fork down Lower River Road, figuring there was no way he'd go up to the Tall Pines since he'd hit a dead end there.

"I followed the road out about two miles, but still, there was no sign of the vehicle. So, I turned around and headed back up to the Tall Pines. Nothing there either, and no tire tracks.

"I'm sorry, Grady. But after the vehicle left Main, I never saw it again."

"Did you get a plate number?"

"No. He had his lights off, and it was too far away. I couldn't make it out."

"Did the vehicle meet the description I gave you?"

"Yeah. Clara's been getting us a list of all older model black F-100s registered in this and the surrounding counties. They'll probably be more than a few to check out."

He was right about that. Grady took another sip of his coffee. The caffeine was starting to help him think clearer. He'd been in the office late, calling local sheriff's departments to have them be on the lookout for the vehicle. He'd waited around hoping to get a callback. When none had come by 4 a.m., he'd gone home to get some sleep.

"What kind of resources do you want to expend on this, Grady? I mean, it was probably just a teenager taking a joy ride. If he comes back into town, we'll get him."

"Or her. We didn't get a visual on the driver or any passengers." At least he hadn't.

He really needed to speak with Candi, not only to see how she was, but also to get more information about what she'd seen. He still didn't understand how she'd gotten such a good look at the truck when all he'd seen was a blur. He also didn't know how she'd managed to get him out of harm's way. She was such a little thing, and he weighed two-twenty naked and soaking wet.

"You may be right, Woody, but for now, I want to keep digging. I was thinking that today we could patrol town and the farms and houses out beyond the railroad tracks, and everything in between to see if we can find that truck."

"And we could head up into the mountain communities this side of the lake to have a look there, too. If we talk to a few people and let them know what happened last night, who knows, maybe if they see the truck, they'll give us a call."

"Yeah, maybe." Grady swiveled in his chair and stared out the window as he finished his coffee. Looked like rain.

"You all right, boss? If you don't mind me sayin', you look like a long stretch of bad road."

"I had a late night. Nothing a little coffee won't cure." He lifted his cup in a salute. "I hope there's more where this came from."

Woody stood. "I'll put on another pot."

"Thanks."

He drained his coffee and rolled the mouse on his computer to disengage the sleep mode. He'd been here so late, he hadn't bothered to shut it down. He pulled up his email and scanned the subject lines. He opened several and read.

No information on any Candi — or any variation on the name — Heart from East Tennessee, Western North Carolina, or Southwest Virginia. Candi Heart became a resident of Angel Ridge only yesterday, and already he had two unsolved mysteries. There was nothing he hated more.

He started typing. A few more inquiries, and then he'd make his rounds in town and head out on patrol. He was determined to get some answers today. He wouldn't rest till he did.

"Miss Estelee, I'm fine," Candi repeated. My shoulder's just a little sore. Nothing some arnica rub won't cure."

"Doc Prescott said you should take it easy today."

"And I will. I just have some things to take care of in town. Nothing too taxing, I promise."

Miss Estelee sighed. "Let me get my coat."

Lordy, any more hovering and she'd smother! "Please, don't trouble yourself."

"It's no trouble. I walk into town most mornings. I need to see if that nice Cole Craig got the chrysanthemums I ordered put in at the angel monument. Once we get to town, you can go your way, and I'll go mine. We can meet back up at the diner for lunch if you'd like."

"All right," Candi relented. She'd looked forward to some time alone. She was used to being the caretaker, not the one that needed taking care of — not that she needed to be cared for. With Aunt Ruby being so old, she'd been tending to herself since she was just a little girl. She didn't know how to let someone else worry and fuss over her, and she had to admit, she didn't much care for it.

They walked into town in silence. It looked and smelled like rain. She was glad she'd put on her jacket with the hood. She'd need it before she headed back. When they walked past the spot where the car had jumped up onto the sidewalk, Candi slowed her step. There was a dent in the line of boxwoods where she and Grady had sailed through to the lawn on the other side. An unsettled feeling pressed down on her. The man in that truck hadn't been driving erratically. He'd pointed his truck at her and Grady intentionally.

Who would want to hurt Grady? She should warn him, but how would she explain such a thing. He'd think she was crazy. Didn't she have enough to deal with getting settled into a new place and setting up a new business? Grady had enough unanswered questions about her. She didn't need to add to them.

A black cat darted out of the bushes right in front of them, crossed the street and dove down the bank leading to the river. Instinctively, Candi grasped Miss Estelee's arm to keep her from tripping and from crossing the cat's path.

"Well, if that don't send a chill up your spine, I don't know what will!"

"Are you superstitious, ma'am?"

The older woman hitched her purse up on her arm. "No sense in testing fate, I always say. How we gonna get into town now? There's no way for us to get there without crossing that devil's path."

Linking her arm in Miss Estelee's, Candi said, "Guess I'll have to conjure up something to ward off bad luck."

"You get right on that, then."

Both women stepped over the spot where the cat's feet had touched the sidewalk.

When they got to town, she and Miss Estelee said their goodbyes, and Candi went straight to the hardware store. As she entered, a bell tinkled announcing her arrival. Only a few shoppers browsed in the aisles. Candi peered around the merchandise looking for Mr. DeFoe.

She found him in the back sitting among a small circle of men; all looked to be about the same age as him. She approached quietly, not wanting to interrupt. They seemed to be in the middle of an intense and serious conversation. Maybe she'd just look around until they finished.

She had just turned to look at a display of paint brushes when Mr. DeFoe stood and said, "Candi! Miss Heart! Good morning."

She turned back to the group of men. Mr. DeFoe had stood and was smiling at her. The other men stayed seated. Several of them looked equal measures of surprised and curious as they looked her over, still others frowned as if perplexed. What a strange reaction. She wondered if they responded this way to all newcomers or if it was just her.

"Come on over here, hon, and let me introduce you to this ragtag group."

Candi approached slowly. "Oh, I don't want to interrupt."

"You're not interrupting anything. We was just chewing the cud as we're like to most mornin's." He pointed to the man at his left and said, "This here's Patrick Houston. He's the mayor of our fine town and the youngster of this bunch."

The younger man stood and extended his hand. "Pleased to meet you."

She shook his hand, and said, "Thank you." He had kind blue eyes, but sadness shaded them and stooped his shoulders a bit.

Moving around the circle, Mr. DeFoe continued the introductions. "This is Albert McKay. He runs the bank in town."

"Mr. McKay," she nodded. "I think I may have met your wife yesterday. Harriet McKay?"

The distinguished-looking older gentleman stood and extended his hand to her. "Do I need to apologize?" he said with a smile.

Candi smiled as well. "Of course not. Why do you ask?"

The group laughed as if they knew some joke she didn't. Mr. DeFoe said, "Go on and apologize, Bert. You know it's just a matter of time."

Mr. McKay hung his head and shook it. "Sad but true."

He sat down again, just as another man in the group stood. Candi recognized him as the older gentleman she'd seen yesterday outside the grocery. He had that same look on his face; like he was about to bolt.

"This is Jim Wallace. Him and his wife run Wallace Grocery here in town."

"I'm pleased to meet you. Wallace . . . are you related to the sheriff?"

He stood looking at her, eyes wide, not speaking. Mr. DeFoe nudged him with an elbow. The gray-haired man blinked and said, "Grady's my nephew." He cleared his throat and said, "Excuse me," and brushed past her on his way to the door.

"Well, he's actin' odd today," Mr. McKay said.

"Wet weather triggers his arthritis," Mr. DeFoe said. "Anyway, this is Dan Harris."

The man from the lawn she'd landed on last night stood and extended his hand.

"He was just tellin' us about the mishap you and Grady had at his place last night."

"I hope you weren't hurt, ma'am."

Candi shook his hand. "I'm afraid your boxwoods got the worst of it."

"Don't you worry about that. I just hope Grady and Woody found whoever nearly ran y'all over."

"Yes," Candi agreed.

"And last but not least, this is Leroy Ferguson."

A strikingly handsome, very tall man with salt and pepper hair stood and shook her hand. "Ma'am. Welcome to Angel Ridge."

"Ferguson. Are you related to Dixie?"

"Afraid so. She's my youngest. Do *I* need to apologize as well?"

Candi laughed. "No. I met her yesterday. She's been very kind to me."

"That's my Dixie. She can be very helpful . . . among other things."

Everyone laughed at another one of those inside jokes shared by people of long acquaintance.

"Is there anything I can do for you this morning, Miss Heart?" Mr. DeFoe asked.

"There is, but it can wait until you finish your conversation."

"Nonsense." He moved to stand next to her, took her arm and walked a few paces away. "What can I do for you?"

"I wanted to talk to you about the shop I looked at yesterday."

"You've made a decision then?"

"Yes. I'd like to lease it if your offer still stands."

He clapped his hands, a big smile lighting his face and eyes. "Absolutely. I still have the keys right here." He dug in his coat pocket and pulled out the ring of keys she'd used yesterday. He pressed them in her hand and steered her toward the paint display. "If you'll pick out colors, I'll get Cole Craig right on getting a coat of paint on the walls. You just pull these cards and write the room name right on the color you like."

"Okay. Thank you."

"Thank *you* for renting the place. I couldn't be more pleased. We need some new businesses in town."

"Can I get these back to you this afternoon?" she said, speaking of the paint chips.

"Sure, sure."

"Also, I'm not going to need the beauty shop equipment in the back room. Do you think you could have someone move it out?"

"Yeah, but I'll have to have a look at the sinks and those pedicure chairs. They're plumbed and will be a mite harder to deal with."

"Whatever you think will be fine."

"What'd you have in mind for that room?"

"I thought I might turn it into a tea room."

"Tea room?"

"Yes. A place for ladies to come and enjoy a relaxing cup of tea, maybe read or meet with other women."

Mr. DeFoe nodded. "That sounds right nice."

"I have things in storage and need to hire someone with a truck to bring them over to the shop. Could you recommend someone?"

"Yeah. Cole Craig does odd jobs around town. He comes by most days. You want me to send him to Miss Estelee's to see you?"

"Just send him over to the shop. I thought I'd get a start on cleaning it up."

"Are you sure you're okay? You look a little banged up."

Candi held up her bandaged hands. "I must look a fright, but these don't hurt at all."

"Well," he rubbed his chin, "if you're sure. Let me get you some supplies, then."

"I prefer eco-friendly cleaners. Do you have any?"

"I just got a new line of that in."

"And brooms and mops made of natural materials."

"Not a problem. I'll have it all delivered over to you within the hour. I'll also get the lease filled out and bring that over for you to look at and sign."

Without thinking, Candi held out her injured hand to shake on it and said, "Thank you."

She was going to enjoy doing business

with Mr. DeFoe. She'd been naturally cautious of him in the beginning, what with the strange way he looked at her. But now, she had a good feeling about him. Aunt Ruby had taught her to trust her instincts, so she wouldn't question it. She had too much work to do to worry unnecessarily.

She walked the short distance to her shop. *Her* shop. She was so happy she could just sing and dance around town square, but the sight of a serious-looking Grady Wallace coming towards her pulled her up short.

Grady removed his hat and raked a hand through his hair.

"Mornin', Candi."

"Good mornin', Sheriff."

An appealing smile transformed his worried expression.

"I know you said it would take some weeks before you could call me 'Grady,' but I think savin' my life should accelerate the process, don't you?"

Candi tucked her head and tried one of the several keys she had in the lock. "It wasn't quite so dramatic as that." When that key wouldn't turn, she tried another.

"No down-playing allowed." He leaned a shoulder against the building and touched a gentle finger to the scratch on her cheek. "It's not every day a man gets to thank a pretty lady for savin' his life."

She felt warmth flood her face at his compliment as the key turned in the lock, and she opened the door. He followed her inside.

"So, I guess this means you're renting the place."

"Yes."

"I'm glad you and Bud worked something out."

"Sheriff, I have a lot to do today; errands to run before I can get started putting things to right here. So, if you'll excuse me . . ."

Grady spun his hat on his hand. "Actually, this isn't entirely a social call. I need to ask you a few questions about last night."

"I don't understand." He'd been there, too. Seen what she had seen.

"I was wondering if you got a look at the driver."

Shaking her head, she said, "I'm afraid I didn't. I just focused on getting us off the sidewalk. I'm sorry."

"No apology necessary, ma'am. I'm grateful for what you did." He rubbed his jaw and asked, "Could you tell if the driver was a man or a woman?"

"It was a man."

"You're certain."

"Yes," she said impatiently. She didn't

have time to be standing around here playing twenty questions with Grady Wallace, much less having to repeat herself. She started to shift from foot to foot, anxious to be on her way. Hopefully, he'd get the message.

"Anyone in the truck besides the driver?"

No such luck. She hitched her purse up on her shoulder. "No. No one else."

He shook his head and chuckled.

That cut it. "Something strike you as funny?"

"Not at all. It's just, I don't know how you did it?"

Here we go, she thought. *Another of his fishing expeditions. Well, not today.* "Could we do this another time?"

"Ah, there she is. The woman of mystery."

Candi lifted a shoulder. "If you call being busy mysterious."

He straightened as if just remembering she was in a hurry. "Of course. I'm sorry to keep you."

Finally. Still she couldn't keep herself from adding, "I would like to make a suggestion."

"By all means."

"When you want to learn something about someone or solve a mystery, as you put it, often it's more useful to watch and listen instead of peppering someone with questions they're not inclined to answer."

His smile was unrepentant. "I suppose I'm just not that patient."

She paused, considering, and just looked at him for a long moment. When he began to fidget, she leaned back and took a cleansing breath. "More's the pity." She spoke the words softly, more to herself than to him. He had such potential, but like so many, he didn't care enough to meet it. Such a waste. Still, no reason for her to be distracted from meeting her potential.

She jangled the keys to the shop to ground them both in the moment. She walked outside, and again, he followed. "I have workers coming this afternoon and, as I said, errands to run. So . . ."

Grady put his hat back on, and looked down at her. The bright sunshine had her squinting. "If you remember anything else —"

"Yes. I'll let you know," she finished.

His smile flashed white against his ruddy complexion. Her pulse picked up, making her breath catch in her throat.

"I'll look forward to it," he said in a slow drawl.

He nodded and crossed the street towards the diner. As she watched him move away without a backward glance, she had to force herself to look away, even out her breathing and her heart rate.

As she got her feet moving, she had to wonder . . . what had caused that strange reaction in her? So much for getting inside his head. That had clearly backfired.

"Women . . ."

Grady took a long draw on his coffee, enjoying the caffeine burn on the back of his throat. What had happened back there? First, he'd seen Candi standing outside Madge's old shop, looking incredible in a long dark green sweater belted at the waste, some kind of dark tights and lace up high heeled boots. Why was it that every time he saw her, she got more attractive?

"You say something?"

He took another drink of his coffee. "Just thinkin' out loud, Dix."

"Wanna bounce whatever it is off me?"

He thought about that for a second, and then figured it couldn't hurt to get a female perspective.

"I just came from Candi's shop."

"So, she signed the lease."

"I guess so. I ran into her as she was going in. I had a few questions I needed to ask her and wanted to make sure she was all right after last night." Funny. She'd looked so good that he'd never gotten around to asking her how she was.

"Whoa! Back the bus up. You mean last night after you and Candi left here?"

"Yeah."

"What happened?"

"Oh, I forgot. You don't know."

Dixie smacked the counter in front of him. Grady sat up straighter and leaned back.

"Tell me now before I have to strangle you."

"Isn't it a little early in the morning for assaulting a public servant?"

"Grady!"

"All right," he held up his hands. "Simmer down. When I was walking Candi over to Miss Estelee's, a reckless driver came barreling up Ridge Road and jumped the curb to the sidewalk."

"Dear Lord! Was Candi hurt?"

"Thanks for your touching concern for my well-being."

"*You* are clearly fine."

He took another sip of coffee in an affected attempt at nonchalance. "Thanks to Candi."

"Spit out the rest of the story already!"

He set his cup down. "She saw the truck before I did. Tackled me and sent us hurdling over the Harris' boxwoods."

"Did she hurt herself?"

Just to annoy her, he said, "I'm fine, thanks."

"Grady!"

"She has a few scratches. Probably some bruises, too, and last night she was a little dizzy, but Doc checked her out. She seems fine today." A little on edge, but fine.

"*Seems* fine?"

"Well, she's a hard woman to get information out of. She had a lot to do, and I didn't get to ask her outright . . ." he stumbled over the excuses. *How are you?* should have been the first question he'd asked.

Dixie grabbed her purse and headed for the door. "Where is she now?"

"I don't know. She chased me out. Said she had errands to run."

"Let's go. I'm closin'."

"It's 9:30!"

"And you're the only one still loiterin' instead of workin'."

He picked up his hat and followed Dixie to the door. "What's with you women today?"

"Us women?"

"Yeah. *You* women. You're all acting like I did something wrong, and Candi's giving *me* advice on how to conduct an investigation."

Dixie set the keyed deadbolt and said, "What are you going on about now?"

"Candi. She said I ask too many questions." Now that he thought about it, he started to get worked up. "What other way is there to conduct an investigation? You have to ask questions if you want answers."

"Well, what do you know?" Dixie put a hand on her hip and smiled at him.

He knew Candi was driving him nuts. He also knew she was hiding something. If she thought he was going to just sit back and wait for her to tip her hand or reveal all her many secrets, she had another think coming. He was a man of action; not a man who sat around waiting for things to work themselves out.

"I think Candi's got you pegged. She also rescued the rescuer, and you don't like either of those things. So, the question is, how are you going to handle it?"

"I don't know what you're talking about."

"Then you must be in denial, because I know you're not that dense."

"Think what you want." He jammed his hat onto his head. "I've got a reckless driver to track down."

"*Mmm-hmm* . . . good luck with that."

"Oh, Grady! There you are."

Geraldine Wallace crossed the street to the diner with Miss Estelee right beside her. So much for beating a hasty retreat.

"Mornin', Mama," Grady took his mother's elbow and kissed her still smooth cheek. As long as he could remember, the familiar scent of White Shoulders had wafted around her. He straightened and nodded to her companion, "Miss Estelee."

She frowned at him. "Sheriff."

Great. She was probably here to give him a piece of her mind about last night. Well, maybe some other time. "If you ladies will —" his getaway excuse hung on his lips as his cell phone's ring tone, *Born to Be Wild,* cut him off. "Excuse me.

"Hello?"

"Hey, boss. It's Woody."

"Yeah, Woody. What's up?"

"Clara's husband just called. Said he saw a truck meeting the description of the one we been looking for, abandoned down near the lake front near Billy Joe Maguire's place."

"Let's go take a look. I'll swing by and pick you up."

"10-4. Oh, and Grady?"

"Yeah?"

"Your mama's looking for you. According

to Clara, she's been calling here every five minutes since you left."

"She found me. I'll be there in a couple of minutes."

Grady disconnected the call. The women were gathered round him in a semicircle blocking his way to the courthouse.

Before he could excuse himself again, his mother gave him a woeful look. "Grady, I've been trying to reach you at the courthouse for hours."

He hadn't been gone for hours, but it made the fact that she couldn't reach him more dramatic. That was his mom. Everything was an emergency. "Sorry, Mama. I've been really busy this morning. Is everything all right?"

"Well, no! Everything is not all right. That's why I've been trying to call you!"

"You could have reached me on my cell."

His mother began to wring her hands. "Grady Wallace, you know I can't remember that number, and watch how you speak to me. I am your mother no matter how old you get or who you are in this town."

He put his hands on his hips, hung his head and took a deep breath. He did not need this right now . . .

Miss Estelee cleared her throat.

He looked up. "Sorry, Mama. I don't

mean to sound disrespectful. What's happened?" He tried to school his features as she took out her handkerchief and rubbed her nose. Last time she had been looking for him, there'd been a mouse in the pantry. He wondered what had her worked up this time.

"I changed the sheets this morning, put them in the washer, and ran it. After they'd finished washing, I put the sheets in the dryer, set it for sixty minutes, pushed the button, and it didn't start. I opened the door, closed it again, and pushed the button, but still, it wouldn't start."

"I have a lead on a case that I need to check out right now, but I'll come by just as soon as I get back to town and have a look. You probably just tripped a breaker."

"No! I need you to come now!"

Her voice rose to that shrill pitch that put him in mind of nails on a chalkboard. "I'm sorry, Mama, but I can't come right this minute. It'll wait till I get back."

"If those sheets sit one second longer, they're going to smell musty, and I'll have to wash them again. All that water, detergent and fabric softener just going to waste! Oh . . ." She waved her handkerchief and started sniffling in earnest. "It's a terrible thing to be old and all alone in the world with a son who has no time for his mother."

"There, there Geraldine," Miss Estelee patted her quivering shoulders. "Bring those sheets down to my house. You can use my dryer. Just go to the back door. The laundry room is just inside." She shot Grady a stern look. "I knew I left that door unlocked for a reason, this mornin'. Now you see? Things always work out just the way they should. Something you'd do well to take to heart, Grady Wallace."

Whatever that was supposed to mean. "I'm sorry. There's a break in the reckless driver case — the one that nearly killed me and your grandniece last night, Miss Estelee? I need to get going. Ladies."

He put a finger to his hat, then stepped off the sidewalk to head for his Jeep.

"Grady Wallace!"

Miss Estelee called after him. He pulled to a stop with another heartfelt sigh. "Ma'am?"

"I need to have a word with you. I'll expect you at my place sometime this afternoon."

"Yes, ma'am." He looked at Dixie and raised his eyebrows, knowing she had to have something to say. She always did.

"Well, what are you waitin' on? Get to gettin'. You got crimes to solve, after all. Don't let us *women* keep you."

What was with the women in this town today? It was like they'd all gotten up this morning and decided to give him hell. He shook his head, wondering if he'd ever understand them.

He and Woody easily found the truck just where the tip had said it would be. It was parked on the side of a deserted road that led out to the Maguire place. No skid marks, no sign of foul play. A search of the vehicle showed some empty beer cans and the keys still in the ignition. The license plate was missing.

"You think the suspect took off from here on foot?"

"That seems likely. Call the VIN number in to Clara and see if she can get us a name and address for who it's registered to while I have a look around."

"I'm on it."

Grady walked away from the truck, looking for anything that might give them an idea of which direction the suspect had taken. The tracks led down to the riverbank. Then they continued in a parallel line to the bank, like someone had been walking back and forth. Grady stood there, looking across the cove. It was a narrow stretch of the Little Tennessee, back water really, but too deep to cross on foot. In a few weeks, they'd change the lake levels and this cove would be nearly drained.

He stopped and held his hand in the icy water, wishing it could speak. No way someone would swim across. There was nothing on the other side anyway — just woods and Laurel Mountain. A small rowboat would do, but there wasn't one in sight. The truck hadn't been hauling one either.

He stood and strolled back toward the truck. No trash. No other debris in sight. He called out to Woody, "Anything from Clara?"

Woody rubbed his chin, frowning. "It's the dangdest thing, boss. The owner of this truck is . . ." Woody clamped his mouth shut, took off his hat, and raked a hand through his sandy blond hair.

"What is it, Woody?" Something was wrong. Really wrong. Every instinct he had was screaming inside him. He stood toe to toe with his deputy. "Talk."

"This truck has had only one owner, and it was purchased new in 1957. Grady, the owner's been dead more than twenty years."

"So, someone never registered it."

"How could you drive a vehicle for more

than twenty years without getting caught?"

"There's a lot of isolated area around here, Woody. A man could get use out of it and never bring it into town. No one would ever know."

Woody started to pace. Now that Grady was taking the time to really look at him, Grady noticed that all the color was gone from his deputy's face. "Who did this truck belong to, Woody?"

The younger man just kept pacing. Grady grabbed his arm, halting his progress. "Who, Woody?"

"Big Tom Hensley. The man your daddy shot and killed was the only owner of this truck."

Chapter 7

Tom Hensley? The man his daddy had shot and killed owned this truck. Grady turned and looked out at the cove. *Think, Grady.* This made sense. Maguire was Hensley's next of kin. "Well, then. Guess that solves our mystery. The only living kin of Tom Hensley lives just up the road."

"Billy Joe Maguire? He hardly ever leaves his farm except to go fishing. Why, I don't even know what the man looks like. His wife Verdi was my third grade teacher, but nobody ever saw her husband." Woody laughed. "I think driving down this road to his place is a teenage boy's rite of passage. If you ain't been shot at by Billy Joe Maguire, you ain't a man."

"Maguire was Hensley's kin. The truck must be his." Grady strode over to the Jeep and opened the door. "Let's go."

Woody got in. Grady fired the engine and slammed it into gear. He took off down the old dirt road towards the Maguire place.

"Grady, where are you goin'?"

"To talk to Billy Joe Maguire." He'd have thought that much was obvious.

"Are you crazy?" Woody's voice climbed up an octave. "I don't want to die today, Grady."

He slammed on the brakes. "If you're afraid, then get out and walk back to the truck, call for a tow, and get it impounded."

"I'm not afraid, Grady, but you can't just go out to the Maguire place without lettin' them know you're coming, not unless you got a death wish."

"And give Billy Joe the chance to run?"

"Billy Joe Maguire don't run from a fight."

"What do you know about him? I thought you said you'd never seen him."

"Yeah, but everybody in town knows that. You're upset. Cool down and think this through."

He leaned in towards Woody. "Last I checked, I was the sheriff and *you* do what I say. Now either shut up or get out."

"I'm not about to let you go up there alone, but let me at least have Clara patch a call through to their house to let them know we're coming."

Grady put the car in drive and spun out before the Jeep shot forward. "Fine, but you better get it done. I'll have us there in less than five minutes."

Billy Joe Maguire had been Tom Hensley's brother-in-law. That family was a legend in Angel Ridge. Big Tom had stood more than six and a half feet tall. A moonshiner who lived on Laurel Mountain, and had gotten sideways of the law in Angel Ridge more often than not. The law in Angel Ridge had been Grady's father, Fred Wallace. The disagreement that resulted in the fatal shooting of Tom had had something to do with Hensley's daughter. The details had never come to light. All the men of his father's age had been tight-lipped about it, but the speculation was that his father and some of the other men in town had spent time with her. She'd died not long after she left Angel Ridge. An apparent drowning victim with no foul play indicated. Case closed. His father had led the investigation. He'd read the file many times. There were more unanswered questions in the case than facts.

When Tom Hensley had come to town, it hadn't been to get answers, but rather satisfaction. The older man had been fatally wounded and his father critically. Grady's dad had died of his wounds three years later, bitter and in a wheelchair; not that he hadn't been bitter without the wheelchair. His father had been a hard man.

Woody made his call. Just as he hung up, Grady pulled into the long driveway that led to the Maguire place. When Grady stopped the Jeep, Maguire came out his front door toting a shotgun. Typical.

Grady got out and slammed the door shut. "Mornin', Billy Joe."

"State your business."

The old man was tall and thin, wearing overalls and a checked shirt. His gray hair stuck out in all directions, and it looked like his face hadn't seen a razor in awhile. "Mind puttin' that shotgun down? I don't believe you'll be needin' it today." Woody got out of the Jeep and slowly moved to stand beside him.

"Not as long as your deputy there has his hand on his gun."

"Woody."

"When he puts down that shotgun," was Woody's response.

"What do you want, Wallace?"

"There's an old Ford F-100 parked just off the road down by that back water cove about half a mile back. You know anything about it?"

"What's it to you?"

A lazy hound dog got up off the porch

and came to stand next to his master. A low growl meant to threaten turned into a huge yawn, killing the effect. He laid back down, but kept his eyes trained on them.

"I'm about to have it towed and impounded because it's got no tags. I was just wonderin' if you knew who it belonged to."

"It ain't nothin' to me. Now, get off my property."

"What would you say if I told you the last person who registered it was Tom Hensley?"

"I'd say you're a damn filthy liar just like your daddy. Now get off my property. I won't say it again."

Well, I tried, Grady thought. He turned and walked back to the Jeep. He hadn't expected the old man to be helpful, but he wouldn't be doing his job if he hadn't at least asked. "You have a good day, Billy Joe. Give our best to the missus."

Maguire spit a line of tobacco juice onto the ground at his feet, letting Grady know what the likelihood of that would be.

Once they were on their way out and Woody seemed to be able to breathe normally again, he said, "Hey, Grady. You mind dropping me off at my place? I think I need to change my underpants."

Grady chuckled. "Call Clara and tell her to have Fuzz impound that truck. I'll drop you off to wait with it. I don't want Maguire coming out and moving it."

"This day just keeps getting better. I might need the rest of the day off, or a hospital bed, if he decides to come out and do something with that truck."

"Geez, Woody. Why didn't I know you were this . . . this . . ."

"Chicken? I don't know, because I've never made a secret of it. And I want full credit for ridin' out there with you on that fool's errand and covering your hind parts."

He fell in with the banter to lighten the mood. "I'll give you a commendation if you want, 'cause I'm the sheriff, and I can do that."

"I'd say that's the least I deserve."

"We'll both stay until Fuzz comes. Neither of us should be alone to deal with the likes of Maguire."

"Now you're thinking clearly."

"You sayin' I wasn't?"

Woody paused before continuing. "Going out there alone wasn't a good idea and you know it."

"Yeah, I know. It's been a crazy couple of days."

"You know, we haven't had this much excitement in years, Boss."

He chuckled. "Yeah, not since someone

put underwear on the angel monument in town square."

"I don't think I've ever seen Miss Estelee that livid."

"She's pretty particular about the angel monument. It's like it belongs to her or something."

They pulled in next to the truck and parked.

"So, what do you think's really going on here, Grady?"

"I think this truck belongs to Maguire."

"So, you think he tried to kill you and Candi?"

"It's more likely that a teenager took it for a joy ride, and they ran off the road because they were drunk."

"Right. I mean, why would Maguire come after you out of the blue after all these years?"

Why, indeed? Still, Grady couldn't rule it out as a possibility.

Candi finished running her errands sooner than she'd expected. Getting the business license had been simple. Even better, they hadn't required personal identification. She'd had to have identification to open the bank account, but bank records were confidential and the checks would only have the business name on them.

The business name. It had hit her what she would name the shop as soon as the clerk asked. Heart's Desire — a shop where women could find everything their heart desired. It was perfect, and it tied in nicely with her new name.

The shop was the center of a flurry of activity when she arrived late that afternoon, thanks to all the calls she'd made on her new cell phone this morning. Cole Craig had returned from picking up the things at her storage unit and was stacking boxes inside. Blake Ferguson had come over to have a look at the back room to figure out what needed to be done about the sinks and foot baths. Mr. DeFoe had called them pedicure chairs.

When Blake hadn't been paying attention, she'd opened the back door to the alley to see if Uncle Billy had brought her supplies from the spring house on Laurel Mountain. The three boxes, stacked neatly next to the door, contained all of her essential oils and herbs, dried flowers and cuttings for a garden in the spring.

She lifted the first box and almost collided with Grady Wallace as she walked back inside. "Sheriff! What are you doing here?"

"I came to help."

She brushed past him with the heavy box and moved in the direction of the large workroom off the salon.

"Here, let me help you with that."

"Thank you, but I've got it."

"I insist."

He grabbed the box, but she didn't release it.

"I just came from Miss Estelee's. She gave me strict orders to make sure you didn't lift anything. Something about a shoulder injury from last night."

She stood there looking at him, she holding one side of the box, he holding the other. "My shoulder is fine."

"Is it?"

For some reason she would take time to examine later, she couldn't lie to him while he stared intently into her eyes. They were flecked with more gold than green today. "It's just a bruise," she confessed.

"From the fall or from tackling me?"

She felt her cheeks heat.

"I'm sorry. Sorry that you were hurt and sorry that the first thing out of my mouth when I saw you this morning wasn't a question about how you were. It was thoughtless of me."

"There's no need to apologize. It's just a little bruise."

"Humor me."

She didn't know what to say.

"Say you accept my apology, then let me carry the box."

"I accept your apology, but I would really be more comfortable carrying this myself."

"What's wrong? Afraid I'll drop it?"

"Yes."

"Precious cargo, then?"

"Very."

"I promise to be very careful."

"Thank you, but —"

He pulled. She tugged. The box fell.

She panicked, but Grady, cool in a crisis, squatted and deftly caught the box just before it hit the floor. The bottles inside rattled, then settled while she held her breath.

"I've got it," he said unnecessarily.

Candi let her breath out in a rush as he stood with the box secure in his arms. He could have let it fall. What did he care if everything in it broke? He had no idea what the contents meant to her and her new business, but he'd reacted automatically to save it nonetheless.

As if reading her thoughts, he said, "I told you I wouldn't drop it, and I'm a man of my word."

He looked at her intently allowing his

words to settle around them, and then turned to carry the box into what would become her workroom. Candi followed.

"It's my turn to be thanking you now. I'd say that you saving that box makes us even."

Grady laughed. "I wouldn't equate catching a box and you saving my life, but I'd settle for you calling me Grady."

Folding her arms in front of her, Candi said, "You are like a dog with a bone in that regard."

"Right, and I'm not lettin' go. So, you might as well start callin' me 'Grady.' "

That huge smile broke across his face causing her heart to jump and hit that funny rhythm it had earlier. Candi sighed. She didn't like the way this was going. Everywhere she turned, it seemed, Grady Wallace was there. He kept showing her glimpses of the man he was meant to be, but he also struggled against becoming that man. She did not want to get caught in that kind of a struggle with any man, and particularly not a lawman. Still, there was no reason she couldn't lower her guard enough to be friendlier to him. After all, she *had* saved his life.

"What's that smile about?" he asked.

Ever observant. Well, except for when he'd missed seeing that truck. "I did save your hide last night."

"So you're gonna rub it in now?"

His smile and relaxed stance didn't fool her. "Rubs you the wrong way doesn't it? Having a woman come through in a crisis and save *you* for a change."

The smile froze on his face, and he unconsciously jerked his head to the side, making the bones in his neck pop.

She should have let it go, but some demon made her say, "How could you, the town's sheriff, have missed that speeding and weaving truck, headed straight for us?"

One long step brought them toe to toe. At least a foot taller, he loomed over her, but she refused to be intimidated and held her ground. She stretched every inch of her five foot two frame and looked him straight in the eye.

He held her gaze for a good while before finally saying, "That works pretty well for you, doesn't it? You're like a porcupine. When someone gets too friendly or too close, you puff up and get all prickly to keep them at a distance. Makes a person wonder what you're hiding to want to keep everyone at arm's length."

"Everyone?"

He spoke softly and leaned in. "Are we back to that? Never trust a lawman?"

"I can't shake the feeling that you're only being nice to me because you don't trust me."

"Hazard of the job. When people avoid answering questions, there's usually a reason."

Candi leaned in this time. They were so close, she could feel his breath on her face. "Did it occur to you that I might just be a private person?"

"Simple as that?"

It wasn't that simple, but it wasn't a lie. "Yes."

He nodded slowly, and then said, "Before long, I'll earn your trust, and you'll tell me all of your secrets."

"And if that doesn't happen?"

"It will."

His deep voice rumbled between them; confidence radiated from him despite the fact that she'd thwarted every attempt he'd made to get information from her. "What makes you so sure?"

He touched the scratch on her cheek with the back of his fingers and focused on her lips. Candi sucked in a ragged breath. Grady lightly grasped her chin and tilted her face up. He wouldn't . . .

"I'm sure because I'm a good guy. You're

smart enough to figure that out . . . eventually."

She ran the tip of her tongue along the crease of lips that had suddenly gone dry. "Too bad you're not a patient man."

He edged closer. "Someone pointed that out to me recently, and I've never been able to resist a challenge."

"Is that how you see me?" she breathed.

He dragged his thumb across her lower lip. "That's part of the problem. Every time I see you, I find something new to pique my interest."

"Sandwich break!"

Dixie breezed into the back room carrying a box, Cole and Blake close behind. Grady took a step back and swept his hand toward the door to the back room. "After you."

Candi spun and preceded him out of the workroom. This wasn't over. He'd wanted to confront her about using a false name, but in the end decided not to play that card too soon. A grin lifted the corner of his mouth. Maybe he would take her advice after all and watch, listen and wait to see what happened. Keeping a close eye on Candi Heart, or whatever her name was, certainly wouldn't be a hardship. He liked the way her long, inky black curls bounced around her shoulders as she walked.

"What's in the box?" Blake asked his sister, peering over her shoulder.

"My famous chicken salad sandwiches, chips, sweet tea, and coconut cream cupcakes."

"Nothin's better than your chicken salad, Dix."

"Thank you, Cole. Y'all dig in."

"This is so kind of you, Dixie," Candi said.

"It's the least I can do after what happened last night."

"Please, don't mention it," Candi insisted. "It was my pleasure, especially after I took you away from your business all afternoon."

"While I appreciate your help last night, I was referring to you getting hurt on your way home. If I'd driven you —"

"It could have been a lot worse," Grady finished the sentence for her.

Dixie cocked a hand on her hip. "Right. And who would have thought the sheriff of this fine town couldn't see a lady home safely?" Dixie shook her head. "Y'all both could have . . ."

Candi held up her hands. "Please, both of you. Stop laying blame. We're both here, no worse for the wear. Let's just be thankful for that."

"Beautiful and wise," Dixie said. "Candi,

the more I get to know you, the more I like. Come on, now. Sit down over here and eat."

"I need to get a couple of boxes in first," Candi said, "but please, you all go ahead."

Grady laughed. Blake and Cole had already downed most of their first sandwich. "I'll get the boxes. Go on and eat."

The look of concern on her face was almost comical. You'd think her boxes were filled with gold and precious jewels. "I'll be careful," he promised.

Candi sat and took a sandwich from Dixie, but she kept a close eye on him as he transferred the boxes from the alley to the workroom. When all three were safely in the workroom, only then did Candi unwrap her sandwich and take a bite.

Grady made a beeline for the box, hoping to get a sandwich before Blake and Cole ate them all. Dixie chatted about the plans for the shop while Candi ate. Grady unwrapped his sandwich, but just as he was about to take a bite, his cell phone rang.

He unclipped the phone from his belt and said, "Wallace."

"Hey, Boss. It's Woody. Fuzz and I went through the truck at the impound lot. We didn't find much to help figure out who might have been the driver. We did find the registration, but it was under Tom Hensley's name and dated mid-80s. Not much help since we already knew that it hadn't been registered to anyone else since then."

"All right. I'll be back in the office in about half hour or so."

"Right. You should know that Jenny Thompson was just here asking questions about the truck and the incident last night. I guess she saw it coming through town on the wrecker."

"No need wonderin' about how she found out. You know she hears about everything. I don't know how she does it."

"Yeah. It's like she has ESP or something."

"Well, thanks for the heads up."

Grady disconnected the call and took a bite of his sandwich. The last thing he needed right now was Jenny Thompson nosing around for a story to run in her newspaper.

"Knock, knock! Anyone here?"

Speak of the devil . . .

"Back here!" Dixie said.

"Hey, y'all. What's going on?"

Jenny Thompson drifted into the room, all southern grace and charm. She wore her shoulder-length blonde hair straight. A crisp cream-colored suit, several strands of pearls different lengths, a shiny gold shirt with matching shoes, and oversized leather purse completed *The Angel Ridge Chronicle* editor's professional look.

Dixie managed the introductions. "Jenny Thompson, this is Candi Heart. She just rented Madge's old beauty shop. She's also Miss Estelee's grandniece. Candi, Jenny runs the town newspaper."

Jenny held out a hand and with a big smile said, "I'm pleased to meet you. Candi Heart . . . I must say, that's an interestin' name you have there."

Candi smiled as well. "Mothers. What can I say? It could have been worse."

"Oh, absolutely!" she enunciated the words in her slow, southern drawl. "It can always be worse. Well, welcome to Angel Ridge."

"Thank you. Would you like to join us? We're having a late lunch. Dixie brought chicken salad sandwiches and sweets."

"Thank you, darlin'. I've eaten already, but never let it be said I turned down a dessert Dixie Ferguson made."

"You have excellent taste, Jenny," Dixie said. "You're looking fabulous, as always."

"You're a doll. You know we do what we can."

Dixie delved into the box and handed Jenny a cupcake and napkin. Grady contented himself to lean back against a counter, listen and observe. Maybe Jenny would forget he was here.

"Pleasure to see you here, Sheriff," she said. "I was just down at the courthouse looking to speak with you. Then I saw all the activity over here and thought I'd see what was going on. Looks like I'll be able to kill two birds with one stone."

Jenny took a bite of her cupcake and managed to smile while she chewed, her gaze not leaving his. "I heard you brought in an abandoned truck this morning that you found out near Billy Joe Maguire's place."

"Word travels fast."

Jenny never stopped smiling, even when she spoke. "I also heard that truck was being driven recklessly here in town last night."

"That's right."

"You found the truck?" Candi interjected.

Grady nodded and took another bite of his sandwich.

"Any idea who the driver was?" Jenny asked.

"Not at this time."

"Any promisin' leads?"

Grady took the last bite of his sandwich, chewed and swallowed before responding. "Sorry, Jenny. As I'm sure you know, I can't release details while the investigation is ongoing."

"Who was the truck registered to?"

"No comment." Tenacious. Jenny Thompson was a shark in heels.

"Would you like to confirm or deny that the vehicle was seen on Ridge Road and on Main here in town, weaving and traveling at high speeds last night about eight o'clock?"

Grady sighed. No sense denying it. She'd just find someone else to confirm that detail. "That's right."

Shaking her head, she took another dainty bite of the cupcake she held. "It's a wonder no one was injured."

"Absolutely," Dixie said. "Candi and Grady were walking down Ridge Road when that truck came outta nowhere and nearly ran them down."

Jenny looked from Grady to Candi and back to Dixie. "Do tell."

Grady groaned. No way to put this cat back in the bag.

"There's not much else to the story other than that," Candi said.

"I'd say those scratches on your face and hands say a lot. You're a lucky woman that you had the sheriff here as your escort to save the day," Jenny said evenly.

"Yes."

Candi's agreement surprised him. In fact, shocked him. Why would she want Jenny to think he'd saved her rather than the other way around?

"Oh, no. *Uh-uh.*" Dixie stood and put her hands up. "Sorry, Candi, but we don't play that here." Dixie turned to Jenny and supplied all the details the reporter wanted. "Candi here saw the truck coming for them and tackled Grady — who didn't see the truck, I might add — and vaulted the two of them right over the Harris' boxwoods and out of harm's way."

Grady groaned. This was just what he needed in the paper. A reckless driver on the loose and him useless in an emergency. His cell phone rang again, thank God.

"Sorry to bother you again, Boss."

"No worries. What's up?"

"Your uncle. He came in about five minutes ago, agitated and actin' real strange. He's goin' on about the truck we brought in. I think you better get over here."

"I'll be right there." He disconnected the call. "Sorry folks. Duty calls." He turned to Dixie and said, "Thanks for the sandwich." He put his hat on, and nodded to Jenny and Candi. "Ladies."

"Sheriff," Jenny gave him a long look that traveled from his head to his boots as the word slowly rolled off her tongue.

Candi looked up at him, her green eyes apologetic. Curious. Given her antagonism towards him, why would she care if the town knew she'd been the hero last night? Candi Heart — layers of mystery in a very appealing package. A lethal combination for him.

"Uncle Jim," Grady said as he walked into the sheriff's department, "this is a nice surprise."

Jim Wallace and his wife, Sadie, had run the town grocery for decades. Like most businesses in town, generations of Wallaces before him had run the grocery, or general store, as it had once been called. He had to say that his uncle looked pretty strung out. His thin gray hair was mussed, his shirt was wrinkled and untucked on one side. As he drew closer to the pacing man, he caught a whiff of alcohol. *A little early in the day to be drinking.* Grady frowned. He'd never seen his uncle like this.

"Something troubling you, Uncle Jim?"

"Could we talk in your office, Grady?"

"Of course. After you." Grady followed his uncle into his office and closed the door behind them. "Have a seat." Grady removed his hat and jacket, hung them on the coat rack, and then sat on the edge of his desk facing his uncle. "What can I do for you?"

"I saw that truck you brought into town."

"Did you?"

His uncle scrubbed a hand down his face. A day's worth of whiskers shadowed his normally clean-shaven jaw. "That's Boots Hensley's old truck. Why'd you bring it in? Where'd you find it?"

Grady held up a hand to slow the stream of questions. "Hold on there. What makes you say that truck belonged to Hensley?"

Uncle Jim looked away. His face showed each of his nearly seventy years; something awful haunted his eyes. "I'd know that truck anywhere."

Grady waited as myriad emotions flashed across his uncle's face, none of them pleasant.

"Boots and your daddy were at odds for years. There wasn't a car in the county that could outrun that truck. The man was crazy. Afraid of nothing and no one, including the law. He hated the Wallaces."

"Daddy's been gone a long time, Uncle Jim."

"Seems like yesterday," he said softly. "That girl shows up in town, and next thing you know, that truck." He shook his head. "Can't no good come of it. I tried to tell 'em."

Grady frowned. "Tell who what? What are you talking about, Uncle Jim?"

The old man didn't look at him or even appear to have heard what he'd said.

"She was a wild, beautiful thing. Every man in town fell under her spell, even the married ones. She flirted and teased until she had us all in a frenzy."

"Who are you talking about?"

He continued, again, without hearing him.

"We all should'a stayed away from that place . . . all the women gossiped about her. She was like a fever that infected everything in town."

Grady waited as the troubled memories filtered through his uncle's mind.

"Months passed with all of us addicted to her show. Then one day, she was gone. It was like she just disappeared into fog that rolls in off the lake in late summer. Things should'a settled back to normal, but it was like all the color in town went with her."

He looked up at Grady, his eyes dark and empty. "Then she came back — washed up dead. Drowned, that's what your daddy said. An accident. But I knew better. We all did. It couldn't a been that simple, not after all she'd seen and done.

"And now that woman shows up and that truck. It's like it's all come back to haunt us. Can't no good come from it, I tell you! No good can come —"

Grady stood and held out his hands. "Easy now. You're gettin' yourself all worked up over —"

"You're not listening!" Uncle Jim vaulted to his feet. "Just like *they* wouldn't listen! She has to go back to where she come from before it's too late."

What was his uncle talking about? It was like he was stuck in something that happened years ago, reliving it. "Why don't you let me take you home, Uncle Jim." He grasped his uncle's arm, but he wrenched it away.

"Get your hands off me! And stop looking at me like I'm some crazy old man!" He pointed a crooked finger at him. "You'll wish you'd listened to me. Mark my words! You don't want to get mixed up in this."

He jerked the door open so hard that it bounced off the wall. Woody stood, ready to stop him. Grady held up his hand. "Let him go."

When his uncle had gone, Grady turned to Clara and said, "Get my Aunt Sadie on the phone, would you Clara?"

"I already got her on line two."

"Transfer it in here."

Woody stepped inside Grady's office.

"What was that about?"

"I have no idea."

His phone started ringing. When he picked up the receiver, Clara said, "Here you go."

The line clicked, and he said, "Aunt Sadie? This is Grady."

"Oh, Grady. Hello, dear. How are you?"

"Fine ma'am. I'm calling about Uncle Jim. He was just here at my office. Aunt Sadie, he was real upset, going on about something that didn't make much sense. I think, well, that he may have been drunk."

"Oh! Oh my . . . I'm so sorry, dear. He's been upset about something since yesterday morning. I couldn't get him to tell me what was wrong, either. Drinking, you say?"

"Yes, ma'am."

"Could you see that he gets home safely?"

"I'll have Woody try and catch up to him," Grady pointed towards the door, and Woody left in a hurry. "But I have to tell you, I tried to get him to let me bring him home, and he got real angry and left."

His aunt sighed heavily. "I'm so sorry you had to see your uncle that way. He hasn't touched alcohol in years — not since your daddy was shot . . ." She added the last almost to herself. "I can't imagine why he's behaving this way."

"Would you like me to come over and help

you with him?"

She paused, as if she were considering. "No. No, I can handle him."

He wasn't sure about leaving her to deal with Uncle Jim alone, so he said, "All right, but promise you'll call if you need me?"

"Of course. Grady, I'm so pleased that you overcame your troubles to become such a fine young man. You had us all concerned there for awhile."

"Thanks, Aunt Sadie. My mama's real glad, too. I'll call and check on you both later, all right?"

"Thank you, dear. Oh, your uncle's here now." She pulled the phone away from her ear. "Get yourself in here right now, James Wallace. What in the world has gotten into —"

She disconnected the call. Grady chuckled and hung up the phone. Maybe his very proper, soft-spoken aunt could handle his drunk uncle after all. He wondered what had caused him to start drinking again. The crazy story he'd been trying to relate had made no sense. Some siren coming to town, driving all the men wild, then turning up dead. He frowned and rubbed his chin . . . the woman here again, he'd said, and the truck, too?

Grady shook his head and sat. No point

in trying to make sense of it. Just the drunken ramblings of an old man. He rolled the mouse and cleared the screen saver on his computer. He had a reckless driver to track down.

CHAPTER 8

A woman sits alone on a porch, looking down the mountain through barren trees to the lake below. It's gray and dreary like she's felt every day since she left Angel Ridge. Dark roots stand out against her bleached hair. She's not brushed it in awhile or changed her dress. No matter. Nowhere to go. No one to see. No one to love . . .

"Baby's cryin'," Mama says from inside the house.

Baby's always cryin', the mournful sound makes her soul ache. She can't look at her 'cause when she does, she sees him.

She stands and starts down the hill. The closer she gets, the quieter the crying becomes. At the water, she looks out across the cove. There's a dirt road on the other side. If she walked across, she could follow it till she reached town. The Flood Board draws the lake levels down this time of the year, leaving the cove with only a small

amount of water in the center.

She wonders how deep it is. If she walks out into it, will it come up to her knees? Her chest? Her neck? Or will it be far over her head. She could walk out and see . . . sink into the water and stay there . . . suspended . . . floating . . . weightless with no cares, no more sadness pressing against her weary heart.

Her knees buckle, and she lands hard on the cold ground. Tears stream down her face unchecked. Weeping . . . The weeping of a soul mourning, the sound so sad it hurts to hear it.

Trees and water . . .

A woman sitting among the shadows.

Crying . . .

Waiting . . .

Water far away from the shore.

Crying . . .

Waiting . . .

My heart . . . oh, my heart . . . she moans.

She stands, moving among the trees. The water rises up to reach the river bank now.

Crying . . .

Pacing . . .

Waiting . . .

Stillness . . .

She steps onto a dock, looks over her shoulder to the trees as if she's not comfort-

able outside of their shadows. Mist swirls up from the rising water that's now almost even with the wood planks she stands on.

Her eyes change. She looks straight ahead.

Hope . . .

A smile breaks on her pretty face.

Love . . .

She holds out her hand and takes a step forward.

My heart, oh my heart . . .

She takes another step forward. The weathered, narrow dock sways and creaks, but she takes another step anyway, an unearthly smile transforming her face.

My heart . . . oh, my heart. You've come back to me!

Another step. A horrible crack. She slips into the water in one fluid motion, the smile still on her face, love shining in her dark eyes.

Ripples circle out around the spot where she sinks.

Ripples . . .

Quiet . . .

Stillness . . .

"Hough . . ." Candi sucked in a breath as she sat up in bed. She looked around her room. Miss Estelee's house. She raked the hair out of her eyes. Gray light filtered in around the shade and lace curtains at the

window. She pushed back the covers and sat on the edge of the bed. The long hours she'd spent at the shop yesterday hadn't helped her soreness. She stood and padded over to the door, grabbed a robe, and headed for the bathroom. Maybe she'd have a soak before she headed out to work in the shop again today.

She shuffled down the hall to the bathroom at the end of the hall. The house was hushed and still. If Miss Estelee was up and about, she'd been quiet about it.

Candi ran hot water in the claw foot tub, threw in a scoop of lavender Epson salts, undressed, and sank into it. Her thoughts returned to the dream, still vivid in her mind's eye. What did it mean? She'd dreamed it both nights she'd spent in this house. Why did the sad woman look so much like her? She rotated her neck and took several long, deep breaths to chase the troubling thoughts away.

She grabbed her shower cream and a washcloth and began to scrub her skin. No time to ponder a silly dream when another dream, one she'd had most of her life, needed her focus.

She finished her bath, dressed, and pulled her long hair into a ponytail at her crown. She chose jeans, a blue t-shirt, and a thick green sweater today. She pulled on cotton socks and blue and green tweed flats.

She made her way carefully down the stairs, grabbed an apple and a bottle of water, and continued out the back door. Her bicycle that Cole had brought from her storage unit was parked just outside. She put her purse and her snack in its basket and hopped on. The short ride to town and her shop took less than five minutes. She couldn't help smiling. Even an overcast day in Angel Ridge was ideal as far as she was concerned.

She parked her bike near the front door of her shop. Retrieving the keys from her purse, she turned to unlock the door, but found the door open a crack. She frowned and pushed it open.

"Hello?" She walked in, alert to any sound. She set her purse down on the counter just inside the door. "Anyone here?" Maybe Blake or Cole had come early.

No response. No sounds at all.

She walked quietly down the hall, pausing to look inside the identical rooms on her left and right. She noticed some overturned boxes in one of the rooms, its contents littering the floor.

Continuing to the back room, everything looked normal except that the door to the workroom was open. She was certain she'd closed it before leaving last night. The sweet heavy aroma of vanilla hung in the air. And roses. Oh no . . .

She entered the workroom. A box was upended, its contents scattered across a wooden table in the middle of the room. Several broken bottles that had been filled with oils, herbs and spices littered the floor.

"Oh, no . . ." She knelt, ran her hand through some of the oil, and lifted her hand to her nose. A wave of electric sensation rocked her body. She stumbled out of the room and wrenched the back door open. Out in the alley, she bent, her hands on her knees, dragging in great gulps of the cool morning air.

What to do. She should call Cole and Blake first to let them know they wouldn't be able to come in today. Then she should call the sheriff's office to report the break-in. Grady . . . she closed her eyes, leaning against the cool rough bricks of the building. Images of him flitted across her mind's eye. His eyes, intense and full of emotion. His strong arms pulling her hard up against him. His face closer and closer until his warm, soft lips touched hers . . .

She opened her eyes and pushed away from the wall. No, no, no. It was the oil.

Just the oil. She'd never have such thoughts about the sheriff otherwise. Absolutely not.

She paced rapidly up and down the alley, stopped, and jumped up and down. She shook her hands and head, trying to scatter her thoughts, but her hormones had a mind of their own.

She sucked in another deep breath and hurried through the back door, leaving it open. She held her breath and rushed back to the front of the shop. She retrieved her cell phone from her purse, and walked out onto the sidewalk.

She called Blake and Cole first. That done, her breathing was still uneven. She should call the sheriff's office now, but she didn't want to see Grady. Not now. She had to let someone know that there'd been a break-in at her shop. She took another deep breath. This time, she felt much calmer. More settled. She could do this. It was Saturday. Maybe Grady didn't work on Saturday. Maybe she'd get the deputy or the constable instead.

Candi dialed the number.

"9-1-1. What's your emergency?"

Grady's voice rumbled through the phone line and fired her already heightened senses. Great.

"Well, it's not really an emergency. I guess

I shouldn't have called 9-1-1. I'm sorry."

Grady checked the Caller ID. Heart's Desire. "Candi? What's wrong?"

"Sheriff Wallace?"

"Grady," he corrected on a sigh.

A beat of silence hummed over the line, and then, "Sorry. I didn't expect you to answer the phone."

"Why'd you call 9-1-1?" Another silence ensued. Grady frowned, his instincts screaming at him. "What is it, Candi?"

"Oh, sorry. I'm not feeling quite right. I apologize again, Sheriff. I believe someone broke in here —"

"A break-in?" The cop in him torpedoed to full alert. "When?"

"I'm not sure. Maybe last night?"

"Listen close, Candi. Don't move and keep quiet. I'll be right over."

"Oh, no! You don't —"

Grady hung up and called out to his deputy, "Catch the phone, Woody. I got something I need to check out."

"You need back-up?"

"No, I got it."

Grady took the stairs that led out the back of the jail two at a time. He hit the sidewalk at a full-out sprint. The morning breeze stung his arms, but he barely noticed.

He saw Candi outside her shop, leaning

up against the building. He skidded to a stop. She looked completely out of sorts. He touched her shoulder, but she jerked away from him like he'd shocked her. "You okay? Did someone hurt you?"

"No, no," she said quickly.

He pulled the gun from his shoulder holster and clicked the safety off. "Stay here."

Candi held out a hand. "There's no need for guns, Sheriff. Please put that away. There's no one inside. I looked already."

"You what?"

"When I got here, I saw the door was open. I went in, called out to see if anyone was inside. I thought Cole or Blake might have come early."

She was talking so fast he could hardly keep up. Very unusual for Candi. He frowned, trying to follow.

"When no one answered, I went towards the back and saw some boxes had been turned over in one of the middle rooms, off the hallway? In the back room, the door to my workroom was open and I'm sure I closed that door before I left. So I went inside and boxes had been upended, bottles broken . . ."

"Are you crazy! You knew someone had broken in, and you went in there alone?"

Her green eyes were dark and opened wide as she stared back at him. The words having finally run out, she just looked at him. He narrowed his gaze. Her eyes were dilated. Some scent wafted around her, firing his senses in a way they shouldn't be firing at the moment.

He shook his head to clear the inappropriate thoughts threatening to override the saner ones that demanded he check out her shop, which was a possible crime scene. "Stay here," he repeated.

"No! Please, Sheriff. You can't go in."

She followed close behind, grabbed his arm and tried to restrain him. What had gotten into her? Lord, she looked good with her hair pulled back like that, her neck bare and inviting. "I thought I told you to stay put," he said harshly.

The feel of her small, soft hand on him felt like a physical shock. He sucked in a deep breath as an intense feeling clenched his gut. He wanted her. Badly.

Forcing himself to focus, he dragged in a breath and set Candi away from him with his free hand. Pinning her with a "no arguments" look, he repeated, "Stay here."

Grady turned, steadied the gun in both hands, and stalked through her shop. He entered both the side rooms, saw the overturned boxes, and searched the area for signs that someone was hiding. Nothing.

In the back room, the first thing he noticed was that the back door was open. He walked over to it, went outside, and scanned the alley. Nothing.

Going back inside, he closed the door and walked over to the workroom. A heavy, sweet scent similar to the one he'd noticed on Candi hung in the air, getting stronger as he approached the workroom. The room was trashed: boxes turned over, plants and broken bottles everywhere. The boxes Candi had been so worried about the day before. This had to be what was upsetting her — what had her acting so odd. It did not, however, explain his sudden, strong reaction to her. A reaction he was having trouble grabbing the reins on, even with her two rooms away.

He walked back to the front of the building to find the room empty. Looking through the nearly floor to ceiling window, he saw Candi standing outside. He took a deep breath and joined her on the sidewalk. "All clear."

"Excuse me?"

"Your shop. There's no one inside."

"Oh," she waved a hand, "yes. I knew that."

Despite the cool morning air, she'd removed her sweater and stood there in just a thin t-shirt that hugged her body in all the right places. He dragged his gaze away. What was wrong with him?

He holstered his gun and pulled a notepad out of a pocket. When he looked back at her, ready to ask the necessary questions, she was looking at him . . . no, devouring him with her eyes. First they were on his face, and then they moved lower to his waist and back up again, lingering at the open collar of his shirt. Her tongue darted out to moisten her lips. Seeing the tip of her pink tongue against shiny red lipstick nearly made him come unglued.

She looked away, embarrassed, chewing on that full lower lip now. He wondered what it would taste like if . . .

Grady blinked and cleared his throat. "So, what happened, Candi? Anything missing?"

"*Um,* I haven't checked yet, but my workroom is in pretty bad shape."

Uncomfortably warm now, Grady tugged at his collar. "Yeah, I saw. Anything else you noticed?"

"The front door was ajar when I got here this morning."

He made a note on his pad. "Did you forget to lock it last night?"

"I don't think so, but I had trouble getting it to latch. Guess it's the cooler temperatures. The wood's probably contracting."

Turning, Grady examined the front door of the shop. "Looks like it may have been jimmied."

Candi peered around him just noticing the scratches he was rubbing his thumb across. "Those don't look fresh."

She was right. He wasn't thinking straight. "I guess with the door not latching right, it would make it easy for someone to get it open." He turned back to Candi. "You'll need to have the door adjusted."

She nodded.

"I'd tell Bud. Since you're renting the place from him, he'll fix it."

Candi nodded again. "Is there something I need to sign?"

"There will be. After I get the report written, I'll bring it by, but before I can write this up, we'll need to go through the shop, make a list of everything that was damaged."

"I can do that and get it over to you."

"It's part of the investigation. By going over the shop more closely, I may be able to gather evidence and get clues about who may have done this."

"But, you can't go back in here, Sheriff."

"Grady," he corrected. He put his pad away and rested his hands on his hips. He looked at the shop, then back at her. "Look, I get that for some reason you don't trust me, but I'm just trying to do my job here. I have your best interest at heart despite what you may think."

"Of course."

She chewed on her thumbnail, considering . . .

"So, I'll just finish my investigation and —"

He pushed the door open and went inside. Candi trailed in behind him, halting his progress by reaching out to grasp his wrist.

"You *really* shouldn't be in there."

There it was again, the feel of molten fire running through his veins when she touched him. Could she feel it, too? Was that why she was acting so oddly, looking at him like she wanted him, too?

"It's for your own safety," he said softly. "What if they decide to come back?"

She stepped back and ran a hand around the back of her neck. The action stretched her t-shirt across her chest. He should look away, but couldn't seem to make himself. She was stalling, and he didn't care. He could stand here looking at her all day.

Hang the investigation.

She closed her eyes and moaned. "Aunt Ruby always said not to mess with love potions. Why didn't I listen?" she mumbled.

"Excuse me?" Had she said *love potion?*

She closed the front door and leaned against it. "Sheriff, all those boxes in the workroom, they're full of things I've been gathering since I was in school working on my merchandising degree, hoping and waiting for the day I'd open my own shop.

"After I graduated, I went back home to help take care of an elderly relative. During those years, I spent quite a lot of time growing and gathering herbs and flowers to use in natural skin care, perfumes."

"That's what was in those boxes in the back? The ones you were so worried about?"

She took a slow step forward. "Yes. Some of those bottles held a special formula I was working on for a perfume. They contained the concentrated ingredients for a . . . a, *um,* kind of love potion."

"I thought that's what you'd said." She kept moving towards him in slow movements that seemed designed to make him lose his mind.

"I want to have a shop for women, Sheriff," she said softly. "So, all the things I've collected and been working on are for women. I was going to make a perfume out of the potion."

She was close enough now for her to feel his body heat. His breathing was slow and deep when her gazed dipped from his face to his chest. She lifted a hand and touched a finger to the scorched skin in the V of his open neckline. She drew her hand back immediately.

"I'm so sorry. I didn't mean to do that, but it's like, I can't help myself," she sighed and shoved her hands into the back pockets of her jeans. "The formula must work only on women."

He closed the gap between them, wrapped an arm around her waist and hauled her up against him. He bent his knees to align himself with her, chest to chest, thigh to thigh. "Oh, no. It's workin' on me just fine."

He took her lips, his mouth open and hot, sliding his tongue against the seam of her lips. She opened, her tongue tangling with his. He groaned. She tasted sweeter than anything he'd ever known.

She arched her back and wrapped her arms around his neck, her fingers sliding into the hair at the back of his head. She chased his tongue with hers, swirling it around his and then withdrawing, his close behind.

He lifted her and spun around until he had her pressed against a wall, then broke the contact to drag his mouth, hot and open, down her neck to the edge of her collar. He yanked at the hem of her shirt until he found the silky, soft skin at her waist. He groaned again.

"I'm so —" she'd sucked in half a breath when he took her earlobe between his lips then swirled his tongue to touch all the places his teeth had. "So sorry," she sighed.

"I'm not." And he wasn't. This had been building ever since he'd met her. Potion or not, it would have come to this sooner or later. Sooner was real fine with him.

He slid his hands from her waist to the backs of her thighs and hitched her up higher. She wrapped her legs around his waist and hung on as he spun around until his back was at the wall this time.

"It's the pheromones." Her mouth was hot and open on his neck now.

He shook his head, his hand at the back of her head and his thumb lightly caressing her jaw. "It's you. Us." He kissed her lightly this time, softly, savoring the feel of her warm, pliant lips.

"It's not real," she whispered.

But she made no effort to stop kissing him. He closed his eyes and just felt. The way they fit together was perfection. This was so right. More right than anything he'd ever known. It was a heady thing, being so sure about something after so many years of living a life that wasn't his own.

"Hello — Oh! Oh my! Sheriff," Mrs. McKay said. "What is the meaning of this?"

Chapter 9

Well, hell. Leave it to Harriet McKay to enter the proceedings at the exact wrong moment to shock him and Candi apart. The look on Candi's face was pure mortification. He eased her feet to the floor, then grasped her wrist and pulled her behind him to give her some privacy while she straightened her clothes.

"Harriet," he said. "I suppose you never learned to knock." A harsh tone edged his words.

"The door was open!" she exclaimed, "And this *is* a place of business."

"This shop clearly is not open for business. So, if you don't mind?"

"And shouldn't you be working, Sheriff, at this time of the morning on a weekend, especially after what recently transpired here in town."

"I put in plenty of hours. No need to

worry yourself about that. Now, if you don't mind?"

"Harrumph!"

The older lady pressed her thin lips into an even harsher line, spun on her serviceable heels and marched out the door. Grady followed and made sure the door was locked and latched this time. When he looked back at Candi, she appeared to have regained a small measure of her composure.

"Sheriff —"

Grady laughed. "You're still calling me that? After what we just did?"

She looked completely horrified, and he was immediately contrite. His mother raised him to be a gentleman, even though he sometimes forgot it. He took a step forward, holding a hand out towards her like he would to a skittish animal. "I'm sorry. That was rude."

She took a fortifying breath. "I just wanted to say how sorry I am . . . about what just happened. This is my fault. I shouldn't have left something like that oil lying around, even in a locked shop."

He felt his anger rising in direct proportion to the desire he'd just felt for her. "You're so sure of this potion you cooked up."

"Well —"

"You must not know much about men, because if you did, you'd know that you don't throw down a challenge like that."

"Challenge? I don't understand."

Clearly. He took a step into her space and slowly leaned in. He enjoyed her sharp intake of breath that brought the heat of her body closer to his. She liked it, too — or at least her body did, even if she wouldn't acknowledge it. Her body relaxed into his, but he didn't take her into his arms, didn't touch her at all. He nearly grazed her ear with his lips, but pulled back moving down towards her neck then over to the other side and back up to her other ear. "This dance we've been doing since you got into town has nothing to do with oil spilled in your workroom, lady, and everything to do with the fact that *we* want each other." His cheek brushed the softness of her hair, and he inhaled the scent of roses in the heat of summer.

She turned into him, her mouth seeking his neck, but he stayed just out of her reach. Frustrated, she grabbed his shirt with both hands. He grasped her wrists gently and stepped back, when all he wanted to do was love her until they were no longer Grady and Candi, but something that had its own identity. The oil may have cut the flimsy curtain of their resistance, but underneath, all along, had been this powerful thing that neither of them could deny. He wasn't about to let her deny it either.

"The next time this need between us gets more than either of us can stand, you're gonna tell me you want me — in detail — so that when this happens again, and you can be sure that it will, you'll know exactly why."

He jammed his hat on his head and walked to the door. Unlocking it, he turned and said, "I'll send Woody over to finish the investigation. From here on out, our relationship won't have anything to do with who I am in this town. Your body knows me. Your head just needs time to catch up." He looked her up and down. "Looks like I'm about to learn that patience you've been telling me I need."

When the door clicked shut, Candi slumped against the counter, willing her body back under her control. It was all she could do to keep from going after him. This was insane. The head should rule the body. Trouble was that her body presently had the upper hand.

First things first. She had to get that oil out of here, and as soon as it was gone, there'd never be any more. She was done playing with that brand of fire.

"Mornin' glory!"

Dixie breezed into the shop with a bag looped over her arm and a cup of coffee in each hand. "Was that Grady I just saw leavin' here whistlin' a happy tune and with a little extra lift in his step?"

Candi raised a hand to her forehead to rub the ache that was settling there, and then remembered that she still hadn't washed up. "Stay here. Please, don't leave this room. Promise me."

Dixie frowned, but said, "Honey, I'm not going anywhere. I smell a juicy story. I'll be right here waitin'."

Candi hurried out of the room, trying to come up with a plausible explanation for what had put the sheriff in his present mood. She ran to the back, holding her breath, closed the door to the workroom, and then washed up at the sink in the back. She rubbed her hands down her legs, and realized she'd probably done that before she washed her hands. A change of clothes was also in order. There was probably something in one of the boxes from storage that would do. First, she had to deal with Dixie.

"Sorry about that, Dixie," she said when she went back into the front room. "What brings you over?" She affected a causal pose leaning against the counter. "I would have thought Saturday mornings would be a real busy time for the diner."

"One day's as busy as the next, and Mom and Dad work on Saturday mornings so I can take off. I thought I'd come by with coffee and muffins and then help you get this place in order. And if I might say so, you look like you need this."

Candi took the coffee from Dixie and said, "Thanks." She started to take a drink, but stopped, unsure what kind of effect caffeine would have combined with the pheromones and the aftermath of Grady's kisses.

"So, what's up with Grady?"

Candi shrugged. "Who knows? I can't seem to say or do the right thing around him."

"*Uh-huh.* Why is it I just don't buy that?"

A knock on the front door saved her from having to answer. "Come in," she said.

"Mornin', Ms. Heart. Dixie. I'm Woody Ragan, deputy sheriff here in Angel Ridge. The sheriff sent me over to get a report on a possible burglary."

"Burglary?" Dixie exclaimed. "What?"

"Thank you for coming over, sir. But no real harm was done. I won't be filing a report."

"Well, I'm glad no harm was done, ma'am,

but a crime's been committed. I'm afraid a report has to be filed."

"But, you can't be in the building right now. It's not safe."

"Excuse me?"

Candi sighed and hung her head. "You shouldn't be here either, Dixie."

Dixie put her hand on Candi's shoulder. "Honey, what's going on?"

Looking at Dixie, she said, "Someone broke in last night. Whoever it was broke some glass bottles in the workroom that contained a dangerous substance."

Woody tried to get out a pad of paper, but in his haste and enthusiasm, lost his grip and slung it across the room. He quickly retrieved it, rifled noisily to a blank page, and began writing furiously. "Do you think that's what the burglar could have been looking for?"

"They'd have been more careful to not break the bottles if that's what they were after," Dixie said.

The officer shrugged. "Maybe something scared them, and they dropped the bottles."

"No, no. It's nothing like that. The labels on the bottles didn't indicate what was in them. No one but me would have known."

"I see," Woody said. "Then what was in the bottles?"

"Pheromones suspended in vanilla oil," she said absently, still distracted by thoughts of Grady.

Dixie's eyes nearly bugged out of their sockets. "Come again? Pheromones?"

"Yes. I was working on a formula for perfume. One that would, *um,* drive men wild."

Dixie roared. "Well, I must say, I would have never guessed *that* was the source of the trouble over here. No wonder Grady was whistlin' a happy tune when he left."

"Dixie, what are you talking about?" Woody asked.

"I should say that a crime being committed here was the least of Candi's worries after Grady Wallace blew through here."

Dixie started laughing — uncontrollably. Could this get any worse?

"And now she just wishes we'd all clear out so she can clean up that oil spill." This made Dixie laugh even harder.

"It does need to be cleaned up before anyone else is exposed."

"Exposed," Dixie roared. "Ha!"

"But you can't clean it up," Woody said. "That would compromise the crime scene before it's been properly examined."

"I'd say Grady already had a thorough examination of something over here!" Dixie slapped Woody on the back. "Better break out a HazMat suit, or you might just suffer the same fate, and I don't believe that girlfriend of yours would appreciate it. Y'all got one of those over to the sheriff's office?"

This triggered another fit of laughter. Candi smiled. It was kind of funny. "What's a HazMat suit?"

"Hazardous materials," Woody supplied, frowning. He clearly wasn't following. "And no, we don't have one yet."

"Well, you can't go anywhere near the back room without the proper protection," Dixie said and then collapsed into another fit of laughter. "Proper protection. I'm really on a roll!"

Woody and Candi just looked at each other, and then Woody's face flushed bright red when he got the joke.

"*Um,* I do have latex gloves, an aspirator I use when I mow, and some coveralls," Woody said as he backed towards the door. "Why don't I just . . ."

He thumbed at the door, and then was gone.

"Candi, I must say, you sure know how to clear a room. Now dish."

"Dish?"

"I presume you came in this morning, realized there'd been an intruder and called the sheriff's office."

"Yes."

"Grady came over."

Candi nodded.

"And then what happened."

"I can't really say."

" 'Won't' is the word I think you're looking for. Won't say. That's okay. I have a vivid imagination. Good thing I'm not the jealous type."

"Jealous? You mean you and Grady?"

"We go out from time to time as a matter of convenience. We've known each other since we were kids. He's about the best friend I got, but don't worry. I'm not opposed to sharing, especially since the kissing thing *so* didn't work for us. It was like kissin' my brother." She shuddered.

"Dixie, I don't know what you're talking about."

"Honey, it's all right."

Dixie squeezed her arm in a way that was meant to be reassuring. Who was she kidding? She knew exactly what Dixie was talking about. She was attracted to Grady, but she couldn't afford to be. The timing couldn't be worse.

"Oh, Dixie . . . what a mess. This was the last thing I intended. Seems like there's been nothing but trouble since I got into town."

"Don't you worry none about that, now. What you call trouble, we call excitement, and it's been years since we've had any of that. You're good for this town, don't you doubt it." She shouldered her purse and said, "I'm goin' down to the hardware to get some rubber gloves and aspirators so we can get that oil cleaned up. Need anything else while I'm there?"

"Bleach?"

"Done. Now, you have some coffee and a muffin, and by the time you're finished eating, I'll be back, we'll get things cleaned up, and start putting this place together."

"It seems I'm in your debt again."

"Girl, please. That's what friends do." She opened the door. "I want that bag one muffin lighter when I get back, you hear?"

"Yes. I'll be sure that it is."

As she left and hurried up the sidewalk, Candi thought she heard her say, "Wise woman . . . knows how to pick her battles and do what's sensible. Yep, we're gonna get on just fine."

Chapter 10

Candi and Dixie had gotten a lot accomplished after cleaning up the spill. Dixie called Blake and Cole to come over after they'd finished. Blake got the sinks out and, together with Cole, dealt with the plumbing issues that came with doing that. He'd left a long counter and a small kitchen area that would work well for making tea. She'd just need to find some tables and chairs, and she'd be able to open a tea room.

Cole had brought something called a power roller and had gotten the painting finished in record time. She and Dixie had been able to spend the day sorting stock and deciding what would go where. She'd gotten some of her paints out and worked on a sign for the front of the building. Dixie had wholeheartedly approved of the name, *Heart's Desire.*

Candi had been concerned that Dixie might say something about certain items she planned to sell, like how some people in town might consider them inappropriate. Dixie just laughed it off. She happened to know that a number of the ladies in town who had a need for "naughty" items like sensual lingerie, creams, oils, and, well, special aids, went to a store in Maryville for them. They might never admit it, but they'd come in and pick up what they needed, especially if there would be a discreet way to do so. There was no shame in it. A girl had to do what a girl had to do after all, right? Might as well do it in town where the treasury would benefit from the tax dollars. Why, if they could sell Viagra over to the drug store, what was a little flavored oil and some edible panties?

Besides, she'd also be selling clothing made of natural materials, a full line of herbal skin care and perfumes that she made herself. And then there were the flower arrangements and door wreaths made of fresh flowers, dried, and silk. She'd also be selling homemade chocolates and fudge. The tea room in the back would be a gathering place for women where they could sit and visit. Women needed a place to gather and talk, share their wisdom and pass it on to younger generations.

Dixie knew where Candi could get a good

deal on some small, round tables and chairs from a supplier she knew that had picked them up from an ice cream shop. At this rate, she'd be open inside of two weeks, maybe sooner.

She stood before the full-length mirror in her room at Miss Estelee's considering her outfit. What did one wear to a cookout with a family she'd never met? She wondered again if this was a good idea.

Dixie had insisted she come over to the Ferguson farm for a cookout that was doubling as a "welcome to the family" celebration for Dixie's brother who had just eloped with his third wife. The family didn't want to make a big fuss, but did want to get to know the girl.

All of the Fergusons would be there and a few close friends of the family. Candi had tried to beg off, but Dixie wouldn't hear of it. Miss Estelee and Doc Prescott would be going as well, so it would be rude to not invite Miss Estelee's house guest.

What if Grady was there? Candi just didn't know how she would face him after the kiss they'd shared this morning. Well, if he was there, she'd be safe enough in such a big crowd of people. She probably wouldn't even have to talk to him, much less worry about his promise that she would admit her attraction to him if he had anything to say about it. It'd be a cold day in an East Tennessee summer before that'd happen. She wasn't about to get involved with anyone, much less a lawman, no matter how appealing.

"Honey? You ready?" Miss Estelee called from downstairs. "Doc's here."

"Coming!"

One more look in the mirror. A little make-up helped cover up the scrape on her check, and she'd removed the bandages from her hands. Jeans and a button-up cotton shirt with chunky silver jewelry from a line she'd carry in her shop and a warm wrap-style shawl that was a pretty shade of blue. Hopefully, this would do.

The drive to just outside of town took just under thirty minutes. The Ferguson farm consisted of expansive rolling hills dotted with cattle, horses, a grove of fruit trees and an old two-story white farmhouse with a wraparound porch. Several tables with bright white tablecloths had been set out on the front lawn. Adults and children filled the yard to overflowing. Candi had to press her hand to her heart to keep it inside her chest. Growing up, how she wished she truly belonged in a scene like this.

She took a deep breath. She was good at

pretending. Growing up, the world of imagination and make believe had been her only means of entertainment, so thankfully it came naturally to her.

Dixie met them at the car. "Welcome, welcome." She linked arms with her and propelled Candi towards the front lawn. "Let me introduce you to everyone."

There were the senior Fergusons. Of course, Candi had already met Mr. Ferguson at DeFoe's. Mrs. Ferguson was clearly the center of the family, as mothers should be. She was thin, not as tall as Dixie, but she had the same spiky hairstyle, only hers was silver.

She'd also met Dixie's older brother, Bill, when she'd helped out at the diner. His wife, Margie, raced by, with a baby on her hip, running after a dark-haired boy that looked about three. He squealed with glee, staying just out of her reach. Bill hitched the twin he carried up on his shoulder and said, "I better help her corral that one. Nice to see you again, Candi. Glad you could come."

"Hey, Candi. How's it goin'?" Blake said.

Blake was standing next to his mom, with his arm looped around her shoulders, drinking a beer. Candi was amused. The Fergusons must attend the free-thinking Presbyterian church in town. Most of Angel Ridge's other denominations took a dim view of alcohol.

"I'm good. Thank you all for having me."

Everyone was dressed similarly to her. Well, except for the men who seemed to all be wearing jeans and t-shirts, and she wasn't about to pretend that they didn't all look good in their jeans and snug t-shirts. The Fergusons were a handsome family.

"Let me introduce you to my baby brother and his bride," Dixie said.

A man sitting at the table with his arm around a lovely woman stood. "Please, Dixie. I'm three years older than you."

"Yeah, but you're the youngest of the boys. Candi, this is Cory and his wife, Bebe."

Cory offered his hand. He wore a pastel pink polo-style shirt and khaki slacks, and he reeked of cologne. "You must be the new beauty in town everyone's talking about. It's a pleasure."

His gaze began at her chest, slid down her body and back up, but never quite made it to her eyes. This must be what they call a player. "Hello."

"Easy, killer," Blake said, "your *wife* is sitting right beside you."

"Surrounded by so many beautiful

women. We're lucky men, Blake."

Blake took a slow draw on his beer. "That we are."

"All right, boys. Time to put up or shut up," Dixie interrupted to ease the tension. The two men clearly didn't get along. "There's a game of football to be played. Are y'all men ready to get your behinds kicked again?"

"Little sister, that's not about to happen. You're dreamin'."

Dixie cocked a hand on her hip. "Really? Are you gonna stand there and act all full of yourselves? Did y'all or did you not get your butts handed to you last time we had a cookout?"

"Yes, we did," Blake said. "But we have a couple of ringers this time."

"Bring it on. Won't matter, 'cause we got Candi here."

Candi choked on her orange soda and squeaked, "Me?" She'd never played football in her life. Had never really even watched a game.

"That's right," Dixie said confidently.

"Dixie —"

Blake laughed. He was more than a foot taller than her. They all were, except for Cory, and even he was taller than her. Everyone was taller than her, but that was no reason to laugh. She was stout. Her Aunt Ruby had made sure she knew how to take care of herself. She had, after all, tackled the sheriff and saved his life as well as her own.

"Fine, Sis. Bring your little friend and come on. You can line her up against Grady, or better yet, Jonathan. You remember Jonathan? He was about the best football player to ever come out of Angel Ridge High; played for the University of Tennessee and then went to the pros?"

"Sounds familiar."

"He's back in town. I invited him to join us tonight."

To say Blake's smile was smug would be an understatement. Dixie, however, didn't miss a beat. "As a matter of fact, I do remember Jonathan. Maybe *you* remember that he took me to his senior prom when I was a freshman. I thought you'd beat him into a bloody pulp when you found out he'd dared to look at me, never mind invited me to the prom."

"It's my job to look after my little sister," he grunted.

"Please. I haven't ever needed 'looking after' and you know it."

"One of these days you're gonna realize that a man appreciates a woman who not only likes men, but actually needs them for something."

Dixie looped her arm around Candi's shoulders. "Oh, we need you for something, it's just not protection."

Candi wondered how she'd gotten sucked into the sibling banter that had morphed into men's men who beat their chests and have no idea what women need, as if that even matters. She'd never played football, but she knew in that moment that she'd do whatever was needed to wipe that smirk off Blake or any other man's face that cared to wear it, including Grady Wallace or this Jonathan person.

"Now y'all play nice," Mrs. Ferguson said, "I've worked hard to see that we have a perfectly pleasant evenin', and I'm not about to let you use a football game to ruin it."

"Just a little friendly competition, Mama," Blake said.

"Do I look new to you? Now listen here. I expect you men to act like gentleman and you women to act like ladies."

"No worries, Mom. I can kick a boy's rear in high heels and not mess up my lipstick."

"Oh, it's on," Blake said.

Dixie just laughed. Candi leaned in and whispered the obvious. "Dixie, we're the only women here besides your mom, Miss Estelee, Margie — who clearly has her hands full with all those babies — and Cory's wife, and I don't mean to be ugly, but she doesn't look like she'd risk breaking one of those red nails in a football game."

It was like a boulder rolling down a mountain; once it got started, there was no stopping it. Candi walked across the lawn to the area where the men had gathered. Grady stood with a man she'd never met, a hulk of a man with the broadest shoulders and arms the size of small tree trunks. This must be the football player.

The man with the shoulders and crew cut came forward when they got near. "Hi, I'm Jonathan Temple."

Her hand felt like the size of a child's inside his. "Candi."

"I'm pleased to meet you." He swung his gaze to Dixie, "Hello, Austin." His words were softer, lower when he spoke to Dixie. To her credit, she met all of his intensity with some of her own.

"Jonathan. I heard you were back in town."

"You're lookin' . . ." he took in everything about her in one sweeping glance . . . "well."

"Thank you."

No comment about how he was looking,

which seemed to agitate him. Interesting.

She noticed that Grady wore an old t-shirt with holes in it and threadbare jeans which also had several tears. The only time she'd seen him out of uniform, he'd been wearing fishing gear. This didn't compare. He looked so good it made her teeth ache. This would never work. He just stood there staring at her without moving one well-developed muscle.

"Let's get this over with," Dixie said. "Mom will have supper ready in fifteen minutes."

"Plenty of time for the men to teach you *girls* a lesson."

Dixie turned to Candi. "Oh no he didn't!" she said with lots of attitude.

Candi played along. "Oh yes he did," she returned with equal attitude.

"Looks like it's four against two. Want us to give you Bill?"

"That won't be necessary. Mom and Margie are joining us."

The two women appeared on cue with Mr. Ferguson right behind them. He wore a referee's whistle around his neck.

"Okay, let's get this game started. I got potatoes in the oven, and I don't want them to overcook. Huddle up."

Candi kicked off her clogs, hopping on

one foot to peel off her socks and shove them in her pockets. She had no idea what she had gotten herself into here, but she was having more fun than she could remember ever having.

The women circled up. Mrs. Ferguson put her hands on her knees and leaned in towards the center. "Okay, here's how this is going to go. Margie, you line up against Bill, Dixie, you have Johnny T, and Candi, that leaves you with Grady. I'll take the hike and will either run it in or pass to one of you if you get open."

"Hey," Blake said. "Why do they get the ball first?"

"Ladies first, son," Mr. Ferguson said.

Mumbling followed that pronouncement.

"Questions?" Mrs. Ferguson asked.

Candi tentatively raised her hand.

"Yeah, hon?"

"How do we get past them? They're huge."

With a big smile, she turned to her daughter. "Dixie? It's your game plan. You share it."

"They're men. They all have the same universal weakness."

Candi leaned in, ready for this great revelation.

"Boobs. Unbutton your shirt."

"Pardon me?" Surely she'd heard wrong,

but both Dixie and Margie were unbuttoning their shirts and both were quite impressively endowed. "You're serious." Candi had never . . . she couldn't imagine . . .

"Oh, absolutely. Refuse to lose." She held up a fist in a symbol of solidarity.

"I don't know . . ."

Dixie snorted. "*Aw* come on, Candi. It's just a little harmless fun, and the looks on their smug faces will be worth it."

Candi was not convinced. After the encounter she'd had earlier today with Grady, she couldn't imagine taunting him. Even now, she could feed the fire of attraction between them.

"It seems unfair."

"As you said, they're bigger and more athletic. Consider it leveling the playing field."

"Let's get this show on the road," Bill said.

"Yeah, the sooner we beat you," Blake chimed in, "the sooner we can eat."

"Pay them no mind," Mrs. Ferguson said. "Honey, if you're not comfortable, don't feel pressured, but you'll have to come up with another strategy for beating Grady off the line. And I'm warning you, he's pretty hard to beat."

Candi thought about it a second. "I have an idea."

"Well all right. Are we set?"

The three women nodded, clapped, and shouted, "Break."

"Oh, that's low," Blake said referring to the ladies' plunging necklines.

"It certainly is," Jonathan agreed with a smile. When Dixie stood in front of him, he added, "You sure grew up nice, Dix."

"If you came home more often, you'd have noticed that before now."

"Playin' in Seattle makes it hard, but you can be sure, I would if I lived closer."

"Foul play!" Bill chimed in. "I haven't seen boobs since before the twins were born."

"That is so not true and you know it," Marge replied.

"Okay. How 'bout if I say it's been awhile since I've seen boobs without babies a few feet away?"

"Your mama's keeping the kids tonight. Maybe you'll get lucky."

Bill shuddered.

Candi stood before Grady, just looking at him while he looked back. His gaze lowered chest high and back to her eyes. "Somethin' wrong with your buttons?"

"I thought I'd try a different tack."

"I had a thought of my own. Men?"

He looked at the other guys, and in one

motion, they swept off their shirts. Candi sputtered, "What are you doing?"

"Shirts and skins. You're the shirts and we're, well, I think that's obvious."

Candi tried to look away, but couldn't drag her eyes from Grady. She had grown up alone with her grandmother. When she'd gone to junior college she'd stayed with her aunt and uncle, who didn't have children living at home. She'd never been this close to a man without his shirt on, and she was struck by the beauty of Grady's body. He was all tan skin stretched tight across rippling muscles. Now she knew what tongue-tied meant. Dixie seemed to be suffering from the same affliction. Margie, however, had no trouble finding her tongue.

"Woo-hoo, baby. I ain't seen this much skin since before the babies were born. Honey, you still look good! These boys here got nothin' on you."

Bill preened under his wife's attention. The other men chuckled, all but Grady. "Like what you see?"

"Let's play ball," Dixie said, saving Candi from having to find her tongue. Focus. She'd had a plan. A plan . . . what was it? Sheez, it had to be a hundred degrees out here.

"Down!" Mrs. Ferguson said, and the

women bent resting one hand on the ground and the other arm rested across a thigh. Candi did the same. She looked back at Grady. He had a self-satisfied smile on his face that helped her focus. So, he thought he'd outsmarted her, did he? She'd show him.

"Hut one, hut two, hike, hike!"

Dixie hiked the ball to her mother and dove straight at Jonathan. Candi did the same except she pivoted at the last second, throwing Grady off-balance. She spun around him and sprinted ahead. When she turned to look back, Grady was sitting on the ground scrambling to get up and the ball was coming right at her. She held out her hands and it hit her in the chest, nearly knocking the breath from her. Everything became a blur then. Grady was on his feet and heading for her, fast.

"Run, Candi, run!" Everyone yelled at her. She turned and got her feet moving. She had no idea where she needed to go, but Mr. Ferguson was there to point her in the right direction as he sprinted alongside her. She ran as fast as her feet would carry her. The finish line, marked by two trees spaced far apart, were in her sights.

She looked over her shoulder just as Grady dove for her. She side-stepped and ducked. He flew over her shoulder, hitting the ground hard, and Candi sprinted to the goal line.

"Touchdown!"

Mr. Ferguson blew his whistle and raised his hands in the air. Her teammates joined her shouting, jumping up and down, and hugging her. Candi looked back at her defender. Grady, face down in the grass, pounded the turf. The other men stood over him laughing. Laughing! Would Candi ever understand these men?

Jonathan hauled Grady up. "I never thought I'd see the day that Angel Ridge High's all-time leading rusher would get beat by a girl!"

Blake joined in adding, "And not only did she beat you, she outsmarted you. Man, that's a lethal combination — brains and beauty. You better steer clear of that little wildcat!"

"Let's eat," Mrs. Ferguson called. "Everybody get cleaned up."

They all moved off towards a spigot at the side of the barn to hose off their hands and forearms. Candi still clutched the football in the "end zone" while Grady stood looking at her, hands on his hips. His stance was casual, his expression one of bemusement. A fine sheen of sweat covered his chest.

"Nice moves," he said.

Candi approached slowly. "You all right?" On closer inspection, she saw that his chest had a few blades of grass stuck to it, and there were ugly red marks in several places.

"I'm fine. My pride, of course, is in shreds. Those guys will never let me live this down."

"I would apologize," she teased, "if there was anything to apologize for."

He took a step closer. "No apology necessary."

His gaze slid to the front of her shirt. He boldly ran a finger from her collar along the opening and slowly lower. "You lost a button."

Candi, struggling to breathe, looked down. His hand so near her skin, but not touching, looked big and tan and very masculine. She *had* lost a button, exposing an expanse of skin plunging to below her breast. Good thing the shirt was a tight fit or she'd be showing more than she was.

So much for not using her assets to her advantage. His scent was warm male, fresh air, grass and a hint of spicy cologne. *Hmm* . . . what an incredible cologne that would make. Mix the natural elements with

Grady's own pheromones. She inhaled . . . devastating combination.

She ran her fingertips along a red mark across his ribs. "You're going to have some bruises. I have a good cream that will help them not be painful."

Grady took another step towards her. "Will you rub it in?"

She smiled into his eyes. "That I bested you? Oh, yes."

He leaned in nudging her nose with his, breathing warmly against her lips. Dear Lord, she wanted to kiss him more than she wanted to breathe. The knowledge rocked her.

He widened his stance until his face was on level with hers. She dropped the football and clung to his smooth shoulders. She swept her tongue across her upper lip, anticipating the taste of his kiss. Grady grasped her waist firmly, and the next thing she knew, he tossed her over his shoulder, his strong forearm holding her thighs firmly to his bare chest. She bounced on his shoulder as he turned to walk back up to the barn.

"What are you doing?"

"Catching *you* off guard."

Candi pressed her hands against his warm, bare back and tried to twist around. That earned her a swift smack on the rear. “Settle down and enjoy the ride, darlin’.”

“Ow! Put me down,” she complained, but she had to admit, the view of his backside was amazing.

“Sorry. If you think that’s gonna leave a mark, I’ll be glad to rub some of that cream you were talkin’ about on it.”

Well, there was more than one way to skin a cat. She bent her knees against his arm, pushed upright, and twisted hard. He grabbed her calves and slid her down so that he had one arm around her shoulders and had the other under her knees. Not satisfied, she pressed against his shoulders. “Put me down right now, Grady Wallace.”

“Now she uses my name. Stop squirming. You are a little wildcat.”

“You have no idea,” she warned.

“You’re gonna hurt yourself if you fall.”

“I’ll take my chances.” She wiggled around, doing her best to get out of his arms, but he was just too strong.

“All right,” he said agreeably, and dropped her.

She felt herself falling and instinctively grabbed for his shoulders, but her hands slipped, and with no shirt, he had nothing but skin for her to grab onto. She braced herself to hit the ground, but at the last second, he caught her, laughing.

She smacked his shoulder. "That's not funny!"

They'd arrived at the barn, and he set her feet on the ground none too gently. "Really? Well maybe you'll think this is."

He grabbed the hose and hit her with the spray.

"Ah!" she exclaimed, shocked when the ice-cold water hit her face and chest.

"Nice."

Candi held her hands out and turned away. "Stop it!"

"I would, but I'm having too much fun."

This man desperately needed to be taught a lesson about dealing with a girl who grew up in the mountains. Tenacious, resourceful, and wily all could have been her middle name. She ducked, spun, and got behind him, then wrapped an arm around his waist while grasping his wrist with her other hand. Surprise was in her favor, and she was able to turn the spray on him, drenching him at close range from neck to knee.

She jumped back and, on her way, turned the water off. She pressed her forearm against her waist and doubled over laughing, until she straightened and looked at him. Really looked at him. His skin glistened in the sun and the wet denim clung to the curves and angles of his hips and thighs.

Grady dragged a hand down his face to clear the water out of his eyes. "Very funny."

"Don't play with fire unless you're prepared to get burned," she said breathlessly.

"Lady, you should come with a warning label."

Struggling to breathe, she countered, "It's not like I haven't been trying to discourage you."

He took a step forward, or did he draw her to him? He pushed a lock of hair behind her ear. "Darlin', if you were payin' attention, you'd have figured out by now that it's gonna take a lot to discourage me. I'm finding that the more I'm around you, the more I want to know everything about you."

"Why?" she breathed.

He cupped her cheek. "If I knew that, maybe I could walk away."

Candi closed her eyes and leaned into his touch. "I can't do this. It's not in the plan."

"Plan?"

She grasped his wrist and pulled back enough to look up at him. "To get settled here and open a shop. A man's not part of the plan."

He pressed his forehead to hers. "I don't think you can plan for something like this."

She took a step back. "I can't."

"Can't or won't?"

She shoved her hands into the back pockets of her jeans. She took a few more steps back even though everything in her wanted to run to him. "There's no difference."

"There's a world of difference."

"Not for me. You don't want to know me, Grady. You won't like what you find, so please, stop looking."

Chapter 11

Grady followed Candi up to the house. She went inside to find a towel, and he followed. She wandered around downstairs, but Grady, having practically grown up in this house, knew where they were. Finding Candi, he handed her one.

"Thank you," she said automatically.

She dried her hair, but there was no help for the shirt. "You're gonna need to borrow a dry shirt."

"No thanks to you," she grumbled.

Now, there was the Candi he knew. "Am I supposed to apologize?" he said, stepping into the role of antagonist even though all he wanted was to kiss her until she had no more fight left in her. But he'd made her a promise he intended to keep.

She shrugged.

He took her arm and led her towards the stairs. She moved away from his touch. Grady turned and looked back at her. "I'm just offering to show you where to get a shirt."

"I should ask first."

"Mom Ferguson," he called out.

"Yes, dear?"

The voice came from the kitchen as he knew it would. "Candi needs a dry shirt."

"Well, show her where to find one. You know where they are."

He swept a hand out in front of him. "After you."

Candi preceded him up the stairs. When he reached the top, he indicated the direction of Mom Ferguson's room. Inside the bedroom, he opened the drawer of a tall chest while Candi stood in the doorway like she was afraid to walk inside. He pulled out a plain pink t-shirt and tossed it to her. "There's a bathroom across the hall where you can change."

She turned and went inside without saying a word. He pulled the tail of his t-shirt out of his back pocket, put it on, and waited. When Candi emerged from the bathroom, he had to admit that she looked nearly as good in Mom Ferguson's pink t-shirt as she had in her damp button-up shirt with the missing button. Well, maybe not almost, but she could make anything look good. He never would have imagined himself going for a petite, curvy woman, but he loved everything about how Candi looked, how she felt in his arms . . .

"You didn't have to wait. I can find my way back downstairs."

The only sound in the quiet room was the clicking of a ceiling fan. "I stayed because I wanted to talk to you before we rejoined everyone."

"I'm not in the mood to undergo another round of interrogation, Sheriff."

He sighed. "Please don't go back to calling me 'sheriff.' "

"Fine. Grady, then. I'm not answering any more of your endless questions, so stop badgering me."

"I don't intend to badger you. I'm sorry if that's how I've made you feel." The apology seemed to catch her by surprise, so he pressed on while she had nothing to say. "You're wrong about me, you know."

"Whatever you say."

Ignoring that, he said, "A person can't earn your trust if you won't give them the opportunity to prove they're trustworthy."

"This doesn't have anything to do with trust. It's all about the fact that I don't need you, and you're not used to that. I might be attracted to you, and I might enjoy your touch, but I don't need *you.*" She took a step closer. "What I'm trying to say, Grady, is that I don't want or need any man. So, please don't take it personally."

"Well, hell, Candi. You'd think I just proposed. I'm not asking you to make a commitment, but it might be fun to spend time together. I think we just saw that when we both let our guards down, we enjoy each other's company."

"I don't have time to spend with you. I have a shop to get in order so I can open it."

"With what I hear from Blake and Cole, that's pretty well in hand."

"True, but starting a new business will be time-consuming, and then there's the matter of needing to find somewhere to live. I can't stay with Miss Estelee forever. I need my own place."

"I'm not about to stop you from doing any of those things."

Candi sighed and raked a hand through her hair. "Why can't you just walk away?"

"I could," he admitted, "but I don't want to."

"Why?" she repeated.

"We have a connection, and I don't believe that kind of thing is random."

She looked away then, but he could tell she'd taken his words in and was considering, carefully.

"Just think about it," he suggested.

"Has anyone ever told you that you're relentlessly persistent?"

"No, but I'll take that as a compliment."

"It wasn't meant as one," she mumbled.

Grady chuckled. "Supper'll be gettin' cold, and there's nothing more upsetting to Mom Ferguson than good food going to waste."

She smiled hesitantly, but it was definitely a smile. "Then I guess we'd better get out there."

"After you."

As he followed her down the stairs, he felt almost hopeful for the first time since he'd met Candi that maybe, if she got comfortable, she'd open up and share her secrets with him. He didn't fully understand it, but he knew that learning her secrets was not simply a matter of curiosity for him, but that it was somehow essential for both of them.

"Where'd y'all get to?" Dixie asked when Grady and Candi made it back to the picnic tables outside.

"Someone," Candi looked pointedly at Grady, "drenched me with the water hose, and I had to go find a shirt to change into."

"And since I was the one that got her all wet, I felt obligated to help her dry off."

"Grady!" Candi exclaimed. "It wasn't like he's making it sound, Mrs. Ferguson."

"That was real obliging of you, Grady," Blake offered.

"Well, I did learn the finer points of bein' a gentleman right here at this table," Grady said.

Dixie chimed in. "A gentleman wouldn't have turned the water hose on a guest, and particularly on a lady."

"Well, what can I say? We got to horsin' around, and I guess I just got carried away," Grady admitted.

To his surprise, Candi added, "A little water never hurt anyone. I won't melt. I'm sorry we were late comin' to the table ma'am," she said to Mrs. Ferguson.

"Well now, don't you worry none about that. Here's you a plate. You can sit right there at the end. There's plenty of room for the both of you, that is, if you want to sit with Grady after having to put up with his hijinks. If you can't reach something, just ask somebody to pass it."

"Thank you, and thank you again for inviting me to your home."

"You're more than welcome anytime. Now, eat."

Candi began filling her plate. Grady was surprised to see that, unlike most women, she didn't eat like a bird. He had to admit, he kind of liked that about her. Honestly, there wasn't much about her that he didn't like, except that she had secrets.

"Where did Miss Estelee and the Doc go?" Candi asked.

"Oh, while we were playing football," Mrs. Ferguson said, "Doc got a call to go up in the back country to deliver a baby. Don't worry, though, we'll see that you get home safe and sound."

"Oh, thank you — I think," she said around a wry smile she shot Grady's way.

He pointed a plastic fork at her. "Don't start, now."

Candi just laughed.

"Did I miss something?" Mom Ferguson said.

"I should say," Dixie supplied. "Our brave sheriff here was charged with getting Candi home 'safe and sound' the other night, and the next thing you know, they were both nearly run over by a reckless driver."

"My word," Mom Ferguson said with a hand pressed against her chest. "What in the world?"

"Yeah, Grady," Dixie said. "Have you found the driver yet?"

"No, but we did find out who the truck was registered to."

Grady scooped two heaping spoons of potato salad onto his plate. He loved Gran Ferguson's recipe for mustard potato salad.

"Well, don't keep us in suspense," Dixie said.

"Yes," Candi agreed.

"Turns out it was registered to Tom Hensley."

"Boots Hensley?" Pop Ferguson said. "How can that be?"

Dixie reached over and grasped his wrist. "Are you sure?"

"Yeah."

"No. That's just not possible. It has to be registered to someone else," Mom Ferguson said.

Grady looked over at Candi, who was surprisingly quiet. Of course, as a newcomer to town she wouldn't know anything about Tom Hensley or the fact that years ago he exchanged gunfire with his daddy and had died of his wounds, while Grady's daddy had been paralyzed. She sat very still with her hands clasped in her lap, looking at him expectantly.

Grady chuckled. "It's registered to Boots, all right. Poor Woody thinks maybe that truck had a ghost drivin' it."

"Haint," Candi said softly.

"Excuse me?"

"A haint is a spirit that means to torture someone. A ghost is well, just a lost soul wandering the earth."

He frowned. "A haint, then. Thanks for clearing that up." Sometimes, he forgot that mountain ways were a part of who Candi was, and then she did or said something to remind him.

"Grady?" Dixie said, her look all concern.

"Come on, y'all. There's a simple explanation for this that has nothing to do with the spirits of dead people roaming around Angel Ridge. Someone's been usin' that truck all these years and never bothered to register it. We figure out who that was, and we figure out who nearly killed me and Candi the other night."

"You're right. Of course you are," Mom Ferguson said. "It's just such a shock to hear that name again after all these years. I'm so sorry for you, Grady, to have to deal with this."

Grady stared at his food, uncomfortable with the turn of the conversation. "Of course I'm the one to deal with it. I'm the sheriff. End of story."

"So, Mama," Dixie said, "you goin' to the

Founder's Day committee meetin' tomorrow?"

Dixie to the rescue. She knew him so well.

"I reckon so, but I tell you, I'd just as soon jump off a cliff. Mrs. McKay and her entourage, forgive me Grady, drive me right up a slick wall."

"No offense taken," Grady said. He knew his mother was in thick with Harriet McKay, always had been. He'd never understood it. His mother didn't really agree with most of the craziness that Mrs. McKay supported, but she always went along. It was like being Mrs. McKay's friend gave her status or something. No one needed that kind of status, but he guessed his mom was too old to change her ways now.

"Oh, Candi!" Dixie said, "You should fill out an application for a booth at the Founder's Day celebration. People come from all over. It'd be a great way to promote your shop."

Mom Ferguson nodded. "Yes, dear. We take over Main Street, set up tables and sell some of everything. There are crafts, candles, music, and food. But the applications are due tomorrow morning. We'll be reviewing and approving them tomorrow night."

"Okay. How do I get one?"

"I'll print you one off the Internet. You can fill it out and turn it in to Mama before you leave."

"Great. Thanks, Dixie."

"Who's the headliner going to be for the concert this year?" Blake asked.

"Miranda Lambert."

"Oh, I love her," Dixie said. "She's a kick-ass girl, and you know we love that."

Jonathan laughed. "Some things never change."

Dixie jabbed him in the ribs. He doubled over in pain even though it would take a lot more than that to truly injure one of the NFL's leading fullbacks.

"Glad you could make it to town for a visit, Jonathan," Pop Ferguson said. "You should come in more when you have games in Nashville."

Jonathan gave Dixie a long, loaded look. "Yeah. I just might do that."

He could have sworn that Dixie Ferguson just blushed like a schoolgirl and his best friend had *never* blushed like a schoolgirl.

"So, Candi, what kinds of things are you going to sell in your shop?" Mom Ferguson asked.

"I'm calling it Heart's Desire, and I'm going to sell everything a woman's heart desires. Clothes, jewelry, flowers, candy, perfumes, and natural skincare."

"*Uh-huh.* You should see some of the clothes she's carrying." Dixie wiggled her eyebrows.

"What?" Mom Ferguson said.

"Let's just say, that room where she's got said items should be for people over twenty-one only."

Now that piqued Grady's interest, as if it wasn't already piqued. Before Candi could respond, Dixie said, "Well, a girl ought to be able to buy a satin teddy or some nice silk thigh-highs with a lacy garter belt without having to go to Knoxville, don't you think?"

Dixie was looking at Jonathan, who was presently choking on his burger. Grady covered his mouth with a napkin and slid his surprised gaze to the woman sitting next to him. Well now, he'd never have pegged Candi for selling sexy lingerie in her store, but he had to admit that notion certainly added dimension to the inappropriate thoughts blooming in his mind about her. He bet she'd look real good in a satin teddy, silk stockings, and a lacy garter belt.

"I'll also be selling flannel pajamas and cotton underwear. All of the clothing will be made from natural materials."

"Yep," Dixie added, "even the candy underwear."

Now *all* the men were choking, including Pop Ferguson.

"Well, isn't that nice," Mom Ferguson said. "What flavors do those come in?"

All surprised eyes swung to the woman at the head of the table. "What? I always wondered. Do they come in sugar-free for people that are hypoglycemic?"

"Yes, ma'am," Candi responded with a smile.

"What are you doin' in the space where the beauty parlor was, in the back of the shop?"

"I'm going to open a tea room. I thought it'd be nice to have a place where women can gather, like the men do at the hardware, to talk and relax."

"Oh, we've needed something like that in this town for a long time. Why didn't someone think of it before now?"

"Because we were waiting for Candi to come along and fill the need," Dixie supplied.

"Well, welcome, Candi. You are a refreshing addition to Angel Ridge."

Grady raised his glass and said, "Here, here."

Everyone at the table lifted their glass in a warm welcome that seemed to please Candi.

They finished the meal, and the men gathered to start churning the ice cream. Candi stood and joined in with clearing the table.

"No you don't." Mom Ferguson said. "The first time you eat at my table, you're a guest. Next time, you're family and you'll be more than welcome to help clean up. Grady, why don't you show Candi around the farm? By the time you get back, the ice cream should be ready."

He turned to Candi. "Would you like that? I could take you home if you'd rather. I know you've had some long hours working on your shop."

He liked the way she leaned into him and softly said for him alone, "I'm not ready to go home yet. I'd love to have a look around." She looked up at the house, a dreamy look clouding her clear green eyes. "It's so peaceful here."

He took her hand and helped her stand. "Let's go then." Grady took her back down to the barn, walking close beside her, but not touching.

"I've seen the barn."

"You've seen the spigot and the hose, but you haven't seen the inside." He leaned down and spoke quietly. "And our ride is inside."

"Ride?"

"Yeah. There's too much property to cover it on foot unless you're planning on taking much longer than we have before that ice cream is ready." He walked inside and Candi followed. They both stood for a moment, waiting for their eyes to adjust to the dimness after being in the late afternoon sunlight.

"What do you think?"

"It's big, but very much like a barn."

"The lady's hard to impress. This is an exceptionally fantastic barn — a dozen stalls, water, electricity, tack room, full loft. There's not one to compare to it in the county."

"It's very nice."

Grady just shook his head. "So, you're not a farmer. I get it."

"Is it necessary to have a barn to be a farmer? Do you need one if you have livestock — wait. Are you fishing for clues about me?"

Busted. "What makes you say that?"

"Do I strike you as unintelligent?"

"No, not at all."

"Then don't insult my intelligence."

"I wasn't fishing for clues. I'm just making a comment about you not being impressed with barns."

She didn't look convinced, but didn't

comment. "Are we riding horses, then?"

"No. They're all out to pasture."

She put a hand on one very shapely hip. "You said our ride was in here."

"It is. Be right back."

He disappeared around a corner, fired up the John Deere, and drove over to meet Candi. She looked up at him and laughed.

"Something funny?"

"Yeah. You on a tractor."

He laid a hand on his heart. "Now, that hurts. It truly does." She just stood there, looking up at him, still amused. He held out a hand. "Your chariot, ma'am. Climb on up."

She needed no help and was quickly standing beside him. "Know your way around a tractor, I see," he said.

"*Mmm* . . . fishing again, I see."

He shook his head. "Just can't help yourself, can you?"

"Help myself?"

"From thinking the worst of me. Is it so hard to believe that I don't always have ulterior motives?"

"Yes."

He took her hand and tugged. She hadn't been expecting that and landed sideways across his lap. He wrapped an arm around her waist, settled her against his chest then let off the brake.

"I'm not sure this is a good idea," she said, but looped an arm around his shoulder and rested a hand on his chest.

"Oh, see now, that's where you're wrong. This is a great idea. It's a beautiful evening, this is an amazing farm, and there's nothing better than seeing it on the back of a John Deere."

"Surely you don't expect me to believe you grew up on a farm."

"No, I don't, because I didn't. I grew up in town, but I wished I could have grown up on a farm. When the Fergusons moved to town and bought this place, I became friends with Blake and Dixie, spent as much time here as I could." He shrugged. "It was the next best thing."

"You would never be a farmer. You're not the type."

"You don't know me well enough to say that."

"Right. What did your father do for a living?"

Grady hesitated. Even after all these years, it was still hard talking about his father. "He was the sheriff."

"See," she said confidently, "it's in your blood. Your destiny."

Yeah. That's what everyone thought. Too

bad it wasn't true. Time for a change in topic. "The Fergusons raise Holsteins. They also have quarter horses. The cattle are in the fields there to the west. The horses are on the other side of the farm. Nine Mile Creek runs through the property, and there are three ponds."

"Do they grow any crops?"

"Just hay."

"That's too bad."

"Crops aren't as profitable as the cattle."

"What's that over there?"

She pointed toward the house by the creek. "That's the old homeplace. When the original owners first built here, that was where they lived. When their family outgrew it, they but built the farmhouse that the Ferguson's live in now. Would you like to see it?"

Candi smiled and nodded. He could feel her excitement in the way she strained against his arm, in the way she smiled, and focused on the little house on the edge of the creek.

Grady pulled up near the house and killed the engine. Candi scrambled down and went straight to the cottage. The white clapboard house had stood on this spot for the better part of two hundred years. Blake and Cole had used their carpentry skills to keep the old place in good shape. A part of Angel Ridge's history they say needs to be preserved.

"Does someone live here?"

Grady climbed down from the tractor and joined her on the front porch. "Not now. Blake was living here, but he bought a place in town, one of the big Victorians. It needs a ton of work, but he's determined to save it . . . and fill it with a big family."

"Oh, that's nice."

They both leaned against the porch railing and looked out at the creek just on the other side of the little yard that stretched out in front of them. Red and gold leaves from huge oak trees drifted to the ground.

"It's peaceful here."

"It's one of my favorite spots."

Candi turned and looked up at the house. "It's a shame no one lives here." She walked over to the window, cupped her hands, and leaned in.

"Would you like to see the inside?"

She turned with a contrite look, like she'd been caught doing something she shouldn't. "I wouldn't want to intrude."

"Please." He felt around on the frame of one of the windows and found the spare key. Unlocking the door, he turned and held out a hand. She walked shyly toward him and stepped inside. He flipped a switch, flooding the room with warm, golden light. "It's small, but adequate for someone who doesn't need a lot of room. There's the sitting room here, a kitchen, and the bathroom's over there. Upstairs, there are two bedrooms."

"Who lived here?"

"You mean before the Fergusons?"

"I mean originally."

She wandered around the parlor, trailing her hand across a table, then a chair.

"This was Houston property."

"Isn't the mayor in town a Houston?"

"That's right. There's been a Houston in that office since the founding of Angel Ridge."

"Like the sheriffs are Wallaces?"

He chuckled and rubbed his chin. "This is probably not a good time to mention it, but the Wallaces and Houstons are cousins."

"That doesn't surprise me. Most folks in small towns are related."

"True," he agreed.

"So, why didn't the mayor's family hold onto this property? It's gorgeous."

"There were a lot of Houstons. The first family of them had nine kids, including Sam Houston. Patrick's arm of the family didn't own this."

"An aunt or uncle then?"

"Or a cousin. Who knows?"

They both laughed.

She walked back outside, and Grady followed. Standing on the porch, she leaned against the railing and turned to him. "Can I ask you a question?"

"Careful. If this keeps up, we might actually get to know each other. That is, if I get to ask questions, too."

She folded her arms and threw back, "We could head back."

He heaved an affected sigh and looked heavenward. "Ask away."

She hesitated.

"Go on," he encouraged. Something was definitely on her mind.

"Everyone acted strange at dinner when you said that truck that nearly hit us belonged to Tom Hensley. What was that about?"

"Well, Tom Hensley's been dead a long time."

"I figured that much when you said Woody thought a ghost was driving the truck."

Grady turned and looked out across the lawn to the creek flowing by so peacefully, but the water churned and ebbed a lot like his gut at the mention of that name. "Hensley was a colorful character around here.

He was bigger than life, literally. The man had to have been six and a half feet tall. He lived up on Laurel Mountain all his life, ran moonshine back in the day."

"So he'd been crosswise of the law?"

"Yeah. I guess you could say he was a thorn in my daddy's side."

"Had you seen him before?"

"Who?"

"Tom Hensley."

"Sure. I saw him around town some when I was young."

"No. I mean, since he died. Have you seen him before now?"

"You mean have I seen his ghost? Well, sure. The spirits of all the lost souls buried in the cemetery at First Presbyterian rise up out of their graves on Halloween and dance around town square."

Grady laughed at his own joke, but Candi didn't seem amused. People from the mountains usually weren't amused by such talk. Ghosts, or "haints" as she'd called them, were part of mountain lore.

"No, of course I haven't seen him before now, and I didn't see him the other night drivin' his truck, either. But you did. You know," he leaned towards her and spoke softer, "I could show you an old mug shot of Boots. Maybe you could ID him.

Wouldn't that make for a great headline on the front page of *The Chronicle*? "Sheriff and Young Woman Nearly Killed by Ghost."

Candi slid her hands into the pockets of her jeans. "Restless spirits come back to where they were last, to settle unfinished business. If Tom Hensley was roaming around the Ridge, would he have a reason to?"

Grady rested a hip against the railing and crossed his arms. "First, you'd have to believe that was possible, which I don't. But if it were possible, I reckon Boots would have as much reason as anybody else, given his history."

"Because he was a moonshiner, and your daddy, I guess, fined and arrested him a few times."

"I don't remember specifics about that, but I suppose it's possible. That and the fact that he and my daddy had a shootout on Main Street that left Tom Hensley dead."

CHAPTER 12

Candi stopped breathing. Grady's daddy had shot her granddaddy? She couldn't process that piece of information, much less respond.

"Hey," Grady placed a hand on her arm, "you okay?" That crooked smile of his slanted across his face. "You look like maybe *you* just saw a ghost."

She rested a hand against her racing heart and managed to breathe. "Your daddy killed a man in cold blood, right out on Main Street?"

"Well, when a man walks down the middle of town with a shotgun on his shoulder and calls the sheriff out, I wouldn't describe that as getting shot down in cold blood."

"Oh." What in the world would cause her granddaddy to do such a thing?

"You think that might cause the guy's ghost to come after me?"

Grady was all smiles and good humor.

How could he talk about such a thing so casually when she felt the world had just radically shifted under her feet? When she looked closer, deeper into his hazel eyes, she saw something raw that time hadn't begun to heal.

"Your daddy was hurt in the shooting, wasn't he?"

All signs of humor drained from his face. "How would you know that?"

She shrugged and spoke softly, because he looked ready to bolt. "Just a guess. He wasn't killed, was he?"

Grady turned and stepped off the porch into the yard. Candi followed.

"My dad didn't die from his injuries, but it might have been better if he had. He was never the same."

Candi bit down hard on her lower lip to keep the tears that rushed into her eyes from falling. Could this be real? Her grandfather and Grady's daddy in a fatal confrontation? She wanted to ask why, but at the same time, she couldn't hear the answer to that question. Not right now. Plus, she had to remember that no one knew her connection to Tom Hensley. She didn't want to ask too many questions and make Grady suspicious.

"What's that building over there?" she

said, pointing to a log structure that sat back away from the house about two hundred yards yards.

"A springhouse."

She continued to worry her lower lip. Nervous habit. This place was ideal, like a place out of time. Peaceful, secluded.

"What's going on in that gorgeous head of yours?"

She had to do the near impossible and force thoughts of her granddaddy out of her mind. So she said, "I'm just thinking, I need somewhere to live and this is perfect. I could have a garden, could store my oils and creams in the spring house." She turned to him. "Do you think they'd consider renting it?"

He tucked a curl behind her ear. "I don't know why not. It's never good to leave a house standing empty."

"You think it'd be okay for me to ask?" She turned towards him as she spoke, but couldn't quite meet his eyes. The secret of her identity took on new meaning given what she'd just learned. Her granddaddy died a violent death at the hands of the sheriff of Angel Ridge. She couldn't process it. She needed time and questions answered she couldn't ask Grady.

"Sure, why not? That is, if you're really

interested."

She looked back at the house. "I would love living here."

"Then it's settled. Let's head back. I bet the ice cream is ready by now." He started back to the tractor, but Candi lagged behind. The easy camaraderie they'd shared before she'd asked too many questions had evaporated like mist on the river in the morning sunshine.

"You coming?"

Lord, how she dreaded getting back on that tractor with him. How could she act like nothing had changed?

"Hey, where are your shoes?"

Pretend. It's what she did best, after all. Compartmentalize the information and store it away for now. She joined him on the tractor, all attitude and spunk. "Someone threw me over their shoulder and hauled me off before I could retrieve them after a football game. A football game where, I might add, someone was soundly beaten — by women."

"Oh, yeah?"

"Yeah."

He looped an arm around her waist and pulled her close. She sucked in a shallow breath, her hands pressed against his chest. The now familiar pull between their bodies made her shiver against the warmth strumming through her body. Unable to resist, she looked into his eyes. Unguarded this time, she realized two things: that they'd both been victims hurt by their parents' actions which had nothing to do with them; and he wanted her — maybe as much as she wanted him.

All pretense fell away as she trailed a hand down the back of his head to his neck. His arms tightened around her waist. "I'm sorry," she whispered near his ear as she settled her head against his and held him close. Imagining him having to care for his injured father, a man who had probably been bigger than life to his son. How he must hate the man who'd injured his father. This time when emotion rose in her chest, she let the tears fall.

"Hey . . ." He leaned back and brushed the back of his hand across her cheek. "What's this about? Why are you sorry?"

"About your daddy and what you must have suffered when he got shot."

A series of emotions flitted across his face so quickly she couldn't begin to identify them. "That was a long time ago."

"That kind of thing's not something you just get over; I don't care how long it's been."

"I hadn't thought about it in years."

"And now you have to because of the investigation."

"It's my job," he said, but he gritted his teeth against the words.

He might not want to admit it, but the hurt was still there. She wrapped her arms around him again. "*Shhh* . . . let me comfort you." No one had probably ever comforted him. As a male and an only child, he'd probably had to grow up instantly, taking on adult responsibilities as the man of the house. She wondered how old he'd been and how soon afterward he'd become sheriff.

Grady smoothed his hands from her shoulders to her hips. "Darlin', if you feel the need to comfort me, I'm not about to complain."

"Don't talk. Close your eyes and feel . . ."

Candi focused all her energy toward touching the hurt in his soul. After a few moments, she felt his shoulders relax. People carried hurts around in their bodies. All those aches and pains were the body's way of urging a person to deal with things. But instead of listening, they mistakenly think the pains are because of sitting at a computer too long, or maybe an old injury. If they only realized those injuries happened to get their attention, and still they don't listen. If people could just learn to drop their guard and get in touch with their bodies . . .

She felt Grady shift and tense. Men. Too used to being the ones to comfort women, they got uncomfortable with the roles reversed.

He pulled back and looked at her. The shutter to his soul had closed. "We should get going. Everyone will wonder where we are."

Candi just nodded, but she eased her arms around his waist and rested her head against his shoulder. She had to close her eyes against the waves of desire that rolled over her. What was it about this man? He touched something deep inside her that had never been touched before. She sighed and leaned into the feeling.

As if sensing that something had changed, Grady breathed her name into her hair. Unaccountably, she wished he'd said "Lark," instead of "Candi."

Grady touched her chin with his fingertips. "I don't know what to make of you."

She traced the line of his jaw with a finger. "Then don't try."

"I wish I were wired that way, but I'm not."

She couldn't hold back the smile. "Ah, the never-ending search for answers."

"Yes, and you'd do well to remember that you don't like me."

His stern expression almost made her laugh. Almost. He was right. She didn't have any business trying to comfort and heal him. She'd lost her focus for a moment, that was all.

"We should get back. Like you said, people will wonder where we are, and I don't want that . . . people wondering about us."

He laughed. "It's a small town. Gossip runs up and down Main Street like the river flows. It ebbs with the seasons, but it's always there, getting everything wet. Worrying about what people think is a recipe for frustration."

He fired up the tractor. "Let's go get your shoes." He got them moving and headed toward the field where they'd played ball before supper.

"I want people focused on my shop, not who I may or may not be involved with."

"Right. Business first."

"Yes. And you should be focused on finding that reckless driver and the person who broke into my shop."

"Of course," he agreed.

He pulled to a stop near where she'd left her shoes. When she got down to retrieve them, he disengaged the break and drove back up to the barn. She didn't protest being left to walk up the lawn to the farmhouse, and he hadn't apologized for leaving her there. After all, she didn't want people to get ideas about them. She should go back to the party alone.

The only trouble with that was that she could still smell his scent on her clothes, feel the imprint of his hands on her body, the rasp of his whiskers on her neck, reminding her that their hearts had spoken to each other. That wasn't something she could just forget, but she had to.

Candi had planned to speak with Miss Estelee about the details of what happened between her granddaddy and Grady's daddy last night when she got home, but she'd already been in bed when Candi got there. This morning when she left for the shop, Miss Estelee had been gone. She hoped she'd see her in town sometime today, but she wasn't sure it was something they should get into without privacy, of which there had been precious little.

There'd been a constant stream of people in and out of the shop all day: Blake and

Cole were nearly finished, delivery people had been bringing things in, while she had been unloading, stocking, painting mosaics on the walls, oh, and the tables for the tea room had been delivered. Candi stood back and looked at everything with pride. It was better than she could have imagined. She couldn't wait to open this weekend.

She'd spoken with Mr. and Mrs. Ferguson last night about renting the house by the creek, and they'd happily agreed to have her there. The rent was more than reasonable. The problem now was finding time to move.

Speaking of Mrs. Ferguson. "Good morning, Candi! Oh, my . . . look how lovely your shop is! Why, I hardly recognize the place! I can't wait to have a look around." She breezed into the shop and gave Candi a warm kiss on the cheek.

"Good morning, ma'am. Feel free to look all you want."

"I certainly will, right after I give you one approved application for your booth at the Founder's Day Celebration. Congratulations! Of course, you'll have the stretch of sidewalk outside your shop."

"That's wonderful. Thank you so much for your help with getting the application processed."

"I was glad to do it. So, Dixie tells me the grand opening is this weekend. You have sure gotten this place together in record time."

"I've had a lot of help. I don't know what I would have done without Mr. DeFoe, Cole, Blake and Dixie."

"You should do some flyers and distribute them around town, dear."

"That's a great idea. I'll work on some tonight."

"Oh, and I wanted to let you know that since you are just setting up house, I've taken the liberty of putting together enough furniture for you to go ahead and move in to the old homeplace. Now, it's nothing fancy, mind you. Just some mismatched pieces I haven't had the heart to get rid of over the years. But it's all clean and comfortable. There's chairs for the living room, two beds for upstairs, a desk, a kitchen table, dishes and some pots and pans." Mrs. Ferguson came over and took her hands when she saw Candi's eyes fill with tears. "Oh dear . . . have I overstepped?"

Candi sniffed. "No, ma'am. I'm just, well, I don't know what to say. I hadn't even begun to think about furnishing the place. I've been so busy here."

"Well, of course you hadn't. That's why

Mr. Ferguson and I took care of it for you. Now, you feel free to use those things as long as you want, and if you decide to get your own furnishings, just let us know, and we'll move the other out. All right?"

"Yes, ma'am. I don't know how to thank you."

"You can thank me by getting your things together and moving in as soon as you feel comfortable. I hope you'll come up and visit me as often as you can. It's been so lonely since Blake moved into town. Dixie's been living here for a few years now."

"That's very kind of you. I'll need to speak with Miss Estelee about moving. I haven't had a chance to talk to her since last night."

"Oh, I just saw her at the drug store. She was pleased as punch about you movin' out to the farm. She asked me to see you settled and to tell you she's going south for a few weeks."

"South?"

"Yes. She said with the cold comin' on, her bones were achin' something fierce. Said to tell you she'll see you when she gets back."

Candi frowned. "She did say her arthritis was bothering her." How odd for her to just up and leave without saying anything.

"She usually goes 'south,' as she puts it,

for a few weeks this time of year. Comes back fit as a fiddle. None of us will be able to keep up with her." Mrs. Ferguson patted Candi's hand. "Not to worry, you're in good hands with the Fergusons."

"I am indeed," Candi agreed.

"You just come on whenever you want. Here's the key. Same one works for the front and back door. And there's one there for the springhouse, too."

Candi took the keys. "Let me give you a check for the first two month's rent. I wrote it out this morning." She walked behind the counter and pulled out her new checkbook.

"Thank you, hon. I'd better get going now. I'll be back on Friday with *my* checkbook for the grand opening!"

Candi smiled. "I appreciate that."

Mrs. Ferguson waved as she left. Candi jingled the keys, then palmed them. Her own place. Things were working out well . . . almost too well, but Aunt Ruby had always said that when you do what you're meant to, things just fall into place. It's when you try to force things that you'll find trouble at every turn.

She shook her head. What was wrong with her, standing around gathering wool with so much work to be done? She had merchandise to display. She was elbow deep in a box of lingerie in the Naughty Shop when the bells she'd wrapped around the doorknob out front jingled.

"Back here!"

"Well, hello."

Candi turned to see Grady standing in the doorway and her with a lacy bra in each hand, one silver, the other purple. She added them to a display on a satin-covered round table and stood. "Sheriff."

He put his hands on his hips and hung his head. When he looked back up at her, he said, "Are we ever going to get past that?"

"That depends. Are you here on business or for some other reason?"

He strode into the room, stopping in front of her. "Actually, I came over to offer to help you move into your house."

"Mrs. Ferguson told you."

He nodded, but his attention had shifted to the displays of underwear she'd gotten out, bras, panties, thongs — lace and edible. She'd hung silk stockings from the branches of a shiny metallic tree. The garters were scattered around the bottom. He was fingering one of the lace bras she'd just been holding. "Nice . . ." his gaze shifted from the bra to her, landing somewhere south of her eyes . . . "merchandise."

"Thank you." Her voice had gone all

husky, so she cleared her throat. "Men won't be allowed in here unless they're shopping for someone, and definitely not when women are here."

"So many rules." He held up a lacey black bra. "How do you think my mom would like this?"

She didn't want or need this kind of distraction. "This is not something a son buys his mother, and you know it." She put the bra back on the display. "As for you helping me move, I'm not sure when that'll be. I'll have to get over to the utility board to pay the deposit and schedule a date for them to turn the electricity on."

"They can usually go out same day if you ask."

"That's good to know." He'd moved on from the bra display to the edible thongs and massage oils. It might be a good idea to get him out of this room. Check that, essential to get him out of this room. Watching him move among the feminine things was doing strange things to her breathing.

Just as she took a step towards the door, she heard a crash in the back of the shop. "What was that?"

One second Grady was on the other side of the room looking at the teddies, and the next he was in the doorway pulling her behind him. "Stay here."

Hand on his gun, he stepped into the hall and hugged the wall as he quietly made his way to the back room. Candi wasn't about to stay put. What if Grady decided to shoot someone? That was the last thing she needed to happen right before her grand opening.

He stopped at the end of the hallway, looked in the back room, then went in. Candi followed. Something else crashed to the floor and shattered. "In the workroom," she whispered.

"I told you —" but then he just shook his head and sidled up to the workroom's closed door. Candi was right behind him. Hand still on his gun, he slowly turned the doorknob and pushed the door open. "Police. Come out with your hands in the air."

Nothing. No sound.

Grady had taken one step inside when a big, furry opossum waddled between his feet and out of the workroom. "What the —"

Candi laughed. "Well, hello big fella. How long you been hidin' out in there?"

The furry gray opossum looked up at her with big brown eyes, clearly frightened.

"Careful, Candi. He might bite. We don't know that he's not rabid."

Grady drew his gun and pointed it at the animal.

"Put that away."

"I'm not taking any chances. I don't want either of us to be injured."

"Just stand back and don't frighten him."

Candi maintained eye contact while she backed slowly to door. The opossum eyed her progress, but didn't move. She opened the door to the back alley. "Come on, buddy. There's fresh air and sunshine out there." She eased out the door, and the opossum took a step towards her. "Good boy. Come on."

He took another step, then picked up speed until he was outside and scurrying down the alley to freedom. Back inside, Candi closed the door and went to the workroom to assess the damage.

"What do you know? We got ourselves a bonafide opossum whisperer. That's a skill that could come in real handy 'round here."

"Funny. At least you can close the case of who broke into my shop."

"True." Grady followed her inside. "What'd he break this time?"

"Just some glass jars. After the last mess, I was more careful about what I kept back here."

"Smart."

She swept up the broken glass and dumped it in the waste basket.

"Why don't you take a break? We could walk over to the utility board so you can get your lights turned on, and then we could get some lunch at Fergusons."

Tempting, but it would take too much time, and there was the matter of distractions she didn't need. "I brought lunch to eat here when I get hungry. I hadn't planned on taking a break. There's so much to do before Friday."

"Don't you want to get moved?"

"Sure, but I really can't spare the time until after the grand opening." Truth was, it wouldn't take much time at all. For that matter, she really didn't need help.

"With the place furnished, all you need to do is move your clothes. If you have anything else you want to take over, I could help you with that when you're finished here."

"You know everything don't you?"

He smiled and rocked back on his heels. "Like I said, it's a small town, and I spend a lot of time with the Fergusons."

"Right. You and Dixie see each other a lot."

"We've been friends for a long time."

"But you go out too, right?"

"Sometimes."

"What is it they say? Friends with benefits?"

"It's not like that. So, what do you say? Deal with the utility board and then lunch?"

Candi sighed. Trying to resist Grady Wallace was like trying to push against the wind. "How about if I go to the utility board to get the electricity scheduled to be turned on, you can go get something to eat, and then I'll meet you at town square for lunch."

"All right. What can I get you?"

"Nothing. I'll eat what I brought."

"You sure?"

"Yeah."

"All right. Meet you in ten minutes then?"

Candi nodded. She grabbed her purse and keys, then walked out with him. They parted ways after she locked up. It wouldn't hurt to have lunch with him. She'd been wondering where he was in finding the reckless driver. She also wanted to find out more about what happened between her granddaddy and his daddy. With Miss Estelee gone, she might just go over to the newspaper to see if she could look up old stories about it. Surely there'd been some. That kind of thing going down right on Main Street had to have been big news in this town.

She shook her head to scatter her troubled thoughts. It was a beautiful day. The fresh air and sunshine'd do anybody good. She needed to get her mind off everything, including the crazy dreams she kept having about a woman who looked like her, wandering riverbanks looking for lost loves right before she drowns.

When Grady arrived at town square, he found Candi sitting on a park bench gazing up at the angel monument. It was a scene right out of a Hitchcock movie. Leaves from the big oak trees on the square fell in a steady shower of gold and red while the mysterious stranger sat on a park bench feeding huge black crows like they were pigeons. Just to make the picture complete, a black kitten sidled up to her to see if she had something for it to eat, too. No one else was in the square. Everyone strolled along the sidewalks observing the scene, probably thinking the same things he was. Fanciful nonsense.

When Grady stepped into the square and neared Candi, the crows scattered. He sat next to her and asked, "Get everything taken care of at the utility board?"

"Yes. They're going to turn the electricity on tomorrow."

"Great. I'm sure Mom Ferguson has already gone over and cleaned."

"She's a nice lady."

"The best." He looked over at her sandwich and said, "What have you got there?"

She held up a wheat pita. "Cucumber, tomato, lettuce, and ranch dressing."

He wrinkled his nose and said, "Yum."

Candi laughed. "What did you get at Ferguson's?"

"Let's see . . ." He opened his bag and pulled out a thick sandwich wrapped in foil. "Turkey club, chips, and brownies — one for me and one for you. Looks like you're gonna need it with all that health food you're ingesting there."

"I'm not opposed to a good brownie," she said as she munched on a carrot stick.

"Tell me you're not on a diet."

"Heck, no."

"Good, because there's absolutely nothing wrong with your figure." He let his gaze slide down her body. She was wearing some kind of dark, stretchy pants that clung to her legs and a long, soft sweater that stopped mid-thigh. She'd settled a jaunty purple beret atop her glossy black curls.

"Do you eat like that all the time?"

She shrugged, but didn't elaborate. Some things didn't change.

She tossed a piece of bread to the mewling kitten. "Mind if I ask about the reckless driver investigation?"

"Not at all."

"Any new leads?"

"No. Nothing. I keep hitting dead ends. The sweep of the vehicle didn't turn up anything either, not even a fingerprint." He took a bite of his sandwich and chewed. "*Mmm* . . . best sandwiches in Tennessee. Want a bite?"

"Sure."

He held the sandwich toward her, and she broke off a corner. He watched as she took a bite, which gave him an excuse to focus on her mouth — which rocketed him back to that kiss they'd shared at the shop the day of the oil spill in the workroom. He licked his lips. "Good?"

"Delicious." A few moments passed. "Did you say that there was someone you were going to question about the truck?"

Had he? It was hard to think straight with her sitting so close he could smell that spicy perfume that put him in the mind of humid summer nights and the two of them rolling in the sweet-smelling grass of a creek bank.

"Yeah, I did," Grady said, "but that conversation didn't go far."

Candi just nodded, still looking up at the

angel monument.

"He's something, isn't he?"

"Yes."

The bronze warrior standing on a brick pedestal was the focal feature of town square. "He's been here for over a hundred years. Miss Estelee's particularly fond of him. Says he reminds her of a long lost love."

"Miss Estelee?"

Grady nodded. "She makes sure Cole plants flowers around him in the spring and fall."

She didn't comment, just kept staring up at the statue as if mesmerized, or maybe it was a way to keep from looking at him. The black crows started gathering again. The kitten, oddly not at all tempted by the birds, jumped up on the park bench to sit next to Candi. She absently stroked its fur. A crow lit on the angel's shoulder. Odd . . .

"You know, they say that an angel appeared to the Craigs, the first settlers of Angel Ridge, and saved them from an Indian attack. That's why they named the town Angel Ridge. Legend has it that they still watch over the town and guide what happens around here."

"Do you believe that?"

"It's just a legend. Doesn't mean it's true."

"Most folks would say crows and black cats were a bad omen."

He rested an arm along the back of the park bench and leaned toward her. "I'm not most folks."

"That you're not, Sheriff — Grady."

That made him smile. She corrected herself without him prompting her. Now that was progress. He held his sandwich out to her. "More?"

"No thanks."

He continued to eat his sandwich. She fed the crows and the kitten.

"People are staring," she noted.

He chuckled. "Are you surprised?"

She stood. "I should get back to the shop."

Grady grabbed her hand to keep her from bolting. "Hold on. You've not had your brownie." Okay, so he hadn't thought touching her through, because the contact made him want to hold her in his arms, and the thought of holding her in his arms had him thinking of kissing her.

He tugged at her hand. "You know you want it." She looked to be considering his words, so he added, "It'll taste so good."

She sat, and taking her hand back, dug into the bag between them. "Okay, but then I really need to get back to work."

He smiled. "Dixie said you're opening this

weekend."

She nodded because she was sighing into her first bite of brownie.

"Good?"

"Mmm . . ."

She liked chocolate. He filed that away for future reference. "Dixie also said you're doing something tomorrow night."

She nodded again. "She had a great idea about inviting the ladies in town for a preview. It's a good way to advertise through word of mouth."

"Good idea." She was licking her fingers now, and he was about to embarrass them both right here in the middle of town, with everyone staring. "Women only?"

"Yes."

God help him . . . she was licking crumbs off her lips now. He stretched an arm across the back of the park bench and leaned in.

Candi stood. "I really need to go."

Grady clinched a fist, willing control into his limbs and stood as well. "I'll walk you back."

"Thanks, but you really don't need to do that. I'm sure you're busy."

He grabbed the bag and took her arm. "It's no trouble. Besides, I want to check to see if there's some way your furry tenant is getting in and out. You don't want him showing back up when you have customers, do you?"

Her shoulders lowered in defeat. "All right."

They turned in the direction of her shop and stopped dead in their tracks. Tom Hensley's truck was parked right in front of Heart's Desire.

CHAPTER 13

"What the hell?"

Candi took a step back and stumbled. Grady grasped her arm more firmly and put an arm around her waist. "Is that —"

"No, it can't be. Fuzz Rhoton impounded that truck for me. It just looks like the same one. Lots of trucks like that around, I'm sure."

Candi looked up at him, a weak smile playing around her lips. "Who are you trying to convince? Me or you?"

Grady wasn't sure. "Come on. Let's check it out."

They walked the rest of the way to the shop. Candi gave the truck a wide berth, and he was about to have a look inside when Candi exclaimed, "Grady!"

She pulled up short and grabbed his arm with both hands, stopping dead in her tracks. He looked back at her, taking in her wide green eyes filled with fear. He grasped her shoulders. "What is it?"

She pointed. "The door to the shop is open. I'm sure I locked it."

Grady glanced at the open door. "Did Bud adjust it?"

Candi nodded.

"Stay here. I'll check it out."

She grabbed his arm again. "No, Grady. Don't go in there. I have a bad feeling."

Woody came skidding to a halt beside them, out of breath like he'd run full out all the way from the courthouse. "Your Uncle Tom called. Said Boots Hensley's truck was parked right in the middle of town. I saw it as soon as I stood on the courthouse lawn. I got here as quick as I could."

"Easy, Woody. You're gonna give yourself a heart attack. Let's all just calm down. You know as well as I do that truck's impounded. This one has to belong to somebody else."

"But —"

"There'll be time to worry about the truck later," Grady said to his deputy. "Looks like someone just broke into Candi's shop. Back me up."

Bud DeFoe joined them next, with several others moving in their direction. "Bud, stay with Candi and keep these people back. Someone may have broken into the shop.

Woody and I are going in."

Bud nodded and put an arm around Candi.

"Be careful," Candi whispered.

Grady unholstered his gun. Woody did the same and followed him as he shouldered the door the rest of the way open. The glass display cases were broken. Glass crunched under their feet. Merchandise was strewn everywhere. "Police! Come out with your hands up!"

No response. Adrenaline pumped through his veins, his heart raced, and blood pounded in his ears. He quickly moved over to the long hallway that led to the back of the shop and eased forward to have a look. "Clear."

They moved in unison down to the two shops that opened up off the hallway. He signaled for Woody to take one and him the other. They both looked inside the rooms, went in. The place had been torn apart as if someone had been looking for something, but it was unoccupied as well. Someone had spray painted in red on the wall, "Go home witch." Bile rose in the back of Grady's throat, but he backed to the doorway. When he saw Woody across the hall, he nodded towards the rear of the shop. Woody nodded as well.

Grady looked into the hallway, made sure no one was there, then gave a hand signal for them to move out. A sweep of the back confirmed the shop was empty. The back door was open. Grady checked the alley, but found it deserted.

He holstered his gun, took off his hat and scrubbed a hand down his face.

"This is really bad, Boss," Woody said unnecessarily. "Who could have done this?"

Grady jammed the hat back down on his head. "Let's check out that truck."

A crowd had gathered on the square behind the vehicle. Candi looked white as a sheet. When she moved to go in her shop, he held out a hand. "Please, wait right there." He looked in the window of the truck while Woody went to the other side. There was a shotgun laying across the seat. He joined Woody and spoke in low tones. "Call Maryville PD, then get the forensics kit and some tape to cordon this area off."

Woody shot off towards the courthouse, cell phone in hand. Grady saw Dixie pushing her way through the crowd of rubberneckers. He motioned for her to come to him. He pulled his cell phone out of his pocket and dialed the Angel Ridge Corner Market.

One look at his face, and Dixie said, "It's bad."

"Go to Candi and, whatever you do, don't let her go inside that shop."

"Corner Market."

"Hey, Cathy. It's Grady Wallace. Is Fuzz in?"

"Hey, Grady. Yeah, Fuzz is here. Let me holler at him. You doin' all right?"

"I been better."

"Well, I'm sorry to hear that. Here's Fuzz."

"Hey, Grady. I was just about to call you. Dangdest thing has happened."

"Just tell me Tom Hensley's Ford is locked up in your impound lot."

"That's just it. It's gone, and there's no sign of anybody breakin' in. The place is locked up tighter'n a drum. It's like it lifted off the ground and flew out of here like a ghost or somethin', and I don't mind tellin' you, it gives me the heebie-jeebies. I think you and Woody oughta come over and have a look."

"Yeah, we will, but we got a situation in town right now."

"Can I help?"

Fuzz had been a security specialist in the army. "It wouldn't hurt havin' another set of eyes and hands. I think half the town's on the square."

"I'm on my way."

Grady ended the call and turned toward the curious bystanders. "There's nothin' to see here. Y'all just go on about your business."

Everybody just looked at each other, but no one made a move to leave.

"What is it, Grady?" someone said.

"Is that Boots Hensley's truck?" someone else said.

"Did that new girl's shop get broken into?"

"Yes, do tell, Sheriff."

Jenny Thompson joined him on the street by the truck. He stepped between her and the vehicle before she could see what was inside. "This is a crime scene, Jenny. I'm going to have to ask you to step back."

Jenny smiled, all sleek southern charm. "I gathered that much, Sheriff." She pulled a digital camera out of her oversized leather purse and started snapping pictures, of the truck, of Candi, the shop. Damn, he'd just noticed that the big window in front was broken and "WITCH" had been written across her new sign.

"What's going on here?" Jenny snapped another picture of the front of the building.

"That's what we're trying to figure out,"

Grady said.

He shifted his attention back to Jenny and did his best to corral her, but she was slippery as the material of her rain coat. "Maybe I'll just have a word with Miss Heart."

Grady grasped Jenny's arm. She looked at his hand pointedly. He broke the contact. "This is an official investigation. You can't talk to her until I've taken her statement."

He was talking straight out of his rear, but protecting Candi was a priority right now. This was going to devastate her. She'd worked so hard to put that shop together, and now . . .

Fuzz careened onto Main Street on two wheels, lights flashing, parked his tow truck diagonally in front of Boots' truck, hopped out, and immediately took control. "All right, everybody. Back it up. There's nothing to see here. Go back to your business and let the sheriff do his work. I'm sure you'll be able to read all about it in *The Chronicle* tomorrow." He held out his arms and walked towards the retreating crowd. "That's right. Move along."

The crowd started to disperse just as Woody and Clara arrived on the scene.

Grady approached Candi slowly. He didn't want to tell her this, but he had to.

"Dixie, can you occupy Jenny for a minute? Maybe try and figure out a way to get her out of here?"

"That's not about to happen, but I'll distract her as long as I can."

"I appreciate it. Hang close." He gave her a long steady look. She nodded, getting his nonverbal message that Candi was going to need a friend.

"Jenny, that coat is fabulous. Where did you get it . . ."

Thank God for Dixie. "Bud, why don't you give Woody a hand taping the area off?"

Bud looked at Candi, and then back at Grady, concern etching his face. Grady squeezed the older man's shoulder, trying to reassure him that he had the situation under control when the truth was things had been out of control since Candi Heart arrived in Angel Ridge.

Bud looked at Candi. "I'll be close by. If you need anything, just holler."

Candi attempted a wobbly smile. "Thank you, sir."

He strode off, and Grady took Candi's hand, pulling her to the side so no one would hear what he had to say. When he looked at her, he couldn't get any words out. She was still unnaturally pale. Her clear green eyes were huge and held a vulnerability that tugged at his heart. On top of that, she was trembling. Gray clouds had rolled in off the lake bringing a chill breeze along with them.

Grady shrugged out of his jacket and draped it around Candi's shoulders. He rubbed his hands up and down her arms to try and warm her up.

"Tell me," she said.

He sighed and just managed to maintain eye contact as he said, "I'm afraid there's a lot of damage to your shop."

She took the news like a blow, slumping against the brick building at her back. "And the truck?"

"I'm not sure yet, but it could be the same truck that ran us off the sidewalk the other night."

"How can that be? You said it was impounded."

"It was. We're trying to figure out what happened. Looks like someone stole it and drove it over here."

"Grady, we were sitting right over there the whole time." She pointed at the park bench where they'd just shared lunch. "How could we not have noticed that truck coming through town and someone breaking windows?"

"We weren't over there the whole time.

You were at the Utility Board, and I was at the diner part of the time."

"It couldn't have been more than fifteen minutes, and we weren't the only ones around."

"I know." He continued to rub her arms.

She straightened, stepping away from his touch. "I want to go inside."

Out of the corner of his eye, thankfully, he saw Woody taking the shop sign down. "I'd rather you go with Dixie and come back later, after we've had a chance to investigate the crime scene. We've called the forensics unit at the Maryville Police Department. They've got more sophisticated facilities than we do here." As he spoke, he could hear the sirens as the unit neared.

"It's that bad?"

He hated to erase the last glimmer of hope from her eyes. "I'm afraid so. I'm sorry, Candi."

"Why? Who could do this?"

"I don't know. I thought after we found out that truck belonged to a man my daddy shot and killed that someone was after me, but it may not be me they're targeting."

"I thought the same thing at first," she agreed. "But it doesn't make sense. I'm new here. No one knows me."

"I have to ask you, is there anything or

anyone in your past that may have followed you here?"

She crossed her arms in front of her. "No. There's no one. I lived alone in an isolated area with my grandmother before I came here. Now that she's gone, I don't have any other family."

"Where is she now?"

"She died."

"I'm sorry." But after a second, he asked, "No old boyfriends? Others who stood to inherit when your grandmother passed?"

Candi laughed. "I never dated or had friends. It was just me and my grandmother."

"What about money? Mountain folks sometimes keep money hidden."

Candi chewed on her lower lip.

"I need you to tell me everything, Candi. It's critical so that I can track down whoever did this and keep you safe until I do."

She jerked her gaze up to his. "You think I'm not safe? Why would you say that?"

He grasped her arms, but she wriggled away from him. "What aren't you telling me?"

Somehow, she got around him, dodging his hands, and shot straight into the front door of her shop. Damn it!

Grady hurried after her, but she had disappeared into the hall by the time he reached the front room of the shop. He picked up his pace to keep her from seeing the messages left for her on the walls. When he skidded into the shop with the slinky lingerie, she was on her knees staring up at the hateful words written in red across the newly painted wall.

"Oh, my Lord . . ." she mumbled through the hand she'd pressed against her mouth.

Grady lifted her into his arms. She came willingly, settling her face against his neck. He carried her straight through the back and out into the alley. Rain had started to fall, but neither of them cared. He couldn't let the people out front see her like this. He gritted his teeth as he felt her tears scald his neck, her body trembling with emotion. He could kill whoever had done this with his bare hands.

He continued to the end of the alley, looking around to see if anyone was there. When he didn't see anybody, he hurried to the back of the Presbyterian Church. The side door, as usual, was open. He took her in and sat down with her in the back pew.

He stroked her hair, holding her close until she had her emotions under control. He reached into his pocket and pulled out a handkerchief, for once glad that his mother had taught him to carry one. “You never know when you might need to give one to a lady who needs it,” she’d always said.

Candi took it and pulled away, wiping her eyes and nose. She slid off his lap to sit on the bench beside him, but he kept his arm around her.

“I’m sorry,” she whispered.

He brushed her hair back over her shoulder so he could see her face. “Don’t apologize. Anyone would be upset by something like this.”

She dragged in a shaky breath, and then another, until she could breathe more evenly. He didn’t want to leave her alone, but at the same time, he needed to get back to direct the investigation. He wanted to personally see that nothing was missed.

“Sheriff? Is that you?”

Grady stood. “Reverend Reynolds.” He shook hands with the pastor of the First Presbyterian Church of Angel Ridge.

“It is indeed you. How are you, Grady?”

“Well, considering.”

“Yes. It appears there is a bit of trouble in town.”

“Unfortunately.”

“And who do we have here?” he said, looking at Candi.

She stood and held out her hand. “I’m

Candi, sir."

"Candi has just moved to town, and unfortunately, her shop has been broken into. I hope you don't mind me bringing her here. She needed to get away from the crowd gathered in the square."

"Of course not." He took her hand in both his. "I'm sorry for your troubles, dear. You're welcome to stay here as long as you'd like." To Grady he added, "I'd be happy to sit with her while you tend to your business. That is, if you don't mind, Candi?"

She stole a glance at Grady. He squeezed her shoulder. "You'll be safe here. No one will bother you. I'll come back for you when things are more settled, all right?"

She nodded.

"Thank you, Reverend."

"Of course. Good luck."

Candi watched Grady go. When she was alone with the pastor, she wasn't sure what to do. So many unsettling things raced through her mind, she had trouble focusing on anything, much less, proper etiquette in a church with a pastor she didn't know.

Reverend Reynolds extended a hand. "Please, sit, sit."

Candi eased back into the old, wooden pew. The man was portly and not very tall. Bald on top with salt and pepper hair and a beard, he had kind blue eyes.

"Can I get you anything? Water?"

"Yes, thank you." While he was gone, she wiped her eyes one more time and blew her nose. She needed to compose herself so she could keep up pretenses with yet another stranger when all she really wanted to do was run back to Aunt Ruby's cabin on the mountain and hide her face in her grandmother's skirts. How she missed her!

"Here we are."

Candi took the bottle of water, uncapped it, and took a long drink. The cool liquid helped ease the constriction in her throat a bit. Reverend Reynolds sat in front of her, leaning an arm across the bench. He smiled and said, "You must be the owner of the new shop in town. Heart's Desire? I saw the sign this morning. Lovely artwork."

"Thank you."

"Did you do it yourself?"

"Yes, sir."

"I understand that you're Miss Estelee's grandniece."

She would surely go to hell for telling lies to a pastor in church. "Yes." She said the affirmation, but couldn't meet his eyes when she did.

"What a fine woman, Miss Estelee. A bit unorthodox, and always one to speak her mind." He chuckled. "One never has to guess at her opinion."

Candi smiled. Not knowing what to say, she stared at the bottle of water in her hands.

"Have you visited Angel Ridge before?"

"Yes, but it's been some years back." That was true enough. She wondered what Grady and the police officers from Maryville were doing. Would they take her merchandise as evidence? There was no way she could replace everything. She'd collected things for years in anticipation of the day she'd have her own shop.

"It's usually a peaceful place. A good town to live in and raise a family. Are you married?"

"No, sir."

He nodded. "I see. Perhaps it's your first time away from home?"

"No. I attended junior college a few years ago. I stayed with an aunt and uncle then."

"Ah, so you do have family. Where are you from?"

"I grew up in the mountains."

"Yes, I detected a hint of the hills in your accent. Laurel Mountain?"

That guess caught her off guard. "*Um,* I —"

"It's all right, dear." He reached over and

patted her hand. "Whatever you tell me is in confidence. I would never repeat anything you share with me."

"I'm sorry. I never went to church, and it's not easy for me to talk to strangers or confide in people I don't know."

"I've asked too many questions then and made you uncomfortable. You don't have to tell me anything you don't want to, dear."

She breathed a bit easier at that. "Thank you."

"Would you rather I left you alone to your thoughts?"

Normally, she'd like nothing better, but after what she'd been through in the past few days, she found she didn't want to be alone. "No."

"All right, then. Perhaps you'd like to tell me what's on your mind."

"I've dreamed of having my own shop here in town most of my life. When I was young, my aunt and uncle took me to Asheville. We walked up and down the streets looking in all the store windows." Once the words began, they tumbled out of her. "I'd never seen so many colors, or so many happy people with bags full of store bought things."

She fiddled with the locket she wore that held her mother's picture. "I never had things. I only had what I needed. My clothes were plain and made by my grandmamma. This locket was the only thing of value I owned."

"It must be very special."

Candi nodded. "I don't mean to sound ungrateful. I had clothes, shoes, a warm bed, and plenty of food, but the colors . . . there were no colors except when the seasons changed.

"I'm so close to having a shop with all the things I never had, but it seems someone doesn't want me here." She laughed. "I was just thinking last night, that everything had come together so easy. I found a shop and rented it my first week in Angel Ridge. I've been able to stay with Miss Estelee and just found my own place. I've made friends. And now this."

"If I may?"

She nodded.

"We are, none of us, here by accident. We were all placed here on this earth to fulfill a purpose. When God puts it in our hearts to do something related to that purpose, we're not promised there won't be obstacles. In fact, at times, the way may be quite perilous, and we might even lose heart. But if you are doing what it is God intends you to do, He'll make a way."

"My grandmother always said, 'Trust your instincts. They'll never lead you down the wrong path.' "

"Your grandmother sounds like a very wise woman."

"People came from all over to get her advice. She said we had the gift of discernment."

"One of the gifts of the Spirit."

"Not everyone understands."

"Understands?"

"Some call it soothsaying — fortunetelling."

"What would you call it?"

Candi stared at the stained glass window beside her. The colors were cool blues, sapphire, amethyst, green, and gold. "It's a deep knowing. A feeling you get, and you just know. I don't understand it, but I've learned not to question it."

"And do people come to you for advice, Candi?"

Still staring at the patterns in the window, she whispered, "No one knows."

"There's always someone who knows. You can only hide your true self for so long. And besides . . . God knows."

A tear fell. She brushed it away quickly, hoping he hadn't seen. Reverend Reynolds took her hand between both his and waited for her to look at him. His soft blue eyes held only love and acceptance. That reminded her of Aunt Ruby.

"I can never reveal my true self. People won't understand. Bad things will happen. Bad things have already happened, and I was so careful."

"Dear one, *you are fearfully and wonderfully made.* You were made exactly the way you are, on purpose, for a purpose. Never doubt it and never be ashamed. If God can lay the foundations of the earth and place everyone and everything in it, then he will make a way for you out of this present trouble."

His words comforted her, gave her a deep peace she hadn't felt in a very long time. "Reverend Reynolds, would you mind if I came back to talk to you from time to time."

"I'd like that very much. You are also most welcome to attend worship here. We meet Sunday mornings at ten."

"Oh, I don't know. I like to worship the Creator in my own way."

Reverend Reynolds chuckled. "So like Miss Estelee."

Candi hated maintaining the lie, but was it really a lie? Miss Estelee was the closest thing she had to family, next to Uncle Billy and Aunt Verdi.

"Hello, Reverend Reynolds."

The pastor stood and held out his hands. "Dixie . . . how are you, my dear?"

The two clasped hands, and Dixie gave the pastor a kiss on the cheek. "Good, good. I see you've met my new friend, Candi."

"I have. We were having a nice chat."

"Well, I hate to interrupt, but Grady asked me to come and get you. He wants to talk to you down at the station."

"Me? Why?"

"Oh, you know, something about needing some information for his reports."

Candi stood. "So, they're finished going over the shop?"

"Not quite, but they should be by the time you finish speaking with Grady."

"All right." She turned to Reverend Reynolds before she left. "Thank you so much."

"I'll look forward to your visits. And if I can help in any way with putting your shop back in order, please let me know."

Candi smiled and walked with Dixie out of the church. As soon as they made it to the sidewalk, Jenny Thompson greeted them. "Hello, ladies."

Candi narrowed her eyes on the woman. She was like a bad penny that kept turning up. A very attractive, blonde penny with beautiful clothes and perfect make-up. The first time she'd met her, Candi had gotten this feeling that she might have an eye for Grady. For some reason she couldn't understand, Grady didn't seem to be interested. For another reason Candi didn't want to consider, that knowledge made her happier than it should.

"I need to get Candi over to the Sheriff's Office. Grady's expecting her."

"I was just wondering if Candi would like to comment on the events of the day. Honey, I am so sorry for what happened. You must be heartbroken."

"It's very upsetting."

"Candi," Dixie said, "you should know that anything you say can and quite possibly will end up in the newspaper."

Jenny just smiled and continued as if Dixie hadn't spoken. "Just a few days ago, you were nearly killed by a reckless driver —"

"That's overstating it a bit, don't you think?" Dixie countered.

"— and now this. We don't normally greet newcomers in this manner."

Not knowing how to respond, Candi didn't. She and Dixie kept walking, and Jenny followed.

"Why do you think they would paint the word 'witch' on your sign, Candi?"

"I'm sure it's just a prank, Jenny. It is

about to be Halloween. You know how kids are."

"So, do you think that's what this is then? Teenagers?"

"Your guess is as good as anyone's at this point, Jenny. Now, if you'll excuse us?"

They took the steps down the hill to the back of the courthouse and entered the Sheriff's Office. Grady met them in the outer office. He took in everything about Candi's appearance in one all-encompassing look. How in the world had she ever been able to hide anything from him? Even as she asked herself the question, she knew the answer: by keeping him at arm's length. Trouble was, that was getting harder and harder when all she wanted to do was run into his arms.

"I'll leave y'all to it then," Dixie said. "I got a dinner crowd to get ready for."

"Thanks, Dix," Grady said.

"Anytime."

To her he said, "Come on in my office and have a seat."

Candi walked in and took a seat in a green padded metal chair that matched the metal desk Grady leaned against. His office was sparsely furnished with just a couple of filing cabinets and a coat rack that held his jacket and a couple of gun holsters.

"I'm sorry to be so much trouble to you."

His smile was wide and appealing. "Please. I haven't had this much fun in years. There hasn't been a crime to investigate in ages, and since you came to town, there's been nothing but mysteries to unravel."

He looked completely relaxed and in his element. Whether he could admit it or not, being a lawman was in his blood. She remembered the way he carried her out of the shop and into the cool, dark interior of the church. He'd been so tender and yet strong. She needed some of that strength right now.

"We're almost finished going over your shop. Woody and Clara are questioning all the other shop owners in town to see if they noticed anyone acting strangely today. We hope that someone saw who did this. I want you to know, that I have a whole team of people lined up to help put your shop to rights. We may not be able to get it ready for the preview you'd planned for tomorrow night, but we will be sure you have your grand opening this weekend."

Emotion clogged her throat, but she managed to say, "I don't know how to thank you."

"No thanks required. When a neighbor's in need, you help them out because you know they'd do the same for you."

Candi smiled. She had always loved Angel Ridge, now she knew why. Reverend Reynolds was right. Trusting her instincts was the thing to do. She had nothing to be ashamed of.

Grady stood and moved around to the other side of his desk. He sat and took up his pen. "I just need to ask you a few more questions, and then we'll head over to the shop so you can have a better look around — tell us what's missing. That is, if you're up to it?"

"Yes. I'm feeling much stronger now."

"Good. I'm glad." He looked down and then back at her. "Did you notice anything or anyone unusual this morning?"

"No."

"Take your time. Give it some thought."

"No. I was inside all morning. You were the only person who came to the shop today besides delivery people, Cole and Blake."

Grady nodded and made a note. "I asked you earlier if you had any enemies, and you said you didn't know anyone. What about your family? You've told me you lived with a grandmother."

"Yes."

"Would she have had anyone that would have wanted to harm her or her family?"

She shook her head. "Everyone loved her."

"What was her name?"

Candi sat straighter, uncomfortable with the direction his questions were taking. "Why is that important?"

"I may need to do a background check. Maybe she had secrets. Things she kept hidden from you."

"No. That's not possible."

"Candi, parents, even grandparents, sometimes keep things from their children to protect them."

"No. There was nothing. I would have known if she were keeping things from me."

"How?"

Oh, boy. "I just, *um,* know things."

Grady looked up at her, confused. "You 'know' things?"

"Yes."

"Could you explain that? I'm not sure I understand."

"I know when people aren't being honest, when they're hiding things, when they're . . . not what they seem. I know when to trust someone and when to have my guard up."

He took a moment to digest that, but looked intrigued. "You were wrong about me."

"No. I wasn't."

"You can trust me, Candi."

"That may be true, but I can't afford to."

"Why not?"

She shifted in her seat. "Is this part of the investigation?"

"We're working from the outside-in right now." He stood and walked around his desk. Candi stood as well. She didn't like having him tower over her, even though she knew he wasn't intentionally trying to intimidate her. Or, maybe he was. "Why can't you afford to trust me?"

"There are things about me and my family that I don't want anyone to know, and that includes you."

She moved over to the window. It had started raining again. A red bird was sitting in a boxwood just outside the window. Her coat was a brownish-red; camouflage so she could protect herself and her babies from predators. Candi wished she could disguise herself as well.

"Candi?"

Grady was standing behind her, so close she could feel warmth from his body. She closed her eyes and battled the urge to lean into him and settle there, sheltered from all the evil surrounding her. But she couldn't. She couldn't depend on him or anyone else to take care of her. She had to take care of herself. She was more than capable because

Aunt Ruby had taught her well, by example and by her teachings.

When she didn't respond, he touched her shoulder. She sighed and turned to look at him. His hazel eyes had deepened to a dark green that reminded her of the moss that grew along Laurel Branch. "I won't tell you my secrets. I can't."

"You have to. It's the only way I can keep you safe."

"I don't need you to keep me safe, Grady."

"Candi, whoever is doing these things is filled with hate and rage, and it's all directed at you."

"I know."

"Do you know why?"

"I think so, yes."

He grasped her shoulders and flexed his fingers to keep from squeezing too hard. His body reverberated with intensity. "Please . . . I need you to tell me."

She looked up at him, considering. Long moments passed, and then finally, she said, "All right. I'll tell you my secrets, but first, I need you to tell me something."

"Ask."

"Why did Tom Hensley shoot your father?"

Grady blinked, then frowned, clearly surprised by the question. "Tom's daughter,

Hazel, died under questionable circumstances. Her body was found here in town. My father investigated and declared her death an accidental drowning. Hensley believed she was murdered."

Candi's knees weakened, and she had to grab the window seal for support.

"He also thought my dad knew she was in danger and did nothing, and then wouldn't investigate the people who he thought were responsible. Hensley came to town and called my father out. I think you know the rest of the story."

Candi swallowed hard and nodded. "Who did he think was responsible?"

"No one knows, or if they did, no one would say. Any other questions?"

She shook her head.

He touched her arm. "You look like you need to sit."

Still grasping the window seal with both hands, she shook her head again. "No. I'm fine. I'm sorry, Grady. Watching your dad go through something like that couldn't have been easy."

His laugh was harsh. "Nothing about my father was easy." She must have looked surprised, because he added, "We weren't close."

"I see." She should say it now. She'd made

her deal, after all, but forming the words was another matter.

"Your turn," he prompted.

Candi took a deep breath, let go of the window seal. She stood her full five feet nothing and looked Grady Wallace right in the eye when she said, "Hazel Hensley was my mother."

Chapter 14

"Dear God . . ."

Candi felt like the world had just spun her around and spit her out. She was going to be sick. "Maybe I do need to sit."

Grady took her arm and walked with her to the chair she'd occupied earlier. He knelt on one knee in front of her, a hand on each arm of the chair. The look of concern on his face touched something deep in her heart causing the words to spill out. "Aunt Ruby told me my mama drowned. I never questioned whether it was accidental or oth erwise."

"How old were you?"

"I was just a baby. I have no memories of her, only what my grandmamma told me."

"Ruby Hensley was your grandmother."

Candi nodded. "I don't want anyone to know."

"Why?"

"Surely you know why."

"You mean that superstitious junk about her being a witch?"

Candi nodded. "And not just her, but all the women in her family."

"You believe that?" Grady asked.

"Of course not, but I understand mountain ways. Outsiders don't."

He gently framed her face with both hands. "You're afraid people here will think you're a witch if they find out who you are?"

"Clearly, someone already does."

"Maybe," he shook his head, "but not me." He sank his fingers into her hair and leaned in close. "Do you believe me?"

She chewed her lower lip and blinked several times. She wrapped her hands around his forearms and whispered, "I want to."

He took her hand and held it against his heart. "You said you know things; that you have instincts about people, who you can trust, and who you can't. Why can't you let yourself trust me?"

Candi closed her eyes, unable to look at the pure honesty in his.

He wrapped a hand around her neck. "Look at me, Candi. Please."

After a moment, she opened her eyes.

"Why? Tell me."

She tilted her head. She could hardly bear

the pleading she saw in his eyes. She brushed the backs of her fingers along his cheek. "I'm Hazel Hensley's daughter, granddaughter of the man who shot your daddy. You can't tell me you don't hate my family for what we did to yours."

"So, you're saying you can't trust me because my father killed your grandfather?"

"No!"

"Good, because my father and your grandfather shooting each other has nothing to do with us."

He paused then to give her time to consider that. She'd thought the same thing when she'd learned the truth the other night at the Fergusons, but she hadn't known how he felt. Relief washed over her like a cool, cleansing rain.

"Is there some other reason you can't trust me?"

Falling back on what she'd been taught, she said, "You're a lawman, and lawmen can't be trusted. They don't understand our kind." She said the words, but they felt bitter on her tongue.

"Candi — is that even your real name?"

She looked at her hands and shook her head.

"What's your name? Is it Hensley? Or do you have your father's name?"

"I don't know who my father was."

He squeezed her neck. "I'm sorry, darlin'."

She eased out of the chair and knelt on the floor with him. If anyone were to walk in, she was sure they'd find their behavior highly inappropriate, but she didn't care. She wanted to hear him say her name, wanted the comfort of his arms around her, needed his kiss like she needed to breathe. Dear Lord . . . when had she fallen in love with the sheriff?

She wrapped her arms around his neck and whispered her name in his ear.

"Lark," he murmured against her cheek.

She closed her eyes and sighed against the sound of it spoken in his deep, southern drawl.

"What a beautiful name." He took her face, looked in her eyes and said it again. "Lark. It's as beautiful as you . . . I never thought Candi fit."

"It's a nickname Aunt Ruby gave me when I was little."

He brushed his lips across hers. "Your lips are sweet."

Candi sighed and leaned into him. When he swept his tongue into her mouth, she pressed herself as close to him as she could and held on against the tide of desire that threatened to pull her under. How could she have ever denied this sort of deep, intense feeling? It was as natural as breathing.

He kissed her over and over, taking her bottom lip into his mouth, then the other, sweeping both spots with his tongue. He stood slowly, bringing her with him. Resting his forehead against hers, he raised her hands to his lips so he could cover her fingers with more soft kisses.

After a long while, Grady eased her back into the chair and leaned against his desk. She read his mind as surely as if he'd spoken the words. This wasn't the time or the place, but the promise of later was in his eyes.

"I called the Utility Board and asked them to go out and turn your power on today. I don't want you staying in town. I need you somewhere that no one knows about so whoever is doing this won't know how to find you."

"Good, because I don't want to stay in town either, especially since Miss Estelee is gone. She left this morning. Said she was going south for a few weeks."

"It's settled then. We'll get started putting things to right at your shop, then we'll go by Miss Estelee's to get your things."

Candi nodded. "All right."

"I'm curious about why you called your grandmamma 'Aunt Ruby'?"

Candi shrugged. "That's what everybody called her."

"Did she tell you how your granddaddy died?"

"She said he died of a broken heart after my mama died. She was heartbroken, too. She lost her only child and her husband all at the same time. So, I never questioned her about it. I figured I knew all I needed to."

"You said you went to school. How did you manage that?"

"You mean regular school or trade school?"

"Both."

"I had an aunt who was a school teacher. I guess you could say she homeschooled me. When I was eighteen, I went to live with her and my uncle for eighteen months to go to vocational school and get an associate's degree in business and merchandising. When I finished, I went back to the mountain to stay with Aunt Ruby. She wasn't in good health and should have been somewhere they could take care of her proper, but she wouldn't leave. I looked after her and the property until she passed a few months ago."

"You've not had an easy life."

"It's all I ever knew. I didn't see it as a hardship."

He nodded, then asked, "Did you know that truck belonged to your granddaddy?"

"No. I never saw it."

"Your uncle didn't have it?"

"Not that I know of, but I didn't go snoopin' around his place, even when I lived there. He wouldn't have appreciated that."

"I'm assuming the aunt and uncle you were talking about living with were Billy Joe and Verdi Maguire."

Candi nodded. "Who do you think's behind all this?"

"Well, at first I thought it was Billy Joe, but now that I know he's your uncle and you've been close to him and Verdi over the years, I'd say that's unlikely." He paused, rubbing the scar on his chin in a now familiar way. "Tell me, do you look anything like your mother?"

"Aunt Ruby and Miss Estelee say I'm the spittin' image of her."

Grady nodded. "That explains why my Uncle Jim's been actin' all crazy since you came to town."

"Who's he?"

"He runs Wallace's Grocery."

"Oh, yes. He looks like he's just seen a

ghost every time I get near him."

"Yeah. I may need to get the old gang together and ask some questions."

"Old gang?"

"All the men in town who were contemporaries of my daddy."

"What do you think they know?"

"I've read the file. Your mother's case was pretty much open and closed, and I can tell you my dad wasn't above covering up the truth if it suited him. I need to find out what she did here in town, who she spent time with. If we can find out more about her, maybe that'll help us figure all this out. It's thin, I admit, but it's all we have right now."

Oh Lord, Mama, Candi thought, *what were you mixed up in that's come back to haunt us all after all these years?*

Candi spent the rest of the evening cleaning up her shop. Most of the merchandise was salvageable, but a lot of things like creams, lotions, and perfumes that had been in glass containers had been destroyed. She'd have to round up more containers to replace the stock from the larger containers she had in the storeroom, and she wasn't sure if she had time to do that before Saturday.

Dixie, Cole, Blake, Mr. and Mrs. Ferguson, Mr. DeFoe, Woody, Clara and her husband, Fuzz and Cathy from the Corner Market, Reverend Reynolds and Grady worked right alongside her all evening. Grady primered the wall with the warning spray painted in red and got it back to the color it had been originally. No one mentioned the message or asked what it meant. Candi was glad for that.

The help started trickling out sometime around nine. Dixie and Woody were the last to leave at ten, but she and Grady kept working. With so many people helping, the store was almost back to the way it was before. Even the window in the front of the shop would be replaced tomorrow morning. Mr. DeFoe had seen to that. The display cases would take longer to fix.

She was working on repainting the shop sign when Grady approached her. He wiped his hands on a utility towel. "Come have a look at the paint in the — what is it you're calling that shop?"

Candi smiled. "The Naughty Shop."

A wry grin full of meaning turned up one corner of his mouth. "Don't get me wrong, now. I feel like if a lady wants to wear that kind of stuff, I'm all for it. But you know, the church ladies are gonna have six fits over that room."

As Candi followed Grady down the hall,

she couldn't help appreciating the way he filled out the threadbare jeans he'd chosen to wear tonight. One pocket was torn and hanging loose. A tear on the leg revealed an enticing bit of thigh. She blinked, forcing herself to refocus. "Church ladies?"

"Yeah."

They walked in the Naughty Shop. Candi couldn't get over how orderly it was after the chaos of before. "Wow. That wall looks just as good as it did before."

"Well, personally, I think it looks better."

She looked again, and said, "You know, I think you're right," even though it did look exactly the same as it had. How could a freshly painted wall look better?

He smiled, pleased at her compliment. Aunt Ruby had always said it never hurt to exaggerate when praising someone.

"It's almost eleven, and we've both had a long day. Let's lock up and head home."

"I'll have to go pack my things."

"No need. Doc Prescott took care of that earlier. Your suitcase is tucked in the backseat of my Jeep."

"Oh. I didn't know you'd seen him. Did he know Miss Estelee left town?"

Grady tucked a curl behind her ear as if it were the most natural thing in the world. The simple act was so intimate, it had a devastating effect on her heart rate.

"Yeah. He took her to the airport. Doc apologized for not helping out at your shop, but he was all tuckered out from doing rounds all day. So after he got your things, he said he was going home."

A bath and a soft, warm bed sounded like heaven. She turned her neck from side to side, kneading the muscles with a weary hand.

"Let's go," Grady said.

"Do you mind putting my bicycle in the back of your car?"

"No, not at all. Where is it?"

"In the Nice Shop, just inside the door."

Grady got her bike while she turned out lights and checked locks on the exterior doors. She lifted her purse straps up to her shoulder, but before she could lock the front door, Grady took the keys from her. "I'm capable of locking a door, you know."

"I know, but I want to be sure it's sound."

"Evenin' ma'am, Sheriff."

An older man stepped out of the shadows. Candi nearly jumped out of her skin, but now that he was standing in the glow of the old-fashioned oil burning street lamps, she could see that he was wearing a policeman's uniform; one that was a bit more formal than the ones Grady and Woody wore.

"Sorry. I didn't mean to startle you."

"Candi, this is Constable Henry Harris. Henry, this is Candi Heart."

The man removed his hat and extended a hand. "It's a pleasure to meet you Miss Heart."

"Thank you," she said, shaking his hand. Candi sighed. He had that look in his eye, the one that said she looked awfully familiar. He must have known her mother, too.

"The constable patrols the town at night. He's going to make sure no one bothers your shop tonight."

"I appreciate that."

"Think nothing of it. I'm sorry about the trouble you've had. You're certainly in good hands with the sheriff, here. There's none finer. He'll get to the bottom of the matter, you can be sure."

Grady clapped the man on the shoulder. "Thanks for the vote of confidence, Henry. Well, we'd better be going." Grady looked back at Henry as he helped her into his Jeep. "I'm not sure if I'll see you in the morning, but be sure to speak with Clara or Woody to let them know how it goes tonight. And of course, if you need me, just call my cell."

"Of course. Have a restful evening."

He touched the brim of his hat and strolled off down the sidewalk.

When Grady was in the Jeep, Candi said, "Is the constable related to the Harrises whose boxwoods we vaulted through the other night?"

"Henry and Dan are brothers."

Candi nodded. "He knew my mother."

Grady gave her a quick look, then refocused on the road ahead. "What makes you say that?"

"The way he looked at me. You know, you can't call the older men of the town together — the ones you suspect knew my mother."

"Why not?"

"I told you earlier. I don't want anyone knowing who I am."

"Candi . . ."

"I mean it, Grady. You have to promise me."

He sighed, turning his head until his neck made a popping sound. "Be reasonable, Candi. What if one of those men is behind this?"

"Why would it be one of them?"

"I don't know, that's why I want to talk to them."

"Surely you have a theory."

"I prefer to deal in facts, and right now, there are precious few of them." Grady touched her hand. "Darlin', the only way to get to the truth is to ask questions."

"Well, you're going to have to figure out a way to ask them without bringing me into it." She crossed her arms, breaking contact with him.

"You are a stubborn woman, you know that?"

"Yes, I think you mentioned it a time or two. You got a problem with that?" she challenged.

He chuckled. "No, ma'am. I like women with spunk."

She narrowed her eyes on him. "Don't you dare laugh at me, Grady Wallace!"

"I wouldn't dream of it, Lark Hensley."

"Candi Heart. And you'd do well to remember to call me that so you don't slip up and call me anything else. No tellin' who might be listening."

She could see he was smiling in the glow of the cab lights. "I bet, true to your name, you can sing."

He *was* laughing at her! She pressed her lips together and turned away from him, staring out the passenger window into the dark. Outside of town, there was only the occasional street lamp, with farmhouses spaced pretty far part.

"I'm just teasing you, darlin'."

"Don't call me that, either." Her voice sounded sulky. She hated people who sulked, not that she had much experience with them, but she knew she didn't like that.

"All right," he said in measured tones. "I'm just teasing you . . . Candi." He said her name slowly, emphasizing the syllables. She liked the way he said "Lark" much better, especially when he was holding her close and whispering it in her ear.

"I'm sorry. You've had a difficult day. I shouldn't be teasing you. I forget some people don't take to it."

She wouldn't know. No one had ever teased her. Aunt Ruby had been the serious sort. Her aunt and uncle had been much the same. Miss Estelee was about the only lively person she knew, and she had to be a hundred if she was a day. Handsome men kissing and bantering with her was not something she knew anything about. She didn't know how to act or what to say.

"I don't have much experience with men teasing me," she finally said softly.

"That's all right, because I'd much rather flirt with you."

She chanced a look at him out of the corner of her eye. He was wearing that crooked grin that did weird things to her pulse. "I don't have much experience with that either."

"You strike me as a quick study. I'm

thinkin' you'll take to it real well."

She did look over at him then, and she could have sworn he winked at her. He pulled off the road onto the long drive at the Fergusons' farm. Halfway down it, he turned again and followed a dirt road that wound through the trees until he came to a stop at her new home.

Grady parked beside the house and cut the lights. Someone had turned on a porch light and had also turned on a lamp inside. Must have been Mrs. Ferguson.

She walked up onto the porch while Grady got her suitcase. She put the key in the lock and opened the door. The house smelled of lemon and pine from the fresh scrubbing Mrs. Ferguson had given the place. A plate of oatmeal cookies sat on the table with a note that read, *Welcome home. The kettle just needs to be heated. Tea's in the crock beside the stove. — Mom Ferguson*

Candi dropped her purse in a chair at the kitchen table and moved into the little parlor. It held a two-person couch, a rocking chair, and a recliner. A small television and a radio sat on a table in the corner. A cozy fireplace made from old brick stood in the central wall. The oak mantel shone in the warm light of the lamp. She wondered if there were fireplaces upstairs in the bedrooms as well . . .

"Cookies . . . nice." Grady set her suitcase at the foot of the stairs and helped himself. "*Mmm* . . . oatmeal chocolate chip. My favorite."

"I don't think Mrs. Ferguson was expecting you."

"Still put out with me, I see," he said around the bite of cookie in his mouth.

"I'm not put out, just . . ."

"What?"

"Just tired, I guess."

"I suppose one excuse is as good as another, but don't expect me to hide my disappointment. After the kiss we shared this afternoon in my office, I'd hoped we had moved past the hostility."

Candi picked up a glass paperweight on an end table and pretended to be fascinated with the flower suspended in it. "I was just feeling vulnerable after what happened to my shop. I was in shock."

"Oh, sure, and I suppose you're going to say that I was the big bad wolf who took advantage of the damsel in distress?"

Was that what she was saying? Thinking that certainly was easier than thinking about the feelings she'd unexpectedly developed for him.

She put the paperweight back on the

table. She should ask him to leave, and then go to bed. She had long days ahead of her and couldn't afford to be exhausted. The dreams came every night, interrupting her sleep. She prayed that they hadn't followed her here.

When she looked up, she found that Grady stood right next to her. He took up all the space in the small room and most of the air she was trying to draw into her lungs.

"What kind of thoughts are running through that beautiful head of yours?" He touched her hair, then her cheek and neck. Candi sighed and swayed into the contact. If she could bottle the attraction between them, she'd be rich.

"You have to talk for me to know what you're thinking."

Candi found her tongue and said, "I was just thinking about a new perfume for the line I'm selling at the shop, and maybe a formula for some men's cologne."

"You don't expect me to believe that do you?" He breathed the words against her cheek as he snaked an arm around her waist and pulled her up against him.

"You should be getting home."

He tipped her face up with a thumb at her chin. "I'm not going home. I'm staying here with you."

Chapter 15

The look on Candi's face was something between shock, desire and horror, but he wasn't taking "no" for an answer. He kissed the spot between her ear and cheek and enjoyed her little intake of breath. "Given the circumstances, you shouldn't be alone, especially at night."

"But you said yourself that no one knows I'm here."

"I'm not willing to take any chances with your safety. So, I'm afraid you're stuck with me until this case is closed." He took her earlobe in his mouth and tugged.

"You can't stay with me, Grady. It's not . . . appropriate — *Mmm* . . . What will people think?"

"We've been over that." He pressed hot, open-mouth kisses down the column of her throat. Sweet mercy, she tasted and smelled so good. "People will think what they will." He pushed her collar back and tasted the juncture between her neck and shoulder. When she arched her back, her long, soft hair brushed against his forearm, and he nearly came unglued.

"The Fergusons will know."

"They'll agree that it's a good idea." He sank down onto the sofa and pulled her on top of him.

"Oh, no . . ." she pressed against his chest creating distance between them which was the last thing he wanted at the moment.

"What?" He tried to pull her back into his arms, but she pushed harder, until she was sitting on the loveseat next to him.

"It just hit me that I could be endangering them and you, too."

He smiled. Leave it to her to worry about everyone but herself. "That would be why you need me here." He flexed his bicep. "I'm the muscle."

Leaning forward, she put her head in her hands. Clearly, she didn't appreciate his humor, so Grady ran a soothing hand up and down her back. After a few moments, she sat back and rested her head against the cushions. Grady did the same.

"How can a person's life come apart like this in less than a week?"

He rolled his head to face hers, only a few inches separating them. He understood now why they called these things "loveseats." The thoughts running through his head about all the things he could do with her on this couch had him worked up and restless.

"Everything will get better once your shop's opened."

"That's just going to draw more attention to me."

He touched her face. So soft . . . so lovely. "Exactly. Making it harder to get you alone or do anything to the shop. I'm also hiring Fuzz Rhoton to temporarily help beef up patrols during the day."

She twined her fingers with his and smiled. "Fuzz. That's a funny name."

"That's calling the kettle black, 'Candi.' "

"Lots of people go by Candi."

"You should have picked a different last name."

"I know, but it's too late now."

A bubble of intimacy sheltered them in the moment. He trailed a fingertip along the arch of her brow. She had amazing eyes. He'd never seen anything like them, had never met anyone like her.

"Where are you going to sleep?" she quietly asked.

So, she accepted that he was going to stay with her. Good. "Down here."

"This couch isn't big enough for you to

stretch out."

"I'll use the recliner, or maybe I'll just roll up in a blanket and sleep on the porch."

"Both sound really uncomfortable, and the nights are getting too cold to sleep outside with just a blanket to keep you warm."

"I could think of other ways to stay warm."

He was half a second from kissing her for the second time today when she smiled and asked, "Is that teasing or flirting?"

She should talk! Grinning, he said, "A little of both."

"See? I'm catching on."

"You certainly are." He leaned in slowly giving her time to move away, but she surprised him by meeting him halfway. He pulled her full lower lip into his mouth and tasted it with his tongue, then swept the V of her lip. He didn't know if the sound between them was her moaning, him, or a combination of the two.

His cell phone rang, and Candi nearly jumped out of her skin.

"Easy." He settled her close to his side, and grabbing the offending object that had "Born to be Wild" blasting out of it, punched a button and said, "Hello?"

"Grady? It's your mother."

"Mom? It's 11:30. Why aren't you in bed?"

"I heard something outside my window. Can you come over and see what it is?"

"Mom, come on. You know that bush outside your window needs to be trimmed. It's probably just a branch scrubbing against the screen."

"Oh, you mean you haven't trimmed it yet?"

He sighed. "No . . . I've been a little busy."

"Yes, I heard there was some sort of ruckus in town today. Something to do with that new shop that's opening up where the beauty parlor used to be?"

So that was it. She was fishing for information. He didn't comment.

"Where are you, dear? I called your house, and no one answered."

Candi stood and pointed upstairs. He nodded. After she'd disappeared, he said, "I'm going to be staying at the Ferguson's for the next few nights."

"Whatever for?"

"Mom . . ."

"Well, it's just that everyone is so on edge with all the strange happenings in town. Harriet McKay told me she saw the new girl who's opening that shop sitting in town square today feeding black crows and black cats. Well, anybody knows they're both bad luck, especially with Halloween coming on. And wouldn't you know, right after that, someone broke into her shop and it not even open yet."

"I suppose Mrs. McKay also told you I was sitting in town square with her today. Her name is Candi, by the way."

"Well, I wasn't going to say anything, but since you mentioned it, I just have to say that I do hope you're not seeing that young lady. Rumor has it that she's selling, *um,* unmentionables in that shop of hers."

She said the last on a whisper as if she was afraid someone might overhear her saying a curse word. Heaven forbid that anyone should know that women buy and actually wear bras and panties! Of course, it wouldn't bother him none if certain ladies didn't wear either. Ah, the mind could be such a dirty thing . . .

She continued as if she hadn't heard him. "There's something not right about that young lady. I mean, who feeds crows in the town square? They'll never leave, and everyone knows that it's a bad omen when you see them. Why, I heard the robbers spray painted the word 'witch' all over her shop."

"Mom, you know how I dislike it when you start with the superstitions. I hope you're not repeating these things among your friends."

"Well! I know that *my* son did not just suggest that his mother would spread rumors." She was in a high huff now.

"I'll let you go. Will you be coming by tomorrow to mow and trim that bush?"

"I don't know. I've got a lot going on."

"Oh, well then," she sniffed, "don't trouble yourself about it. I'll just lie here and listen to that branch scrape my window all night. I probably won't get a wink of sleep. Maybe the neighbors won't mind if the grass isn't trimmed for another few days . . ."

"I just cut the grass last weekend, Mom. It can't be that high."

"Yes, but it rained today, and you know how that makes the grass grow."

"Fine. I'll hire a kid from the high school to come over and take care of it and the bush."

"Now, Grady, you know how I dislike having strangers in my house."

"You won't have strangers in your house, Mother. They'll be in the yard."

"It's the same to me." She punctuated the end of the sentence with another sniff.

"Then it'll just have to wait until I can get to it. Goodnight."

He disconnected the call and raked a hand

through his hair. The joys of being an only child were never-ending. Candi had already come back downstairs and was heating water for tea. When she saw that he wasn't on the phone, she asked, "Do you want a cup?"

"No, thanks, but I sure could use something stronger." He walked over to the fridge and, looking inside, blessed whichever Ferguson guessed he'd be by here tonight. He pulled a longneck out, uncapped it and took a long draw. He held it out towards her, "You don't mind do you?"

"Of course not."

She had changed into pajamas, not that he could tell what they looked like. Her oversized, thick, fuzzy robe hid everything but her head and lower legs.

"Everything okay with your mother?" she asked.

"Nothing's ever okay with my mother." He propped a foot on one of the chairs at the kitchen table and rested his arms on his thigh. "She does whatever she can to get me to come by. I don't think she ever got over me growing up and moving out."

Candi stirred a teaspoon full of sugar into her tea. "At least you had a mom, and a father, too. I always wondered what it would be like to have a normal family with a mom and a dad and brothers and sisters."

He dropped his foot to the floor. "It's not the fantasy you've probably made it out to be." He took another draw on his beer. "My mother wasn't Donna Reed, and my father wasn't Andy Taylor." A harsh sound pushed its way up his throat. He remembered watching that old black and white show on television with the kind sheriff full of folk wisdom who went fishing most days with his little boy. That sort of idyllic life in a small, southern town had been far from his reality.

"I found a blanket and pillow upstairs and brought them down for you."

Her words pulled him back to the present. "Thanks."

"You know, there is another room upstairs. I suppose you could sleep up there."

"Tempting as that sounds, I don't like the idea of being upstairs. If someone tries to break in here, I want to be between them and the stairs."

"All right, then." She took a sip of her tea, then put a cookie on a napkin. "I think I'll go up."

"I'll just check around outside, then lock up."

"Thank you." She padded across the kitchen floor, but stopped when she was next to him. Easing up on her toes, he bent towards her so she could give him a chaste kiss on the cheek. "Goodnight," she whispered. "Sleep well."

Because he couldn't resist, Grady turned his head and brushed her lips with a quick, easy kiss that didn't near satisfy, but it'd have to do for now. "Goodnight."

He watched her until she disappeared up the stairs and heard her bedroom door click shut. He drank the rest of his beer in two sips. Smiling, he set the empty bottle on the counter. He'd give her till the end of the week. There wasn't a woman alive who could resist a Wallace once he set out to win a woman.

CHAPTER 16

Grady woke with a crick in his neck. He tried to roll it out, but it seized with a spasm that made his fingers numb. He rubbed it until the pain passed. There was an old Army cot in his mom's storage building. He'd be picking it up before he came back here tonight.

A glance at his watch told him what he already knew. Six-thirty. The sun and his internal alarm had gotten him up at the same time since he'd become sheriff of Angel Ridge.

He threw off the quilt Candi had given him last night and stood, twisting to pop the stiffness out of his back. He shuffled into the kitchen to put some coffee on, but stopped cold when he opened the cabinet beside the sink. Outside, mist rose from the grass and swirled about Candi as she twirled and danced, her arms outstretched, palms up. A sheer, white cotton nightgown flowed out from her legs and clung to her body. Tousled hair hung to her waist in a jet-black curtain of loose curls. He moved quietly to the front door and eased it open. The words of a song in her sweet, soprano voice floated to him as she danced, moving barefoot across the dew-kissed grass to the quick rhythm of it. *Up on Sugar Hill we'd go walkin'* . . . She hummed the next line, twirled all the way around, then stopped abruptly when she saw him standing on the porch. Grady stepped into the grass and strode to her. When he stood in front of her, he took her hands and started dancing with her. He sang the next verse of the old Dolly Parton song about teen lovers planning their future. He and Candi then sang the chorus together.

They both laughed and stood still as the song ended. "When I went to make the coffee, I thought I saw a wood nymph out here dancing. Do you always come out first thing in the morning in your nightgown with no shoes to dance and sing in the wet grass?"

Her smile was pure and unrepentant. "As often as I can. We spend so much time in shoes, walkin' on paved roads and brick sidewalks, that we lose touch with nature.

This helps me stay connected to what's truly real."

"I was right," he breathed, still holding her hands. "You have a beautiful voice." He was afraid to let go of her for fear she'd vanish in the mist. She looked like something from another place and time, but here she was, standing in front of him, her hands in his, with the most peaceful smile on her face.

"You're not so bad either."

Autumn's chill was in the air, but he hardly noticed. He couldn't help admiring the way her white nightgown clung to her body leaving little to the imagination. "Aren't you cold?"

Her gaze slid from his face, over his bare chest, to the waistband of his jeans and back up. "I could ask you the same."

He pulled her unresisting into his arms. "Maybe a little," he lied, "but I know a sure way to keep us both warm." He flexed his knees until his face was level with hers, then took her mouth in a hot, passionate kiss that turned the fire that had been banked inside him for days into a firestorm. He lifted her off the ground and tilted his head to gain better access.

He swept his tongue in and out of her mouth in a rhythm that had her clinging to him and meeting each thrust and retreat of his tongue with one of her own. She swirled her tongue around his, over and over again making him crazy with wanting her.

Grady slid a hand to the back of her thigh, and she wrapped her legs around his waist. He broke the kiss, gasping for air, but Lark was intent on covering every inch of his face and neck with butterfly kisses. He carried her up on the porch and into the house, kicking the door closed behind them.

He eased her onto the kitchen counter, and then kissed her again, his desire raging like wildfire on a parched meadow. He should stop now before he did something neither of them was ready for. Last night, she'd told him she was vulnerable, and even though he wanted her more than he'd ever wanted anything in his life, he didn't want her to regret anything that happened between them.

Grasping her shoulders, he slid his mouth from her lips to her ear and said her name . . . he gripped the edge of the counter with both hands, willing control into his body, his mind. Unfortunately, her body wasn't getting the signal yet. She plunged a hand into his hair and raked her nails down his chest, then cupped his nipple. Heavy eyelids hooded her eyes that had turned a deep emerald, but did nothing to conceal the desire in them.

He grasped her shoulders and eased back a little. Pushing the hair off her cheek, he said, “You are exquisite.”

She leaned forward and bit his lower lip, then tugged it into her mouth. “I don’t need pretty words.”

Grady didn’t think he had it in him to be noble with a woman like Candi, but he had the small comfort of knowing he was doing the right thing. They barely knew each other, had only just gotten to the point where they could almost have a civil conversation with one another. Sex would just be another excuse to avoid honesty.

“You deserve pretty words and more.”

“You don’t want me.”

Candi eased off the counter and crossed her arms over her breasts, embarrassed and ashamed. What must Grady think of her? She sat in one of the chairs at the table and pulled her knees up to her chin. She’d lost her head. It was the only explanation for it. She covered her face with her hands. How could she have behaved this way with someone she barely knew? The fog was clearing now, but shame and humiliation rushed in to replace it.

Grady knelt in front of her, his hands on

either side of her chair. "Darlin', I want you more than you could possibly know. The timing's just all wrong."

Candi folded her arms around her knees and looked at him. He was absolutely the most beautiful man she'd ever seen. Dark russet-colored hair with unruly waves that it would be a shame to trim, a sexy shadow of whiskers the same color emphasizing the strong angles of his face. Muscular arms and chest that made her feel dainty even though she knew that she was anything but. The freckles that sprinkled his cheeks, nose, shoulders, and forearms were the only thing that saved him from being model perfect.

"If you keep looking at me like that," he warned in low tones, "I'm gonna forget that my mama raised me to be a gentleman."

"You should put on a shirt, then, if you don't want me lookin' at you."

"I think I'll go take a cold shower. When I come out, I promise to be properly covered."

"See that you are."

His warm laughter lingered in the kitchen even after he closed the door to the bathroom. As she made the coffee, her body still humming from his kisses and strong hands on her body, she heard him singing the Dolly Parton love song again.

■ ■ ■ ■

After Grady dropped Candi and her bicycle off at Heart's Desire, he continued over to Ferguson's for his morning cup of coffee and donut.

"Mornin', sunshine," Dixie said. "It's a beautiful day to be alive and living on Angel Ridge."

Dixie was impossibly perky in the morning. It usually annoyed him, but somehow today, it didn't. Still, he gave her his usual reply, "Yeah, yeah. Just pour the coffee, would ya?"

Dixie cocked a hand on her hip. "Would you like to rephrase that?"

Grady removed his hat and sat it cap down on the counter. "Just pour the coffee — please?"

Dixie rolled her eyes, but set a thick white mug in front of him and filled it with strong, steaming liquid. He took a long sip. *Ahh . . .* there was nothing like caffeine burn to get you going.

Removing a donut from the cake plate, she set it in front of him on a napkin. "How late did you and Candi stay at the shop last night?"

"Till about eleven."

Leaning on the counter and facing him, Dixie just shook her head. "I was sound asleep by then."

Grady rubbed his stiff neck. "You got any aspirin?"

"Of course." She opened a cabinet behind the counter and handed him the bottle. "Too many hours painting without a break will do that to you."

Grady let her think what she wanted. He popped the pills into his mouth and took another sip of coffee, then unfolded the newspaper someone had left on the counter.

"I don't think you're gonna like Jenny's lead story . . ." Dixie warned.

The headline read, *"New Shop on Main Vandalized"* and was punctuated by a photo of a distraught Candi in front of the sign for Heart's Desire hanging askew with the word "witch" spray painted in large, hateful red letters.

Grady's blood boiled as he read the first bit of the article, written, of course, by Jenny Thompson.

A new shop on Main Street was set to open this weekend, but vandals may force a postponement of the grand opening. Heart's Desire, which occupies the former Madge's Beauty Shop, was broken into yesterday around noon. While customers and shop owners went about their business, criminals were destroying property and defacing signs as well as the walls of Heart's Desire with hateful messages such as, "Witch Go Home."

Sheriff Grady Wallace stated that the investigation was on-going and declined to make a statement. The sheriff also would not allow access to the shop owner, Candi Heart.

With hate crime rampant in the business district of Angel Ridge, shop owners and customers are warned to be on their guard and to take any means to protect themselves and their property.

Grady let lose a stream of curses so disparaging of Jenny Thompson's conduct and parentage that they should have blistered the paint on the walls of the diner.

"Easy there, big boy."

"She makes it sound like the town has to take the law into their own hands to protect themselves and their property since, clearly, I can't do my job!" He wadded the paper in his hand and marched to the door.

"Grady, you need to calm down before you go over there," Dixie warned, but he was too angry to listen.

He slammed into the offices of *The Angel Ridge Chronicle* and didn't think of stopping until he stood in front of Jenny Thompson's sleek, modern desk. A sputtering Jolene Smith stood in the door apologizing for letting him get past her, as if she or anyone else could have stopped him.

"It's all right, Jolene. Close the door, would you, sugar? There's a dear." Relaxed, Jenny leaned back in her chair and smiled up at him. "Well, what brings you by my office this fine mornin', Sheriff Wallace?"

Grady slapped the paper on her desk, scattering several items. Jenny sat there, nonplused, in her peach jacket and skirt, legs crossed, lipstick a perfect match to her suit. "You know why I'm here."

"Oh, so you've seen my lead story. I thought the picture of Miss Heart really captured the depth of her despair, didn't you?"

"You are a low-down, bloodsucking leech, *Ms.* Thompson." Emphasis on the 'Ms.' "How could you have printed a picture of that sign with what was written on it?"

"Well, Sheriff, everyone saw it, and I'll accept your apology for the name-calling. That was absolutely inappropriate, and do call me Jenny."

He braced his hands on her desk and

leaned in. “If you’re waitin’ on my apology, you’re gonna have a long wait. You’ll just have to be content in knowing that was the watered-down version of what I really want to call you.”

Jenny flipped her long blonde hair over her shoulder, her smile never cracking. “I can see that your emotions are running high on this case. I also noted that you stayed at that shop last night with Miss Heart until the wee hours, helping her clean up.” She leaned forward, resting her arms on the desk, until they were practically nose to nose. “Tell me, Sheriff, do all the businesses in town get this kind of service from the Sheriff’s Department?”

He straightened, nauseated by her perfume. “I’m just a regular citizen helping out a member of our community, which is more than I can say for you. If this article damages Candi’s business, she’d be well within her rights to sue you for libel.”

“And will you be advising her to do that, Grady? Because I do believe that giving legal advice is outside your purview.”

“You’re too right, Jenny. But you know, my best friend has a brother who’s a lawyer. I’m sure you know Cory Ferguson.”

“I can’t say that I’ve made his acquaintance.”

"Then I'd say it's high time."

He tossed the paper at her and slammed out of the office back onto Main. His blood still boiling, he turned and went straight to his office. As soon as he got in the door, Clara stood and said, "Grady, there's —"

"Not now, Clara."

He removed his hat and raked a hand through his hair, pulling up short when he saw Mrs. McKay perched on the edge of the chair in front of his desk. "It's not a good time, Harriet." He hung his hat and coat on the rack behind his desk and sat.

"I'm here as a courtesy, Sheriff, to inform you there will be a special called meeting of the town council this evening at seven. Your attendance is mandatory as the meeting has to do with the rash of crime here in town. Please come with copies of the reports of the recent incidents to provide for the council men and women. I'm sure we'll also have a number of questions for you."

"I won't be able to make it. Now, if you'll excuse me."

"You most certainly will not be excused. How dare you, young man? Who do you think you are to address me in such a manner?"

"I am the sheriff of this town, and I have a job to do, namely seeing that citizens of

Angel Ridge are safe, which I cannot do if I'm to be called on the carpet of the town council when you'd be better served if I were here and out on the streets pursuing leads in these ongoing investigations."

Mrs. McKay sat back at his stern tone, unaccustomed to being denied a request of any kind. "This is not open for discussion, Grady."

"Good, because I don't have time to discuss anything with you at the moment." He started reading through the constable's reports and also summaries Clara had typed out from where Woody and Fuzz had questioned people in town yesterday.

"I must say, Sheriff, you have ample time to help paint graffiti off walls and seem quite happy to do so in lieu of working your ongoing investigations."

"And yet she's still here and still talking," he mumbled under his breath. "Clara?" he called out to the clerk in the front office. She came into his office, deposited a cup of coffee, and held out a hand toward the door. "I'll show you out, Harriet."

Mrs. McKay stood and clearly had "bees in her bonnet," as his mama would say. She tugged at the hem of her unflattering gray jacket that was buttoned all the way up. "Grady Wallace, you are employed by the

Town of Angel Ridge, and this town is run by a Mayor and town council. Should we wish to speak with you, we are within our rights, as your employer, to request an audience, and you will comply."

Grady just kept reading through the reports. "If you would like to speak with me, I'm afraid you're going to have to follow proper procedure and make your request giving forty-eight hours' notice, in writing, which is set out in the Council's bylaws." He lifted his coffee to his lips and took a long sip. After he'd set it back down, he looked at Mrs. McKay and said, "That means that the earliest you can call a meeting is Monday. That's the first business day after forty-eight hours has passed."

"You are a coarse, insufferable young man."

"You made the rules. Don't blame me for following them."

Clara took a step towards the door. "After you, ma'am."

"I'll expect an agenda as well," Grady added, "and ask that you hold the meeting to under an hour. There are too many other pressing matters demanding my attention for me to spare more time than that."

Amid much huffing, sniffing, and "wells," Harriet McKay was finally out the door. He took another sip of coffee. The McKays might practically own this town, but they didn't own him.

"Clara?"

"Yes, Grady?"

"Could you get me the file and the evidence box on the drowning of Tom Hensley's daughter? I'm not sure what her name was. Helen . . . Holly . . ."

"Hazel."

"Excuse me?"

"Her name was Hazel Hensley."

"You remember it?"

"Sure. That was a trying time in Angel Ridge, what with a young woman turning up dead, and then her daddy coming to town and getting shot and killed right here on the lawn of the courthouse. I'd daresay that the people who witnessed it will never forget."

He had to agree with that. He'd been doing community service for shoplifting by picking up trash in town square the day after a Fourth of July celebration. Boots Hensley had roared into town in that truck of his, got out and started shouting for the sheriff to come out and face him like a man. Grady leaned back and rubbed his chin. Man, he'd forgotten about having seen that truck before until just now.

He shook his head to clear the memory. "What do you recall, Clara?"

"Not much. Nothing but gossip really, and you know how reliable that is. I do know that my mother and many of the women in town said nothing good would come of that woman — Hazel. She didn't belong here was what they said."

"I don't remember her, do you?"

"No. Like I said, just what I heard my mom and her friends say about her. Apparently she was young and beautiful and captured the attention of all the men in town. None of the women liked it."

Like mother, like daughter. He wondered what his mama might have to say about it. "Thanks, Clara. If you could get me those items, I'd appreciate it."

"I'll probably have to go to storage for them."

"Make it a priority, all right?"

"I'll head over there now."

"Thanks."

Maybe he should go to his mom's today to trim that bush after all.

Candi walked down the street towards the offices of *The Angel Ridge Chronicle* to discuss buying an ad for her grand opening. As soon as she entered, Jenny Thompson came out to meet her. "Candi! How are you, darlin'? Have you recovered from that terrible ordeal yesterday?" She continued before Candi could speak. "Come into my office, and let me get you a cup of tea."

Candi followed the fashionable woman into an elegantly decorated office. Today she wore a pretty peach suit that shimmered when she walked. Her blouse was coral satin. She looked like she'd stepped right off the cover of a fashion magazine. Candi would love to look that cool and sophisticated, but only a tall woman could pull it off.

"Thank you, Jenny, but I can't stay. I need to get back to the shop. I just dropped by to see about running an ad in the paper tomorrow advertising the grand opening of Heart's Desire this weekend. I hope it's not too late."

"Oh no, sugar. We'll do up somethin' real nice for you. So, the break-in won't delay the opening. I'm so glad." She picked up a pad and pen from her desk and said, "What do you want the ad to say?"

"The name of the business is Heart's Desire. Tomorrow night, there'll be a preview from six to nine for women only, with complimentary tea and cookies. All purchases will be twenty-five percent off. Then we'll open for business at our regular business hours on Saturday, from ten to six."

"And of course you'll be closed on Sunday."

"No."

"No?" Jenny pulled her zebra striped reading glasses off, surprise making her blue eyes large. "You're going to be open on Sunday?"

"Yes, but the hours will be one to six because I know a lot of folks 'round here go to church."

"But not you?"

Candi hedged. "I'm new in town."

"Of course." Jenny replaced her glasses and asked. "What about graphics?"

"I hadn't thought about that," Candi frowned. "Maybe a flower border?"

"Something old-fashioned?"

Candi nodded.

"Do you have a logo?"

"No."

"All right. We'll just use a nice script for the business name. Now, what do you want to list as the types of merchandise the shop will carry?"

"Floral arrangements, hand-crafted chocolates, herbal teas, antique knick-knacks, organic skin care, and clothing."

"Perfect. I'll have advertising do something up right away. Can you come back after lunch to have a look and approve it?"

"Of course. Thank you so much for doing this for me."

She turned to leave, but Jenny said, "Candi? I just wanted to say that I hope the article that I ran in the paper didn't offend you in any way. The break-in at your shop yesterday had to be reported."

"Oh, no," Candi said. "I'm not upset. You were just doing your job. It was kind of odd, though, reading about it like that."

"What do you mean?"

"It was so cold and impersonal. I could almost pretend I was reading about something happening in Knoxville, but it wasn't Knoxville; it was here. And it wasn't some stranger being talked about; it was me."

Candi held Jenny's gaze for a long silent moment, and then turned to leave. It was a sad thing that people could talk about someone's heartache and personal tragedies like it was some distant happening on the national news, but she tried not to take it too personally. Candi believed that, deep down, Jenny was a good person. But like most folks who hadn't dealt with much hardship in their lives, she could be insensitive to those who had.

And after all, Candi was just a stranger in town.

CHAPTER 17

Candi was putting another pan of cookies in the oven when she heard someone pull up outside. She laid her oven mitts aside and went to the door. Just as she pushed the curtain aside, she saw Grady step up onto the porch. He looked exhausted.

She unlocked the door and opened it. "Hi."

His smile was weak, but it was there. "Hi."

Candi stepped aside. Grady walked in, taking his coat off as he moved. "Something smells amazing."

"I'm making cookies for the shop's preview tomorrow. Are you hungry? I made some chili earlier. I could warm up a bowl for you."

"You must be tired. I can do it."

"Don't be silly. Sit."

He did as she said without a fuss. He eased the holster off his shoulder and laid it in the chair with his jacket. Candi put a bowl of chili in the microwave, got a beer out of the refrigerator and handed it to him. "If you don't mind me saying so, you look like nine miles of bad road."

He uncapped the bottle and lifted it to her in a salute. "Thanks."

"You okay?"

"Yeah. I get like this when I sit behind a desk all day. Nothing a good night's sleep won't cure."

"Not much chance of that happening if you sleep in that recliner again."

"Aw, man . . ."

"What?" The microwave bleeped, and Candi got his chili.

"I meant to pick up a cot at Mom's, and I totally forgot."

A smile tugged at the corners of her mouth. "So, you went by and trimmed that bush, did you?"

"Yeah. I wanted to talk to her, but she wasn't home."

She handed him a spoon and napkin, then joined him at the table.

"This is really good," Grady said around a mouthful of food. "Do you have any cheese and corn chips?"

Candi wrinkled up her nose. "No. Why?"

"That's what I usually eat in my chili. That and sour cream. I used to eat the combination at the ball park when I was in Little League. The concession stand people named the chili-cheese-chips-sour-cream mix 'A Homerun.' "

"Sounds disgusting. I made some pones. You want one of those?"

"You mean cornbread."

"What else would I mean?"

"Sorry, it's just I haven't heard that word in a long time. My grandmother said that instead of 'cornbread,' too."

Candi stood and went to the breadbox. Great. She sounded like his grandmother.

"I'm sorry, darlin'. I'm not making fun of you. I'm just tired and my filter isn't working."

She shook her head. Lord, would she ever understand the way city folk talked? "I don't know what that means."

"It means I'm not thinking before I speak, and I'm sorry."

"It's okay. Eat."

She gave him the cornbread, as he called it, and the butter dish. He ate and she put the cookies on a rack to cool, wiped off the pan, and sliced more to go in the oven. She put two on a plate, glazed them and set the dish in front of Grady.

He gave her a doubtful look. "You think I

can stop at only two? After the day I've had?"

She sat and sipped a glass of milk. "Eat those, and we'll see."

A comfortable silence filled the room while he devoured his food, and Candi enjoyed watching him eat. She could get used to having a man in her kitchen, chatting about his day and hers, settling on the couch after, snuggled in each other's arms.

The buzzer on the oven interrupted her ill-advised fantasies. Just the thought of having Grady around full-time made her heart clench painfully. *Slow down there, Lark. One thing at a time.* A few kisses, and she was already imagining what it would be like to share a life with him. How could she be so naïve?

Something inside her whispered, *because you never got to be a child or dream about your future . . . you're long overdue.* It's just that it was happening so fast.

"Earth to Candi, or should I call you 'Lark' if I want you to respond?"

She set the pan of cookies on the hotplate and put the next batch in. "Sorry?"

"Where'd you go just now?"

"Oh, you know, I've been by myself so long, I just get lost in my own thoughts because I'm so used to wandering through them." She pointed at his empty bowl. "Do you want some more?"

"No, but I would love a glass of milk to go with these cookies."

"Are your legs broken? The glasses are in the cabinet and the milk's in the fridge."

"Wow. Those must have been some ugly thoughts."

"What I was thinking has nothing to do with the fact that you are fully capable of getting your own milk. This is a self-serve kitchen."

"Except that you got everything else for me."

Candi crossed her arms, not knowing which she hated more: acting illogically or that he was right. "So, what were you saying that I didn't hear?"

"It's not important."

"Suit yourself."

She transferred the cookies onto a rack and iced them. Let him sulk. She didn't have the inclination to coax him out of whatever kind of mood he was in. Why would she? Why should she want to?

"Aren't you curious?"

Well, that was an open-ended question if she'd ever heard one. Of course she was curious. She was curious about a lot of things, and with him sitting at her kitchen table eating the food she'd made, she couldn't focus on one thing but him.

She jammed the spatula under one of the cookies and broke it. "Dang it!"

"Easy there. I got tender ears, you know." He stood and came up beside her. "Guess we'll have to eat that one."

He picked up one of the pieces and took a bite. He held what was left to her mouth. She looked up at him. That was her first mistake, because seeing the way he was looking at her made her go all weak in the knees. And when she opened her mouth and took the bite of cookie, he rubbed the backs of his fingers along her cheek, down her neck, and then back up under her chin. He smiled. "I know what's got you so cranky."

"I'm not cranky."

"*Hmm* . . . Well, if what I'm about to do improves your mood, I'm going to have to insist that you admit it."

"Admit what?"

He cupped the back of her head, tilted his face close to hers, and nuzzled her nose with his. Then he kissed her, and she realized he was right. *This* was what she'd wanted from the moment he'd walked through the door. Even though her head hadn't acknowledged it, her heart and body had. Denying them what they wanted had made her testy.

She sighed into his kiss; she couldn't help herself. He tasted and felt so good. If she were truthful, she'd have to admit that she'd thought about him all day, wondered what he was doing, if he'd come by to see her, but he hadn't and that had put her on edge, too. Truth was, she hadn't felt anything from the time they'd parted ways this morning until he walked through her door tonight.

He held her secure and tight in his arms. "I missed you today," he whispered. "I wanted to come by, but I was so busy."

His admission made her heart sing. So much so, she reluctantly made an admission of her own. "I missed you, too."

Grady pulled back a little and looked at her. "You don't sound happy about it either."

"I don't want to miss you. It wasn't part of the plan."

He sighed. "It wasn't part of my plan either, but I'm not near as miserable as you seem to be. In fact, I'm settlin' into this a lot easier than I would have expected."

She played with a button on his uniform. "Why do you think that is?"

He shrugged. "The heart wants what the heart wants."

"I don't understand why you'd want me.

I'm backwards and close-mouthed and surly."

"A woman of mystery, yes. You're distant because you don't want to answer people's questions. That's how you were raised. It's not your fault, and there's not necessarily anything wrong with it as long as you can tell the difference between the people you shouldn't trust and the ones you should."

She kept playing with the button, but considered what he was saying.

"Tell me what you want, Lark." He ducked his head so that she had to meet his gaze or step out of his arms — and she didn't want that.

"Did you come here to have a business and nothing else? I mean, what makes a woman who's spent her whole life on a mountain alone with an elderly woman want to do something like live in a town around a lot of people and run a business dealing with people?"

She bit down on her lip hard to keep the tears that flooded her eyes from falling. Swallowing hard, she said, "When a person spends all their time alone, it does something to them. You have to find a way to entertain yourself, and I made up worlds in my head. Beautiful, magical worlds that I lived in that were colorful and filled with happy people. I dreamed those dreams, moved around in them, but then I'd hear Aunt Ruby calling me back to my reality. 'Get yer head outta the clouds, girl. Them fantasies o' yours'll lead to nothin' but heartache.' And she never said it, but I know, in her head, she was addin', 'Look at what happened to your mama and what heartache that caused.' "

"So, you knew she lived in Angel Ridge for a time?"

"Oh, yes. It was Aunt Ruby's constant warning for my life; to not overreach. My mama tried that and got nothing but disappointed." Her laugh was bitter. "You know what I always thought when Aunt Ruby said that to me?"

Grady shook his head.

"I'd think to myself, she came out of her disappointment with me. Was that so bad?" She shrugged. "It suppose it musta been, because she died before I knew her." Candi's eyes widened with understanding. She stepped back, out of his arms.

"The dream . . ."

"What dream?"

The woman in the dream who looked like her was her mother. She came to Angel Ridge and fell in love, but her man deserted her. He didn't stand by her when she got pregnant with his baby. And after she had the baby, her child wasn't enough. She wanted him more, so she searched for him every day, hoping he'd come to her. Her longing for what she'd lost killed her in the end.

"Candi?"

She walked away from Grady, into the parlor. The dream was a warning . . . a warning to learn from her mother's mistakes and not want everything at once. If her mother had found her place in Angel Ridge and *then* fallen in love, things might have been different. If she'd had something in her life besides him, she might have had something to live for when he abandoned her. And then her mistakes led to her granddaddy's death, leaving Aunt Ruby alone with no husband and no daughter. Just a baby to raise, and Candi had never been able to fill the voids.

Grady grasped Candi's shoulders and turned her around. "Talk, Lark."

"Candi. I'm not that girl from the mountain, Grady. I can't be. I have to walk a different path than my mother did, or I'll be fated to repeat her mistakes."

"I don't understand."

She stepped away from his touch. "You don't need to."

"If you don't want to be that girl from the mountain, then stop acting like her."

She spun to face him. "What is that supposed to mean?"

"Get out of your head and interact. If you're not going to let anyone get close to you, you might as well have stayed on the mountain alone."

"I need to make my own way. I don't want to depend on anyone but myself. Once I've made a life for myself, then and only then, will I begin to consider if I want a man to share that life."

One long step brought him close to her. "You don't have to go through this alone."

She smiled. Men. They thought a woman couldn't make her way in the world without their help. "I'm not alone. I have Miss Estelee, Doc, Dixie and the Fergusons, Cole, Mr. DeFoe. I have so many people helping me, I'm trippin' over them."

"But no room for me?"

"Sure, there's room for friendship, but nothing more."

He motioned between them. "What's going on between us has nothing to do with friendship. This wasn't my intent or yours. It just is."

"Yes," she whispered, "but just because there's attraction, and maybe feelings, does not mean we have to . . . to give in to those things."

The buzzer on the oven went off. Candi edged around Grady and went back into the kitchen. "That's the last batch. I'm going to go up as soon as I ice these and put them in containers."

Grady didn't respond.

"You don't have to stay."

"I'm not leaving you."

"That's your choice."

"I don't think we have a choice, Lark. If you were as perceptive as you say you are, you'd know that." He leaned against the counter and crossed his arms. "Or maybe you do know it and just don't want admit it."

Candi rolled her eyes. "We always have choice, and I'll thank you to not speak for me." She iced the last cookie and closed the plastic container she was putting them in.

"Goodnight, Grady."

"If you think I'm going to give up on us that easily, you underestimate me."

Candi smiled as she climbed the stairs. Grady was hotwired to be tenacious and solve mysteries. She hadn't expected him to just walk away. The question then became, how was she going to keep the tempting sheriff at arm's length?

■ ■ ■ ■

Early the next morning, Candi stood in her bedroom trying to decide what to wear. This was a big day. She wanted to look just right.

Her cell phone rang. Who would be calling her so early in the morning? She dug for the phone in her purse.

"Hello?"

"Candi? Good mornin'. It's Jenny Thompson."

Candi frowned. What could she possibly want at this hour? The sun was barely up.

"Hello," she said coolly.

"I'm sorry to call so early, but I was up all night, and the longer I go without sleep, the more wired I get, you know?"

She didn't, but asked, "Is something wrong?"

"I believe so, but before I get to that, I want to apologize to you — for the article that I ran yesterday about your break-in." She chuckled. "I have to tell you that this is a first for me. So, you'll have to forgive me if I don't do it well."

Candi waited while Jenny found her words. "I've never run an article that I couldn't stand behind, and that was the case with the one I ran yesterday. And yet . . .

nothing about it jived. It felt awkward and wrong to me, even though the facts in the article were accurate."

"I'm not sure I understand."

"Oh, that's all right, darlin'. I'm not sure I understand myself. That's why I've been up all night. There are a lot of pieces to the puzzle, but I can't seem to make them fit together. That's what was wrong with the article. There were holes. The facts are all there, but a lot of things are missing. You see, I had questions about Tom Hensley — they called him Boots. I asked around about him to some of the older folks in town, but no one would talk. In fact, everyone was unusually tight-lipped about him.

"That made me ask 'why?' Long story short, I've been combing through microfilm at the paper since the wee hours."

"What does this have to do with me, Ms. Thompson?"

"On the surface nothing, but my gut tells me different, and I never ignore my gut, if you know what I mean."

She did.

"I know you have a full day getting ready for your preview this evening, but I was wondering if I could buy you a cup of coffee at the diner this morning."

Candi didn't know what to say.

"Oh, please say 'yes.' I really want to apologize in person and show you what I've found. I think you'll find it very interesting."

Good Lord . . . why couldn't people just live in the present instead of digging up the past?

"All right, but we'll have to make it quick."

"Of course. I understand completely. I'll meet you there in forty-five minutes? And I'll bring several copies of the paper with your ad in it. I think you'll be pleased."

"All right."

"Thank you, darlin'."

Candi disconnected the call and stared at the outfit she'd laid out on the bed. She couldn't help thinking, what could she wear that wouldn't make her look short and frumpy next to Jenny Thompson?

When Candi walked into Ferguson's, it was packed and buzzing with activity. But when she walked in, it seemed that conversation stopped and all eyes settled on her. Dixie came from around the lunch counter and took her arm. "Well, don't you look fabulous! That color is great on you."

"It sure is," Jenny Thompson agreed. She leaned down and air kissed Candi's cheek. "Burgundy is definitely your color, and that eye shadow really makes your eyes pop."

"I picked that out for her."

"*Mmm* . . . I bet browns would be good, too." Jenny fanned a hand in front of her as if she was clearing the air. "Look at us standing in the door like tourists. Come on over her, darlin'. I got us a booth in the back where we can talk."

"I'll bring y'all some coffee and menus."

"Thanks, Dix."

Candi sat, apprehension making her entire body tense. Sensing it, Jenny reached over and patted her hand. "Please don't be concerned. I promise you, everything I've done has been because I wanted to see things go easier for you in Angel Ridge from here on out." She chuckled. "You've had more trouble than you can shake a stick at. You're overdue for a little peace."

"I can't disagree with that."

Dixie laid menus on the table in front of them and poured coffee. "You ladies know what you want? I have some mixed berry muffins I just took out of the oven."

"Oh that sounds grand. Bring us a couple of those, some scrambled eggs, and do you have melon?"

Dixie nodded. "Cantaloupe."

"Perfect. How does that sound to you, Candi?"

She was starved. Just the thought of food

and the aromas coming from the kitchen made her stomach rumble. "That sounds good."

"Coming right up."

"Thanks, Dixie," Jenny said. "Now, Candi. I know your time is precious, so I'll dive right in, if that's all right."

Candi nodded.

"I pulled some old newspaper articles on Boots Hensley. He was quite the interesting figure here in town. Turns out he lived up on Laurel Mountain with a wife and daughter, and that back in the day, he made moonshine until he figured out he could make more money as a runner. Let's just say he was crosswise of the law more than a few times."

Candi sipped her coffee, but chose not to comment. She had to concentrate on composing her features so she didn't give anything away.

"He was less active in the years before he died, I guess because he was getting elderly. But what piqued my interest was how he died. Turns out he came to town, called out the sheriff — Grady's daddy — and got himself killed, but not before he paralyzed the sheriff.

"So, and this is the really interesting part, he called the sheriff out because his daughter had washed up in some backwater cove, on the back side of the ridge, dead. The sheriff conducted an investigation and declared her death an accidental drowning, an outcome Boots took issue with. *He* maintained that his daughter was murdered."

Candi leaned back in the booth, feeling her throat tighten, which made breathing nearly impossible.

Dixie brought their food and topped their coffee off. "Y'all just give me a wave if you need anything else."

"Will do, doll," Jenny said before continuing. "So, I did some digging on Hensley's daughter."

Candi pulled off a piece of muffin and put it in her mouth. It could have been sawdust, but it gave her something to do.

"Well, this just can't be described, and words rarely fail me. Let me show you."

She opened a file and set it in front of Candi. She looked down at the black and white newspaper clippings photocopied all on just a few pages, but what leaped out from the page was a black and white photo of Hazel Hensley. Of course she'd seen pictures of her mom. She'd been younger than she was here and had dark hair. This woman was blonde, wore a formal dress, a crown and sash.

The caption read, *Hazel Hensley crowned Miss Knoxville.* "She was a beauty queen?"

"*Uh-huh,* and that's not all. Turns out she surrendered her crown for undisclosed reasons and the first runner-up took her place."

"I suppose that's a bit odd?"

"It was the only time in the history of the pageant that such a thing happened. That was about a year before she died. So, I did some more digging and came up with this."

An advertisement listed Hazel as the featured performer at some place called the Chota Gentleman's Club.

"That club was legendary around here. They served alcohol in a dry county and had adult entertainment." She pointed at the photo. "This Hazel Hensley did a fair impersonation of Marilyn Monroe, the Playboy version, if you get my meaning. That would explain why she had to surrender her crown."

Oh, Lord . . .

"And it wasn't easy to dig up, but I found out when she left the mountain, she came to live here in Angel Ridge with an aunt and uncle, Billy Joe and Verdi Maguire. Unfortunately the paper trail ends there."

Candi put another pinch of muffin in her mouth.

"Well?" Jenny prompted.

Candi just looked at her. She had nothing to say to Jenny Thompson, or anyone else for that matter, on the subject of Hazel Hensley. "I don't understand what this has to do with the reckless driver or the break-in at my shop."

"I think it's all related."

"I don't follow."

"That club had all manner of shady people as clientele: bootleggers, drug dealers, loan sharks, the real dregs of society. My understanding is that the sheriff over in that county was well-paid to look the other way. Maybe Boots Hensley's daughter got caught up in something that spun out of control. Maybe that's why she 'drowned.' " She punctuated the word with hand gestures.

She swallowed back the emotion bubbling up inside. *Stay calm . . . look disinterested. You're not supposed to know anything about Hazel Hensley.*

"I still don't follow."

"All right, I'll spell it out for you then. This Hazel lived here in Angel Ridge. People in town were sure to have known about her working over at the Gentleman's Club, especially since I'm sure there were men from Angel Ridge who went there on occasion. You know the women who lived here had to have made her life hell. Look who we'd be talking about — Mrs. McKay, Sadie and Geraldine Wallace, and I bet several other church ladies jumped on the bandwagon.

"And there's the matter of her body being found here in town. That made it the jurisdiction of Grady's dad. If there was foul play involved with some of those characters at the Gentleman's Club, he might have been afraid to conduct a thorough investigation. Thus her father, Tom Hensley, coming to town to demand justice." She shrugged. "Who knows? His next stop might have been that club if he hadn't gotten himself killed."

Talking about this as if it had nothing to do with her was taking its toll. "I still don't see what that has to do with what's happening here now."

"Call it a hunch. That's why I wanted to talk to you. You said you're from the mountains, but you didn't say where. Did you know the Hensleys? They were from Laurel Mountain."

"No," she lied. Picking up her fork, she took a bite of eggs. They tasted like cardboard on her tongue, but the food was something to focus on besides Jenny.

"Well, here's what I think. Hazel stopped working at the club not long after these ads appeared, and then less than a year later, she was dead, the victim of an unexplained drowning. The obituary said that she lived on Laurel Mountain, and that she was survived by her parents and a daughter named Lark. I think I'll pay a visit to Billy Joe and Verdi Maguire today. See if I can find out why she left Angel Ridge. I've also put out feelers to find her daughter."

"Feelers?" This was going from bad to worse.

"I was an investigative reporter for the *Knoxville News-Sentinel* before I bought *The Chronicle* and settled in Angel Ridge. I'm trained to find the truth, and I will."

"What exactly are you trying to find, Jenny?"

"I think Hazel Hensley either got involved *in* something shady or *with* someone shady. If they murdered her to keep her quiet, they could be back in town looking for something — like money or valuables that they gave Hazel for safekeeping."

"Are you saying you think whatever this is might be hidden in my shop?"

"Can't rule it out."

"I've been over every inch of that shop. I

didn't find anything unusual."

"It could be in a wall or under a floorboard."

"So why not look when the building was empty?"

"Why indeed?"

There was the shrewd look again. Too shrewd. "What about the reckless driver?"

"Well, see, you were part of my theory. I thought you might be somehow connected to the Hensleys, which would give these people a reason to come after you, now that you're more accessible than you would have been in the mountains. Guess I was wrong about that."

Jenny picked up the photos of Candi's mom and studied them. She had to get out of here before Jenny got another of her hunches. The walls felt like they were closing in on her. "I should be going." She took some money out of her purse and laid it on the table.

"Keep your money, darlin'. This is on me."

Not wanting to argue, Candi put the money back in her bag.

"I'll see you tonight at the preview. I'm looking forward to it."

Her smile was tight, but she managed one. "Thank you for breakfast. I'll see you tonight."

Jenny lifted her orange juice in a salute. "Wish me luck. I'll keep you posted."

Candi beat a path to the door. Outside, she stepped out into the street, heading for the shop without looking to see if it was clear. A car horn blared and tires screeched. "Sorry," she said, and hurried over to her shop. Inside, she leaned back against the door. Only when she was alone in the darkened shop did she realize that her cheeks were wet.

Her mother, an exotic entertainer at a club with criminals? What if Jenny was right? What if they knew who she was and they were coming after her because they were looking for something? She dropped her purse on the counter and leaned against it. The money in Aunt Ruby's strong box and the other stash they kept in the springhouse . . . she'd thought it was from her granddaddy's moonshining days. What if it wasn't? What if, all these years, she and her grandmother had been living off some criminal's money?

Why was this happening now, after all this time? Now, when she was so close to having everything she'd always wanted?

Maybe she'd pay her own visit to Uncle Billy and Aunt Verdi. She needed some answers. Now.

CHAPTER 18

Candi waited and watched out the window of her shop all morning. When she saw Jenny pull up in her white Mercedes convertible and park in front of the newspaper offices, she waited ten minutes after Jenny went inside to be sure she didn't leave again.

When she was certain the woman would stay put, she locked up and tossing her keys in the basket, hopped onto her bicycle and pointed it towards Ridge Road. She crossed the railroad tracks and took the right fork that went down into the heavily wooded area near her aunt and uncle's farm. Fifteen minutes later, she approached their farmhouse cautiously, making sure they didn't have company.

No cars were parked in the driveway, so she rode up to the front porch and parked her bike. She took the front steps two at a time to the porch and knocked on the screen door.

"Lark, what a surprise!"

Aunt Verdi opened the door and folded her into a tight hug. Candi sighed. She'd missed her aunt, but visiting her had been too much of a risk, was still a risk now.

"It's good to see you, Aunt Verdi."

"Come in, come in. I made plans to come to your preview tonight. I figured it would be safe enough with so many other people coming. You must be terribly excited. Can I get you something to drink?"

Candi sat on the couch in the parlor, shaking her head. "No thanks. Is Uncle Billy in?"

"Oh, no honey. He's fishing. Is something wrong?"

The warmth and concern in her voice were almost her undoing. When Aunt Verdi sat and reached out to touch Candi's hand, the tears that had been threatening all day filled her eyes and spilled over. "Oh, Aunt Verdi. Why? Why didn't anyone tell me the truth about my mother?"

"Oh. Oh, my. What's brought this on?"

"You've read the paper, so I'm sure you know that a reckless driver nearly killed me last week, and yesterday, my shop was broken into. If it weren't for the help of all the nice people I've gotten to know in town, I wouldn't be having a preview tonight."

"Yes, dear. I did hear about that. I've wanted so badly to come to you, but Billy wouldn't let me. Said you needed to figure out for yourself that you . . ."

Candi swiped the tears with the back of her hand. "That I what?"

"That your coming to Angel Ridge was a bad decision."

"Yeah, he warned me no good could come of it. It would have been more useful if he'd told me why."

"Honey, Aunt Ruby wanted to spare you. She thought it was bad enough you had to grow up without your mama. So, we honored Aunt Ruby's wishes, even after she passed. Being who she was, we never dreamed of questioning her."

Aunt Verdi pressed a wad of tissues into Candi's hand. She blew her nose. The wise woman of the mountain. Candi wished she had some of that wisdom now.

"I never would have dreamed my mother was someone like, like that."

"I know, dear. It must be such a shock."

"I'm surprised that Uncle Billy let her live here while she worked there."

"Well, honey, after she began working at the club, she didn't spend much time here. The church ladies in town made it real hard for her to live in Angel Ridge, even with us living all the way out here."

"Aunt Verdi, did she get involved in anything illegal? Get mixed up with the wrong people? Is that why she went back home to Granddaddy and Aunt Ruby?"

"No, darlin'. She went back home because she was pregnant with you. After all she'd done, she couldn't stay here and have a child out of wedlock. I know it was the Eighties when most people were less judgmental about things like this, but the folks in Angel Ridge have always been so conservative."

Candi dragged in a long breath. "Do you know who my daddy was?"

"Your mama never said, and we didn't ask. It was clear she was heartbroken, I can tell you that much."

"Did she walk the riverbank looking for him? My daddy? Hoping he'd come find her? Is that what she was doing when she drowned?"

Both Candi's hands were in her aunt's now. "I'm sorry. We just don't know what happened, darlin'."

"But granddaddy went into town and called the sheriff out. He must have had some idea of what happened."

She shook her head. "I talked to Aunt Ruby about it, but you know how tight-lipped she could be. She wasn't about to talk ill of the dead and especially not her husband and only child."

"Damned mountain ways," she mumbled, then immediately apologized.

"Darlin', it's enough to make anyone want to cuss, especially with that newspaper lady snoopin' around."

"She took me to breakfast this morning. Told me she's determined to find out what happened with Hazel Hensley and to find her daughter."

"Well, she didn't find anything out from me, but you should be more concerned about someone following you out here. This was very risky."

Candi squeezed her aunt's hand. "I had to ask what you know. I'm trying not to worry, but do you think someone is after me because of my mother? Or granddaddy?"

"There's no way to know, but Grady Wallace and Jenny Thompson are good people. They'll get to the bottom of this."

Her laugh was harsh. "I guess people finding out that my grandmother was Ruby Hensley is the least of my worries now."

"I'll talk to your uncle as soon as he gets home. If he tells me anything that would be helpful, I'll call you at your shop."

Candi chewed her lower lip and started

shredding her tissues into a pile in her lap. "I don't know if I should go ahead with the grand opening. Maybe I should just stay out here with you and Uncle Billy until Grady and Jenny figure something out. No one would think to look for me out here now."

"Unless Jenny finds out you're Hazel's daughter, and then she'll be the first one at our door, demanding answers."

"Uncle Billy was right. I should have never come here. I could be putting so many lives in danger."

"Or this could have nothing to do with you. No, you get back to your shop and go ahead with your opening just like you planned. It'll cause more suspicions if you disappear."

Candi stood and walked outside with her aunt. They shared a long, comforting hug. "Thank you, Aunt Verdi."

"Don't you worry, now. Everything is going to turn out just fine. You'll see. Trust what your grandmamma taught you. If you have a feeling or if you get any kind of message, trust it. Don't question. Promise me."

Candi nodded. "I will." She mounted her bike and looked back up at her aunt.

She waved from the porch. "I love you!"

"Love you, too." Candi pedaled away from

the house. In the shade of the trees that lined the dirt road, everything seemed to crash in on her at once. The tears came so fast and hard, everything in front of her blurred.

The trees opened up and a cleared, grassy shoulder took their place. Candi steered her bike into the grass and fell to the ground, sobbing all the pain that had welled up inside her. All the weeks of hiding her identity, nearly being killed, her shop being vandalized with the word "witch" written everywhere in red. Why? Who would do this? Who knew her secrets?

She pressed clinched hands to her eyes, then looked up to heaven and asked God, "Why? All my life, I've tried to do what was right. I lived alone with Aunt Ruby when I should have lived in a normal house with a mom and dad. I should have been able to go to school with other kids, gone to prom, had boyfriends."

A flash of white on the other side of the cove caught her eye. She blinked and wiped the tears out of her eyes. She must be seeing things. This was back water for the lake. This time of year, when they lowered the lake levels at the dam in Lenoir City, hardly any water filled little coves like this.

She saw it again. Standing, she took

several steps forward. Yes, she'd definitely seen something.

Lark . . .

Her name carried across the cove on the current of a light breeze that lifted the hair off her neck. She moved closer to the muddy riverbed, but then she saw a flash of white and blonde hair. A woman —

I'm sorry . . .

"Mama?"

Lark . . . forgive me for leaving you . . . I didn't want to . . .

The woman's soft, lyrical voice enticed Candi. Mud sucked at her shoes and ankles, still she kept moving toward the mesmerizing motion on the other side of the cove. Just then, she noticed an old, narrow dock just like the one in her dreams.

"Candi, stop. Come back! It's not safe."

Grady's heart nearly stopped beating as he watched Candi slogging closer and closer to the water in the center of the cove. Those waters could be deceptively deep, and he knew she was fixing to step in a hole.

"Candi, please! Stop!"

She kept going forward as if she didn't, or couldn't, hear him. She was waist deep in muddy water now and mumbling something, her focus on the far riverbank. He'd taken two steps towards her when she disappeared below the surface. He lurched towards her, but the mud slowed his progress. She still hadn't broken the surface when he got to the water. Shrugging out of his jacket, he dove. The water was so muddy, it burned his eyes and he couldn't see a thing.

He came up to get a gulp of air, then dove again. He reached out with his arms, moving forward until he hit something solid. He wrapped his arms around the body and immediately knew he had her. He encircled her waist and tried to pull her to the surface, but she didn't budge. Following the line of her body, he checked her feet. Her foot was wrapped in something. He pulled at the weed that held her until she was free and shot to the surface with him close behind.

Choked, she coughed and sputtered, spitting dirty water out of her mouth. Grady put an arm around her, treading water for them both, and held her neck steady so he could get a good look at her. "Talk to me, darlin'."

She began to struggle. "Let go of me! I have to get to the other side. She's there! I heard her, saw her!"

"Stop fighting me, Lark."

"I have to go to her before it's too late!"

He hitched her higher against his chest.

"All right, I'll get you to the other side, but you've got to be still or we'll both drown."

"I've been alone my whole life. What makes you think I suddenly need you or anyone else?"

His feet touched the bottom and he swung her up into his arms, cradling her against his heart. "Did it ever occur to you that I might need you? That we might need each other if you'd just let yourself feel something besides wariness and mistrust?"

Grady set her on her feet as soon as they got to the riverbank. When her knees nearly buckled, he steadied her with a hand on her arm. When she got her legs under her, she shrugged out of his grasp. She went right into the trees, weaving in and out of them. Grady followed, not willing to let her out of his sight.

"What are you looking for?"

"I saw my mother. She spoke to me."

Dear Lord, was she seeing ghosts now? With all the other freaky things going on, he didn't know why this should surprise him. He hoped she hadn't snapped under the pressure, especially in light of what Jenny had dug up.

He followed her, but the search was useless. No one was here but the two of them. He was right there by her side when she slumped to the ground.

"I saw her. I did, Grady. She was wearing white and she looked just like her pictures."

He rubbed her cold hands, trying to get some warmth back into them.

"You think I'm crazy, don't you."

"No, darlin'."

"You should have let me drown, just like her. Just like in my dream. It would solve all our problems."

"*Now* you're talking crazy."

"If I wasn't here, they wouldn't have anyone to go after, and no one would be in danger. The town would be safe."

"First off, we don't know that whoever is behind the reckless driving and the vandalism is targeting you. It could all be a decoy to throw us off what they're really trying to do."

"Then why was I part of both incidents?"

"I don't know, but I'm going to find out, I promise you."

She blinked back tears. He automatically reached into his pocket, but his handkerchief was soaked and useless. He tossed it aside and pulled her into his arms.

Stroking her back as he spoke, he said, "This involves both of us, Lark. My daddy investigated your mother's death, and the mistakes our parents made have come back to haunt us. That has a way of happening when things are left . . . unsettled. Things this big, this important, can't just be covered up or ignored as if they didn't happen. We're in this together, and until we both have answers, I'm not leaving your side. I can't lose you. I won't."

She clung to him, emotion shaking her body as he rocked and soothed her. "I'm here," he whispered over and over. "I'm here. You're not alone anymore."

After awhile, she quieted in his arms, but he kept her close. The feel of her in his arms, pressed against his chest, did things to him that went beyond anything physical. He needed her. He didn't know when it had happened, but she'd slipped into his heart and filled all its empty spaces with emotion, tenderness, protectiveness, excitement, anguish, urgency, intensity and need. All rolled together — all at once.

He pressed his lips to a spot where her hair met the soft skin of her forehead. "We should get back. You've got a preview to host."

She shook her head. "I can't go back. It's too dangerous. What if Jenny . . ."

Grady leaned back so he could look at her. "I spoke with Jenny. We're working together. She understands the importance of keeping your true identity a secret."

"You told her?"

"She already knew. You look like her, you know."

Candi nodded.

He paused, pushing her wet, matted hair back from the side of her face. Mud streaked her face and clothes, but still, just looking at her made his heart race. "I'm afraid your outfit's ruined."

She looked down at herself then and tried, unsuccessfully, to run her fingers through her wet, tangled hair. "I must look a fright."

Grady tipped his head to the side, considering her appearance. "I don't know. I'm beginning to see how some people enjoy watching women's mud wrestling. If you were only wearing a bikini . . ."

She looked up at him, shocked at what he'd said. He just smiled and waited until she realized he was teasing her. The smile came first, and then the warmth of her laughter. He kissed her because he couldn't help himself. "That's better."

She looked across the cove to where her bike and his truck were. "How are we going to get back?"

"I know this river and its coves like the back of my hand. I know where it's shallow, where it's deep, and where there are holes to avoid."

"How did you know I was here?"

"I was on my way to your uncle's to ask him some questions. I guess you had the same idea."

Candi nodded, her gaze moving from his to the tree line. He placed a finger under her chin and brought it back. "What did he tell you?"

"Nothing. He wasn't there. I spoke with my aunt . . . about my mom." She clinched his wrist and swallowed hard, tears filling her eyes. "It's all true, what Jenny said about her. I had no idea. No one ever told me."

"I'm sorry," he said softly.

She pulled her upper lip into her mouth. "You know what this means, don't you?"

"No, what?"

"You see, I had this crazy fantasy that I'd come to Angel Ridge and maybe find my father. In my dream, she left without telling him she was pregnant and he'd never known anything about me. When he learned the truth, I thought he'd be so happy. We'd get to know each other and do all the things a daughter does with her dad."

Grady squeezed her shoulder, emotion tightening his throat. When dreams shattered, devastation followed. Candi had had more than her fair share of that reality.

She looked up at him, her eyes huge in her face, the hurt there jagged, raw and exposed. "Any number of men could be my father. I'll never know who he is." Her laugh sounded bitter and lifeless. "We could be cousins, Grady."

He shook his head. "No, that's not possible."

"How do you know? You're related to half the town." Her laugh turned edgy and a little hysterical. "You could be my brother."

He grasped her shoulders and shook her a little until she stopped laughing. "Listen to me. We're not related. I know this for a fact because I was adopted."

Chapter 19

Why couldn't she make him see? "Your being adopted has nothing to do with your father's ability to have a child, Grady."

"But it does. You see, my daddy was in Vietnam. A shrapnel injury left him sterile."

Her shoulders slumped, his words leaving her limp with relief. "Oh, thank goodness."

He chuckled at that.

"I mean, it's terrible your dad was injured and couldn't have children —"

"But good that it means we can't be related? Careful, Lark," his voice dipped an octave and he leaned close, "you're gonna have me thinking you have feelings for me."

She framed his face with her hands. "Are you just now figuring that out? Boy, for a trained investigator, you're awfully blind to clues that give a person away, and the ones you've gotten with me haven't exactly been all that subtle."

She kissed him then, hard and long, so

there was no mistaking her feelings for him. After several moments had passed, they both had to break the contact to get their breath.

He pressed a trail of hot, open-mouth kisses from her lips to her ear. "Use your words, Lark. I need to hear them."

"I care about you, Grady, and — and — I *could* need you." There. She'd said it. She'd never needed anyone. Growing up without parents taught you that the only person you could depend on was yourself. "I could need you," she repeated, "and it scares me to death because everyone I ever allowed myself to need either left me or never showed up."

"I'm here, Lark. I'm not going anywhere."

"Life's too uncertain for that promise to hold any truth."

"There are no guarantees in life, that's true. But as long as I'm breathing, I promise, I'll be here for you."

He looked sincere, but doubts and second-guessing were part of who she was at her core.

"You still don't trust me," he said as if he were reading her thoughts.

"Don't take it personally. I've never really trusted anyone but myself."

"Well, you're in luck, because one of the

things I do best is show up. I'm reliable and dependable. Those traits were engrained in me from an early age. In fact, I think I was born with a sense of responsibility. Six generations of sheriffs in one family seal the deal. Whether you want to or not, whether it's in your blood or not, when the time comes, Wallaces do their duty. The security of the town and the safety of its citizens sit square on your shoulders, and it's not something to take lightly. So, you see, I have great references."

His smile was wide and confident. "Now, two things are about to happen if we don't do something about it right away." He stood and helped her up. "First, it feels like it's about twenty degrees out here," he exaggerated, "and if we don't get out of these wet clothes, we're going to have pneumonia. Neither of us has time for that. Second," he swept her up into his arms and walked out into the squishy riverbed, "if I don't get you back now, there's no way we're going to make your preview."

She wrapped her arms around him and nestled her face into the space between his shoulder and neck that she just realized had been made for her. It was a perfect fit. He navigated the cove so that the water never rose above his waist. She arrived at the opposite riverbank no worse for the journey, because that's what love did. It carried you, through treacherous waters and the other hazards of life, safely to the other side.

Grady stowed her bike in the back of his Jeep and took her home so they could both shower and change. She chose a mint green sweater that matched her eyes and a long chocolate-brown skirt and boots to wear for the opening. She'd used the blow dryer on her hair, leaving it to hang in long, loose curls down her back. She picked up her purse and a cashmere shawl and went downstairs to find Grady.

He had showered and put on a fresh uniform and stood staring out the kitchen window. He turned when he heard her footsteps on the stairs, coming over to meet her when she reached the bottom.

"Have I told you lately how incredibly beautiful you are?" He leaned down and kissed her cheek, then stepped back to look at her. She loved that he liked the way she looked.

"You clean up pretty good, too," she said.

"*Aw,* shucks, ma'am," he teased, "I ain't nothin' compared to you."

Candi gave him a sideways glance, rolling her eyes. "Right. I'm sure you never noticed how women act around you." She walked past him to the door. He followed her out onto the porch, turning to make sure the lock was secure.

"How's that?" he said.

Leave it to a man to make a girl spell it out. Grady took her arm and walked her to his Jeep. When she was settled and he was behind the wheel, Candi said, "Don't be dense. You know how Dixie and Jenny act around you."

He swung a skeptical look in her direction as he turned his car around and headed down the drive. "Dixie and Jenny?" And then he started to laugh.

She failed to see the humor. "What's so funny?"

"Just that I've known Dixie half my life. She's like a sister to me. And Jenny," he laughed harder, unable to finish the sentence.

"She gets all girly and flirty every time you're around."

"She's like that with everybody."

Candi shook her head and mumbled. "Men can be so blind."

He lifted her hand to his lips. When he had her attention, and he did — have her full attention — he said, "You're the only woman I've noticed since you got to town."

"I haven't been here long."

"And there wasn't anyone before that. I mean, I'm not gonna lie to you. Dixie and I tried dating once." He shuddered. "It was like kissing your sister."

Candi remembered Dixie saying something similar about him, but she still couldn't resist teasing, now that she was getting better at it, "How would you know? You don't have a sister."

"I know," he said, all warm intensity, "because I've kissed you."

Candi melted. Who knew she'd be one of those women who'd go all gooey inside at sweet words. She undid her seatbelt and scooted across the bench seat until she was right up next to him, shoulder to shoulder. She squeezed his hand and wrapped her arm around his.

"It's against the law in Tennessee to not wear a seatbelt."

She propped her chin on his shoulder and smiled up at him. "I know the sheriff in this town, and since he's clearly got a thing for me, I'm thinking he won't write me up."

He smiled at that, doing his best to concentrate on the road instead of her. "He might lock you up, though."

She squeezed his arm. "Really?"

"Mmm-hmm."

She traced the line of his five-star badge.

"I wouldn't mind, if you were the guard keeping a *close* eye on me."

"Keeping a *close* eye on prisoners is one of my specialties."

She snuggled closer. "That sounds . . . promising." She was really good at this flirting thing.

"Lark Hensley —"

"Candi Heart," she corrected.

"Whatever your name is, then. You're under arrest for violating the seatbelt law and for operating a business under an assumed name."

"There's nothing illegal about how I'm operating my business. The bank account is in the business's name."

"Who signs the checks? Lark or Candi?"

"Lark, for now. I haven't changed my name legally — yet."

He looked at her then, like he was surprised she'd considered changing her name legally. "What? It's not expensive to change your name, and you don't have to have a lawyer. I can even do it in Knoxville so no one here will know. I was thinking of keeping 'Lark,' though. Candi Lark Heart, or maybe Lark Candi Heart. But we've gotten off point. I do have a question."

"Ask."

"If I'm truly under arrest," she traced the

handcuffs attached to his gun belt, "does that mean you're going to use these on me?"

He chuckled and squirmed in his seat. "I think you've got a little of your mother in you after all."

She swatted at his arm. "Grady Wallace."

"*Ow!* Don't go gettin' all upset. You're not gonna hear me complainin', but I'm warning you. You sure are givin' me ideas that aren't very respectable."

She was ashamed to admit it, because her Aunt Ruby had raised her right, but she liked teasing and flirting with Grady. "I'm new to this, Grady. I don't know the limits, so you'll have to tell me if I go too far."

He kissed her hand again. "You just have to remember that I'm teasing you, too. When we're flirting like this, don't take what I say too seriously. I'm the man in this relationship," he looked at her then and repeated, "and this *is* a relationship. It's my responsibility to treat you with the respect you deserve. So you don't have to worry about pushing me too far or of me taking advantage of your lack of experience."

Candi sighed. He was too good to be true. There had to be a catch, but she was too happy to think about it right now. With so many bad things happening and so many hard truths being revealed, she needed a safe place where she felt comfortable and safe. Being with Grady like this felt so right.

"I love you," she sighed. Saying the words came naturally and without forethought as to the possible repercussions.

Grady parked in the alley behind the shop and shut the car off. He turned and pulled her into his arms. "What did you say?"

She panicked then. She hadn't thought he'd hear her. "What?" she hedged.

"Say it again," his warm breath teased her mouth with the promise of a kiss.

She melted into him, trying to close the distance between their lips, but he countered every move she made.

"Say it again," he insisted.

She blinked through the desire fogging her vision, trying to focus on his eyes instead of his mouth. "Grady, please don't press me. I shouldn't have said that," she whispered.

He let out his breath and kissed her then, a long, sweet embrace filled with promise and all the feelings that swirled between them.

"I never dreamed this could happen for me," he said. "I'd pretty much given up hope of finding someone this late in the game."

She smoothed the material of his jacket.

"Oh, right, you're so old."

"Most guys my age are married and have kids."

"Well don't go gettin' any ideas, Grady Wallace. I'm not intending to marry you, especially seeing as you aren't declaring yourself."

"Oh, I got plenty to declare, but right now, we both have work to do." He kissed her again, and promised, "Later."

Lordy, how could she have gotten so carried away that she blurted out that she loved him when it was clearly too soon to do such a thing? Too much happening all at once had her emotions raw, that's what.

He got out of the car. The time it took him to come around to open her door and help her out of the Jeep, gave her half a second to compose herself, put her mask of pretense in place.

He caressed her cheek with the backs of his fingers. "Now, don't go talking yourself out of it, Lark."

"Candi," she automatically corrected, as she exhaled most of her tension. "I think I'll see about getting it changed next week."

"I'd hold off on that if I were you. Filing a court document is a sure way to help someone who's looking, find you. Knoxville's not that far away."

He was right about that.

"And when and if you do change your name, I'm still going to call you 'Lark.' " He adjusted his gun belt low over his hips. She'd never seen him wear his gun that way. He usually carried it in a shoulder holster.

He followed the direction of her gaze. "I want whoever's after us to know that I'm armed and ready for them."

"Now, you're scaring me. I wouldn't be able to live with myself if something happened to you, or anyone else in this town, because of me."

He tapped the front of his jacket. "I got Kevlar sewn in here. It's bulletproof. But don't worry, I know how to take care of myself. You got your keys? I want to sweep the shop before you go in."

She dug in her purse and gave them to him. She waited by the door, antsy, nervous, scared, and excited. She so wanted tonight to be a success.

Grady came back outside. "Come on in."

Candi walked straight to the front and stashed her purse. Then she put on an apron and went to the back to put cookies on plates. The plastic cups and plates were already in place. Lacy tablecloths covered small round tables, some with candles and others with fall colored chrysanthemums in vases.

"What can I do to help?"

"Go open the front door and make yourself scarce."

She set out the pitchers of tea she'd put to chill in the refrigerator earlier, then walked to the front turning on lights as she went. Grady trailed behind her despite her request. She turned and said, "The front door?"

"Oh, sorry."

Candi frowned. He must have been preoccupied with the investigation. Now that they were back in town, his mind had probably shifted gears.

When she made it to the front of the shop, she was surprised to see that Grady was still there and talking to Woody and Constable Harris.

She greeted the men. "Woody, Constable. What are you two doing here?"

"I was just giving them their instructions," Grady said.

"What instructions?"

"Henry is going to patrol town square and Main, and Woody's going to be in the alley during your event. I'll be here, inside the shop."

"This is for women only. I don't want a

man with a big gun in here making everyone nervous."

"I'll be inconspicuous."

Candi laughed. "Grady, you are about the least inconspicuous person I've ever known. I mean, look at you! If you wanted to be inconspicuous, you should have worn casual clothing."

"She's got a point there, Boss," Woody agreed.

"And did I mention," she added, "this is a women-only event? Any man would stand out."

Stepping close to her so only she could hear him, he said, "I'm not leaving you here alone. We agreed. Until we find who's behind all this, I'm not leaving your side."

Candi touched his cheek with her fingertips. "Woody and the constable will be right outside. If anything happens, they'll call you. I'm sure you have work to do at the office since I kept you away most of the afternoon."

"I don't like changing a plan at the last minute," he grumbled, running his hands up and down her arms.

She touched his jacket and tilted her head. "It's not like you're going to be in the next county."

She knew he was going to give in when he

sighed, heavily. "You are one headstrong woman, you know that?"

"Yes, I believe someone recently told me that. Now, git. I've got work to do." She looked up and smiled when she saw a line of ladies coming up the sidewalk towards the shop. "And customers to greet." She squeezed his arms and pulled him down for a quick kiss. "See you at nine."

"Eight-thirty," he countered.

"Fine, just go!"

"Break a leg, darlin'."

He turned and motioned to a shocked-looking Woody to follow him to the back of the shop. When they'd disappeared in the hallway, Dixie walked in with her mother and sisters-in-law close behind her. "Well, don't you look cute!" She kissed Candi's cheek and folded her into a warm hug.

"Thanks! I'm glad you're here."

While Candi was greeting the other Ferguson women in similar fashion, Dixie said, "The shop looks fabulous."

"Go on and browse," Candi suggested. "The candies and floral arrangements are here in front. Down the hall, to the left is a shop with traditional clothing. To the right, is a shop where, *um,* well, you'll find a little something naughty, if it suits your tastes."

The women giggled.

"In the tea room out back, there's cookies and iced tea, and tables where you can sit and chat. I was just about to boil some water for hot tea, if you'd prefer."

"Oh, that sounds great," Dixie said. "Well, come on girls. I got my credit card, and I plan on doin' some damage. Point me to the Naughty Shop!"

"Dixie!" Mrs. Ferguson chided, while the other women laughed and followed her down the hall.

Four more ladies came in then. "Welcome to Heart's Desire. Thank you for coming. I'm Candi, the owner."

"Well, hello dear. Isn't that a perfectly precious name, Cathy? Candi."

"Yes, indeed. It's as pretty as you are, dear." The beautiful lady with short, stylish hair began the introductions. "I'm Cathy Rhoton. My husband, Fuzz, and I own the Corner Market just outside town. This is Wanda Jenkins."

"Hello." Wanda nodded and smiled, her red curls bouncing.

"This is Jan Reid." A tall thin lady smiled shyly at her and nodded.

"And I'm Kay Rhoton. I don't need an introduction. Everyone knows who I am."

"Well, that's certainly true, Mama Kay," Cathy said, "but Candi is new in town. She doesn't know *any*one. Kay's my mother-in-law," Cathy tried to add, but was interrupted.

"Well, now she does. What's this store about, honey?" Kay asked.

Kay was petite, with short, silver hair and astute blue eyes that missed nothing. She wore a blue top with matching pants and pink plastic clogs. Interesting . . .

"I named the shop 'Heart's Desire' because I sell everything a woman's heart desires. Here in the front, I have handcrafted chocolates, floral arrangements, and wreaths. Down the hall, there are two shops; in the one to the left, you'll find traditional clothing and skin care, and candles; in the one to the right, you'll find, *uh,* less traditional clothing, perfumes and lotions.

"I only sell things that are made from natural, organic materials, and I make the skincare and perfumes myself."

"Well, I'll be. So pretty and talented to boot!" Wanda, the one with red curls, said. She hadn't stopped smiling.

"Wanda," Kay said, "we did organic in the Sixties. The hippies from that era still do. It's just back in style now."

"Well that don't mean it ain't clever."

"You do hair here?" Kay asked.

"No, ma'am."

"But this is a beauty parlor," Kay exclaimed. "How can you not do hair in a beauty parlor?"

"I've converted the back room that used to be a salon into a tea room."

"A tea room!" Kay exclaimed. "Well, who'd want to drink tea in a salon when they can get something to drink at the diner across the street?"

Cathy touched Kay's arm. "It's not a salon anymore, Mama Kay. Candi here can do whatever she likes in the back room. It's her shop."

"Well, of all the unmitigated gall, to invite the entire town to a preview and choose to tell us, after we've dressed up and come out at six o'clock at night, that she's not runnin' a beauty parlor here. We're all still going to have to go into Maryville to get our hair done!"

"Let's have a look around, shall we," the smiling Wanda suggested.

Jan never spoke.

Cathy twined her arm with Kay's and steered her toward the hallway. "Well, why in the world would I want to look around if she's not going to be doing my hair?"

"There's cookies and iced tea in the back," Candi said. "Feel free to have a seat and visit as long as you like. Everything is twenty-five percent off tonight."

She heard Kay complaining all the way down the hall, just before she exclaimed, "What the H-E-Double Hockey Sticks do we have here?" she chuckled and then added. "Harriet McKay and her gang are gonna have a field day when they see this! Oh, goodie. I'm for sure stayin' now. Wouldn't miss those fireworks for nothin'!"

Speaking of Mrs. McKay, she walked in followed closely by three women wearing demure blouses buttoned up to the neck, sweaters thrown across their shoulders, straight skirts that fell to their knees, hose, and low-heeled pumps. They looked like throwbacks from the fifties, complete with pearl necklaces and earrings. The only thing missing were white gloves, pillbox hats, and pocketbooks that snapped closed.

"Good evening, Mrs. McKay. Ladies. Welcome to Heart's Desire, and thank you for coming." None of them spoke. As they looked around the front room, they did so similarly with their heads tilted back so that it appeared they were looking down their long noses at everything.

One of the ladies stepped forward and announced, "I am Geraldine Wallace. My son is the town sheriff."

Candi smiled warmly at the woman. "I'm

pleased to meet you Mrs. Wallace. I've met your son. He's been very kind to me."

"Yes, which you should appreciate, given the fact that his work has tripled since you arrived in our town."

That took Candi by surprise. "I'm very appreciative for all he's done, ma'am. You must be very proud of him."

"Of course I am. What mother wouldn't be?" Mrs. Wallace spat the words at her, clearly insulted, although Candi couldn't figure out why a woman with a son like Grady would speak to someone this way when paid a compliment about him.

"I'm Thelma Houston. My son, Patrick, is the mayor."

She had kind brown eyes that put Candi at ease, for the moment.

"And I'm Sadie Wallace. My husband and I run the grocery across the way. Welcome to Angel Ridge," she offered as if trying to apologize for the behavior of Mrs. McKay and the other Mrs. Wallace.

"Thank you."

Mrs. McKay reached in her purse and pulled out a pad and pen. "What will you be selling here, Ms. Heart?"

Candi went through the types of items being sold in the front room, then told them about the two shops off the hallway and the tea room in the back.

"What a nice idea," Mrs. Houston said, "a tea room where women can sit and relax to enjoy conversation. Will you be serving biscuits as well?"

"Cookies, yes, but I could look into British-style biscuits and scones. That's a wonderful idea."

"Let's have a look, shall we?" Mrs. McKay led the delegation towards the hallway.

"Everything is twenty-five percent off this evening only," Candi said, but the women ignored her. She thought she heard Grady's mother say to Mrs. McKay. "I would never buy anything on sale! How crude . . ."

Candi slumped against the front counter. They must have gone into the Nice Shop first, because she didn't hear any shrieking.

The bells on the door chimed, announcing more customers. Clara from the sheriff's office came through the door with Aunt Verdi. Thank goodness for friendly faces. "Hello. Welcome to Heart's Desire."

Clara gave her a hug. Aunt Verdi looked unsure of what to do. So, Candi helped her out. "Hi, I'm Candi Heart, the owner of the shop."

"I'm Verdi Hensley. So nice to meet you."

Candi nodded, smiling. "I'm pleased to meet you, too."

She explained the shop to them and invited them to browse. She walked with them down the hallway, then went to the back to put the water on to heat, but Dixie had beat her to it.

"Dixie, please. Let me do that, you go sit with your family and enjoy yourself."

"I wouldn't know how I got this, hon. You go talk to your customers." Dixie elbowed her and added, "It's a good turnout."

Candi smiled. "It is, isn't it?" As she looked around the room, several people had selected a number of items from apparel to skincare and were discussing their choices with their companions as they ate cookies and drank tea.

"Oh! I forgot to hand out the shopping bags!"

She hurried to the front and grabbed the mesh bags she'd gotten for people to put their things in as they shopped. She also forgot to tell everyone that there were dressing rooms in each shop if they needed to try anything on.

"Oh, no, no, no. This will *not* do. This will not do at all!" Mrs. McKay was saying as Candi passed by the Naughty Shop.

She stepped inside and asked, "Is something the matter, ladies?"

"Indeed there is," Mrs. McKay said.

"What is the meaning of this, young lady?"

"The meaning of what, ma'am?"

"Harriet, please don't make a scene," Mrs. Houston said.

"Yes, please," the Mrs. Wallace of Wallace's Grocery agreed. "This is a special night for Miss Heart."

Ignoring them, Mrs. McKay said, "Why, these things," she took her pen and lifted a lacy thong off a counter as if it were contaminated, "are positively indecent. What kind of *respectable* woman would purchase something like this, let alone wear it."

"Yes," Grady's mother agreed. "And there are ones that you can eat inside that case over there. Absolutely disgusting, if you ask me!"

"So, I will repeat my question. What is the meaning of this? A store where adult items and — and — shall we call them 'novelties,' for lack of a better word, are sold."

"I'd call it trash," Grady's mother supplied, "and I'd call anyone who bought *or sold* things like this the same. Trash. And right here in the middle of our town." She clicked her tongue. "Why, I never thought I'd see the day."

"Ladies, it isn't my intent to offend anyone," Candi said. "That's why I have the Nice Shop across the hall, so everyone's tastes are served. You need not shop in here if you find some of the items offensive."

Mrs. McKay snorted. "So, Ms. Heart, if I hear you correctly, you are saying that I should just ignore the fact that you sell these types of things here by shopping across the hall?"

"Yes."

"And yet anything I bought would support a store that caters to a baser element of society, of which I can assure you, we do not have or want in Angel Ridge. Even if I spent my hard-earned money on items that are perfectly appropriate, you could still take that money and purchase —" she scanned the room and settled on a piece of lingerie on a clothes horse — "a 'show and tell' corset?"

"They're called peek-a-boo teddies, ma'am."

"They are indecent, and no woman of character or breeding would think to wear such a thing. No. This will bring a bad element into our town, and we cannot have people like that sullying our image and robbing us blind. Why, it's already happened! Criminals just broke in here yesterday. Right here in our happy, quiet, safe town, right on Main Street, our principle business district." She shook her head. "No, I'm sorry, Ms.

Heart. You may not sell any of the items in this room. I insist you remove them before the store opens to the public."

Candi was speechless. Could Mrs. McKay tell her what she could and could not sell in her shop?

Clara chose that moment, with a silk nightgown in her hands, to say, "She can sell anything she wants, Harriet. It's her constitutional right. Freedom of speech? I'm sure you've heard of it."

"No one asked for you input, Clara."

"I feel certain no one asked for yours either," she said, just before she asked what flavors the edible underwear came in.

Grady's mother expressed her disgust with an intake of breath and also by leveling Clara with a look of contempt. Both were ignored by the shopper.

Mrs. McKay moved to stand near Candi at the entrance to the Naughty Shop, with Mrs. Wallace close at her heels. "Ms. Heart, I urge you to reconsider my request."

Candi did not know what to say, so she didn't say anything. Mrs. McKay nodded. "We'll take this up at the meeting of the town council on Monday, then. I'd encourage you to be in attendance. Ladies?"

Grady's mother left the shop with Mrs. McKay, but the other Mrs. Wallace and

Mrs. Houston stayed.

"Oh, honey, don't you worry any about Harriet McKay," Clara said. "She's three-part hot air and one-part pure meanness. The town council can't tell you what you can and can't sell."

The Mrs. Wallace from the grocery added her agreement. "That's true. Once, the town council tried to pass a referendum to keep the grocery from selling condoms and personal hygiene products, if you can imagine. Well that order wasn't worth the paper it was written on. We had to pay a lawyer to write a letter telling them so, but once they got it, the council backed right down. I can't imagine they'd put themselves through that kind of embarrassment again." She chuckled and said to Mrs. Houston, "Remember that article Jenny Thompson ran in *The Chronicle* about it, Thelma? Why Harriet was so put out, she left and went to Florida for a month."

"Ah, yes," Mrs. Houston nodded. "We haven't had a month of such peace and quiet since." She blinked and came back to the present, "Well, I'm going to have myself of cup of tea. You going to join me, Sadie?"

"Lead the way. Oh, and Candi, would you mind wrapping up that perfume in the red bottle over there? I just love it."

"Of course. I'll bring it back to you."

"Thank you, dear."

Candi took the bottle off the display and offered shopping bags to Clara and Aunt Verdi, who managed to give her hand a reassuring squeeze when no one was looking. Their encouragement helped her put Mrs. McKay, and her threats, out of her mind so she could enjoy the rest of the evening.

All in all, she'd say the preview was a resounding success. Sales were excellent, and the women seemed to particularly like sitting around and enjoying each other's company in the tea room. The sales of the organic herbal teas had been strong, as well.

She was sitting with Dixie and the Ferguson's when Grady strolled in. Candi looked at her watch, surprised that it was already eight-thirty.

"Don't look now," Dixie said, "but a M-A-N is crashing our party."

Candi smiled at Dixie. "I'm just happy he stayed away this long. He wanted to act as my security guard, but I convinced him to go to the office."

"Convinced who?" Dixie asked.

"Grady."

"Grady who?"

Candi laughed. "Grady Wallace. Who do you think?"

"Well, write this one down in the books, ladies. Grady Wallace did something he didn't want to, and at a woman's suggestion no less."

Candi watched Grady's progress as he made his way across the room. Her heart sang at just the sight of him.

The senior Mrs. Ferguson suggested, "It must be love."

Candi looked back at Dixie's mother, flushing scarlet.

"Oh, my," she continued. "And the feeling must be mutual."

"Mom Ferguson," Margie said, "you're embarrassing Candi."

"Oh honey, it's all right. She'll have to get used to it if she's going to be part of our family."

Candi looked up at Mom Ferguson and then at the two other Ferguson women sitting around the table. Part of a family . . . a big, loud, happy, loving family. She hadn't even considered it. After all, they weren't Grady's real family. But having met his mother, she understood why he spent so much time with the Fergusons.

"Evenin' ladies." Grady stood behind Candi's chair. "I hope you've been enjoying yourselves."

"Oh, it's been wonderful," Dixie declared.

"Heart's Desire is officially on the map and open for business." She lifted her tea cup and said, "Here's to Candi. May everyday be as successful as this one."

"Here, here," the other ladies said, lifting their cups in a salute.

Candi wondered if a person could die of such happiness. It really was true what Aunt Ruby had always said. *Don't live in the past, because it's done and gone. Just remember its lessons so when life's blessings come along, you can properly appreciate them.*

Candi lifted her cup to the ladies in front of her. "To blessings. I am truly thankful for the many kindnesses you've all shown me."

"Here, here. This is only the beginning, hon," Dixie said. She looked up at Grady and added, "I think there are many more blessings to come."

Candi turned to Grady, then. His smile was in place, but it didn't reach his eyes. Something was wrong.

"Ladies, take your time," Candi said. "There's no rush. I'll wait for you up front to ring your purchases whenever you're ready." To Grady, she said, "Will you join me, Sheriff?"

"Of course." Grady kissed the Ferguson women, then followed Candi to the front of the shop.

As soon as he got there, Candi said, "What is it? What's wrong?"

He cupped the side of her face because he couldn't go without touching her another minute. "It's nothing that can't wait. I'll tell you on the way home."

"Tell me now if it's bad news."

"You're safe, and that's all that matters to me right now. We'll get through the rest together, just like I promised."

Grady pressed his lips to her forehead. How was he going to tell her what Jenny had found out today? He wondered how many shattered illusions a person could absorb before the weight of it broke them completely.

CHAPTER 20

Grady took one more look around the shop before they locked up. Candi was glowing despite her obvious concern. He wondered if it was from her success tonight or from the feelings developing between them or both. Not that it mattered, he just wanted to hold her in his arms and protect her.

They had barely gotten settled in the Jeep before the questions started. "What's happened, Grady?"

"What was the most popular item tonight? I want to know what one thing all the ladies in town have to have."

She smiled, remembering. "Perfume. They loved the perfumes. I must have sold half the stock."

He looked over at her thinking how stunning she looked in the moonlight. "Did you sell any of the aphrodisiac perfume?"

"No I'll never mess with that stuff again."

"Oh, I bet you would, if someone you

cared about needed it."

She was quiet for a moment. "You didn't answer my question, Grady."

"Did Mrs. McKay and her church ladies come?"

"You mean, Mrs. McKay, your mom and aunt, and Mrs. Houston? Yes."

"How did that go?"

"Not well. In fact, after Mrs. McKay and your mom took one look around the Naughty Shop, I was instructed to get rid of all the merchandise in there or else."

He shot her a concerned look. "Or what?"

"Mrs. McKay said she would bring it before the town council on Monday."

"The town council can't tell you what you can and can't sell in your shop. You're not breaking any laws."

"That's what Clara and your aunt said. Mrs. Wallace — your aunt — said something about the town council trying to pass a law or something to force the grocery to stop selling condoms and feminine hygiene products."

Grady chuckled, rubbing his finger across his lips and thinking about kissing Candi for at least a couple of hours after he got her home. "Is that what my aunt called it? Feminine hygiene products?"

"Yes."

Grady laughed again.

"Why? What was she talking about?"

"*Hmm* . . . how can I put this delicately? It was a common, *um,* lubrication product."

"Oh."

"Yeah. Jenny had some fun with it in the paper."

"They mentioned that, too."

"Jenny does have her moments," he said thoughtfully. He might actually miss her after all.

"And you're still not answering my question. The longer you avoid it, the more anxious I get."

He reached over and squeezed her hand. "We're almost home. I just want to curl up on the couch with you in my arms before we talk, okay?"

She nodded, but worry tugged at the corners of her mouth and eyes. "What do you have planned for the grand opening tomorrow?" He turned into the Ferguson drive. Almost there.

"Pretty much the same except everyone gets to draw a number when they come in that will tell them what their discount is. Oh, and there will be some giveaways."

"Are you giving away anything from the Naughty Shop?" She punched him in the shoulder. *"Ow!"*

"Why, did you see something you liked?"

He parked the Jeep beside the house and turned to her. "Yeah, you, in just about anything in there."

"So, you want a fashion show?"

She got out of the car, and when he caught up with her on the porch, he snagged her hand and pulled her close. "If you insist."

He wrapped his arms around her waist and leaned down to kiss her, but she pressed against his chest and pushed back. "Oh, no you don't. Not until you've told me whatever it is that had to wait until we got here."

He released her. "Stubborn," he mumbled.

She turned and put her key in the lock. "Mountain people usually are."

"Oh, yeah. Forgot." She turned on the lamps in the parlor and laid her wrap on the back of the couch. Leaning a hip against the back of the sofa, she crossed her arms and looked at him expectantly.

Grady touched her elbow with his fingertips. "Let's sit." He walked backwards and Candi followed. When they were sitting knee to knee on the loveseat, he found he didn't know where to start. She was perched stiffly on the edge of the couch.

"The beginning is usually a good place to start."

"Reading my mind now?"

She took his hand in both hers. "Please, my insides are all tangled."

"Well, we can't have that." The attempt at lightening the mood failed badly. "I spoke with Jenny Thompson today. She's learned some more things she thought I needed to know."

"Like?"

"She found some men in Vonore who used to frequent the old Gentleman's Club. So, she went up there today to talk to them. Oh, I almost forgot. She said to tell you she was sorry she missed the preview."

"Go on, Grady. What did she find out?"

Candi was leaning toward him, her eyes wide, curious and filled with worry, all mixed in together. "They remembered your mother. Said she did an amazing Marilyn Monroe. She was very talented, and all the men were in love with her."

Candi looked away. "Is that what she went all the way down there to find out? That all the men wanted to see my mother sing and take her clothes off? That's a given, right?"

He squeezed her shoulder. "You have to ease into things when you're conducting an investigation. If you go in with guns blazin' and ask the hardest questions first, folks clam up."

She raised her eyebrows.

Grady chuckled. "And then there's you, who just clams up no matter what the question is."

"Back to Jenny, please."

"She asked them if the entertainment was the only reason they went to the club. Of course, they said they went there for the food and liquor, too. Vonore's in a dry county."

"Again, not surprising they were serving drinks, legal or not."

"Right. Jenny asked them if the people who went there were all locals or if there were out-of-towners."

"Cut to the chase, Grady. What did she find out?"

"The club was a front for a number of illegal activities. It appears they paid the sheriff well to look the other way."

"Your daddy?"

"No. Different county."

"I don't understand. Why did you think this would upset me? Jenny pretty much told me all of this earlier."

"One of the men who used the club as a front was richer and more powerful than all the rest, and it turns out he had a thing for your mother. He wanted her for himself, exclusively. Problem with that was, she fell in love with another guy she met at the club — a local who really did just go there for the entertainment and food. They said he didn't even drink most of the time. He, *um* . . ." Grady cleared his throat, and then added, "He spent most of his money for time alone with Hazel."

"You mean he paid her for sex."

"No, no. That's not what I'm saying. He paid her for private performances."

Candi looked skeptical. "That's one way to put it, I guess."

"Anyway, the crime boss who had the thing for your mom barred this guy from the club. Hazel got angry about it and went to confront him."

"That doesn't sound smart."

"He was behind closed doors when she burst in on him with a deal going down. Several crime lords were sitting around a table discussing business."

Candi laughed. "You make it sound like the mafia or something."

"That would be a good description."

"In the south? That's something that goes on up north, not around here, and certainly not in Vonore, Tennessee!"

"I know it sounds unlikely, which is part of what makes it brilliant, really. These crime lords from the north came down and opened this gentleman's club, recruited poor white men down on their luck to come work for them. They threw more money at these men than they'd ever seen in their lives. They infiltrated the local sheriff's department, recruited men in local government so they could basically do whatever they wanted and get away with it.

"And this man that wanted your mother, he was the leader of all of them."

"And she went to confront him, saw what was going on and got a good look at all his partners to boot."

"Yes. She was smart enough to know that knowledge was power. So, she pretended to care about the guy, thinking that if she got in good with him, she could get him to let her boyfriend come back to the club."

Candi shook her head.

"Right. That was *not* smart — that and the fact that once she knew all their secrets, she was one of them. And you know, they never let you go once you're in."

"But she did get away. She went home to Granddaddy and Aunt Ruby to have me."

This was the hard part. The part he dreaded most. He held her hands tightly. "Lark . . . he didn't have any use for her after she got pregnant."

"I don't understand. He wanted her to

himself, you said that. Why didn't he marry her? Oh — oh, no." She backed away from Grady. "Is he? No, it couldn't be him." Not him. Anyone but him.

"Why would he just let her go if he'd fallen for her, and she knew too much?"

"He already had a wife and kids — up north."

Candi's head felt like it was going to explode. Her father was a mafia kingpin? She couldn't begin to process this. Walking from one end of the tiny room to the other took about three steps, but she did it over and over and over.

"She pined for him. She went home, miserable and pregnant, had me and then wouldn't have anything to do with me. She kept holding out hope he'd come for her." Her laugh sounded strange even to her own ears. "I suppose she got used to the money and lifestyle he gave her. Going back to the cabin must have been a real shock."

Grady stepped in front of her, bringing her up short. "Don't you see? It doesn't add up. He sent her away. *He* sent her away to have you. If her being pregnant was an inconvenience, she could have come back to him and their life after you were born. But she didn't do that. She stayed on the mountain. Why?"

"I don't know. Maybe he closed up the club and went back home."

"The club did close, but it was a couple of years later. One day they were there and open for business, and the next they were gone. I'm sure they moved on to another town. The Feds must have been onto them. An operation like that can't go unnoticed forever."

She shook her head and bit down on her lip. "My father is a criminal?"

"We don't know." When he reached for her this time, she didn't resist. "It seems more plausible to believe that she was in love with this other man and was already pregnant when she hatched her plan to get the club owner to let him back in. It could be that the man your mother loved never knew she was pregnant."

So there was a thin chance her father wasn't a criminal. That, at least, was something. "But the club owner would have come after her, wouldn't he? Because she knew too much."

He sighed. "Yes."

"That's probably why she went home. The cabin's hard to get to without being noticed, and my granddaddy was a crack shot with a rifle."

"That he was."

"Oh, I'm sorry, Grady. That was thoughtless of me."

"It's okay. My daddy was the one that was the better shot — that day."

Candi looked up at Grady. "What about the other man? The one she loved? When she left, why didn't she go to him?"

"The men Jenny spoke with said the guy wasn't from around here, that he went back home when he found out Hazel was with this rich, powerful, corrupt man who owned the club. He probably didn't even know she left, and if she did try and find him, he'd never have known."

"So you think this man — the one who owned the club — murdered her?"

"That's one possibility."

"What do you think?" She could see in his eyes that he had a hunch. Grady was a lawman with good instincts. "Tell me." *Please, tell me anything else, because the thought of my mother being murdered . . .*

"She could have drowned, like the police report my father wrote up says."

"You don't believe that, though," she guessed.

Grady shook his head. "I think it's more likely she went home and told her folks everything. Your granddaddy would have known about the club she was working at and what they were doing there. He probably tried to drag her out of there on more than one occasion."

Candi could just imagine it. Even though she had never gotten to know him, from all that Aunt Ruby had told her, he didn't suffer fools. He'd stood six foot nine and weighed nearly three hundred pounds. Not many people would think to cross Tom Hensley.

"You still haven't told me what you think happened."

"I think Boots probably told my daddy what was going on over at that club and that his daughter had gotten mixed up in it. He may have even asked him to report them to the sheriff there so that the place would be shut down and the owner put in prison."

"That way my mother would be protected."

"Possibly. These organizations are typically far-reaching."

"But that didn't happen."

Grady shook his head. "My dad knew what was going on over at that club. Everyone did. Hell, I'm sure plenty of the men in this town frequented the place, my dad included."

Candi stepped back out of his arms. "If he knew, why didn't he do something?"

"What could he do? He was one man. He couldn't have taken down something like that on his own."

"He could have asked for help."

"Maybe he did and no one believed him."

"Or maybe he *didn't* because he liked going over there and watching women dance naked."

She stomped over to the kitchen table, pulled out a chair, and then put it back and stomped back to the parlor, looking anywhere but at Grady. She tried to tell herself it wasn't his fault, that he wasn't responsible for what his daddy did or didn't do. And she would believe all that — later when she wasn't so upset.

Grady snagged her arm, halting her pacing. "Listen, I'll be the first to admit that my father was no saint. Fact is, I hardly knew him because he was never home. When he was, he —" Grady clamped his mouth shut to stop the words from coming out.

Something awful hid in what Grady wasn't telling her now. "What did he do to you, Grady?" She grasped his arms. "Tell me."

Grady's gaze skidded to the window darkened by the moonless night. "Most days he beat me till I was bloody and bruised. But when that wasn't any fun, he locked me in dark places . . . closets, the jail at night, the storage shed."

"Oh, Grady." Candi wrapped her arms around his waist and pressed her head to his chest. "I'm so sorry."

He put his arms around like her, not because he wanted to hold her, but more because he needed something to do with them. "He said I was a mama's boy, and he was gonna make a man out of me. If I'd had Wallace blood in me, I'd have been a real man."

Candi leaned back and touched his face. "It's no excuse, but he did those things because it made him feel more a man. It must have killed someone like him to be sterile and likely impotent, too."

"How did you know?"

"They go hand in hand." Candi laid her cheek back on his chest and hugged him tightly. "But that doesn't change the fact that it was wrong, what he did. You didn't deserve to be treated that way."

"I know. But still, following in his footsteps has been harder than anyone could ever know. I don't want anyone to think I'm anything like him, but everyone thinks I am." He stroked her hair and the tension in him lessened a bit. "Most days I want to get on my motorcycle and leave Angel Ridge.

Never look back."

"Why don't you?" she asked softly, a little afraid of his answer. She wanted nothing more than to call Angel Ridge home. If he dreamed of leaving it behind . . . what would she do if he left? She couldn't imagine being like her mother: sad and forlorn, heartbroken and unable to function. But still, his leaving would hurt.

Grady shrugged, still stroking her hair. "The time never seemed to be right. You see, I waiver from content to restless. When I'm restless, I get away for awhile, do things outdoors that I enjoy. But I always come back. I never understood why, but now I know."

He kissed her and lifted her off the floor in one motion that had her pulse pounding. Grady broke the contact just long enough to say, "I guess I was waiting for you. Since I've found you, I've realized that home really is where your heart is. At first, I found it with the Fergusons, and now," he kissed her again, long and slow and sweet, "there's you."

"I've always dreamed of a home in Angel Ridge, Grady."

"Well, I guess since you and the Fergusons are here, that's more than enough reason for me to be content to stay."

Chapter 21

The next day, Candi opened the store with high hopes of scores of customers coming in to shop. Throughout the day, a number of tourists had walked through. A few had bought homemade fudge, but most were just window shoppers.

When Grady came to pick her up at six, she'd been so exhausted, she'd gone home, taken a shower and climbed into bed.

On Sunday, Grady dropped her off on his way to church, promising to bring her lunch at noon. His attempts at talking her into coming with him had met with firm resistance. She'd never worshiped in a church, and she didn't mean to start now, even though, she had to admit she had enjoyed the talk she'd had with Reverend Reynolds. She'd thought about him several times since the break-in. Maybe she'd stop by and see him tomorrow to offer him a gift and thank him for taking her in for awhile that day.

She busied herself cleaning and tidying racks, shelves, and displays. As promised, Grady had brought her lunch shortly after noon, and they'd shared it picnic-style in town square. She sent him off to fish with Doc Prescott, insisting he needed a break from the investigation so he could come back with fresh eyes and ideas. He'd been working such long hours that a heavy tension had settled over him. A few hours fly fishing at the river would do him some good.

As she turned the sign over on the front door that said "Open" in bright cheerful letters, she thought of Miss Estelee. She had missed her since she'd been gone. Miss Estelee had a touch of the gift she and all the Hensley women had. She had likely known that Candi would be in good hands with Grady and the Fergusons looking after her, or she never would have left town so suddenly.

The bell on the front door rang, and Candi turned to see Reverend Reynolds coming in. "Afternoon, Miss Heart."

"Reverend Reynolds, I was just thinking about you and here you are."

"You were?"

"Yes. I had decided that I was going to call on you at the church tomorrow, but you've saved me the trouble."

"Miss Heart —"

"Please, call me Candi."

"Candi, as I said before, you can visit or contact me at the church anytime you like. I'd enjoy that very much."

"Thank you." A genuine kindness radiated in his warm, blue eyes. She was drawn to him in a natural, familiar way, like she'd known him her whole life despite the fact that they'd just met a few days earlier. "Feel free to browse. I'll just be a minute."

Candi walked back to the Nice Shop, going directly to the display case. Opening the back, she reached in and pulled out a long, slim case that contained a wide velvet navy ribbon with an intricately designed Celtic cross. Closing the case, she carried it out front to give it to the reverend, but she found he wasn't there.

"Reverend Reynolds?"

"In here."

Candi walked back into the hallway. He was looking through her Naughty Shop. Interesting. Maybe he was looking for something for his wife. "Can I help you find something?"

"Oh, no dear. I just wanted to see for myself what all the fuss is about."

"Fuss?"

"Yes. Several ladies of the church were

here the other night and came away with a, shall we say, negative impression?"

"Actually, two ladies were offended by the items sold in this shop."

"Yes, well, as I'm sure you know, bad news travels faster than good, and they picked up support along the way."

Candi bit her lip. No wonder she hadn't had very many customers all weekend. It's hard telling what the women who hadn't come in had been told about what she was selling in here.

Reverend Reynolds patted her hand. "I wouldn't worry about it, dear. These little wildfires have a tendency to spread quickly, but they also burn out just as fast."

Candi grinned because he was grinning at her. "And the grass that comes in after the fire is rich and green."

"Indeed. There were plenty of ladies who enjoyed the shop very much. They'll tell their friends, and that will give you a good customer base. You know, you should advertise in the Maryville and Vonore papers."

That was actually a very good idea. Maryville and Vonore weren't that far away. "I think I will." She held out the box to him. "I want you to have this, sir, as a token of thanks for you taking me into your church and speaking with me at time when I was . . . very upset and troubled. Your wise council helped get me through that terrible day, and I thank you."

He seemed genuinely touched by her words and the gesture. "Well," he cleared his throat, "this is very kind of you, Candi."

"I hope you like it."

"Oh, I'm sure I will." He lifted the lid. "Oh, my." He grasped the silver bar at one end of the ribbon and admired the large silver cross at the other end. "What a beautiful bookmark."

"I thought you could use it in your Bible."

He laid the bookmark carefully back into its case, tracing the cross with reverent fingertips. "I'll treasure this. Thank you."

He held out his hand to her. Candi stared at it, then back up into his kind eyes, surprised to find that a fine mist clouded them. She put her hand in his and squeezed. "Reverend Reynolds?"

"Forgive me. It's just that, you remind me of someone I knew a long time ago." He shook his head. "You must think me an old, sentimental fool."

"No, of course not, and you're not at all old."

He chuckled. "Well, thank you for that."

He tucked her gift into an inner pocket of his blazer. When he patted it and winked at her, Candi felt like a little girl. Why couldn't someone like Reverend Reynolds be her father?

He took her arm and walked with her out of the Naughty Shop. "Would you like a cup of tea, Reverend?"

"I'd like that very much, if you'll keep me company."

"Well, since I don't have customers beating down my door, you might just be able to persuade me."

"Excellent. So tell me, did you always want to be a shop owner?"

Before she could answer, a loud explosion shook the building, rattling the windows and unsettling the china cups and saucers she had sitting on the back counter. Reverend Reynolds instinctively put a protective arm around Candi, and they both ducked, covering their heads as plaster showered them.

"What in the world?" the Reverend exclaimed.

Candi turned toward the front of the shop, and the next thing she knew, she was running and didn't stop until she was outside on the sidewalk. Her first thought was to check the courthouse to be sure that it was still there. When she saw it was fine, she turned her gaze to the row of shops across the street. People were running in all directions, some laying on the grass, injured, others coming to offer aid.

"Dear God," Reverend Reynolds breathed.

"Someone get the Doc!" a man yelled as he cradled a woman's head in his lap. Blood trickled from her forehead down her cheek.

"Doc Prescott is fishing with Grady," Candi said numbly.

Candi was glad that the Reverend grasped her arm firmly. Otherwise, she wasn't sure she would have been able to keep upright. She pointed to the gaping hole across the street between the bank and the grocery.

"The paper," he said.

"Jenny," Candi breathed. "You don't think —"

Candi covered her mouth, unable to say the words. Reverend Reynolds was praying, whispering fervently to God about safety and protection for Jenny Thompson. She hoped that prayer wasn't going up too late, but her gut told her otherwise.

She left the reverend to pray. People were injured and needed tendin' till Doc and Grady could be reached. She ran back into the shop, grabbed two large shopping bags and filled them with as many towels as she could get her hands on, went to the storeroom and took down a big tin of natural disinfecting ointment, opened the refrigerator and threw in all the water bottles she could get to, and ran back outside.

She went to the man holding the head of the bleeding and unconscious woman first. "Are you a nurse?" he asked.

"Of sorts." She uncapped a bottle of water and poured some on a towel. She pressed it against the woman's head. The lady moaned. "She's coming around. That's good. Is she your wife?"

The man nodded, his face ashen.

"What's her name?"

"Gina."

Candi lifted the towel and looked at the cut. It was free of debris, and she was going to need stitches, but she'd be fine. She pressed the towel back on the cut. The woman moaned. "What happened?"

"You fell and cut your head," Candi said. "Can you open your eyes, Gina?" Candi checked her for signs of a head injury, but she seemed okay.

"Is she going to be all right?" the man asked.

"She'll need to see Doc when he gets here, but she looks well enough. Hold that towel on her head to stop the bleeding. She'll likely need some stitches."

"And who might you be?"

Candi looked up into the face of a large, very large woman, standing over her, blocking out the sun. She stood and faced the angry Amazon. "I'm Candi. I own the new shop across the way. I know a little about tendin' injuries and thought I'd help till Doc gets here. Who are you, ma'am?"

"I'm Nurse Mable Calloway. I work for Doc Prescott."

"Good. Then you take over, and I'll help." The woman's scowl deepened. "*Um,* if you'd like me to, that is."

"What's in that bag?"

Candi told her. The nurse looked her up and down, then said, "Come with me."

They saw to as many of the injured as they could, quickly assessing them and writing down their names and injuries on a pad of paper. The volunteer firemen arrived along with several ambulances and the rescue squad. She watched as they sprayed down the rubble while others rummaged through it, looking for injured.

She had to look away, praying that no one had been inside. Grady pulled up then, lights flashing and siren blaring. He flung open his door and ran into the chaos, searching the faces of people lining the sidewalks and the injured lying mostly on the grass. She stood and ran to him. Candi jumped into his arms and he squeezed the breath out of her. "Thank God you're all right."

"I'm fine. Go. These people need you."

He set her on the ground and ran over to what was left of the newspaper office. He spoke briefly to the fire chief, clearly not liking what he heard. He pulled out his cell phone and made a call. Doc Prescott joined them, asking his nurse to point out the most seriously injured. She read off the names and injuries, pointing each one out as she did. Candi stood back and let them work. Dixie came over to her then and put an arm around her shoulders. "You okay?"

Candi nodded. "You?"

"My ears are ringing, but I guess that'll stop before long."

"Sweet oil should help them."

"Right."

Enough of the niceties. "Was Jenny . . ."

"I don't know. She wasn't at church this mornin'. I talked to her last night. She was busy working on that investigative piece she'd started after the break-in at your place."

"I wonder if anyone has called her family."

"She didn't have any in town. She has

some people in Knoxville, but I think her parents go south for the winter."

Candi turned to her new friend and said all in a rush, "I can't stand it, Dixie. What if she was in there? What if she got too close to finding something out and they — what if they killed her to keep her quiet?"

Dixie hugged her close, uncharacteristically not saying anything, and Dixie always had something to say.

Maryville PD's bomb squad showed up next. Everyone stood around watching the scene play out like a disaster movie. Grady joined them, his mouth set in a grim line.

"Well don't just stand there." Dixie said. "Tell us what you know and don't leave anything out."

"Jenny called me about thirty minutes ago to tell me she had broken her story wide open. She wanted me to come by, but said it could wait till I fished awhile." He paused, putting his arms around both women. "She was in her office, working on the story."

Dixie pressed her fingers tight against her mouth while tears spilled down her cheeks. Candi reached across Grady to squeeze her forearm. Grady held them both closer. When his cell phone rang, he stepped back to take the call, and Candi and Dixie held each other.

"Wallace . . . who is this . . . what . . . you son of a . . . bring those cowardly threats here and face me like a man . . . hello? Damn it!"

Candi and Dixie both turned to face Grady. "What was that?" Dixie asked.

"The people that blew up the newspaper warning me to not go sticking my nose where she had, or I'd wind up like her."

CHAPTER 22

Two days later, they still hadn't found Jenny or the people responsible for the bombing and the threatening call made to Grady. It was good that they hadn't recovered her body from the rubble, but unsettling to think that someone you saw everyday, who had been such a prominent member of the small community, could just vanish. Rumors swirled that she'd been kidnapped or worse.

Candi had hardly seen Grady. He was so busy, trying to find the people responsible that he only came home to eat and sleep. At his insistence, she hadn't gone into the shop. Business in town had pretty much ground to a halt. The only folks milling about were investigators, workers, and the curious wanting to see *Devastation in a Small Town* as the Knoxville paper had called it.

She and Grady both knew it was the crime ring from the old gentleman's club. The nagging, unanswered question remained.

Why had they come back in the first place? How had they gotten her granddaddy's truck? And why had they trashed her shop and tried to kill her and Grady?

She didn't have any answers, but she knew how to find them. She needed to go back to the mountain, to Aunt Ruby's cabin, to be close to nature, her grandmother's and mother's graves, to meditate and discern the truth.

She packed a backpack with a few clothes and supplies, and got on her bicycle heading for Uncle Billy and Aunt Verdi. Uncle Billy was sitting on the front porch steps whittling when she arrived, his old coon dog laid out asleep in the yard.

"Uncle Billy!" she smiled and waved. The old man looked up, spit a line of tobacco juice into the grass, and stood. Aunt Verdi came out onto the porch and waved as she approached. Candi hopped off the bike and parked it next to the steps.

"What are you doin' here, girl?" Uncle Billy asked.

"Nice to see you, too, Uncle Billy." Candi pressed a kiss to his weathered cheek. The old man in worn overalls and a faded cotton shirt grunted and settled back on the steps. "Hey, Aunt Verdi."

Her aunt pulled her sweater closer. "Hey,

yourself. What brings you out on a cold, dreary day like today?"

"I was hopin' Uncle Billy could take me across the lake to the mountain."

"Told you no good'd come of you livin' in Angel Ridge," he muttered. "Guess you're goin' home now."

"No. I just need a few days on the mountain to figure some things out."

"Well, of course he'll take you, won't you Billy? Now go make sure there's gas in the tank." Uncle Billy looked up at her like she'd lost her mind. "Go on now. Lark needs to go home, and it'll be gettin' dark soon."

Uncle Billy stood and looked at both of them, then turned to walk down to the river shaking his head. She wondered how Aunt Verdi stood living with a mountain man? She guessed they'd made their peace. They'd been married forty-some odd years.

"You have everything you need there? I made some biscuits and just brought down homemade preserves from the pantry. Let me put some in a bag for you."

Candi waited in the solemn quiet outside while her aunt got the food. Her gaze fell on the tire swing she'd swayed on many a starlit night when she was living here. She wondered if her mother had liked it, too.

Probably so. The thought made her feel happy.

"Here you go."

Candi took the bag and said, "Thank you."

"How long you think you'll be gone?"

"A day or two at most."

Aunt Verdi nodded. "I'll see that your Uncle Billy checks on you day after tomorrow. If you need to come back sooner, just make your way over to the cove up the road here. You can cross it safely if you keep to the left as you go."

Candi nodded, remembering the day Grady had carried her safely across. She'd left him a note explaining that she needed to be gone a few days. As busy as he'd been, he'd probably not even miss her.

"Well, come on then," Uncle Billy hollered. "We're burnin' daylight!"

The two women smiled at each other. "See you soon," Candi said and walked down the lawn to the dock where Uncle kept his motorboat.

Later that night, the clouds had cleared, and she lay under the stars trying to count them all, like she did when she was a little girl. Now, as an adult, she knew it was a way to free her mind of thoughts that kept the truth away.

Lead me to the truth became her silent mantra. She said it in her head over and over as she counted. When the truth hadn't come and frost began to fall, she draped her blanket around her and went inside Aunt Ruby's cabin. Filling the stove, she lit a match and held it to the tinder. Soon, flames were licking at the cured wood, filling the room with its scent and warmth.

She sat on the floor and, leaving the door to the stove open, stared at the flames. *Lead me to the truth . . .*

After a time, she put more logs in and closed the door. She curled up on the floor, exhausted, and slept.

She wanders along the riverbank, weaving in and out of the trees. Blonde hair, flowing white dress, creamy pale skin.

My heart, oh my heart . . . why don't you come to me? Where did you go? I linger only because I pray that you'll come. Our love will protect us, all of us.

She's a pretty little pink thing, our baby girl. She's got green eyes like my mama. When I look at her, I only see you, and that hurts too much. Remembering you and the strong love we shared makes my heart break over and over and over again.

I wish you were here, but I guess it's time to stop wishin'. My dreams and wishes have a way of amountin' to nothin' but heartache. So, I'll put them in a box now, and bury it deep in the heart of the mountain. I'll leave a sign for her, and maybe one day, if she has the gift, she'll find it . . .

Maybe she'll find it . . .

My love? Is that you? Have you finally come?

She walks out onto an old dock, the planks creak, the dock shifts, but still, she puts one foot in front of the other.

My love! It is you. You've come for me at last.

A horrible crack. The water rises up to meet her. She disappears below its surface, leaving nothing behind. No sound. Not even a ripple in the water.

Candi sat up on an indrawn breath, wide awake in the pre-dawn gray. The fire had died down and chill morning seeped into the cabin and her bones.

Reaching for her pack, Candi put on another pair of socks and sweater. She quickly ate one of Aunt Verdi's biscuits, not bothering with the jam. Hopping on one foot, she pulled on hiking boots and walked out into the freezing mountain air.

She made her way straight up to the little cemetery on the knoll above the cabin. At the foot of her mother's grave, she said, "Lead me to your truth, Mama."

Her mother's words came to her from the dream: *I'll put them in a box now, and bury it deep in the heart of the mountain. I'll leave a sign for her, and maybe one day, if she has the gift, she'll find it . . .*

A sign. She looked around, turning in a wide circle. She stopped when she saw the old storage shed where Aunt Ruby said Granddaddy had kept his sundries. Ball jars, hoes, shovels, pick axes, tools.

Candi jogged down to it and pulled the door open. Spider webs filled the corners and rafters. She cut through one at the door with her hand and went inside. She moved an old broken chair aside, pushing through the items lining the dirt floor. An old trunk in the corner caught her eye. Candi made a path to it, took several items off its top and opened it.

There were old musty quilts inside, ribbons, hats and gloves, nightgowns and a creamy satin dress. Candi frowned. Was this a hope chest? Could this have been Aunt

Ruby's wedding dress?

She dug a little deeper and found an old doll and an envelope, yellow and brittle with age. She turned it over. Written on the front in neat script was the name *Lark.*

Candi sat back on her heels. She knew in her heart, as she opened the envelope, that she held the truth in her hand.

Fall, 1984

My Little Lark:

If you're reading this letter, I know that you've come in search of truth. Your truth. I asked Aunt Ruby to not tell you anything, because I knew when the time was right, you'd come for this. I'm sorry I didn't get to watch you grow up. I know you must be beautiful and smart. All the things I wasn't. I was fair enough to look at, but I'm ashamed to say I misused that gift. In fact, it caused me nothing but trouble.

You see, I left the mountain for a time. I found love, and I found evil such as I hope that you'll never encounter. It says in books that love conquers all, but I can tell you that there's evil in this world so bad that not even love can penetrate that darkness.

I want you to know that your daddy's name was Robert Lee Reynolds. I called him Rob, and he called me his angel. The evil separated us. When the time came for me to tell him about you, he was already gone.

I wanted to find him at first, but then discerned it would be best if I didn't, lest the evil take him, too. Don't be sad for me, Little Lark. I made sure you'll be protected and provided for. There's a metal box buried under Aunt Ruby's pecan tree where that heavy branch hangs so low. The money in it is what I made working at a club in Vonore. I earned it honest.

Take it and use it as you see fit. The other items I got by not so honorable means, but I figured I had it comin' to me after the hell they put me through. So don't hold back from usin' it. You deserve all this and more. I pray that you find happiness and real, true and abiding love in your life. Please know that I loved you and your daddy with all my heart and soul.

Your own Mama, Hazel Hensley

Candi pressed the letter to her heart. Her mama had loved her, and now she knew her daddy's name. Reynolds . . . the reverend. He was her father. She didn't know his first name, but she knew in her heart, this was her truth.

After a moment, she stood, grabbed a shovel, and walked to the hanging branch of the pecan tree, ducked under it and started digging. About two feet down, she hit metal. Dropping to her knees, she found the edges and used the shovel to wedge the box out.

She stood again, and taking the shovel, hit at the lock. When the latch popped free, she opened it. Good Lord Almighty . . . she'd never seen so much money in one place! Not even in Aunt Ruby's strong box. There were necklaces and earrings and bracelets, all sparkling with jewels that looked real enough. There was a velvet pouch tucked in the corner. Candi picked it up and opened the top of it. Something inside sparkled in the sunlight, glittering like . . . diamonds!

She upended the pouch into the box. There were hundreds, all shapes and sizes. This had to be worth a fortune. How could her mama have gotten this?

Lead me to the truth, Mama.

This must have been what the people who broke into her shop were looking for. She knew it as sure as she knew this mountain. They were looking for them in her granddaddy's truck, too. But how did they know that she was Hazel Hensley's daughter, and how did they know Hazel had them?

"Lark! Are you here?"

Candi's heart nearly leapt out of her chest. Who in the world?

"Lark!"

"Grady?"

"Where are you?"

She scanned the clearing, but didn't see him. "I'm over here, by the big tree sittin' back a ways from the cabin."

Then she saw him. He walked around the cabin, looking in all directions trying to find her. She'd never been so glad to see anyone in her life.

"Up here," she said.

As soon as he saw her, he ran to her. She wanted to run to meet him, too, but thunderheads were gathering on his brow. He pulled her to him roughly. "You scared me to death, do you know that? I thought they'd gotten to you like they did Jenny." He held her at arm's length and looked at her. "Are you all right?"

She touched his forearms. "I'm fine. I left you a note. Didn't you get it?"

"No. I went to the house, found the door standing wide open, and you gone. I went to your aunt and uncle's and forced them on threat of arrest to tell me where you were."

"I locked that door. I'm sure."

"The lock had been jimmied."

Lead me to the truth, Mama. "Someone else may have gotten the note I left you. Someone that shouldn't have it. What if it was them?"

"What did it say?"

"Just that I was going away for a few days, and that I didn't want you to worry."

"You left me?"

She touched his face. "No. I just needed to get away to think. I was coming back."

His shoulders relaxed a little. "The note didn't say where you were going?"

"No, but they could have followed you." She closed the metal box and tucked it under her arm. "Come on. I know where we can hide. If they followed you, we shouldn't have to wait long."

She walked up the big hill behind the cabin to the root cellar that granddaddy had dug out in the side of it. She pulled brush out from in front of it and tried to open the old wood plank door. It stuck against the dirt and grass that had built up in front of it. "Give me a hand here," she said to Grady.

"What is this?" he said instead.

"A root cellar. They won't think to look all the way up here for us. They'll go through the cabin and the shed, then wander off and look somewhere else."

"I can't go in there."

Candi tugged at the door again and wedged it open enough for them to slip in. "Of course you can."

"No. Listen. I *can't* go in there."

Candi looked closely at him. His skin was clammy, eyes wide, pupils dilated. Fear made his features look strained and tense. Then she remembered. He'd told her his father used to lock him up in dark places. How could she have forgotten?

"Don't policemen usually carry flash-lights?"

Grady nodded, and pulled one off his gun belt. Candi took it and clicked it on. "There, we have a light. It won't be so bad with me in there with you."

"Why can't we just hide in the trees?"

"Because, they might come up on us in the trees, and then we'd have nowhere to go." Candi heard movement below, near the cabin. "Listen . . . what was that?"

A voice carried up the mountain. "Little girl . . . come out. Come out . . . Daddy's home."

CHAPTER 23

Candi grabbed Grady's hand and pulled him into the hole cut out in the side of the mountain. The threat of intruders would normally have rocketed him into action, but instead, fear for Candi's safety gripped his chest tight and made it impossible to breathe.

"Pull the door closed," Candi instructed.

He willed his muscles to work, doing as she asked. The ceiling was low and earthen, but the walls were lined with river rock. The room was surprisingly large as she pulled him to the back. She sat and urged him down beside her. Candi held the flashlight so that only a small circle around them was illuminated.

"You're all right. Take some deep breaths," she said.

He breathed in the dank, musty air through his mouth, in short, quick breaths.

Touching his stomach, she calmly said,

"No. You'll hyperventilate if you do that. Breathe in through your nose and slowly out through your mouth." She squeezed his hand. "Close your eyes if it helps."

He did as she said, but instead of closing his eyes, he focused on her beautiful, unharmed, perfect face. With each breath, he felt calmer. More in control. Down below, they could hear windows breaking and things being thrown around. He read the fear on her face. Wrapping an arm around her, he said, "I'm sorry."

She nodded and swiped at the tears. "It's just things."

He reached in his pocket for the ever-present handkerchief and handed it to her. She crushed it in her hand instead of using it, her eyes trained on the door to the cellar.

"Are you all right?" she asked, looking back at him.

The longer he looked at her, the calmer and more focused he became. He removed the gun from his holster and clicked the safety off. If they came through that door, they wouldn't leave alive.

Grady looked around where they sat. There were jugs and jars with clear liquid in them stacked everywhere. "Is that moonshine?" he asked.

Candi looked around then, as if she hadn't

noticed before. Shrugging, she said, "I guess. I don't really know."

"You never came up here?"

"Not much. Aunt Ruby and I used the springhouse to store things."

The racket below quieted. They both listened for any sign of movement outside. After a good stretch of time passed with them hearing nothing, Candi said, "Do you think they left?"

"There's no way to know."

"I guess we should wait till dark before we try to leave."

"Probably," he agreed, though the thought of it made his stomach churn. He eyed the jugs and jars longingly. He could really use a drink, but he shouldn't be impaired in any way. He laughed at that thought — like fear wasn't impairing!

"What's so funny?"

"I was just thinking I could use a drink."

"Help yourself."

"I could just see the headline now. *Sheriff Found Dead in Cellar Filled with Moonshine.* And then of course, the story would list my blood alcohol levels as off the chart."

"We don't have a newspaper anymore," Candi reminded softly.

He tightened the arm around her shoulders.

"Have they found Jenny yet?"

Grady closed his eyes and bit his lip against the urge to tell her everything. Jenny was fine. She'd followed a lead to a man in Vonore who, in return for her keeping the source confidential, gave up the structure of the crime ring that had operated out of the club where Candi's mother worked. It was still active in the area, with arms throughout the southeast, but their leader lived in Florida now instead of East Tennessee. The man gave Jenny names of everyone he knew that was involved, and the list was extensive.

When Jenny called Grady on Sunday afternoon, she told him everything and also that she'd contacted the Tennessee Bureau of Investigation who had been trying to crack the ring for years. He was already on his way back to town to meet with Jenny and the TBI agents, what they hadn't counted on was someone finding out what she'd done and setting off a bomb to try and kill her. Luckily, she'd just stepped out to pick up some lunch, but the explosion kept her from getting to the diner.

After the explosion, Jenny realized it would be too dangerous to stay in town. So, she went to his office and hid out in the jail until he could get in contact with the TBI, who went over and picked her up. She was now in protective custody, with the U.S. Marshall Service keeping her safe. The explosion was a perfect cover to put her into witness protection. A report was being drawn up now declaring her dead. The federal agents would make a statement after as many arrests as possible were made, but with a crime syndicate this large, it would be impossible to get everyone behind bars.

So, Grady could never tell anyone the truth without endangering their lives. The TBI traced the call on his cell phone and made their first arrests as quietly as possible — the same day that the head of the crime ring was also arrested. The story had made national news, but of course, no one knew that the ring had connections in Angel Ridge, and Grady intended to keep it that way, while seeing to it that everyone within a two hundred mile radius of Angel Ridge went away for a very, very long time. He'd stay behind the scenes, with the TBI and the FBI making the arrests, so no one would know he had ever been involved.

"Hey, where did you go?" Candi said.

"Sorry."

"I asked if they'd found Jenny yet?"

"I'm afraid not."

"Her body wasn't recovered, though. She wasn't in her office?"

"They're still sifting through the rubble."

"Do you think she found something awful? Something so bad that they wanted her dead?"

Sighing, he shook his head. "I wish I could give you the answers you need, but I can't."

Candi looked at him closely then, tilting her head to the side in the dim lighting. "I understand."

He nodded, sure that she did, but knowing she'd leave it at that. Just one more reason to love and cherish this woman forever. She was gonna frustrate the hell out of him, but his life would never be boring again!

She shined the flashlight in all directions, stopping at a point on the back wall they were leaning against. "Well, what do you know?"

Grady followed the beam of light. "Looks like a door."

Candi smiled. "It is." She grabbed her mama's metal box and scooted over to it. Unlatching it, she pulled the door open. "It's a tunnel."

Grady joined her looking into the long, earthen passage. "Where do you think it goes?"

"It's only a guess, but I'd bet it goes up into the woods. Come on."

She hunched down and squat-walked about twenty feet away from him. When he didn't follow, she shined the flashlight into his face. "You coming?"

"People can get lost for days in these woods."

She rolled her eyes. "Please. I know these woods like you know the lake and its coves. I grew up here, remember? And I didn't have much else to do with my time besides explore."

His sigh was heartfelt. Hanging his head, he said, "What part of 'I don't do close, tight spaces' don't you get?"

She came back to him and held out her hand. "Just like you got me across the cove safe, I'll get you through this tunnel safe." She squeezed his hand. "Don't you know yet that we can get through anything as long as we're together?"

He put his hand in hers and immediately felt stronger when he was touching her. "You don't think less of me because I have trouble doing this?" He hated showing this particular vulnerability. He was supposed to be tough, unafraid. That's what men were. They didn't get all freaked out about stuff like this.

"I'd worry more if you didn't have any shortcomings. I'm way too imperfect to be with someone who has no flaws at all."

"No worries there. I'm plenty flawed." He holstered his gun and ducked into the tunnel, breathing the way she'd showed him earlier. After he'd pulled the door shut behind him, he said, "So, does all that add up to we're together? Like a couple?"

She looked over her shoulder at him. "Oh, I don't know about that."

He would have pulled her up short and settled the matter then and there, but he just wanted to get out of this place and take a long, deep breath of fresh air in a wide open space. A few minutes later, the tunnel widened and ended. Candi shined the light in all directions, settling on a spot above their heads. "There's the trap door."

Grady got his gun and pulled her behind him. "Let me make sure there's no one around."

Candi didn't resist or complain. He pushed on the door, but it didn't budge. He took the flashlight and tried to get an idea of how the thing worked. There were no hinges. It was just sitting in the opening.

Grady handed Candi the flashlight, and putting his shoulder against the wooden planks, pushed. The heavy door budged a little, so he bent his legs, and pushed again. It wedged open a crack, far enough for him to look in two directions. He put a finger against his lips. When he didn't see or hear anything, he pushed against the door again. This time it came free, and he lifted it to the side. Gun ready, he looked all around. Nothing but the dark green peace of the woods.

Grady hauled himself up, then offered Candi a hand up. She set her metal box at his feet, then took his hand so he could pull her out. He took in that long, cool breath of cleansing air he'd been fantasizing about.

Candi tucked the box under her arm and looked around. "Oh, I know where this is. We're not far from that cove near Uncle Billy and Aunt Verdi's place." She glanced over at him. "You ready?"

"Almost."

He hauled her up against his chest to give her a long, hard, hot kiss, but her box jabbed him in the ribs before he could fully execute it. "*Ow!* What is in that thing you can't seem to let go of."

Candi smiled, resting a hand against the rusty top. "My mama and my daddy."

Grady frowned. "You saying their ashes are in there or somethin'?"

She laughed, and twisting to the side with the box safely away from him, looped her arm around his neck and pulled him down for that kiss. Candi being the instigator ruined the effect he was going for, but he wasn't complaining.

When they broke for air, he kept her close, his hand at her neck and under her chin so he could look into her eyes when he spoke. "Just so there's no confusion, I love you Lark Hensley. You are *my* woman and no one else's. *That* makes us a couple. That and the fact that you love me, too. You said so yourself the other day."

She frowned up at him. "Now look here, Grady Wallace. I won't be manhandled." She twisted her head out of his hand, but pinned him with the full intensity of those gorgeous green eyes. "And when a lady tells a man she loves him, he doesn't wait nearly a week to return the sentiment unless it takes him that long to figure out his feelings. And if it took you that long to decide, I'm not sure if I want to be your 'woman' as you so elegantly put it."

"Stubborn as the day is long," he said, shaking his head. "I tell you I love you, and you get all prickly."

"I've got every right to be prickly. I thought you didn't feel the same way."

"Well, hell Lark. Anybody with eyes could see that I've not been about to look at or think about anyone else but you since we met."

"So you didn't tell you me you loved me because it took me so long to warm up to you in the beginning?"

His lips were soft and gentle against hers. "No. I didn't tell you because I'm an idiot. You have me twisted around so many different ways, I don't know which way is up." He kissed her again. "Forgive me?"

She held her box between them, taking a step back. "Maybe in a couple of years."

"What?"

"And during that time, I expect to be courted proper."

She took another step back, then turned and headed down the mountain, deftly walking around trees, and sweeping the underbrush out of the way as she went. Grady followed, smiling. "Yes, ma'am. I just have one question."

"What's that?"

"Are you going to tell me what's in that box?"

She shot him a saucy look that promised whatever happened between them would be the most exciting adventure of his life.

"Maybe."

DIXIE'S FAREWELL

Well don't that just make you smile? I do so enjoy a good love story.

Grady and Candi — Lark — theirs is a legendary love story in these parts. When they got back to town, she did share with him what was in her metal box. They turned the diamonds over to the authorities. They were from a jewelry store robbery twenty-some years back. The store was so thankful to at last have those diamonds returned, they let Candi pick out one to have set in a ring — an engagement ring.

Grady would have put it on her finger then and there and took her to the courthouse to have the judge hitch 'em, but Candi insisted, as she put it, that he 'court her proper.' And he did. Grady's mother was none too happy about it in the beginning, but the prospect of eventually having grandchildren close by to spoil, softened her to Candi over time.

She stayed in the old home place on my family's property, with Grady just across the creek in his.

Candi showed her daddy, Reverend Reynolds, the letter her mother had written her. You never seen a happier man in your life. He'd told her he'd been heartbroken when he came back from seminary to Angel Ridge and learned that Hazel had died. You see, he decided that if he couldn't have her, he'd become a preacher and give his life over to church work. He never had any idea that she'd loved him like she did and longed for him to come back to her. That made his heart break all over again, but finding Candi and getting to know her helped him heal. Candi did change her name legal, to Candi Lark Hensley-Reynolds.

His congregation had been shocked at the revelation, to say the least; but after all, a person couldn't be held accountable for the sins they committed before they came to know the Lord, even though Mrs. McKay did her best to see that he would. In the end, she was outnumbered and outvoted!

The Reverend and Candi took a long trip that Christmas so she could meet and get to know his family, her family, in Virginia. It's a trip they look forward to every year, which is good for me because Grady has always been my date to the church's annual Snow Ball. Some day Grady'll go with them to Virginia, but for now, they need that time to themselves to catch up on all they missed.

My friend Jenny's body was finally recovered from the rubble of *The Angel Ridge Chronicle.* I can't for the life of me figure why it took so long with half the law enforcement of East Tennessee looking. Her funeral was a sad occasion. Candi plans to lay a wreath at her grave every year in thanks that she helped her learn the truth about her mother. Knowing that truth had given her, at long last, a father to love and had freed up her heart enough to trust and let others in.

Now she has everything her heart ever wanted: a town to call home, a father to love and care for her, friends, a man to share her life with, and a shop full of color and all the pretty, girly things she'd lacked growing up on the mountain. Oh, and in case you were wondering, Mrs. McKay got outvoted on closing down Heart's Desire, too. That made *twice* in one month, if you're keeping count.

In the big bay window at the front of her store, Candi is known for her *Naughty and Nice* displays. Gives Mrs. McKay a fit every time she walks out the front door of her bank. Yep, that Candi fits in just fine around here.

Oh, and Miss Estelee did come home, after all the dust had settled, full of vim and vigor. She came clean about not being Candi's blood kin, but continued to claim her as a grandniece anyway. She never did say where she'd gone. Talk about a woman of mystery!

Well, it's time for me to go. I got the dinner rush to get ready for. I sure do hope you enjoyed your time with us in Angel Ridge. Come on back and visit anytime. You hear?

Dixie

DIXIE'S RECIPES

CHICKEN SALAD SANDWICHES

Ingredients:

- 8 to 12 ounces chopped cooked chicken
- 3 tablespoons finely chopped red onion
- 2 to 3 tablespoons finely chopped celery
- 1 large egg, hard boiled, chopped
- 1 tablespoon dill pickle relish
- 1/3 to 1/2 cup mayonnaise, or as needed
- 1/4 teaspoon salt, or to taste
- 1/8 teaspoon freshly ground black pepper

Preparation:

In a bowl, combine the chicken, onion, celery, and egg; toss to blend. Add the relish, 1/3 cup of mayonnaise, salt, and pepper, blend well. Add more mayonnaise, if desired. Serve on two slices of fresh, toasted white bread.

Serves 4.

Coconut Cake

Ingredients:

- 3 cups sifted cake flour (sift before measuring)
- 2 teaspoons baking powder
- 1/4 teaspoon salt
- 1 cup butter, room temperature
- 1 pound powdered sugar
- 4 egg yolks, well beaten
- 1 cup milk (can substitute coconut milk)
- 1 teaspoon vanilla
- 1 cup shredded coconut
- 4 egg whites, well beaten

Frosting:

- 1 cup sugar
- 1/2 cup light corn syrup
- 3 tablespoons water
- 3 egg whites
- 1/4 teaspoon cream of tartar
- 1/4 teaspoon salt
- 1 1/2 teaspoons vanilla
- 1 cup grated coconut

Preparation:

Cake:

Measure the sifted cake flour into a bowl. Add baking powder and salt. Sift these ingredients 3 times. In a mixing bowl, cream butter thoroughly; add sugar gradually. Continue creaming until light and fluffy. Add the beaten egg yolks and beat well. Add flour mixture alternately with the milk, beating well after each addition. Stir in coconut and vanilla. Fold in egg whites gently. Bake in greased 8-inch pans at 350° for about 30 minutes, or until a wooden pick or cake tester inserted in center comes out clean. Makes three 8-inch layers or a whole slew of cupcakes.

Frosting:

Combine sugar, corn syrup, water, egg whites, cream of tartar and salt in top of double boiler. Cook over rapidly boiling water, beating with electric hand-held mixer until mixture stands in peaks. Remove from heat; add vanilla. Continue beating until frosting is firm enough to hold when spread on cake. Frost cake sprinkle immediately with grated coconut, pressing coconut onto sides of cake with hands.

ICED LEMON COOKIES

Cookies:

- 2 c. sugar
- 2 eggs
- 1/2 c. lemon juice
- 1 tsp. baking soda

- 4 1/2 c. sifted flour
- 1 c. shortening
- 1 c. buttermilk
- 1 lemon rind, grated
- 2 tsp. baking powder

Icing:

- 1 box powdered sugar (1 lb.)
- 2 tbsp. evaporated milk
- 1/4 tsp. lemon extract
- 2 tbsp. melted butter
- Rind and juice of 1 lemon
- Drops of boiling water to thin

Cream sugar and shortening. Add eggs and beat until fluffy. Add lemon juice and grated rind. Sift flour, soda and baking powder together. Add to above mixture alternating with buttermilk. Drop on greased cookie sheet and bake at 350 degrees for 12 to 15 minutes. Cool and ice. Makes 8 to 10 dozen. Icing: Combine ingredients for icing. Mix well. Consistency should be like a thick glaze.

Gran Ferguson's Mustard Potato Salad

- 1 lb. cubed, boiled white potatoes
- 4 boiled eggs, chopped
- 1/2 c. sweet pickle relish

- 1/2 c. mayonnaise
- 1/4 c. yellow mustard
- Salt and pepper to taste

Combine all of the above ingredients. Serve warm or cold. I like to add a little extra juice from the sweet pickle relish to make the salad tangy! Also, the amount of mayonnaise and mustard can vary according to taste. The texture should be creamy, so you may need to add more or use less of either.

Sweet Southern Iced Tea

Boil two quarts of water in a sauce pan. Heat water to just hot enough to boil. Add two cups of sugar or just enough to make your teeth ache when you taste it. Stir until sugar is completely dissolved. Remove pan from heat and add 3-gallon size tea bags. I prefer Luzianne or Lipton brand tea. Cover and let steep until the tea is a deep, rich brown.

Remove the tea bags, squeeze out excess liquid. Pour tea into a gallon tea pitcher, add water, and stir.

Serve over ice. Add fruit if desired. I like mine straight, but some like to add lemon wedges, orange slices, cranberry or peach juice.

DIXIE'S READERS GUIDE

1. Talk about how Candi's upbringing was different from a normal upbringing. Was your childhood normal? If so, what were your favorite things to do? If not, discuss that as well.
2. When Candi was young, she dreamed of owning a shop. Grady had little choice in what he would become, but found that serving the community where he grew up was in his blood after all. When you were young, what did you dream of doing when you grew up? Did you achieve that dream? Why or why not?
3. Life in the mountains was at one time rooted in superstition. What superstitions did Candi subscribe to? Are there any superstitions that you believe in, like not stepping on the cracks in sidewalks or Friday the 13th?
4. Candi and Grady are drawn to each other in ways neither of them fully understand.

Discuss how Candi and Grady come together. Do you think they'll eventually marry?

5. Angel Ridge has skeletons in its closets. Discuss these secrets. Were there any secrets in the town you grew up in? If so, how did they come to light?
6. Candi and her mother wanted to fit into a place they had longed to be a part of all their lives. Discuss the choices they made for fitting into Angel Ridge society. Which choices worked, which didn't, and why. Have you ever wanted to fit in so badly that you did something ill-advised?
7. My diner, Ferguson's, is a favorite restaurant in Angel Ridge, and rightly so. If you sat down for a meal at Ferguson's, what would you order? What is your favorite local establishment to eat at in your hometown?
8. Grady was not close to his mother and father, but integrated into the Ferguson family when they moved to Angel Ridge. Why do you think that was? What was it about his family that was dysfunctional and what was it about the Ferguson family that drew him? Did you have a second family when you were growing up? Remember the joy they brought to your life and discuss them.

9. Angel Ridge is going to need someone to run the town newspaper. Who would you nominate for the job? Should someone be brought in from outside the community or should someone who's lived in Angel Ridge all their life run the newspaper?
10. Talk about your favorite characters in *What the Heart Wants.* Who would you like to see have their own story.

If you'd like to share your answers to 9 and 10 with the author, please email Deborah at dgracestaley@aol.com.

Deborah would love to meet with your book club via Skype. Please contact her via dgracestaley@aol.com or at bellebooks@bellebooks.com to schedule an appearance.

AUTHOR'S NOTE

It took quite some time for *What the Heart Wants* to come to life, mainly because Candi kept changing her mind about who she wanted to be in Angel Ridge. When she at last told me that she was from the mountains and the wise woman tradition, this made sense to me. So, like any author, I immediately began research on wise women, or granny women, as they were sometimes called.

My research efforts were met with frustration. There is very little written information about these amazing women of the mountains who healed the sick because there were no doctors, attended the births of thousands of children, and yes, even saw the future. Perhaps most important, they honored this tradition that was passed to them from the women in their families. There is little written about them because outsiders considered these women witches or people to be looked upon with distrust and suspicion. Within their communities, however, these women were respected, and for that reason, people didn't talk about them to outsiders. Even the women themselves would rarely boast of their special gifts.

In the small amount of information I found, my frustration intensified because I already knew practically everything I read about these women. When asking myself why I knew these things, I realized that my mother had passed this information to me. She had always had an instinct for what to do, and quite often, just simply knew things. How she knew could not be explained. I also remembered that she'd told me that people came to her mother to get advice, that she sometimes read these people's coffee grounds. When I asked my mother if she really read the coffee grounds or if she knew anyway, mom said that the "reading" was just a prop. Some wise women "read" tea leaves or carried animal bones in pouches that they would throw on the ground and read, but as the Dolly Parton song, *These Old Bones,* says, that was just for show.

Surprisingly, my research for Candi turned out to be a delving into my own family history and the line of wise women that passed their gifts and wisdom to me. May I be worthy of this God-given gift. For this reason, I acknowledge the generations of women through whom this wise woman's gift flows: Elizabeth F. Hensley and her daughter, Anna Rebecca Hensley, and her daughter, Tiny Bell Fields, and her daughter, Betty Mae Jones, and her daughters Christy Grace McKinney and me, Deborah Grace Staley.

ABOUT THE AUTHOR

Deborah Grace Staley is a life-long resident of East Tennessee. Married to her college sweetheart for twenty-five years, she lives in the Foothills of the Smoky Mountains in a circa 1867 farmhouse that has Angel's Wings in the gingerbread trim.

In addition to being an award-winning author, in her spare time, Deborah works as a disability services specialist at a local college, enjoys watching her son play college baseball, and is working toward her Master of Fine Arts degree in Creative Writing through Goddard College in Port Townsend, Washington.

The employees of Thorndike Press hope you have enjoyed this Large Print book. All our Thorndike, Wheeler, and Kennebec Large Print titles are designed for easy reading, and all our books are made to last. Other Thorndike Press Large Print books are available at your library, through selected bookstores, or directly from us.

For information about titles, please call:
(800) 223-1244

or visit our Web site at:
http://gale.cengage.com/thorndike

To share your comments, please write:

Publisher
Thorndike Press
295 Kennedy Memorial Drive
Waterville, ME 04901